Love on the Rooftop

Also by Elise Darcy

The Living Apart Together Series

Living Apart Together

It Takes 2 to Tango

Dear John

Love on the Rooftop

The Sunrise Coast Series

New Beginnings at the Harbour Inn

The Secret of the Summerhouse

The Cottage by the Sea

Standalone books

A Mallorcan Affair

Lola & The Man

We'll Meet Again

The Villa in Sicily

AUTHOR'S NOTE

Living Apart Together is a series.
Love on the Rooftop is the final book.

Love on the Rooftop

Living Apart Together

Book IV

ELISE DARCY

Penny Lane Press

For Editor M.

1

Sitting outside Heathrow Airport, parked in the drop-off zone at Terminal 5, John hugged his youngest daughter.

Chloe gave him a kiss goodbye.

He was just opening the car door when Chloe said, 'Have you forgotten something, Dad?'

He turned to look at Chloe and then remembered Mouse. The reason he'd called on Chloe was because he needed someone to pop in every day to feed his pet cat while he was away. John reluctantly gave her the keys to his apartment; he was trying to shake off an inexplicable feeling that leaving his youngest daughter in charge of his place was a bad idea.

John couldn't throw off that feeling as he walked through the terminal, queued at security, handed over his boarding pass, and boarded his flight. However, as soon as he took his seat on the plane in business class for the eight-hour trip to America, a new anxiety reared its head. The trip wasn't a vacation. He was on his way to New York to appear on an American talk show. He'd never been on television before. But it wasn't the thought of being in front of the cameras, on a live show, that was raising his anxiety levels. It was who he would meet on that show – the writer, Love on the Rooftop.

He didn't know her identity. No one did. She was famous because of her blog and magazine column; it was all about how living apart together, or LAT living as she called it, had brought the romance back into her relationship and rescued her marriage. People were clamouring to learn the identity of the woman calling herself Love on the Rooftop, who wrote the successful column that went by the same name. Apparently, she would reveal herself in front of a live studio audience on a talk show in America.

The first John heard about it was when he received a phone call from the assistant editor of the magazine he worked for inviting him on an all-expenses-paid trip to New York, to appear on the show as a surprise guest. The other writer, Love on the Rooftop, knew nothing about the surprise guest – her arch-rival, Dear John. She had no idea he would make an appearance. John wondered what her reaction would be when she found out.

He'd been dying to meet her, his nemesis, the woman for whom LAT living had worked out so well. Like Love on the Rooftop, John had written a blog about LAT living too. Except his blog was all about how living apart together had led to this – John slipped a hand inside his blazer pocket; it was still there, the handwritten note from his wife. It began, Dear John…

John hadn't bothered to read it. He knew what it was: a Dear John letter. This was where he expected LAT living would eventually lead. To the end of their marriage. He'd found the note outside his door, unfolded the notepaper and saw the first two words, *Dear John,* then tossed it over the banisters. It had landed outside the entrance to Sylvie's apartment downstairs.

There was no point knocking on her door, hoping she'd change her mind. Soon after finding that note, he spotted Sylvie getting into a taxi with her suitcases and Alfie, her pet dog. She had left him – for good this time.

After seeing her leave, John didn't bother reading the letter. What was the point? That's when he got the phone call about a trip to New York, all because his blog and subsequent magazine column had become a surprise hit with the magazine's readers. John knew he could be accused of riding the coattails of the other blogger's success, but people wanted to hear the other side of the story; how LAT living isn't always such a bed of roses.

John had kept his identity a secret because he'd been writing all about his wife, living downstairs. But now she'd gone, and he had received his Dear John letter, he didn't see any reason to hang around waiting for the divorce papers to come through. An all-expenses-paid trip to New York was just what he needed.

John thought about the note in his blazer pocket and sighed. The only reason he still had the letter was because of Chloe. When she'd turned up at the house to collect his keys and give him a lift to the airport, she'd spotted the crumpled piece of paper in the hall. Chloe nearly read the note before he snatched it out of her hands. He had yet to tell any of his three girls about their mother walking out. His daughters were still under the illusion that despite living apart, Mum and Dad might get back together.

It wasn't his intention for the house conversion to lead to LAT living. The original plan was to live in one apartment and rent out the other for an additional source of income in retirement. John didn't factor in his wife moving out of their flat and moving into the rental apartment downstairs on her own. He also didn't factor in the final cost of the alterations and the financial implications if he couldn't rent out the garden apartment. He thought she would move back in with him upstairs, so they could rent out the garden apartment and pay off their debts. But that's when Sylvie surprised him. She refused. Instead, she went out and found herself a new job at the age of sixty.

He didn't know what she did for a living, but for the first time in their married lives, she had become the main breadwinner. If it weren't for the money that she was bringing in, he would have found himself back down the job centre in a desperate bid to find work. Instead, because Sylvie took charge of their finances and paid the bills, John had free time on his hands. That's when he started a blog. The success of that blog had led to a second career as a columnist working for a magazine in London.

His only reservation about the trip to New York was the fact that he knew he'd been taking a bit of poetic licence in his blog and column. Or not to put a too finer point on it, he had been telling lies. It didn't start out that way; it began with him writing all about what had been going on in the Baxter household since he converted the house into two apartments, and they started living apart together.

Writing his blog had been working very well, to begin with. One highlight was his piece about Sylvie's house party and the emergence of a new creature living in the downstairs apartment: the neighbour from hell. His loyal readers were lapping it up; they loved that John's blog suggested women couldn't be trusted to behave responsibly and cope on their own without their husbands or partners around. It's just what his readers wanted to hear. But then the tables reversed, and it was John who was acting immature; he had late night parties and played loud music at all hours in a lame attempt to show Sylvie he could have a good time, he could be fun. It was sometime later when he realised what she really thought; that he was playing up because she was still refusing to move out of the rental apartment and back upstairs.

Somehow John had neglected to write that in his blog and forgotten to mention this new turn of events; his wife was out at work paying all the bills. If only she had relented and moved back in with him. They wouldn't have got themselves in a financial mess, and he wouldn't have had to lie to his readers. Perhaps then things might have turned out differently. Maybe things would have turned out like the anonymous writer of *Love on the Rooftop* for whom living apart together had strengthened their relationship, not driven them apart.

Despite getting his act together, any hope of things changing was locked in the past. John heaved a sigh and unbuckled his seatbelt. He was feeling restless. He hadn't flown for years and had never taken a long-haul flight. Fortunately, he was in an aisle seat, so he didn't have to disturb anyone when he needed to stretch his legs. The instant he rose from his seat, a flight attendant was by his side, asking if there was anything he needed.

'Um, I need to use the—'

'The washrooms are right this way, sir.'

John followed the flight attendant, only to discover the toilet was already occupied. He stood there leaning against one of the empty seats, waiting for the door to open. He heard a man's voice from inside the cubicle. 'Stop that, this instant.'

John raised an eyebrow. He heard the voice again.

'No, don't open the door, Henry.' The door opened a crack.

John could see a man by the sink gathering up reams of toilet paper from the floor.

'Henry, how many times have I told you *not* to pull all the toilet paper out of the holder?'

John looked down at a small boy standing by the door. He couldn't have been more than three years old.

He looked up at John and smiled.

John smiled back.

'I'm sorry about that,' said the young man as he exited the washroom, holding the boy's hand. 'Come on, Henry.'

John stood there watching the young man pick the boy up and carry him back to his seat. John's smile faltered. Seeing the young man with the small boy reminded him of Gertie. John recalled that episode when they were landed with the job of looking after their two-year-old grandchild. Their eldest daughter, Harriet, had to return to work.

John assumed he and Sylvie would look after Gertie. That's what Harriet wanted. It was also what John wanted. He thought it would be the perfect opportunity to spend time together and perhaps find a way back to each other. However, Sylvie was too busy with work. John took on the responsibility of looking after their grandchild on his own practically full time. It wasn't an arrangement Harriet was privy too. She was under the misapprehension that both grandparents were looking after Gertie while she was at work. She didn't realise Sylvie was in a full-time job herself, supporting the roof over their head and paying off John's debts. Harriet found out about Mum and Dad's little charade when their son-in-law, Dominic, turned up at their house one day to collect Gertie early.

John walked back to his seat, frowning. It wasn't an episode he could forget in a hurry. It was soon after his blog went stratospheric that he was offered an interview for a job as a columnist for a magazine. The editor of that magazine wanted Dear John to write about LAT living. There was just one complication: his daughter was the editor. She had no clue that the anonymous blogger she was about to interview, known only by his pen name, was none other than her father.

Unfortunately, Harriet then found out about their little deception that Gertie wasn't being looked after by both grandparents as promised. All along, they had lied to her. The consequences were far worse than either John or Sylvie could ever have imagined. Harriet and Dominic withdrew all contact between Gertie and her grandparents in London until they sorted themselves out once and for all.

Harriet blamed her parents' bad behaviour on their bizarre living arrangement – living apart together. They then issued an ultimatum: stop living apart and get back together or split up for good. He guessed they were past caring which one.

John recalled that massive row he and Sylvie had over losing access to Gertie, each blaming the other for the situation they found themselves in. To make matters worse, they weren't even speaking to each other. But that was of little consequence now. They didn't need to sit down and talk things through. He had his Dear John letter, the crumpled note stashed away in his blazer pocket, and that said it all.

2

After another toilet break, John made his way back through the cabin to his seat. He noticed the stranger who had been sitting next to him in the window seat, snoring for the last hour, was nowhere to be seen. He looked about him before he sat down in case the chap was making his way down the aisle towards him. He wasn't. John resumed his seat. He glanced out of the window and gazed at an impenetrable layer of thick white cloud. That's when something caught his eye. He noticed his fellow passenger had left a magazine on the empty seat. John picked it up. He raised an eyebrow. On the front cover were the words *Dear John* emblazoned in bold lettering. He stared at the by-line: *Read the next exciting episode in the saga, Living Apart Together.*

John flicked through the pages and came to the most recent article he had written for the magazine. He sat reading the whole sorry piece, all about how he'd found his Dear John letter. John recalled that he'd abstained from the bottle of booze he craved and had written this article instead.

John finished reading the article and sat there staring into space. His blog about LAT living, and the articles he had been writing on the subject for his column, were coming to an end. It was the reason he'd agreed to go to New York. He was aware that along with the other blogger he would blow his anonymity wide open, but he knew it was time. This chapter of their lives, living apart together, was ending with a capital D, as in divorce. He knew that for a fact because Sylvie had packed her suitcase and walked out that door. His story, their story, was finally over.

'Interesting, isn't it?' A voice cut across his thoughts.

John looked up and recognised the man standing in the aisle. It was the guy who was occupying the window seat.

He glanced at the magazine in John's hand.

'Oh Sorry, here—' John held out the magazine.

'Hey, keep it. I've read it.'

John got up to let the man resume his seat.

They both sat down.

The middle-aged man pointed at the magazine in John's hand. 'You should read that article. It's bloody good.'

'You think so?' asked John.

'Oh yes. I'm quite a fan.'

'You are?' He knew Dear John was popular, but he'd met none of his readers.

'I'd love to meet that writer, Dear John.'

'You would?'

'Uh-huh. I've got some stories about my wife, I can tell you. She's no saint.'

'Do you think Dear John is popular in America?' John had been sceptical about the chat show, wondering how many people would have heard of his blog across the pond.

'Popular? Uh-huh, in my neck of the woods at any rate. I'm from Seattle and all the guys, friends of mine, read it. Our wives are reading the other one.'

'The other one?'

'You know – Love on the Rooftop.' He frowned. 'It's all romantic meals out and walks together along Regent's Canal in London.' He rolled his eyes in exasperation. 'My wife keeps pressuring to do this LAT living nonsense. I think she's under the illusion I'm going to morph into some romantic fool if we live apart.'

John smiled. 'Yes, it is rather far-fetched isn't it, the notion that you would suddenly become a romantic.'

'Exactly. Although I have to say the thoughts of living in my own place, like Dear John, without being henpecked by my wife 24/7 is kinda appealing.'

'Hmm.'

'What's your missus like?'

'Ah, well. The fact is we're getting a divorce.'

'Oh, sorry to hear that.'

John was too. 'And yours?'

'She's a pain in my behind. But I couldn't live without the woman. She's the love of my life.'

'That's nice.' John pursed his lips, wanting this conversation to be over.

'That doesn't mean to say I wouldn't fancy having some time out occasionally.' He looked about him, leaned in towards John, and lowered his voice. 'I have a confession to make.'

John raised his eyebrows.

He whispered, 'I've been reading *Love on the Rooftop*.'

John was taken aback.

'My wife doesn't even know. I've been secretly borrowing her magazines and reading the articles when she's out.'

John didn't respond. He was also guilty of reading Love on

the Rooftop's column every week. In part, it was to keep abreast of the competition. Although he was loath to admit it, he enjoyed her column. Reading those articles took him back to a happier time soon after the house conversion, when Sylvie first moved downstairs. Back then they had enjoyed spending time together, despite living apart. Or was it because they were living apart?

John never had a chance to find out before Sylvie discovered the financial mess he was hiding after underestimating the final cost of the conversion. She jumped to the conclusion that John had an agenda: all those sudden romantic gestures from her husband were just to encourage her to move back in with him upstairs so he could rent out the garden apartment. They weren't genuine, heartfelt displays of affection for the love of his life.

'I haven't told anyone this,' continued the man in the window seat. 'Not even my closest buddies. We've been thinking about giving it a try.'

John raised an eyebrow. 'Giving what a try?'

'You know – living apart together.'

John looked at him, aghast. 'You've got to be joking.'

'Nope.'

'But have you read *Dear John*?' He couldn't believe a fan of his was thinking of defecting to the other side.

'Of course, I've read it. Every single article.'

'Well?'

'Well, what?'

'I'd have thought, after reading *Dear John*, that you wouldn't even consider LAT living if you don't want things to end up in the divorce courts.'

'True, true. But here's the thing, for LAT living to work we believe *both* parties have to want to do it. It's no good if you're both not on board. Do you catch my drift?'

John regarded him thoughtfully.

'My wife believes LAT living works for Love on the Rooftop because both she and her husband want to do it. It's not working for Dear John because he doesn't want to change.'

John stared at the middle-aged man in the window seat with the interesting perspective on Dear John.

He pointed at the magazine on John's lap. 'If you read in between the lines, all Dear John wanted was for things to go back to the way they were. Clearly, his wife didn't want that. She's moved on. He just couldn't see that. Him and his wife don't want the same things. It's little wonder he got his Dear John letter . . .' He shrugged. 'Hey, do you mind if I pull down the blind at the window? I'm going to get some shut-eye.'

John nodded.

Before he closed his eyes, he glanced at the magazine. 'I hope that isn't the end of the *Dear John* column. If it is, I'm going to miss those articles. I'm a real fan. They were a hoot.'

John managed a smile. 'I haven't introduced myself. I'm John.'

'Oh sure, I'm Dan.'

'Is this your first visit to New York?'

'Nope, I've been plenty of times on business. But one of these days I would love to bring my wife. I've held back seeing any of the sights. We're planning to see them together.'

John nodded. He'd had similar plans himself to whisk Sylvie off to New York when he retired. Who knew that when he retired, he would find himself travelling to New York alone?

'Are you travelling on business too, John?'

John hesitated. He could see where this conversation was going. Next, Dan would ask what it was he did for a living. John knew he could lie and pretend he was still an accountant. Instead, he said, 'You know what? I think I'm going to get some shut-eye too.' John leaned his head back on the headrest and closed his eyes.

He heard Dan moving around in the seat next to him, and then everything went quiet. He waited a few more minutes and then opened one eye to peek at Dan. His neighbour was sleeping under a thin blanket from the complimentary travel pack provided in business class.

John opened his eyes and turned his attention to the magazine. He glanced at his neighbour as he unzipped his laptop case and found a pen. John smiled as he wrote a little note on the front of the magazine to Dan and his wife, wishing them a happy future living apart together. LAT living might not have worked out for him and Sylvie, but Dan was right: it didn't mean it couldn't work for anybody else. It didn't mean it couldn't work for Dan and his wife. If LAT living was for them, then he wished them every happiness. They were the lucky ones. However, John wasn't sorry that he had warned him of the risks of going down that road because who knew where it would lead.

He studied the cover of the magazine and then flicked to his *Dear John* article once more. This might well be the last time he saw his writing in print. It was certainly the final *Dear John* article he would write about LAT living.

John signed his name at the bottom of the article. He glanced at Dan as he slipped the autographed magazine into the carry-on bag by his feet. Who knows, perhaps it would be worth something in the future. John smiled. At the very least, Dan would get a kick out of discovering he had spent his flight to New York in the company of Dear John.

He had to acknowledge that it might all be over, but what a way to go, flying on an all-expenses-paid trip to America. John thought he might as well go out in style and enjoy the moment because he imagined when the truth came out, it would spell the end of his dream as a writer and his new career as a columnist.

All this had been going through his mind as he sat on the flight, counting down the hours until he landed at Newark Airport. Dan had provided a welcome distraction. John glanced at him. The American was snoring into his blanket. He was still a trifle concerned that, despite reading his column, Dan and his wife were buying into the message from Love on the Rooftop that LAT living was some sort of panacea.

John sat there mulling over the articles he'd read in the *Love on the Rooftop* column. There were times when he read her column that it just seemed too good to be true. Too much like a fairy tale. It was almost as though she was writing just what women wanted to hear. It made him wonder whether she also had taken a bit of poetic licence. If perhaps she had sugar-coated things for the sake of her readers.

In reality, LAT living wasn't easy. It would never surprise him if it had not gone as smoothly as she liked to make out. Considering his own experiences, it was a question that he was interested to put to her on live television, something he had tried to do through his weekly column.

So far, she had refused to address his questions and criticisms in her column. Instead, she had deflected them by plenty criticising Dear John. In fact, it had become a ritual of sorts – discussing each other's articles and blogs in their own column –

until John couldn't wait to read the next piece by the writer, Love on the Rooftop, just to see what derogatory remarks and counter-arguments she had come up with in response to Dear John.

John then wrote his own article in response to hers, dropping in some choice remarks about Love on the Rooftop, knowing full well she would do the same; read his column and responding to Dear John in her next article. The ball bouncing back and forth. The game afoot.

They were arch rivals. She was his nemesis. And yet their magazine columns were taken up with responding to each other. Both their articles were entertaining, witty, and informative, mostly about LAT living, but sometimes veering off in different directions as the mood took them. John felt as though he was getting to know this writer through her column; each asking the other questions, arguing, sometimes agreeing, mostly not, but revealing a little more of themselves, bit by bit, as the weeks went by.

John was going to miss that when it was all over. Whatever he believed or didn't believe about what had really gone on between this writer and her husband living apart together, that it couldn't have been all plain sailing as she so successfully made out in her blog, the fact remained that her story still had a different outcome to his; she was getting back with her husband. It also meant that her story in her blog and her column about LAT living would, like John's, also be coming to an end. And that spelled the end of this virtual relationship that had been developing between John and this mystery writer.

He had been following her blog, interested to find out when they would finally do it, when Love on the Rooftop and her husband would move back in together. It was only a matter of time. John suspected the writer was just keeping everybody in suspense, waiting for the right moment to announce it. John had a good idea when that moment would be; when she revealed her identity on *The Who's Who Show* in New York. In fact, it would never surprise him if, unbeknown to her, they had arranged for her husband to be there on the show. Perhaps he would sit among the studio audience, ready to surprise her and walk down to join his wife in front of the cameras. Then she would smugly make her announcement that they were no longer living apart.

He could just imagine the show filming them walking together arm-in-arm out of the studio to the sound of clapping and cheering from the studio audience; a perfect ending to an episode in their marriage living apart together. A splendid finale to her blog and her magazine column. And worst of all, John was going to be right there to see it.

John wasn't looking forward to that. The more he thought about it, the less he felt inclined to share how his own story ends, in front of a studio audience, on live television. There was no happy ending for the writer, Dear John, just a Dear John letter in his pocket, divorce papers in the post, and an empty house to look forward to on his return.

John frowned. He was starting to wonder if he had been a bit hasty, agreeing so readily to go on this trip without thinking this through. But it wasn't as though they had given him a great deal of time to mull it over. Besides, John had got carried away, on a high with the thought of an all-expenses-paid trip to New York. Only now, with eight hours to kill and an awful lot of thinking time, John was regretting that decision. He had a feeling in the pit of his stomach that this was all going to turn out a very bad idea. John's shoulders sagged. He couldn't back out now, even if he wanted to. He'd made a commitment to Harriet, to her magazine, and *The Who's Who Show*. On top of which, he couldn't afford to reimburse the studio for the cost of his trip to New York if he backed out. Apart from his pension, John didn't have any money on one side to pay for all this. He'd have to ask Sylvie for the money. He could just imagine her reaction if he asked her to pay for a jolly to New York.

John frowned. He had no choice but to see this through. Unless, by some miracle, he was delayed and missed the show. John raised an eyebrow. That was a distinct possibility. He was aware he was on a tight schedule. Apparently, the other guest on the show, his nemesis, had left that morning and was some hours ahead of him on another flight. John glanced at his watch and calculated the time difference. By his estimate, she would already be approaching New York.

The plan was that a limo would be waiting to take him straight from the airport to the television studios where the show was being aired. It was going to be tight. The producers were aware of this. The studio and everybody at Harriet's magazine were crossing their fingers that there weren't any last-minute delays, and he would make it on time.

John had brought a change of clothes, but he doubted there would be enough time to freshen up before they whisked him to the studio. He wasn't sorry his feet would barely touch the ground before it was all over. In fact, he was counting on it; he was looking forward to spending some free time in New York at his leisure before flying home.

John remembered what the assistant editor had told him over the phone before his trip; the producers of the show were excited at the prospect of getting these two remarkably successful mystery bloggers and columnists, with opposing views, in the same room together. They thought sparks would fly; they were counting on it because that's what made for great television. The fact that they were both revealing their identities in front of a studio audience on live TV was just the icing on the cake.

They had all read the entertaining articles that had resulted from the intense rivalry between these two writers. And if their columns were anything to go by, the producers knew this was going to be one hell of a show.

The producers had kept it a closely guarded secret that he would appear on the show tonight. They wanted it to be a surprise for the studio audience. But more than that, they wanted to surprise their first guest, the writer of the phenomenally successful *Love on the Rooftop* and capture her reaction on live television when she met her arch-rival, the writer of the phenomenally successful *Dear John*.

3

Sylvie listened to the announcement as she sat in business class sipping an ice-cold orange juice. In less than an hour, the plane would begin its final descent into Newark Airport, where she would be met by a limo and whisked off to her hotel. She would have plenty of time to freshen up, change into a new outfit, and have dinner before appearing on *The Who's Who Show* later that evening.

Sylvie didn't know how she had kept all this to herself. The only person who knew about her trip was her best friend, Julia. It made her feel like a child running away from home, not a businesswoman on an all-expenses-paid trip to New York. It all felt very surreal, as though she had stepped into somebody else's life. Sylvie was still getting used to the fact that this was her life now — a writer and columnist, and a phenomenally successful one at that. Sylvie couldn't quite believe she had come this far and in such a brief space of time. She should be elated, but the moment was bittersweet for Sylvie. She realised that as her professional life was on an upward trajectory, her personal life was in free fall.

John had not spoken to her since they lost access to their

only grandchild. Harriet refused to talk to her. Who could blame her after the lies she'd told her daughter every single day when she pretended that she was looking after Gertie? Even Chloe was giving her the cold shoulder after she heard what had happened. Sylvie didn't bother to ring up Jess in Australia. She imagined that Harriet had already been on the phone to her sister about what was going on at home.

As the plane began its final descent into New York, she sat there thinking what was the point of all this success if she had nobody to share it with? Afraid she might burst into tears, she opened her purse, looking for a tissue, and found an unopened letter. It was from Bertram, the man she'd been meeting for lunch at The Rooftop Café in Hanover Square each weekday. If it weren't for her recurring dream where she finds love on a rooftop, Sylvie would not have accepted Bertram's invitation to have lunch together. The fact that they'd met on a rooftop had intrigued her until she found out Julia had got up to mischief and planted them both there to see what would happen.

Something happened all right. When Sylvie discovered her best friend had been meddling, all because she knew about her dream, Sylvie stopped seeing Bertram. It had been entirely innocent; nothing more than some lunch dates and a couple of evening meals together. But it was the dancing that bothered Sylvie. During their first evening out, Bertram had taken her to The Savoy Hotel for dinner. Afterwards, they had danced the night away. To Sylvie's astonishment, they made the perfect partners even though neither of them had danced for years.

However, it wasn't Julia's meddling that put an end to their blossoming friendship or Sylvie's reticence at the prospect of starting a new relationship when she was still married. It was

Bertram's attitude when she told him she'd lost contact with her grandchild. He thought it was for the best. He said, "All that was just getting in the way of us." She remembered his words verbatim. By *all that,* he meant her family. Although he apologised for that off-hand remark, his attitude did not surprise her. From what Sylvie gleaned, he'd had a tough time as a single parent bringing up his only child alone.

Sylvie plucked the letter from her purse. She sat there, staring at the unopened envelope. She didn't know its contents. Bertram had written the letter and passed it to their mutual friend, Julia, to give to Sylvie. Julia didn't know the contents of the note either, but she hoped Sylvie would consider giving him a second chance if that's what he was after. Sylvie wondered if she should have read the letter before her trip to New York. Perhaps if she had, then Bertram would be sitting next to her right now on this flight, and maybe they would stay in one of his hotels together in New York.

Sylvie knew why she hadn't read the letter. She still couldn't let go of that dream; the possibility that she might find love on the rooftop. In her dream, it wasn't a rooftop café where she met *the one,* but a rooftop garden. That made all the difference. That meant Bertram wasn't *the one.* Despite Julia's objections that she couldn't base her life and her future happiness on a vision, Sylvie *still* couldn't get that image out of her mind. Although who that person was on the rooftop garden is never revealed in her dream.

She didn't tell her best friend how she felt when Julia handed her the letter and eagerly waited for Sylvie to rip open the envelope and find out what was inside. Sylvie knew what she was thinking: inside that envelope was a key to an apartment in London, although there was no tell-tale bulge or jingle of keys. It didn't change the fact that Julia was aware Bertram *had* bought Sylvie an apartment. There were no strings attached. He just thought it was about time she stopped living apart together with her husband and moved out of the marital home and into her own place.

Sylvie had been extremely cross with Bertram when she found out. After decades of marriage, she didn't want another man telling her where to live or how to lead her life. She already had a husband who was more than capable of doing that. She was an independent woman now with her own career. The last thing she wanted to become was a kept woman by her wealthy friend.

Bertram said she could pay him rent if it made her feel better. And the landlord even allowed pet dogs, Bertram had joked. Sylvie still wasn't pleased about it, but that didn't mean it hadn't crossed her mind the prospect of starting over somewhere else, where someone couldn't interfere in her life. And by *someone,* Sylvie meant her neighbour, John, living upstairs. What Julia didn't know was that she already had a set of keys to that apartment.

Sylvie's mind wandered back to Julia, handing her the letter. She could tell by the look on her face that Julia was astonished when she stuffed the note into her bag to read later. Only there wasn't a later. With preparations for the trip to New York, she hadn't got around to reading it. However, she had plenty of time to read it on the flight, but something was holding her back. Perhaps it was because she had an idea what might be in that letter: the address of the penthouse apartment, with the rooftop garden, that was waiting for her when she returned from New York.

Sylvie rolled her eyes. Although she'd made Julia promise not to tell another living soul about her trip to New York, Julia had broken that promise and told Bertram. She knew why. It was part of Julia's master plan to encourage her to leave John – for good this time. Sylvie thought of the set of keys that Bertram must have slipped in her purse when they last met. When Sylvie discovered them, she knew what they were. However, she did not know where in London the apartment might be. Sylvie had a feeling that if she opened the envelope, she was about to find out. Perhaps it was that, more than anything, which was holding her back from reading the note. She might just be tempted to take him up on that offer after all.

Sitting alone on her flight to New York, turning over the unopened letter in her hand, Sylvie was wondering whether Julia was right: all because of a ridiculous dream, she had no one to share her success with. She had an opportunity right here in her hands. The question was, should she open that envelope or let a second chance at happiness pass her by?

She was about to tear open the envelope when something she'd said to Bertram came to mind. When she found out he was estranged from his daughter, Sylvie told him that before he embarked on a serious relationship, he needed to sort out his relationships closer to home. Sylvie looked at the envelope in her hands. Perhaps it was time she listened to her own advice.

She put the unopened letter back in her bag and sat there thinking about John. Things had come to a head; the unfortunate incident over Gertie had proved that. For the sake of their family and themselves, she knew the time had come to set aside their differences and face up to the reality of where all this was leading – to a divorce. They couldn't avoid each other forever. And

Sylvie had to face up to something else: the demise of her successful career. She couldn't hide behind her anonymity forever. Once people found out the truth, then her career – like her marriage – was over.

But Sylvie wasn't giving up New York. Before she opened that envelope, and decided on her future, she was going to see New York. If this was all about to end, then it was going to end on a high. And it *was* going to end because she intended to use this trip to tell the whole world and her family that she was the writer, Love on the Rooftop. She was the writer who had concocted a fictional story about two people who converted their house into two apartments and, as a result, found their way back to each other through living apart together. She was the writer who had fooled so many readers, so many women, into thinking that her story was true, and not only that, inferring it could happen to them.

Sylvie knew it would all come tumbling down like a pack of cards once everyone discovered it was Sylvie Baxter who had been writing *Love on the Rooftop*. Once they scrutinised her life, they would discover the reality of her situation couldn't be further from the fictional life she had created for her blog and weekly column.

Sylvie shook her head. For a person who once prided herself on always telling the truth, she couldn't believe just how low she could go. Her new life as this successful writer and columnist was built on a lie. Now she knew the time had come to expose herself as the fraud she was. And she intended to do it in the worst possible way, in front of a studio audience on a live television show for all the world to see.

She was going to tell the truth and set the record straight. It was time to put an end to her ludicrously successful blog. It was time to write that last article, telling the truth for once; the truth about how her story *really* ends. She already knew how her story ends – badly.

Caught up in her own fantasy, writing about that fictional couple who had found love again through LAT living, Sylvie had distanced herself from the reality of her own situation. She had been avoiding John. Perhaps that's why she was determined to make this trip to New York. Sylvie wanted her last hurrah. Her successful career was over, her marriage was over, but Sylvie thought *to hell with it*; she might as well go out in style. She would enjoy the fantasy, and the last vestiges of her fame and success before she revealed her identity and with it the lie that she'd been perpetrating. Sylvie knew this would spell the end of her dream job as a writer and her new career as a columnist.

Sylvie's thoughts turned to that other successful writer whose blog and column, *Dear John,* had become just as well known and successful as her own. She was aware she was the one who had started all this; it was her idea to write about LAT living. To begin with, he was just riding her coattails, providing another perspective – a man's perspective – on LAT living, focusing on when things go wrong. Sylvie knew that without her, this anonymous writer's blog would never have been discovered.

The irony was not lost on Sylvie that when she revealed her identity, when she exposed the deception and her readers found out there was no happy ending, it was going to be her blog and column that bit the dust, leaving Dear John to smugly tell his readers: I told you so. I told you LAT living couldn't work. There would be no happy endings. *Dear John* was right, and *Love on the Rooftop* was wrong.

Sylvie was pleased she would never have to meet that writer face-to-face and see his smug expression when he said: *I told you so.* But that didn't mean she wanted to see the back of him. As much as Sylvie wanted all this to be over, she knew that once she put an end to her blog and her column, it would mean the end of this *thing* between them. She didn't even know what to call it, but they had a connection – of that she had no doubt.

She felt like she was in some kind of virtual relationship. They were arch rivals. The writer, Dear John, was her nemesis. And yet increasingly her articles were taken up with responding to his. As time went on, Sylvie felt as though they were getting to know one another through their columns, asking questions, arguing, sometimes agreeing, mostly not, but revealing a little more of themselves as each week went by. Sylvie was going to miss that when it was all over; she was going to miss *him.* For as much as he didn't understand how LAT living could work in a relationship — he just didn't get it — but he did get *her.* That revelation had come as quite a shock to Sylvie, a blow even when she realised the writer, Dear John, understood her in a way her husband never would.

He was her yin to his yang. It was the way they spun off each other so extraordinarily well. As incredible as it seemed, there were times it almost felt as though they were a writing team; she could imagine them both sitting in the same room together, perhaps even sitting right opposite each other at their laptops, bouncing ideas off each other the way they did in their columns, rather than two anonymous writers, two strangers who had never even met.

Sitting on the flight to New York, mulling all this over, her best friend Julia came to mind. Julia had followed her dream to live on a houseboat and had met someone who shared the same goal. Julia said it was a sign that he was *the one*. It made Sylvie wonder about the writer, Dear John, whether like her, he had always harboured a secret ambition to be a writer.

If she'd told Julia all this, Sylvie knew what she would say: that it was a sign. It was *the* sign that he was *the one*. Sylvie didn't want to think about *signs* and *the one* because what she really didn't want to think about, or acknowledge, was the genuine possibility she was falling in love with somebody she had never even met. Sylvie shook her head. It was a ridiculous notion. Besides, it was one thing having this virtual relationship, but how would it work in reality? How could this mystery writer be *the one* if they had such opposing views on LAT living?

4

Sylvie walked into the hotel ahead of the porter carrying her luggage and paused in the middle of the lobby. She still couldn't quite believe she was in New York. For years she'd dreamed of going on adventures with John to far-flung places.

Living in a city all her life, some might think she would want to escape and relax on a deserted beach somewhere like the Maldives or sail away on a cruise. That wasn't Sylvie's idea of an adventure. She enjoyed the hustle and bustle of a metropolis. Perhaps it had something to do with her age, or maybe it was just part of her psyche, but she loved how a city made her feel so alive, the future filled with endless possibilities.

She recalled when Bertram had offered to whisk her away to New York for a long weekend. They had returned to Bertram's place in London for a nightcap after an evening out dancing together. She was admiring the view of the London skyline from his penthouse apartment when he made that suggestion. He couldn't wait to show her the view of the city skyline from his penthouse suite in Manhattan. Bertram wasn't joking. His driver could take them to the airport and within the hour they could be on their way to New York flying by private jet.

Sylvie was less surprised by the offer – she had grown accustomed to her wealthy friend's flights of fancy – than by her reaction. She would have jumped at the chance to go to New York, without a second thought, if it wasn't for her commitments at home. Bertram assumed she was thinking about her work commitments. Sylvie wasn't. She was thinking about her promise to John and the arrangement they had made to keep up appearances, for Harriet's sake. She couldn't just take off at a moment's notice. She had people who depended on her. Harriet assumed her mum was looking after Gertie while she was at work.

Sylvie inwardly groaned. Her ready smile vanished. She looked around the beautiful lobby, knowing full well she wouldn't be here if it wasn't because she had lost access to Gertie. Sylvie would give up New York in a heartbeat if only she could turn back the clock and make things right with Harriet and her son-in-law, Dominic. But she couldn't. And here she was in a hotel in New York, her career on an upward trajectory while her personal life was a mess.

That wasn't the only reason she wanted to turn back the clock. Perhaps if John hadn't converted the house, it wouldn't have come to this – splitting up. However, she knew if they hadn't started living apart together, she wouldn't be here in New York as a consequence of her very successful column about their unusual living arrangement. That was the price she paid for her success.

The trip was bittersweet for Sylvie. She always imagined that one day she would fly to New York with John, and stay in a plush hotel such as this, spending their days walking together through Central Park, visiting museums, and catching a show on Broadway.

'Excuse me, madam.' The porter motioned for Sylvie to walk this way.

Sylvie snapped out of her reverie and followed the porter to the reception desk. In front of her were three couples waiting to check in. Sylvie frowned. It wasn't the queue that bothered her. It was the thought of all that free time she would have after the show – on her own.

When she first found out about the schedule, Sylvie was pleased that she would get her appearance on the talk show out of the way on the day she arrived. She wouldn't have time to worry and angst over her decision to reveal her identity on live television. The one consolation was the fact that Marcia, her magazine editor, told Sylvie she would have a few days at her leisure in New York after the show before she flew home.

Sylvie was delighted when she first found out she would have some free time in the city. However, now she was here, standing in the hotel lobby waiting to collect her room key, she was a lot less enamoured at the prospect of seeing the sights. The problem was Sylvie always imagined she would share those moments with her other half, with John. Now, after everything that had happened with Gertie, even if the magazine had offered to pay for John to join her on the trip, he was the last person she would want to spend time with, whether it was in New York, or anywhere else come to that.

Sylvie stepped forward as the couple ahead of her collected their room key. She couldn't help but overhear their conversation with the receptionist at the front desk...

'Good afternoon, Mr and Mrs Clark. I have your room key here. Are you staying with us for business or pleasure?'

'Pleasure,' said the hotel guest in a strong southern drawl.

'We stayed here many years ago on our honeymoon.' He put an affectionate arm around his wife's shoulders.

'It's still as amazing as we remember it,' added his wife. 'Don't you agree, hon?'

Mr Clark cast an eye around the lobby. 'Oh, yes.'

'Are you celebrating your wedding anniversary?' asked the receptionist.

'That we are. We're celebrating our Ruby wedding anniversary.'

The receptionist smiled at the couple. 'Congratulations. Have you been married long?'

'Have we been married long?' repeated Mr Clark. He exchanged a glance with his wife, and the couple burst out laughing. 'I take it you don't know how many years you have to be married to celebrate your Ruby wedding anniversary?'

Behind the couple, Sylvie was standing there wishing she wasn't hearing all this. She knew how many years this couple had been married if they were celebrating their Ruby wedding anniversary. That would have been her and John if things hadn't gone so very wrong when he retired.

'Forty years!' exclaimed Mrs Clark, leaning in towards her husband and giving him an affectionate pat on the behind.

Sylvie saw that, raised her eyebrows in embarrassment, and averted her gaze.

'It's quite something, isn't it?' said Mr Clark, blowing his own trumpet. 'Do you know how many couples wind up divorced these days?' he continued smugly.

Sylvie rolled her eyes.

His wife chipped in, 'We're both retired, and this is just the start of many adventures together.'

'Congratulations to you both,' said the receptionist.

Sylvie stared at the couple in front of her. In another life, if things had worked out differently, perhaps that would have been her and John standing there at the reception desk celebrating forty years of marriage. Instead, all that lay ahead of them was a trip to the solicitor to start divorce proceedings.

'I don't suppose you remember which suite you stayed in when you were here on your honeymoon. If you do, then we will try our best to put you in the same room as before.'

A knowing smile passed between them before Mrs Clark said, 'As a matter of fact, we do. Since we got married, every trip we've been on together we kept a scrapbook with our itinerary, photos, postcards – that sort of thing.' She produced an old worn scrapbook from her handbag and placed it on the reception desk in front of her. 'Ah, here we are.' Flicking through the pages, she came to the details of the room they had stayed in on their honeymoon soon after they were married.

'This is amazing. You have photos of the hotel from forty years ago?'

'Uh-huh. Back then, this hotel was the most money we had ever paid out on anything in our lives. We were a young couple in love, and it was quite an experience to stay in a hotel in New York on Park Avenue.'

Sylvie stepped forward and stood on tiptoes to look over their shoulder, which was incredibly rude, but she couldn't help herself. She smiled as the woman flicked through page after page of black and white photos of a young couple very much in love, seeing the sights in New York at the start of their journey together as a married couple.

'How romantic,' blurted Sylvie, forgetting herself.

The couple turned around to look at Sylvie.

'I'm sorry.' Sylvie took a step back. 'I couldn't help overhearing…'

'Hey, no problem,' said the couple in unison. 'Here, would you like to have a look while we finish checking in?' offered Mrs Clark.

'Oh, could I?' asked Sylvie. 'This is my first trip to New York.'

'Well, I'm sure it won't be your last. New York has a way of getting under your skin. It's quite something.'

Sylvie smiled as she took the old scrapbook and held the precious memento in her hands. From what she had seen during her journey in the limo from Newark Airport to Manhattan, she already knew that her free days after the show would not do it justice. She would need more time to see all the sights. Sylvie had already been thinking about when she might return. And who she might return with. Seeing photos of the couple in their younger days exploring the city together, she was determined that next time she came to New York, she would be with *the one* – whoever that might be.

She was flicking through the scrapbook, studying the photos and holiday mementos from their honeymoon forty years ago, when something caught her eye. She flicked back a page to take a closer look. One photo stood out. Sylvie studied the picture for some minutes while the Clarks checked in and were handed their room keys. Sylvie pointed at the page and glanced at Mrs Clark. 'These photographs of a diner in New York…' She wasn't wearing her reading glasses, so she was only hazarding a guess when she said, 'The name above the door of that diner – it isn't Morellis by any chance?'

Mr and Mrs Clark turned from the reception desk. They didn't need to look at the photo before they answered her question. 'Yes, that's Morelli's, all right. In fact, that's on our bucket list of places to revisit while we're here. We're just hoping that the place has survived and hasn't been taken over by a Starbucks or something.'

'That would be such a shame,' said Mrs Clark. She looked at Sylvie and brightened. 'How do you know of it? Have you read about it in a New York guidebook? That would mean it still exists.'

'Er no, I'm afraid I haven't. I just thought I recognised the name – that's all.' Sylvie pursed her lips. She didn't feel inclined to share how she knew the name Morelli. Sylvie would rather avoid that guilty feeling that crept up over her every time she thought of her mother's ashes still sitting in an urn on her mantel shelf at home, waiting for her last wish to be fulfilled.

Her mother wanted her ashes scattered in the garden of a cottage in Cornwall; a place where Sylvie and her mother used to spend time during the school summer holidays. The property was now owned by an American who had the surname Morelli.

Sylvie had sent him a letter seeking his permission to scatter her mother's ashes in the garden of his holiday home. She had heard nothing back. She didn't know much about the owner, apart from two things; they sent any correspondence via his lawyer in New York, and the owner's name –Mr Morelli. That was it. That's why the name of the diner had intrigued her. Perhaps Mr Morelli had some connection with the restaurant. Or maybe it was just a coincidence and the Italian surname, Morelli, was commonplace among Italian immigrants.

'That Italian surname is quite common,' said Mr Clark to his wife, as if reading Sylvie's thoughts. 'She could have heard it anywhere.'

'I know.' Mrs Clark glanced at her scrapbook. She turned to her husband. 'Hey, didn't we have a photo taken of the two of us with Mr Morelli?'

Mr Clark looked at his wife and then raised his eyebrows. 'I think you're right,' he chortled.

'I'm always right – you know that.'

'Oh yes, how could I forget the secret of our long-lasting marriage?' He nudged his wife playfully.

Sylvie managed a smile at their private joke. She couldn't begrudge them their happiness just because things hadn't worked out with her and John. She turned her attention to the old scrapbook and watched Mrs Clark with interest as she flicked through the pages.

'There!' exclaimed her husband, pointing at a photograph.

'Yes, that's the one.' Mrs Clark passed the book over to Sylvie.

Sylvie fumbled in her handbag. 'Just a moment.' She found her reading glasses and put them on. She took the scrapbook and studied the picture closely. The young couple were sitting together at a table, in an old-fashioned booth-style seat. Standing next to the booth, in a black suit with a white cloth draped over his arm, was a middle-aged man.

'Is that Mr Morelli?' asked Sylvie. 'He looks like his dressed as a waiter.'

'I know, but that's the owner, Mr Morelli. Apparently, he insisted on making the time to call in on the diner and serve some of his loyal customers.'

'I think it was quite an honour to be served by Mr Morelli himself,' added Mrs Clark.

Mr Clark turned to his wife. 'I guess it was our lucky day.'

Sylvie took a closer look at the photo of the tall, slim gentleman standing beside the booth where the young couple were seated. He looked handsome, with large dark eyes and black hair slicked back. He wasn't smiling at the camera, but his expression suggested he wasn't unhappy, perhaps a little melancholy. He held his head high and his manner appeared one of quiet confidence. Sylvie wondered whether the diner still existed and what became of Mr Morelli in the forty years since this picture was taken.

Staring at the photo, Sylvie imagined, just for a moment, that this was the Mr Morelli she had written to, requesting to scatter her mother's ashes in the garden of his holiday home in Cornwall.

It was a nice thought while it lasted, but the coincidence would be too good to be true; from Sylvie's recent experiences on the domestic front, things in her life had a tendency not to fall so neatly into place. Besides, this Mr Morelli wasn't a young man in the photograph. Was he even still alive? And if he was, where would he be now? Certainly not serving in that diner, if it still existed – which she very much doubted. Sylvie turned to Mr and Mrs Clark to hand back their scrapbook. 'Thank you for showing me this. Are you staying in New York long?'

'We've got a whole glorious week,' said Mrs Clark.

Mr Clark smiled at his wife. 'We're intending to revisit the places in this book and take some pictures for a new scrapbook to show our family on our return.'

Sylvie smiled. 'That sounds like a marvellous idea.'

'That's if we can tear ourselves away from our hotel room,' added Mrs Clark, glancing at her husband and giving him a naughty wink.

'Ahem.' Mr Clark's face went bright purple.

Sylvie curbed a smile.

Mrs Clark continued, 'We heard the hotel has changed hands in recent years, so we were reticent about coming here again in case it wasn't as nice as we remembered it.'

'Do you think it's changed much since you were here last?' asked Sylvie.

The couple took a moment to glance around at their surroundings. 'It has changed somewhat,' Mr Clark concluded.

'But in a nice way – wouldn't you agree, darling?'

He nodded. 'In fact, I think it's safe to say we like it even more.'

Sylvie looked about her. She wasn't well travelled, and didn't stay in upmarket hotels, but if the hotel lobby were anything to go by, she expected her room would be very much to her liking.

Mrs Clark turned to her husband. 'I wish we'd booked for two weeks.'

Her husband shook his head. 'Ah, New York. You could spend a lifetime here and still only scratch the surface. That's what I love about the place, there's always a surprise waiting around the next corner.'

'And you, my dear,' said Mrs Clark, turning to Sylvie. 'Are you here with someone?' Mrs Clark looked about her as though she expected Sylvie's husband to come and join them any minute.

Sylvie wondered when that would crop up. 'No. I'm in New York on business.' Considering what that business was – outing herself as the fraudster, Love on the Rooftop, who professed that LAT living was the panacea it most definitely was not – she would much rather be in Mrs Clark's shoes right now.

'Business?' said Mr and Mrs Clark in unison.

Sylvie guessed what they were thinking: what was someone her age doing in New York on business?

'What is it you do for a living?'

'I'm a writer.'

'A writer!' Mr and Mrs Clark exclaimed.

Sylvie stared at them. Like most people who found themselves in the presence of a writer, they seemed to develop a sudden bout of self-consciousness as though they are in the presence of a celebrity.

'Are you like, famous?'

Sylvie grinned at Mrs Clark. 'Actually – yes.' She saw no reason to hide behind Love on the Rooftop anymore. In fact, thinking of her alter ego, she thought she'd better hurry and get checked in if she wanted to have dinner before the show. She glanced at the clock on the wall behind reception. 'Crumbs, is that the time? Look, it's been so nice talking to you, but I have to get a move on if I'm going to make *The Who's Who Show* this evening.'

'You're on that talk show?'

'Yes, I'm their star guest tonight.'

'Are you serious?' Mrs Clark squealed.

Sylvie nodded wondering why she told them that.

'We watch that show, don't we?'

Her husband sighed. The bored look on his face suggested he only watched the show because his wife did.

Mrs Clark lowered her voice to almost a whisper. 'They normally announce the guests for the following week but tonight they've kept the guests under wraps.' She stared at Sylvie. 'Who are you?'

'I'm Sylvie Baxter.'

Mrs Clark's face dropped. 'Oh. I've never heard of you.'

'Cheer up, you've probably never heard of her because she's only famous in England,' her husband remarked. 'Remember they said the only detail they were going to give away about their guest on the show tonight was that she was a famous British writer.'

Sylvie nodded. 'That's me!'

Mrs Clark looked disappointed. 'Yes, but rumour had it Love on the Rooftop was going to be on that show.'

Sylvie looked at her in surprise. 'You know about Love on the Rooftop?'

Mrs Clark gave Sylvie a look which said, are you from another planet? 'My friends and I love that column. My husband knows that whatever else I'm doing on this holiday, I'm tuning in tonight to catch *The Who's Who Show*—' She stopped and stared at Sylvie. Then the penny dropped. Her eyes went wide. 'You're her, aren't you? You're Love on the Rooftop.'

Sylvie put a finger to her lips and swivelled her head to check nobody had overheard her being outed in the hotel foyer. She was under contract not to go public before the show.

'I don't believe it! Here, will you …?' Mrs Clark reached into her handbag. Out came the most recent copy of the magazine which featured Sylvie's column. She offered Sylvie a pen. 'Please, may I have your autograph?'

Mr Clark sighed.

Sylvie looked uncomfortable. Of course, she didn't mind giving Mrs Clark her autograph. However, Sylvie wondered what she would think of Love on the Rooftop when she discovered the lies Sylvie had been spinning about LAT living to line her own pockets.

'I'm Ellen, by the way.'

Sylvie took the pen and wrote a brief message to Ellen and her husband wishing them a super Ruby wedding anniversary in New York, before signing the magazine as her alter ego. Sylvie handed Ellen the magazine and pen.

'You have no idea how envious my friends are going to be when they find out I met the writer, Love on the Rooftop, in person, right here in New York before the show.'

Sylvie offered a weak smile in return. After she watched the show, Sylvie guessed that Ellen wouldn't end up sharing that bit of information about her trip to New York.

Ellen caught Sylvie's arm as she turned towards the reception desk. 'Thanks to you, we've been thinking about changing our lives in retirement.'

Sylvie looked at her curiously. 'How so?'

Ellen shook her head as if to say, you need to ask? 'Why, through LAT living of course.'

Sylvie looked at her, aghast. 'Don't do it!'

'What? But I thought—?'

'Trust me, read Dear John before you make the biggest mistake of your—'

'That's what I keep telling her!' interrupted Mr Clark.

Sylvie looked at him askance. 'You know about Dear John?'

'Of course. My buddies and I discovered his blog online, and now we read his column. It's the perfect counter-balance to Love on the Rooftop.' He glanced sheepishly at his wife who was giving him a disapproving glare. He said to his wife, 'Since we started talking about going down that road, I've been pestering you to read Dear John just to find out what happens when LAT living goes wrong.'

She rolled her eyes at her husband. 'I'm a fan of Love on the Rooftop. I refuse point blank to read that garbage.'

Sylvie sighed. 'I agree with your husband, you should read it.'

'You agree?' Mr Clark looked at Sylvie in surprise.

Ellen looked stunned. 'I don't understand...?'

'You will.' Sylvie added, 'What you've got to ask yourself is why I'm here in New York on my own.'

Ellen opened her mouth to say something, but her husband intervened. 'Come on, Ellen, let the lady check in.'

Ellen reluctantly left Love on the Rooftop in peace. Sylvie overheard her saying to her husband, 'But I don't get why she said I need to read Dear John.'

'Let's watch the show tonight,' he replied. 'I'm sure all will be revealed.'

Sylvie stared after them. And no truer words were spoken, thought Sylvie as the receptionist handed her a room key.

5

'Would madam like to reserve a table for dinner?'

Even though she wasn't particularly hungry – the thought of appearing on that chat show was already making her stomach churn – Sylvie looked at the receptionist and said, 'Why not.' Although she'd have no dining companion, she would rather sit alone at a table in a room full of people than stay in her hotel room and stare at four blank walls. She didn't even have her pet dog, Alfie, for company.

Sylvie realised she had been on such a high over the thought of going to New York that it hadn't dawned on her how lonely she would feel when she arrived and found herself in a strange city all on her own.

'Will there be anything else, madam? Would you like a newspaper delivered to your room or a wake-up call in the morning?'

'No wake-up call, thank you.' After the show was over this evening, Sylvie intended to hide away in her room and find an old late-night black-and-white movie to watch on the television, order some food from room service, and raid the mini bar. Then emerge sometime later the next day, when she had slept it off, to do some sightseeing and enjoy the rest of her trip knowing that the show, and the fallout, was behind her.

Thinking of the show, Sylvie said, 'I think I will have a newspaper delivered tomorrow morning.' She thought she might as well read the fallout in the press, then she could see if someone had leaked a photo of Love on the Rooftop to the press. She hoped not. She didn't fancy seeing her face plastered all over the tabloids. However, she needed to know in case she wanted to go out sightseeing incognito. Sylvie had thought ahead when she packed for the trip and remembered to bring a headscarf and large dark sunglasses.

'Will that be all, madam?'

'I think so.'

'Very good, madam. Now, if there is anything else, anything at all, please contact the concierge and he will be happy to help. Just dial zero from your room.'

Sylvie picked up her room key. 'Thank you.'

'Have a nice day!'

Sylvie smiled. She didn't think New Yorkers really said that. She thought it was only something people did in the movies.

Sylvie followed the porter, who was carrying her luggage.

He glanced over his shoulder. 'Your room is on the third floor, so we'll take the elevator.'

'Elevator,' mumbled Sylvie, trying to think like a New Yorker.

They stepped out of the elevator. The porter led the way along the carpeted corridor. Sylvie glanced at one of the gold-rimmed ornate mirrors hanging on the wall as she passed by and caught her reflection. She noted that she didn't look as tired as she thought she would after a long-haul flight.

Fortunately, she wasn't on a night flight. Sylvie doubted she could sleep on a plane, even though she was in business class.

She saw other people lying down for a catnap during the flight. They looked comfortable enough. Sylvie thought perhaps she might have been able to sleep if she hadn't had so much on her mind.

Sylvie caught up with the porter. He'd stopped at a solid oak-panelled door at the far end of the corridor. He turned to Sylvie. 'Sorry about the trek, but the suites are at the end of the corridor, whichever floor you are on.'

'Oh, I see,' said Sylvie, not bothered by the walk. In fact, after eight hours on a plane, and an hour sitting in the back of a limo to get to the hotel, she was quite pleased to stretch her legs.

The porter held the key over the keypad until a light blinked green and she heard an audible click. He opened the door for Sylvie and walked in behind her and straight through another door into the bedroom, where he left her luggage. When he returned, Sylvie was still standing near the entrance, taking in her suite. 'Oh my!'

'Is something wrong?' asked the porter.

'No. Not at all.' Sylvie stared around the room. 'I didn't expect it to be so big.'

'Well, if there's nothing more you need…' He trailed off.

'No, everything is fine, thank you.' She looked at the young man lingering in front of her and remembered that in America it was customary to tip. Sylvie opened her handbag and found her purse. 'Thank you,' she said, handing him a twenty-dollar tip.

'Oh.' He hesitated before taking the note.

'I'm afraid I haven't got change.'

He frowned. 'Neither have I.'

'Ah. I see.' Sylvie held out the note. 'Here, I insist. I've kept you waiting long enough while I chatted to the couple at the reception desk.' She wanted to compensate him for the tips he could have been earning if she'd just got a move on.

The porter gingerly took the note. 'Thank you.' He walked to the door.

She saw him hesitate in the doorway. He turned around to look at Sylvie. 'My mum, she's a big fan.'

'Excuse me?'

'I couldn't help overhearing your conversation. You're Love on the Rooftop.'

Sylvie stared at the young man. She sighed. 'So, you know my secret too.'

'I'm not going to get in trouble, am I?'

'Of course not.' She was wondering if her secret would spread throughout the hotel. At this rate, she wouldn't need to go on the show. Sylvie smiled at the young man. 'Would your mum like an autograph?'

His face lit up. 'Oh boy, I can't wait to tell her who is staying at the hotel.' His face fell. 'I haven't got a pen and paper.'

'Wait there, I can do one better.' Sylvie went into the bedroom and opened one of her suitcases. She returned to the lounge with a copy of the magazine containing her latest article. 'What's your mum's name?' asked Sylvie.

'It's Esme.'

Sylvie wrote a message to Esme, signed it, and handed the magazine to the young porter.

He held it in two hands as though it was something priceless that had to be handled with the utmost care.

She stared at the magazine. After the show, it would probably end up in the trash. Sylvie closed the door behind him, hoping he didn't share his discovery with anyone else otherwise she imagined there would be a stream of people beating a path to her door for an autograph.

Sylvie rolled her eyes. At least after the show tonight, that was one thing she wouldn't have to worry about. She was quite sure nobody would want her autograph when they found out Love on the Rooftop was not enjoying the blissful second honeymoon she'd so vividly written about in her blog and magazine column.

Sylvie locked her door and turned around. The producers on the show hadn't just provided a hotel room for her stay, they'd booked her into a suite. And judging by the size and the furnishings, she guessed this was one of the most expensive suites in the hotel.

Sylvie took a moment to explore her suite. She imagined everything would be on a bigger, grander scale in America, but this was ridiculous. It was larger than her garden apartment back home. There was a huge flat-screen television on the wall in the lounge, complete with two comfortable sofas, two easy chairs, a rug, cushions and expensive-looking oak furniture. There was a large, round oak table and four matching chairs by the window overlooking the street below.

She stepped over to the window to look outside and discovered a kitchenette in a snug around the corner. Sylvie could smell coffee. She walked over to the kitchen counter and found a coffee grinder containing fresh granules. Next to it was a coffee maker, a cup and saucer, and an array of sweet biscuits and pastries. Sylvie switched on the coffee maker and spooned the freshly ground coffee into the filter already waiting in the compartment.

She took a seat at the table by the window while she waited

for the coffee to brew and glanced out the window. Her suite was only three floors up, so there wasn't a view of the New York skyline, but she could see down to the street below and the New Yorkers making their way along Park Avenue. It was already growing dark outside, reminding her that she would have to get ready soon if she wanted to have dinner first before she was picked up by the limo and taken to the show.

She wondered if she wouldn't be able to stomach eating dinner after all. Although she wanted to get the production over with, a part of her wanted something to happen to postpone the show, so she could enjoy her first evening in New York without it looming over her head.

'Huh, chance would be a fine thing,' said Sylvie as she got up from the table and walked into the kitchenette.

She was just pouring a cup of freshly brewed coffee when a phone rang somewhere in her suite. Sylvie put the jug of coffee down and walked into the lounge. She could hear the ringtone more distinctly as she made her way through the lounge toward the bedroom. In the doorway, she spotted the phone on the bedside table beside the huge four-poster bed.

Sylvie raced over and picked it up. 'Hello?' she said breathlessly. 'Yes, this is she… Yes, I accept the call.' Sylvie waited a moment. 'Hello, Marcia. So good of you to call.' Sylvie smiled. She wasn't surprised Marcia had phoned to check she had arrived safely in New York. Marcia wasn't just her editor, but a good friend.

She sat down on her comfortable bed and glanced around the bedroom. 'You'll never guess how big my room is! Well, it's not a room, it's a suite, actually. A limo picked me up from the airport. I've never been in a limo before. They're treating me like royalty. Oops, sorry Marcia, I am so excited I'm not letting you get a word in edgeways.'

Sylvie raised an eyebrow when she heard the reason for Marcia's call. 'What do mean they're postponing my appearance on the show – why?' Sylvie listened, her eyebrows arching. 'What do you mean the other guest has been delayed, so the show can't air tonight?' She frowned. 'But I thought I was their star guest?'

Marcia was just as surprised as Sylvie when she heard.

'So, you don't know who I'm sharing the guest spot with.' It was a rhetorical question. Marcia was as much in the dark over this one as Sylvie.

'Yes, Marcia, I think it's strange too. Why would they keep it a secret?'

Marcia didn't know the answer to that question either.

'Do you know when it's going to be re-arranged for?'

Sylvie wasn't pleased when she heard what Marcia had to say.

'At the end of the week!' She stood up. 'But I was looking forward to having free time in New York after the show…'

Sylvie listened to her response.

'Yes, I know I'll still have some free time, it's just….' Sylvie didn't want to mention that she was looking forward to getting it over and done with because she intended to blow the lid on all the lies that she'd been telling about the idyll that wasn't LAT living. Marcia didn't know that was her intention.

'Okay, Marcia.' She was right: there wasn't a lot she could do about it. 'I guess I'll have to do some sightseeing in New York before the show. Of course, I will. I promise.' She smiled tightly and put the phone down. Marcia reminded her that she wasn't just here for work and made Sylvie promise she would make the most of her trip to New York and have a good time.

Sylvie stood there staring at the phone. The last thing she expected was a phone call postponing the show. But it wasn't that that was really bothering her. 'Who on earth is appearing on the show with me?' Sylvie frowned.

She returned to the kitchenette. Her coffee was now lukewarm. She popped the cup in the microwave and zapped it for a minute or two, then added some cream and sugar. Five minutes later, she had downed the coffee and eaten one too many pastries. She set her empty cup down on the saucer. 'Now what?'

Sylvie returned to the bedroom and started unpacking her suitcases. There was plenty of cupboard space in which to arrange all her clothes. She unzipped one of her cases and found the photo of Gertie that John had framed as a surprise when he started grandpa duty. It was one of the first items she'd packed before she left.

Sylvie sat down on her bed with the photo in her hands. She'd only been gone a matter of hours and yet she missed them all already – her daughters, her grandchild, her colleagues from work. Even – dare she think it – her annoying neighbour in the apartment upstairs. Sylvie glanced at the phone. It was good to hear a familiar voice from home. She wished she could phone her daughters and tell them all about her adventure in New York, but Harriet, Chloe, and Jess had no clue their mother was the successful writer and columnist, Love on the Rooftop. It wasn't something she wanted to share with them on the phone.

She didn't have time to speak to them before they whisked her off to New York. And she certainly didn't want to ring them up and let slip that she was appearing on a chat show in America. The last thing she wanted was for them to find out all about her covert writing career – not yet anyway.

The minute they discovered she was Love on the Rooftop they would realise the lies she had been spinning about LAT living. They already knew the reality – Mum and Dad were separated. However, what they failed to understand was that Mum and Dad were splitting up for good. That was not something she wanted them to find out from some television programme. She hoped Julia kept her promise not to breathe a word about it to Chloe, Harriet or Jess.

In reality, Harriet, a busy working mum, had little contact with Julia. As for Jess, she was living in Australia and, like her older sister, wouldn't be in contact with Sylvie's best friend. It was Chloe that would be the problem. For starters, she couldn't keep a secret. If she found out about Mum's trip to New York, she'd be straight on to her two older sisters. But the only way she'd find out was through Julia, whom Chloe was very close to. That's why Sylvie had been sure to tell Julia to keep her mouth firmly shut for the time being.

Sylvie stared at the photo of her only grandchild. She wished she could ring Harriet and speak to Gertie on the phone, but that was out of the question. She was still in Harriet's bad books. She sighed as she placed the photo frame on the dressing table.

Sylvie returned to her suitcase and rifled through to find a change of clothes for dinner this evening. As she wasn't going anywhere, and her stomach wasn't doing backflips anymore at the prospect of appearing on that show, she thought she might as well keep her dinner reservation in the hotel restaurant.

By the time she had opened her three other cases and found a pair of shoes that matched her dinner outfit, and then retrieved her toiletry bag, makeup bag, and her silk pyjamas for later, she'd had enough of unpacking. The wardrobe and chest of drawers were still empty. Sylvie looked at her three suitcases. They were open and overflowing with clothes where she'd rifled through to find a few items. Sylvie sighed. She knew she should really finish unpacking. She thought to hell with the unpacking and went to run herself a bath instead.

She wanted to take her time getting ready for dinner. First, she was going to have a nice long soak in a luxurious bath. As she lowered herself in the bubble-filled bath that smelled of soothing lavender, Sylvie was thinking about all the things she wanted to see and do in New York over the next few days.

She was trying hard not to let the show at the end of the week put a dampener on things. However, try as she might, her thoughts kept drifting back to her impending appearance on that chat show and the other mystery guest she had no idea she was sharing top billing with. If it wasn't for the fact that this mystery guest had been delayed, and the show had to be postponed, neither Sylvie nor Marcia would have even been aware there was another star on the show. A star whose identity the producers refused to reveal. Sylvie narrowed her eyes. What was the big secret?

6

John was bored. He was restless just two hours into the flight once he'd finished watching a movie and having a chat with his neighbour in the window seat. He then had six more excruciatingly boring hours to go. Now John, and every other passenger on the Boeing 747, was stuck thirty thousand feet above Newark, flying around in circles, unable to land because of a freak thunderstorm.

'Excuse me,' he said to a passing flight attendant.

The flight attendant came to a halt by his seat. 'Yes sir?'

'Look, is there any chance we will land soon because I've got somewhere to be in…' John checked his watch, subtracted six hours from UK time and realised even then he would not make it. He slumped back in his seat. 'Never mind.'

'I'm sorry about the delay, sir. As soon as we receive clearance, we can begin our final descent.'

He nodded and reached for the in-flight magazine, which he'd already read cover to cover – twice. Next time, he would remember to pack a novel. Except there wouldn't be a next time. John sat there and folded his arms across his chest. He imagined Love on the Rooftop was on the show, at this very moment, enjoying her five minutes of fame. Although he was having second thoughts about appearing on the show, he still wanted to meet Love on the Rooftop.

Fifteen minutes later, the captain announced that they had been cleared to land. They began their final descent into Newark Airport. John furrowed his brow, wondering what would happen when he arrived. If he wasn't appearing on the show, did that mean they would put him on the first flight home? He didn't fancy that. He'd been looking forward to his free time in New York after the show.

John passed through arrivals with flying colours, although he felt a bit intimidated by the passport control person who kept asking him questions: how long was his stay? Was he staying with relatives? Was he here on business or pleasure?

He got himself in a spot of bother when he couldn't decide whether it was business or pleasure, and then told passport control he wasn't sure whether he would be walking through arrivals and straight back to departures.

The young man motioned at two police officers standing in the arrival's hall.

John's eyes went wide when he saw the two burly officers with stern faces making their way towards him. He turned back to the young man in the booth. 'Look, I was meant to be a guest on a chat show in New York.'

He caught the sceptical look on the young man's face.

'It's true,' John continued. 'The show was going on air…' John checked his watch, 'over an hour ago, but as you can see, I didn't make it because my flight was delayed. Now I don't know whether they are going to send me straight home.'

'They…?'

'The producers of the show who paid for my trip to New York.'

The bored look on the young man's face said he'd heard it all before; John's was just another one in a long line of cock-and-bull stories he had to listen to all day – every day.

'It's the truth,' John tried to convince him as he glanced over his shoulder.

The officers were fast approaching.

He turned back to the young man. 'Look, I can't imagine they'll let me stay in New York for four days if I don't appear on *The Who's Who Show*.'

A flash of recognition registered on the young man's face. He sat up in his chair. 'Did you just say you were appearing on *The Who's Who Show*?'

John looked at him nervously and nodded. He recalled the confidentiality agreement he had signed. He was not supposed to go public with his identity before the show.

The young man looked past John and shook his head.

John glanced over his shoulder. The two burly police officers came to a halt and turned around. He saw them resume their posts at the far end of the hall, watching the arrivals.

John turned back to find the young man staring at him intently. 'So that's why they postponed the show.'

'Pardon me?' John was about to ask what he was talking about when his phone rang. He'd switched it on as soon as he got off the plane, intending to ring the assistant editor at the magazine's head office and find out what he should do now, since he hadn't made it to the show.

John took the mobile phone out of his pocket and saw the number. He looked at the young man. 'Do you mind if I take this? It's my editor back in London. He might tell me what's happening.'

The young man nodded.

'Great, thanks.' John answered his phone. The first words out of his mouth were, 'I didn't make it to the show, and I don't know what to do!' His mouth felt dry. He'd flown all this way to land in a foreign country, and now he wasn't sure whether the all-expenses-paid trip was off, and he was on his own. John was wondering if he wouldn't have enough money in his bank account for the flight home.

'Pardon me?' John blinked in surprise when he heard what the assistant editor had to say. 'Did you just say they postponed the show because my flight was delayed?' John stared at the young man in the booth, who was nodding his head. 'It's been postponed until the end of the week? Does that mean I can stay in New York?'

John breathed a sigh of relief when the assistant editor confirmed his trip hadn't been cancelled. They'd just reorganised things so he would appear on the show at the end of his stay rather than at the beginning. The assistant editor checked that John was okay with the new arrangements.

'Okay?' repeated John in surprise. It wasn't just okay. It was 'Bloody marvellous!' John was over the moon that they weren't abandoning him at Newark Airport. He glanced at the young man in the booth and said, 'I'm staying in New York!' Then his face dropped. There wasn't much point appearing on the show if he didn't get to meet his nemesis.

John returned his attention to the phone conversation. He

lowered his voice. 'What about Love on the Rooftop?' He listened and nodded his head. 'I see. So, she's staying on in New York until the end of the week to appear on the rescheduled show too... Yes, I agree that's splendid news.'

John listened to what he said next. John's smile faltered. 'Okay, yes I promise.' John ended the call and put the phone back in his pocket. He'd just told the assistant editor that he would make sure he made the most of his time in New York and to remember that he wasn't just here for work; he was here to have a good time.

John knew why the assistant editor had emphasised this. He recalled the last phone conversation they had when he had phoned John with the news that the producers of a talk show in America wanted to fly him to New York to appear on their show. John imagined his reaction to that news was not quite what the assistant editor had expected. Of course, he'd agreed to go, but he hadn't sounded enthusiastic about it. In fact, when the editor had said it was unfair of them to ask him to drop everything at a moment's notice, to appear on the show with Love on the Rooftop, John had rudely snapped at him.

John recalled his retort. "Drop what?" He'd just lost access to his grandchild. Consequently, he'd been suffering from writer's block and was struggling to write his next column for the magazine. And to cap it all, that very morning he'd got a Dear John letter from his wife and then spotted her leaving with a suitcase. The fact that she hadn't asked him to look after her dog suggested she hadn't just gone on a trip, she was leaving for good. The Dear John letter burning a hole in his pocket was all the evidence he needed to convince him that when he returned home, the garden apartment downstairs would be empty.

'Here you are, sir.'

John looked threw the young man in the booth a blank look.

'Your passport, sir.'

'Oh, yes, right.' John's mind was elsewhere. He slipped the phone back in his pocket and took his passport.

The young man looked about him before lowering his voice. 'Look, I shouldn't ask, but before you go, will you do something for me?'

John shrugged. 'Sure – what is it?' He furrowed his brow as he watched the young man get out of his seat. He appeared to be looking for something under the desk in the booth, out of John's line of vision.

His head popped up. The young man's serious expression gave way to a disarming smile. 'Please, can I have your autograph?'

'My autograph?'

The young man looked down at the magazine in his hands. 'You are Dear John, aren't you?'

John followed his gaze to the recent copy of the magazine. The words Dear John were emblazoned on the front cover.

The young man eyed John thoughtfully. 'I knew they had cancelled the show because their mystery guest couldn't make it. I watch that every week. So, when you said you were meant to be appearing on that show, I was sceptical at first. You wouldn't believe the BS that comes out of people's mouths sometimes. But when I saw your name on the passport – John – it got me thinking. It was a British writer that was appearing on the show. That's the only clue the producers would give away as to the identity of their mystery guest. So, I'm thinking – here's a guy who's British. I wonder if he's also a writer.'

John didn't answer. He was going to get himself in a whole heap of trouble if word got out about Dear John's identity before the show.

'You look like a writer.'

'Do I?' John replied before he could stop himself.

'I knew it! You're Dear John!'

John put a nervous finger to his lips in a shushing motion.

'So, can I have your autograph?'

John looked at the magazine in his hands and sighed. 'Have you got a pen?'

'Oh boy, wait till the guys hear about who I met at passport control today.'

'What's your name, son?'

'It's Jensen.'

'Right you are.' John wrote a brief message on the front of the magazine and signed it. He handed the magazine back to the young man. 'I don't mean to sound rude, but how old are you?' John asked.

'I'm twenty-six – why?'

'Well, I imagined it was people from my generation or middle-aged who were reading my column.'

'How come?'

'I suppose because someone older is more likely to have been married for years, or perhaps divorced and embarking on a new relationship. It's those sorts of people I thought might consider LAT living. That's who I wrote my articles for. I wouldn't presume to tell people how they should or should not lead their lives. But I wanted to tell them about my experiences of living apart together – it isn't always a bed of roses that some might lead you to believe.'

John was thinking about Love on the Rooftop's column.

'So, you're wondering why somebody my age is reading your column.'

'Well, yes. You're just starting out in life. You'll meet some-one, if you haven't already, and set up home together. I would have thought living apart would be the furthest thing from your mind.'

'You'd think so,' said Jensen glumly. 'It's my girlfriend. We've been living together for a year. It started off okay. Just recently, she got annoyed whenever my friends come over or when I play my Nintendo. Then suddenly it's like, "You don't pay me any attention. You don't buy me flowers. You don't surprise me anymore with romantic gestures." And I'm thinking: what's this all about?'

John knew what it was about: the honeymoon period was over. They'd got to know each other over the past year living together and probably discovered things about each other that they didn't much like. That wasn't a surprise. Nobody was perfect. Sharing your life with somebody involved a huge dose of compromise; there was no way around that.

He didn't say that out loud or add that things didn't always improve as you got older. In fact, John believed it was par for the course when you'd been with the same person for so long. The trouble was even though you still love them, there were times you just wished to see the back of them.

'She never used to be like that before…'

John looked at him askance. 'Before?'

Jensen rolled his eyes. 'Before she started reading that blasted Love on the Rooftop. You know we split up because of that blog.'

John raised an eyebrow in surprise. 'I'm sorry to hear that.'

'We haven't really split up. I don't know what you'd call it. She's calling it living apart together.'

'Oh, dear.'

'Exactly.'

'The thing is, she makes out that I'm the one who's done something wrong. So, I started reading *Love on the Rooftop* and as luck would have it the writer mentioned some columnist with opposing views called Dear John. That's how I came by your column. And thank god I did. I'm sick and tired of me being the one who's in the wrong with my Nintendo and my mates coming around to watch baseball. I'm no saint, I grant you, but she's got her issues too. I get Dear John, I really do. It's great to hear the other side of the story.'

John nodded his head in agreement. That was the whole idea.

'I've tried to get her to read Dear John, but she's having none of it. In fact, because of Love on the Rooftop, she reckons if we live apart then things are going to go back to the way they were before we moved in together.'

John caught himself from laughing out loud at that ridiculous notion. 'And have they?' he asked. It was a sarcastic rhetorical question. Of course things wouldn't go back to that honeymoon period before they started living together, as Love on the Rooftop would have them believe.

'Well, that's the weird part.'

John frowned at the young man. He hoped he wasn't about to say...

'It's kind of working – living apart together.'

'You've got to be kidding.'

'Uh-uh. I still enjoy reading Dear John, but I must admit, my girlfriend is right. I don't know what our plans are in the long haul, but right now we both agree that LAT living has saved our relationship.'

John stood there, stunned.

'Is there a problem here?'

John jumped at the sound of an authoritative voice. He turned to find the two police officers, who he thought were still patrolling at the far end of the arrival's hall, standing either side of him.

The young man looked at Dear John. 'There's no problem here, officers. This is the writer, Dear John. He was due to appear on *The Who's Who Show*. His plane was delayed. That's why they've postponed the show. He's just received a call from his editor confirming he is staying in New York.'

One officer turned to John. 'Are you going to be on the show this week?'

John rolled his eyes. He couldn't very well lie to an officer of the law. He nodded, hoping he hadn't done something wrong, apart from breaking his confidentiality agreement, that is.

The other officer looked at him. 'Can I shake your hand?'

'Uh, okay.'

The officer shook John's hand enthusiastically.

'He's another fan, if you haven't already guessed,' Jensen quipped.

'Oh... yes... right.' He didn't think anybody would have heard of Dear John across the pond. Little wonder they'd invited him on *The Who's Who Show*. Thinking of which, John was looking about him anxiously. What if his secret spread through the airport? At this rate, he wouldn't need to go on the show to reveal his real identity.

Both officers shook his hand. John knew what was coming

next, so he opened his old British Airways carry-on shoulder bag and found the most recent copy of the magazine, inside of which was his weekly column. John held it up. 'Look, I've only got one to sign.'

They didn't seem to mind, so he wrote both the officers' names down on the front of the magazine and signed it.

In the queue behind him, he overheard one passenger turn to their companion and say, 'I think he's a celebrity. Shall we ask for his autograph too?'

John glanced at them and then down the long line of disgruntled passengers, still waiting to get through passport control. A rumour was spreading through the crowd like wildfire that he was the writer, Dear John.

John hastily zipped up his bag. 'Right, well if we're all done here, I think I better dash.' He glanced at the crowd of passengers and didn't fancy being mobbed by fans. Besides which, he didn't want to miss his ride to the hotel. The show had arranged for a driver to meet him at the airport.

He wished Jensen the best of luck and left through the gate. John slowed. Waiting on the other side of the barrier were people holding small placards. John looked for his name and spotted it on a whiteboard held by a young woman in a smart, black suit.

John stopped in front of her. 'Er, I'm John Baxter. Are you here to take me to my hotel?'

'Yes, that's me.'

'Oh.' He wasn't expecting his driver to be a fresh-faced bronze goddess with a pearly white smile and an infectious laugh.

'Welcome to New York! I hope you've had a pleasant flight.'

'Oh yes, very pleasant indeed,' John lied. He had no idea why he just told a fib to the attractive young lady. Perhaps the smile that lit up her face made him feel less inclined to have a moan.

'I'm parked right outside. Follow me.'

John followed her, wheeling his case behind him. Outside, he saw a row of cars parked in the drop-off zone. He walked past a stretch limousine, shaking his head at the thought of the extravagant fool who was being picked up at the airport in that. John tutted at how many car-parking spaces one vehicle was clogging up.

'Here we are.'

John heard the young lady's voice behind him. He'd been too busy staring at the limo and didn't notice he'd walked straight past her.

John turned around.

She was standing by the limo with the passenger door open.

John's eyebrows shot up in surprise. 'This is for me?' He gaped at the limousine.

'Absolutely.' She nodded. 'Unless there's another famous British writer due to appear on *The Who's Who Show*,' she joked.

There was, but John reserved comment.

'Why don't you take a seat and I'll just put your suitcase in the trunk.'

'There he is!'

John turned around and saw the couple who had been standing behind him in the queue at passport control racing down the path towards him, waving frantically. They shouted out, 'Dear John!'

John climbed into the back of the limo and slammed the door shut.

To his relief, a moment later the young woman opened the

driver's door and got behind the wheel of the car. She turned to look at her passenger. 'Friends of yours?'

John shook his head. He scrambled over to the seat behind the driver and said, 'Um, can we leave now?'

The young woman didn't waste any time. As they sped away from the airport parking zone, John spied the couple coming to an abrupt halt. A small crowd was gathering at the spot where the limo was parked not a moment ago. John thought perhaps it wasn't a bad thing that the show was at the end and not the beginnings of his break in New York. At least he would get to see the sights without being mobbed.

'There's champagne in the fridge to your left.'

'Champagne?'

'Uh-huh.'

John reached for a glass. He needed a drink. John poured himself a large glass of champagne and leaned back on the long leather seat in the rear of the car.

'How do you like it so far?'

'I think it's going to take some getting used to,' said John, wiping his brow. He wasn't used to this – being a celebrity. He much preferred the old John Baxter who lived a somewhat boring life of quiet anonymity at number 67 Penfold Street, Holland Park, W11. John pursed his lips. Perhaps he should have thought of that before he so readily agreed to appear on that show. He rolled his eyes and poured himself another large glass of champagne.

'Not used to a big city, then?'

'Oh, you meant New York.' John stared out of the window. After seeing New York in movies, the city already felt familiar, as though he'd been here countless times before. Perhaps that's what attracted so many Brits to New York, like bees to honey; it was the familiarity of the place. But nothing quite beats seeing it for real.

'Do you mind if I open a window?' After being cooped up in a plane for hours, John wanted to feel the breeze on his face. The windows were tinted so dark he wasn't seeing much of anything.

'Sure. But I think you'll find it's a bit....'

John opened the window and was pelted by rain. He swiftly closed the window. 'Were you going to say rainy?'

'Uh-huh.'

'I must say, I'm surprised by the weather. I was expecting New York to be colder. I thought it snowed here in December?'

'Yes, most often we have terrible winters where it's so cold it takes your breath away. It's unseasonably mild at the moment.'

John helped himself to another glass of champagne. The next thing he knew, someone was shaking his shoulder. 'Mr Baxter, we've arrived.'

'Oh, dear me.' John opened his eyes. 'I must have dozed off.'

The young woman with the pearly white smile was sitting beside him in the back of the limo. 'Here, let me take that.' She took the empty glass from John's hand.

'Crumbs.' I didn't spill anything, did I?' John checked the black leather upholstery. When he looked up, the driver was already outside, standing with his luggage.

John climbed out of the limousine and staggered over to the young woman. 'Oh dear, I don't think I should have drunk three large glasses of champagne on an empty stomach.'

Some passers-by stared at the limousine as they walked by. John caught them checking him out, wondering if he was some sort of celebrity.

The young woman looked up at the hotel. 'The hotel restaurant has an excellent reputation. I would recommend making a reservation for dinner if I were you.'

John's stomach was rumbling. 'Right you are.' He checked the time. He was still on British time, so according to his watch it was almost midnight. Little wonder he had fallen asleep in the back of the limo. He could tell the jet lag was going to catch up with him; in New York, it was only seven o'clock in the evening.

'I'll go ahead and ask the concierge to make you a dinner reservation.'

John nodded and reached down for his suitcase.

'Here, let me help you with that.' A young man dressed in a porter's uniform had appeared outside the hotel. He insisted on carrying John's one small suitcase and his old BA shoulder bag.

John followed the porter into the hotel, asking him what time the hotel restaurant opened. He was famished. He glanced at his watch. He would just have enough time to unpack before making his way down to the restaurant for dinner.

7

Sylvie smiled as the waiter showed her to a small, intimate table for two. He pulled out a chair. She sat down and watched the young man clear away some cutlery and a wineglass, leaving just one place setting for dinner.

Sylvie looked at the empty place opposite her. She'd told the concierge that she would dine alone. Fortunately, she had a table off to one side. Sylvie didn't mind eating alone. She'd heard the hotel restaurant had an excellent reputation. However, she didn't fancy sitting in the middle of the restaurant by herself, surrounded by people dining together.

Sylvie picked up the menu and heard the maître d' greeting hotel guests as they walked into the restaurant. She glanced at a young couple being shown to their table nearby before turning her attention to the menu. The choices were plentiful, and all sounded delicious.

'You know, we really should stop meeting like this.'

Sylvie looked up at the sound of a familiar voice. She turned in her seat to look over her shoulder. 'Bertram!' exclaimed Sylvie in surprise.

'What are you doing here?' they both said in unison.

John precision-folded his pyjamas and placed them in a drawer in the bedside table. That was the last of his unpacking. He walked over to the double wardrobe and adjusted one of his shirts on a hanger before closing the wardrobe door. John looked at the laundry bag in his hand. He'd found it in the wardrobe and decided that as this was an all-expenses-paid trip, he might as well change for dinner and put his clothes out to be laundered. John would have thought twice about the cost if he was paying for it himself.

He left the laundry bag on the bed and was just zipping up his empty suitcase, intending to store it under the four-poster bed, when the phone on his bedside table rang. John raised an eyebrow; he wasn't expecting a call.

John sat down on one of the comfortable wing chairs and picked up the phone. 'Hello?'

It was the concierge telling him he was late for his dinner reservation.

'Crumbs, I didn't realise the time.' He looked at his watch. 'Yes, I still want my reservation. Thank you. I will be along shortly.' John put the phone down. He had been so busy unpacking his suitcase and neatly arranging his clothes and sundry items in the wardrobe, and his toiletries in the bathroom, that he had lost track of time. Luckily, he had already changed for dinner.

John stuffed the clothes he'd worn on the flight into the laundry bag. He stood in front of the long mirror affixed to the wardrobe door and undid the top button of his crisp white shirt.

The chinos were clean too, although he was wearing the same smart-causal blue blazer he had worn on the flight. John frowned at his reflection. He'd forgotten to inquire about the dress code for dinner. John hoped he didn't need a tie. In fact, he didn't own one anymore. After decades working in an office as an accountant, he had ditched the old John who wore off-the-peg suits and scruffy jeans and jumpers at the weekend, which were eons old.

John checked his appearance in the full-length mirror once more. For years he'd been carrying around excess weight thanks to Sylvie's penchant for cooking Italian meals with plenty of cheese sauce, and John's habit of helping himself to large portions – and second helpings. It wasn't the fact that he had to fend for himself when Sylvie moved downstairs that had encouraged his weight loss. John had progressed from TV dinners to homemade chicken pies, which didn't help his waistline. He tried joining a gym, but that ended in disaster when he sprained his ankle on the first visit. He didn't bother going back.

What led him to become leaner and fitter, and drop down to a weight he hadn't been since he got married, was something he couldn't have foreseen. He'd started doing regular exercise twice a day, every day, come rain or shine. But he wasn't going to the gym. He was walking Sylvie's dog while she was at work. Then he found himself with the responsibility of looking after Gertie, their two-year-old grandchild, practically full time all on his own. He was on the go from the moment she arrived, until he handed her back at the end of the day. It was exhausting and demanding caring for a small child at his age, but that played a big factor in the new slimmed-down John. And the new happier John.

He turned away from the mirror and stared at the picture on the dressing table. It was the photo of Gertie that normally had pride of place on his mantel shelf at home. That was the first thing he had packed for his trip to New York. It was the first professional photograph of Gertie that had ever been taken. They gave him three copies of the photo. He then bought three photo frames so Sylvie and their daughter, Harriet, had one too.

Harriet was over the moon when he surprised her with the framed photograph of her only child sitting on a faux fur rug smiling at the camera. However, John neglected to mention just where that photograph was taken. Gertie had attended a photo shoot for a modelling agency that was seeking photogenic toddlers in advertising campaigns for their clients. She passed her screen test with flying colours and was to become their most successful child model. It wasn't long before she jumped straight to the big leagues, filming television commercials and appearing in advertising campaigns for some of the major high street stores.

That was all in the past now, before Harriet found out about their little charade – pretending *both* grandparents were looking after her daughter when all along Sylvie was really at work. The agency had agreed to keep Gertie on their books while John sorted out a little domestic issue, as he called it. John didn't tell them that he didn't know when she'd return, if ever. He didn't know when he'd see her again, let alone whether Harriet and his son-in-law, Dominic, would trust either John or Sylvie to look after her again.

John thought about that first photo shoot he had taken Gertie to which arose from their trip to the job centre one day. He recalled walking into the job centre, determined that if Sylvie could get back into work, then so could he. However, it wasn't John who had walked out with a job, but his cherub-faced grandchild.

It all began as a bit of fun, attending a photo shoot for a modelling agency one rainy afternoon. And the rest is history. She had earned so much money that he went to the bank and opened his grandchild's first ever savings account. John smiled at Gertie's photo when he recalled it wasn't that long ago, before Sylvie started paying off their debts, that Gertie had a healthier bank balance than he did. But he wouldn't have it any other way – after all, she'd earned it.

Harriet and Dominic didn't know about Gertie's extra-curricular activities while John was looking after her. Now he had lost access to Gertie, he wasn't inclined to tell them, just in case it added fuel to the fire and gave them even more reason to continue not letting him see his grandchild. He didn't think it would upset them, though. In fact, he'd been looking forward to showing them the nice, healthy balance in her savings book. He'd tucked it away safely in his desk drawer at home.

When he did get around to telling them, John was going to leave out the part about the reason he signed her up with the modelling agency in the first place. John saw a way of making some ready cash to pay his outstanding bills. It turned out the agency paid very good money *and* a chaperone's fee. At that time John needed money, and if he couldn't find a job, then... John cringed. He couldn't believe how low he could go. He was, without doubt, a first-class schmuck to even contemplate using his grandchild's money to pay his bills. But he had considered it.

In the event, he didn't touch a penny – not even his chaper-one's fee. Thousands of pounds deposited into her savings account continued to accrue until he suddenly lost access to Gertie. John was worried what their reaction would be when they found out he had signed her up to a modelling agency without their permission — and kept it from them for all this time.

John missed his little granddaughter terribly and all the fun they used to have together during Grandpa days, so much so that he decided to call Harriet and try another apology. It wasn't the weekend. He would have to ring her at work. She wouldn't like that. He knew she would be too busy to take personal calls.

John considered whether to contact her about something work-related as an excuse to speak to her. He could do that. He worked for the same magazine even though he now only spoke with the assistant editor because Harriet — the editor-in-chief — was still cheesed off with him over Gertie. But she was still his boss, the person who had hired him as their new columnist when she discovered his anonymous blog online. She would take a work-related call if he said it was important. Then he could steer the conversation to Gertie.

John picked up the phone and glanced at the photo of Gertie as he dialled the number for an outside line. He paused and then slowly replaced the receiver. He didn't want to make things any worse than they already were. What John really didn't want to hear was that he wouldn't be seeing Gertie on his return from New York.

He stood up and walked out of the bedroom, glancing at his watch. John sighed. Now he was late for his dinner reservation, but John couldn't care less. He'd lost his appetite. The only reason he was going to venture down to the restaurant and see if he could still get a table, was that it would be a darn sight preferable to sitting alone in his hotel room staring at four blank walls, wishing he was at home right now knocking on Harriet's door.

John thought he had been cured of his penchant for

perfection when he started looking after Sylvie's dog and their grandchild. With sticky fingers up the walls, dog hairs on his sofa, and his lounge resembling a toy shop, John realised he was fighting a losing battle if he thought he could keep his apartment upstairs looking as pristine as it used to. John thought he would resent all the mess. But it was a small price to pay for Gertie's company. Even the dog grew on him. John didn't do pets. Never had. He didn't see the point of having an animal in the house until he'd spent time with Alfie.

After he lost access to Gertie, he depended on seeing that merry cocker spaniel each morning when Sylvie left him outside his apartment door, before she left for work. Now he didn't even have the dog. Alfie had gone. She'd taken him with her in the taxi the morning John had received his phone call inviting him to New York.

John stood at the door to his suite and stared at the cushions he'd just straightened. He hadn't intended to do that. He just had the impulse to plump up the cushions and position them just so on the sofa, and wipe around the surfaces in the kitchenette even though they were clean. But he had spotted a minute dusting of freshly-ground coffee on the worktop.

It was very thoughtful of the hotel to leave a pot of coffee ready for his arrival. However, he didn't sit at the table by the window enjoying a coffee and eating a pastry or two. No, John had to make sure the kitchen was spotless instead.

He'd been like that most of their married lives. He didn't use to be so pernickety before he met Sylvie. It wasn't her fault he'd become so anal about everything once they married. But John had an agenda, and it was almost as though if everything wasn't in its place, even the small inconsequential things like a scatter cushion on the sofa, the plan for their lives together would fall to pieces.

It wasn't normal behaviour. He could see that. It was a symptom. A manifestation of some deep-seated unhappiness that John could now articulate; despite marrying the woman of his dreams and achieving all the things he had set his sights on in life like having children, a home, and a good job to support his family, he was unfulfilled as a person – always had been.

In hindsight, he didn't think the plan helped. It didn't leave any room for the one thing that scared John the most and yet exhilarated him at the same time – there was no wriggle room for the unexpected. What boring, uptight, stuffed-shirt John had craved all his life was work that was more meaningful than merely providing a paycheck at the end of the month. But that meant taking a risk. And back then he wasn't a risk-taker – far from it. That's why he couldn't let go of the plan. The problem was that the plan for their lives together seemed to take him down a road ever further from his heart's desire.

John had always harboured a secret desire to be a writer, something he never shared with Sylvie because he was afraid she wouldn't believe in his dream; she wouldn't believe in him. What would she have thought of her husband if he told her one day that he wanted to ditch his secure well-paid job as an accountant to be a writer? He could only imagine what her reaction would be because John never had the courage to ask her, let alone follow his dreams. Until one day his safe, comfortable, familiar world fell apart when Sylvie upped and moved downstairs.

That's when John made a discovery. After years of just thinking about being a writer, he had sat down at his laptop and started to write. Then something magical happened: John found his true self. This was what he was meant to do with the rest of his life. The success of his blog and his new job as a columnist was just the icing on the cake.

John's life had taken on a whole new dimension. Working in the evenings, and looking after Alfie and Gertie during the day, didn't leave any time for plumping up cushions that didn't need plumping or wiping kitchen worktops that didn't need wiping. His life over the past few weeks was hectic, exhausting. But for the first time in his adult life John was doing and being all the things he wanted to do and be, and it had cured his insatiable desire for everything to be tidy and in its place. He had put all that neat freak – the world was going to end if he didn't tidy up – nonsense behind him. Or so he thought.

He'd lost Gertie. He'd lost Alfie. And he'd lost the love of his life. And to top that, his new writing career might well be over. Sylvie had walked out that door. They were no longer living apart together which meant, now she was gone he had nothing to write about. John suspected that's why he saw the emergence of the old, unhappy John who had nothing better to do with his time than clean up some minuscule coffee granules.

John stepped out into the plush hallway and closed the door on his spotless suite. He paused outside the entrance to check the time. His watch said half past two in the afternoon. John was still on UK time. He did a quick mental calculation and realised he had lingered too long in his suite. His reservation would most likely have gone to someone else by now. He recalled the young woman who drove him to the hotel mentioning how popular the restaurant was.

John shrugged and decided to go down to the restaurant anyway and see if they could squeeze him in. He strolled down the long the corridor, not in any great hurry. His room was right at the end of the hallway where, according to the porter who carried his suitcase, all the expensive suites were located. There was one suite for special guests on each floor.

'Excuse me,' said John, to a passing porter. 'Could you direct me to the lift to the ground floor?'

The porter looked at John blankly.

'Oh. Pardon me,' said John, realising his mistake. 'Sorry. I think over here you call them *elevators*.'

'You're British, aren't you,' said the porter, smiling at John.

'Guilty as charged,' answered John.

'The elevators are down the hall on your left.'

'Right you are.'

'Er, no sir, I said on your *left*.'

John opened his mouth to say something, then clamped it shut deciding to spare the porter any more British colloquialisms.

John walked along the corridor, pausing to check his appearance in a mirror. He didn't know why he was bothering. It wasn't as though he was interested in meeting somebody now he was newly single, unless their name was Sylvie and they used to live in Holland Park.

John wondered what his soon-to-be ex-wife was doing at this moment or, more to the point, who she was with. He could just imagine she had unpacked her suitcases and was now having dinner with Bertram in her new digs. That's what John was afraid of – she had moved in with that pompous git with the double-barrelled surname, whom she'd met at The Rooftop Café in Hanover Square.

John recalled the paper napkin he had discovered stuck to her fridge door with a fridge magnet. It had the words: *The*

Rooftop Café embossed in thick black lettering along one side, along with his name and number scrawled across the top.

John stepped into the elevator and scowled. He was assuming that Sylvie had moved in with Bertram. John recalled spotting Sylvie loading her suitcases into the back of a waiting taxi after he'd found his Dear John letter. But where else would she have gone? She could have gone to stay with her best friend, Julia. That possibility would have lightened John's mood if it wasn't for one thing that made that scenario implausible. Julia lived on a houseboat. Anyone who knew Sylvie knew her aversion to boats of any kind.

John was back to thinking about Bertram. He stood in the empty elevator and watched the floors count down as he scowled some more. He didn't want the thought of those two together to ruin a pleasant evening meal. It was his first day in New York, and he had travelled thousands of miles to get away from thoughts of his wife leaving him. He resolved to try and not think about them for the rest of his trip.

John stepped out of the elevator and asked a passing hotel employee for directions to the hotel restaurant.

She led him through the impressive, marbled entrance lobby and then along a short corridor towards a set of oak double doors with ornate carvings. The doors were propped open.

As he neared the door to the restaurant, he could hear the distinct buzz of a room full of people, accompanied by the clatter of cutlery on plates. John's mouth watered at the thought of a delicious restaurant meal. He hadn't eaten out in ages, not since he had taken Sylvie to Fellini's in London, the restaurant they used to frequent when they first got engaged. Of course, that was way back when they were still living apart together and were on speaking terms. John rolled his eyes. Now she probably had dinner out in fancy restaurants with Bertram.

Once again John was back to trying to put all thoughts of Sylvie and Bertram out of his mind for the duration of his trip. That was no easy feat when he took a cursory glance around the hotel restaurant, and all he could see were happy, smiling couples enjoying their meal together. John heaved a sigh and resolved not to feel sorry for himself.

'I hope you enjoy your meal,' said the hotel employee.

'So do I,' commented John. He was famished. The food in business class on the flight over was, contrary to expectations, not that bad at all. In fact, John would say it was rather good, but not that plentiful. There was only so much you could vacuum pack in a small foil container.

John joined a small queue, waiting to be seated. He glanced around the room to see if there were many tables free. John was so hungry he would share a table if it came to it. However, it didn't look as though there would be any problems securing one. The restaurant was quite large, and it appeared to be only half full.

While he waited for his turn to be seated, John glanced around the room at some meals that were being served. His mouth watered again. It all looked delicious.

It wasn't long before he was the next in line to be seated. He watched the last couple ahead of him being shown to their table. John saw the waiter hand the couple a menu.

He was just making his way back towards John when one of the diners summoned the waiter. John rolled his eyes – typical. He glanced at the annoying man seated at the table who had called him over. John gasped in surprise when he thought he recognised him. He stepped forward to take a closer look. It had to be a case of mistaken identity. John's next thought was *who am I kidding?* He'd recognise that pompous git with the snow-white hair and bronze tan anywhere – that was Bertram Wyndom-Price!

'What the heck is *he* doing here?' said John under his breath before he remembered what Sylvie had told him. Bertram was a hotelier and owned hotels around the world. John furrowed his brow. Perhaps he was here on business. Or perhaps he owned this hotel. If he owned a hotel on Park Avenue in New York, then John realised he had woefully underestimated Sylvie's wealthy new friend.

John wondered who Bertram's dining companion was. He couldn't see because the waiter was standing in front of them obscuring John's view.

John saw the waiter nod his head and gather up the bottle of wine that was sitting in an ice bucket in the centre of Bertram's table. Perhaps it wasn't to Bertram's liking thought John as he watched the waiter walk off with the unopened bottle still in his hands. John turned his attention to Bertram once again, who was talking to his dining companion. John's eyes shifted from Bertram to see who was seated at his table.

John's eyes went wide in disbelief. 'It can't be!' John took an involuntary step back in surprise. He wasn't just surprised – shocked. 'What the heck was *she* doing here?'

Without thinking, John was about to stride over and ask her, when the penny dropped. He scowled across the room at Bertram. 'That pompous git!' exclaimed John out loud, oblivious to the fact that people at nearby tables had heard him talking to himself.

'So, he'd whisked her off to New York.' John didn't know

why he was acting all surprised. He should have seen it coming. Even so, the irony wasn't lost on him as he backed out of the restaurant.

John's first thought was to confront her. What was she was doing? She was still a married woman, for goodness' sake. John's next thought was that he didn't relish explaining to Sylvie what he was doing here in New York. That's why he was backing out of the restaurant before either of them spotted him.

'Would sir like to be seated?'

John turned around at the sound of a man's voice. He had nearly backed into the young man who was approaching from behind. John shook his head. 'No, thank you.' He stepped aside and then almost careered into the waiter who a moment ago had taken away a bottle from Bertram and Sylvie's table.

The waiter just caught the new bottle of wine in time before it slipped out of his hands.

John saw the label as he brushed past. It was champagne. John groaned as he watched him take the bottle of champagne over to their table. He still couldn't believe Bertram had whisked her off to New York. And Sylvie had agreed to go.

John turned on his heel and shuffled off to the elevator. Of all the hotels in the all the world, thought John miserably, why oh why did they have to be staying in this one?

8

'Of all the hotels in all the world,' said Bertram, smiling. 'I still can't believe you're staying in this one.'

Sylvie returned his smile. 'Yes, it's quite a coincidence, isn't it?'

'I'll say. What happened to, "I can't fly to New York at a moment's notice." Hmm?'

'That was different,' said Sylvie, her smile fading somewhat. 'This is work-related.' She didn't want to think about how things had changed since that conversation with Bertram in his London apartment. She couldn't just take off then, but she could now because she no longer had to keep up a charade for Harriet's sake by making sure she was home by five thirty every weekday evening to hand over Gertie. She regretted not telling Harriet the truth in the first place; she wouldn't be around to look after Gertie with John because she was working. She knew why she'd kept up the pretence: one thing would lead to another and she would have told Harriet what she did for a living.

That didn't bother her. Sylvie wanted to tell Harriet all about her new career. But if she did, then she'd have to divulge who she was, the writer Love on the Rooftop. She couldn't do that because the whole reason Harriet had to return to full-time work was because she had lost her lucrative freelance job to "an anonymous blogger with a ridiculous name." Sylvie recalled her words verbatim.

Sylvie had got herself in a bind and then implicated John in the deception, only for things to turn out very badly indeed. She still couldn't get over the fact that Harriet and Dominic had cut off all contact between Gertie and her grandparents. Sylvie hoped things would change by the time she returned from New York.

'Are you here to write an article for your column?' asked Bertram.

Sylvie pursed her lips. She didn't want to discuss the reason she was here. Sylvie changed the subject. 'So, what about you, Bertram? Are you here on business?'

'No. I'm with someone. In fact,' Bertram glanced at his watch, 'they're late.'

Sylvie looked at him in surprise. She had no idea he was waiting for someone to join him. 'I'm sorry, I didn't realise you weren't dining alone.' Sylvie stood up and glanced around the room for a free table, far away from Bertram and his date.

'Where are you going?'

'I'm going to shift to another...'

'Sylvie, sit down. It's not what you think.'

The sound of a small child interrupted their conversation.

'There you are,' exclaimed Bertram as he rose from his seat.

Sylvie turned in her chair and saw a young couple with a toddler making their way towards them. She recognised the young man. He was carrying a little boy in his arms called Rory.

'Oh my.' Sylvie's face coloured. This was embarrassing.

'Sylvie, I want you to meet my daughter, Amy.'

Sylvie smiled at the slender young woman with short spiky blonde hair and Bertram's soft brown eyes.

'Amy, this is Sylvie Baxter, the lady I was telling you about. She is the one responsible for our reconciliation.'

'Oh, I wouldn't say that.'

'I would.' Bertram beamed at Sylvie.

Sylvie was glad things had gone according to plan. When she found out Bertram was estranged from his daughter and two-year-old grandson, after her own experience losing access to Gertie, she didn't want Bertram to suffer the same fate.

'And this is Amy's fiancé,' continued Bertram.

The young man looked at Sylvie, a flash of recognition in his eyes. 'You're the lady from Hanover Square Gardens.'

Sylvie gave him a tentative smile as she said to Bertram, 'We've already met.'

Ralph shook Sylvie's hand warmly.

'No hard feelings?'

Sylvie felt embarrassed about pretending she did not know who Amy or Bertram were.

'Not at all. If it weren't for you, we wouldn't be here in New York with Amy's father.'

'That's very true,' said Bertram, beaming.

'Hello, Rory.' Sylvie ruffled his hair.

Rory smiled at Sylvie.

Sylvie got out of her seat. 'Well, it was lovely to meet you.'

Bertram looked up at her in surprise. 'Why are you leaving?'

'To let you have dinner with your family, Bertram.'

Bertram rolled his eyes. 'Sylvie, please join us.'

'Yes, please do,' said Amy, glancing at her fiancé and nodding at him to say something to persuade Sylvie to stay.

Ralph saw Amy looking at him with those large brown eyes, egging him on to add his voice of protest to her leaving. 'Oh right, well it's kinda weird bumping into you again in New York, of all places.'

Sylvie caught Amy rolling her eyes at him, suggesting he'd said the wrong thing. Sylvie smiled. She was all too familiar with that scenario. The times John had put his foot in it, and Sylvie just wished he'd kept his mouth shut. Amy and her fiancé were already acting like a married couple.

'Oh, er, what I meant to say was that it's great to bump into you again and it would be grand if you would join us.' He glanced furtively at Amy, checking he had said the right thing this time.

Amy's expression said she approved.

'Well, that's settled then,' said Bertram, waving at a waiter to come over.

'Are you ready to order, sir?'

Bertram shook his head. 'First, we need to be seated at a table that accommodates...' Bertram did a quick head count, 'five.'

'Of course, sir. Right this way.'

When they had all taken their seats at a larger table, Amy said to Sylvie, 'It's our first visit to New York.'

'Mine too.'

'We don't know anyone in New York, besides Bertram, so it's nice to see a familiar face.'

'Here, here,' agreed Bertram, smiling at Sylvie.

Ralph glanced at Rory in his arms and turned to Sylvie seated next to him. 'I promised I'd send my parents a text when we arrived. Would you mind giving Rory a cuddle while I...?'

'I'd be delighted.' Sylvie smiled at Rory. Who could resist an offer like that?

Ralph passed Rory to Sylvie. The little boy had no complaints as he settled on Sylvie's lap and resumed playing with his toy cars on the table in front of her. Sylvie looked around the table at Bertram, Amy, and Ralph, and missed her own family dreadfully.

The waiter reappeared and waited while everybody studied the menu and chose what they were having for dinner. Then he took their orders.

'Are you here on holiday, Sylvie?' asked Amy.

Before Sylvie answered, Bertram interrupted. 'Sylvie is a writer. She's here researching an article for her column.'

Sylvie glanced at Bertram and averted her gaze. She hadn't actually said that in so many words. That's what Bertram had presumed. Sylvie wished it were that simple.

'You're a columnist?' said Amy. 'Do you write for a women's magazine?'

Sylvie nodded her head and inwardly groaned. She knew where this was leading. Next, Amy would ask about her column and which magazine she worked for.

'Which magazine do you—?'

'Here we have the smoked salmon,' said the waiter, interrupting Amy.

'I'm having smoked salmon,' said Sylvie, waving her hand at the waiter as she breathed a sigh of relief. The waiter couldn't have timed it better. The conversation with Amy was steering in a direction she didn't want to go down. Sylvie would rather not reveal she was Love on the Rooftop.

'Here, let me take him,' said Amy.

Rory let out a cry of annoyance when Amy lifted him up. 'Rory, you have to go in the high chair to eat your dinner.'

'Nooo.'

'I'm afraid you do.' Amy gave him a kiss before she put him in the high chair and did up the straps. 'There now, don't fuss.'

Another waiter appeared with a child's meal as soon as Rory had sat in the high chair.

A few minutes later everyone had been served the first course. They'd all agreed to dispense with starters, so Rory wouldn't have to wait too long for his dinner.

Sylvie watched Amy cut Rory's roast potatoes into bite-size pieces. It didn't surprise her that Amy, Rory, and Ralph were here with Bertram. After their reconciliation at The Rooftop Café, she was delighted that Bertram had whisked them off to New York for a break. She couldn't imagine that with Amy's job as a paralegal, and her partner working full time as a painter and decorator that they had many opportunities to take a holiday. On top of which, from what Sylvie gathered, they lived quite low-key and weren't flush with cash. Bertram hadn't given Amy a penny in support since she fell pregnant. She doubted they could afford a trip to New York.

Sylvie glanced at Bertram beaming with pride as he watched his grandchild eating dinner. Although Amy was adamant she wanted to support herself and her son with no help from her father, Bertram must have twisted her arm and persuaded her to come with him to New York. Sylvie was glad he did.

Sylvie looked around the table and thought how wonderful that she should find herself in the company of friends when she was so far from home. As much as New York seemed familiar from the movies, she still felt a foreigner abroad. And to make matters worse, she was not here enjoying New York with her husband as she always imagined she would. It wasn't a holiday. She was here to blow the lid on a lie in front of a studio audience on live television.

Every time she thought of the show, Sylvie's tummy felt as though it was doing somersaults. She wasn't a gregarious extrovert. The last thing Sylvie wanted was to be in the public eye. She was a writer. Appearing on a chat show was way out of her comfort zone. She would prefer to be sitting at home on her laptop, writing. Sylvie willed herself to stop thinking about the show. Although she had wanted to get it over with, Sylvie was relieved the show had been postponed and the next few days were free to spend sightseeing in New York. It made her wonder how long Bertram and his family were staying in New York.

Sylvie turned to Bertram. 'Are you in New York long?'

'Oh, a week – at least.'

'That's great.' Sylvie was rather hoping she could meet up with them again. 'Have you got any plans?'

Bertram exchanged a look with Amy. He said to his daughter, 'Shall I tell her or—'

'Oh, let me,' said Amy, in excitement. She put her knife and fork down and held out her hand to show Sylvie her beautiful engagement ring.

Sylvie didn't let on that she had seen it before when Ralph had shown it to her in Hanover Square before he proposed to Amy. 'It's stunning.'

'I know. I couldn't believe it when Ralph asked my father for my hand in marriage and then proposed to me on bended knee.'

Neither could Sylvie. She had seen that proposal through her binoculars when she was sitting in Hanover Square Gardens spying on Bertram. Sylvie had been over the moon that not only had Amy resumed contact with her father, but her boyfriend had proposed to her too.

'There's more,' said Amy. 'After the proposal, Daddy asked us to come with him to America. We're planning to get married in New York next summer. Daddy said we could use his hotel as a venue.'

'Oh my!' said Sylvie, clapping her hands. 'How exciting.'

'Yes – isn't it.'

Amy smiled at her father.

'Have you seen the hotel yet?' asked Sylvie, looking from Bertram to Amy.

'Oh yes.'

'Well, what's it like?'

Amy furrowed her brow at Sylvie and turned to her father. 'She doesn't know, does she?'

Sylvie looked from Amy to Bertram. 'Know what—?'

Bertram chuckled as he wiped his mouth with a napkin. 'Remember that time I wanted to whisk you off to see the New York skyline from my hotel?'

Sylvie nodded. 'Yes, of course.' Sylvie also remembered how disappointed she was when she realised she couldn't just drop everything at a moment's notice.

'Well, as luck would have it, you are staying in that very hotel.'

'Pardon me?'

Amy said, 'This is Daddy's hotel.'

Sylvie wasn't the only one who was surprised.

Ralph had been cutting into his juicy steak when he overheard Amy's last remark. He looked up. 'Amy, you didn't tell me your father *owns* this hotel.'

Amy looked sheepishly at Ralph. 'I know. I thought it might be a bit much that Daddy has paid for the trip without you finding out that we're staying in one of his hotels too.'

Sylvie was getting the impression that Amy had not let on just how wealthy Ralph's future father-in-law was.

'I thought you might find it all overwhelming.'

Sylvie glanced at Bertram and could see her point. It was enough to meet your father-in-law for the first time and propose to his daughter, without feeling intimidated in the presence of Bertram Wyndom-Price – the second.

'Amy, tell Sylvie about your engagement party.'

'Engagement party?' Sylvie and Ralph said in unison.

'Dad!' Amy rolled her eyes. 'I haven't even told him yet.'

Ralph turned to Amy. 'What's all this about an engagement party?'

'Daddy wants to throw us an engagement party.'

'I see.'

'It's er the other reason we're in New York this week.'

Bertram cut in. 'It was meant to be a surprise, but when I asked Amy if you would both come to New York this week, she wasn't sure whether you could get the time off work. And she's got her evening course and part-time work. So, I had to tell her the reason I wanted you both to accompany me to New York.'

Ralph looked at Amy in surprise. 'When were you going to tell me about the engagement party?'

Sylvie noted a hint of irritation in his voice.

'I thought it was a shame that Daddy had to tell me about the surprise engagement party, so we thought why not keep it under wraps from now on, that way at least the groom-to-be can have a surprise.'

'Oh, I'm surprised all right.'

Amy beamed at her fiancé. 'It's all good then?'

'Of course. Why wouldn't it be?'

Sylvie stared at Ralph. She wasn't convinced it was all good. She glanced at Bertram and wondered if he should have asked them whether they wanted an engagement party before he went ahead and organised one.

Although Bertram had the best intentions, the problem with being so wealthy was that he could make things happen, without a second thought, the moment an idea popped into his head. Sylvie guessed that was how he got to where he was today. He wasn't a successful businessman for nothing. He was used to taking charge and getting things done. However, that was fine for business, but perhaps Bertram needed a different approach in his personal life.

Sylvie knew that over the years since Bertram was left to raise his daughter alone, he hadn't had much of a personal life. It was all about work. It was all about getting results. In Sylvie's experience, Bertram tended to see things in black and white. He didn't stop to consider that things weren't always so cut and dried. Here was a case in point. He was taking charge and making decisions about other people's lives without stopping to consider that perhaps Amy and her fiancé might have plans of their own.

'What a stroke of good luck that you are in New York, Sylvie,' said Bertram. 'Are you here for the next few days?'

'Until the end of the week,' Sylvie admitted. She didn't want to be reminded about the talk show and the price she was going to pay for her all-expenses-paid trip to New York.

'That's excellent news,' exclaimed Bertram. 'I was going to ask you to come to New York with me.'

'Really?'

Bertram nodded. 'I wanted you to accompany me to my daughter's engagement party, but I knew that with all your family commitments you couldn't just drop everything—'

'Drop what?' Sylvie blurted bitterly.

Bertram raised his eyebrows.

'Sorry,' murmured Sylvie. 'I'm afraid I still haven't patched things up with Harriet. So when the magazine I work for got in touch when they received a call from the producers of an American chat show.'

'An American chat show?' said Amy in surprise.

'Oh, er, yes. Didn't I mention that?' Sylvie had just put her foot in it. She didn't intend to tell them that. It just slipped out.

Amy shook her head. 'That's the first I've heard of it. You must tell us all about it,' said Amy, staring wide-eyed at Sylvie.

Sylvie recognised that look in her eyes. Amy was staring at her anew, as though she had just found out she was in the presence of a celebrity. Which wasn't far from the truth.

Sylvie tried to play it down. 'I've been invited to appear on this chat show in New York, so I thought – why not? There's nothing to hang around for at home. I'm free.'

'Are you?' said Bertram, smiling broadly.

'It's no big deal.'

'No big deal?' Amy disagreed. 'You're going to be on television! I wouldn't call it *no big deal*, would you, Ralph?'

Ralph sat there, his fork suspended in mid-air, looking quite surprised that the unassuming lady he had met in Hanover Square Gardens was to appear as a guest on an American television show.

Now Sylvie was feeling embarrassed by all the attention.

'So when is the chat show?' asked Bertram.

Sylvie sighed. 'It was meant to be a whirlwind visit, enough time to appear on the show tonight and have a bit of free time in New York before the flight home.'

'A bit of free time? Oh, that won't do at all.' Bertram shook his head. 'You can't come here and not see the sights.'

'The show was postponed, so I've got all this free time until the end of the week.'

'Excellent,' said Bertram. 'That means you can see the sights and come to my daughter's engagement party.'

Amy turned to Sylvie. 'Oh yes, please say you'll come.'

Much to Sylvie's relief, all talk of her impending appearance on that show was suspended in favour of Amy's upcoming nuptials.

'Please, please, please,' said Amy, bouncing up and down on her chair like an excited schoolgirl.

Rory saw his mum getting excited and got excited too, banging his spoon on the table and sending a dollop of food flying across the room.

Sylvie smiled at them all seated around the table. 'I guess I'm going to an engagement party in New York!'

9

Sylvie changed into her silk pyjamas as soon as she returned to her hotel room after dinner. The next thing she did was check out the pillow menu. She'd never even heard of such a thing until she found one had been left on her bed after the chambermaid had been in to do the turndown service. Intrigued, Sylvie had sat reading it while she ate the delicious foil-wrapped chocolate the maid had left on her pillow.

Sylvie plumped up the two extra pillows she'd ordered from the pillow menu. They were the softest goose-feather pillows, and they were also quite huge, which rather suited her king-sized bed. As she reached over to switch the off the table lamp, she caught sight of the framed photograph of Gertie.

'Goodnight, my sweet.' Sylvie's gaze lingered on the cherubic face of her only granddaughter before she switched off the light. The room was plunged into darkness.

Sylvie put on the eye mask to cover her eyes. She didn't need to wear them as the room was pitch dark, but they had come as a set with her brand new silk pyjamas and Sylvie rather fancied trying them out. The only thing she didn't have were earplugs. She was staying in a hotel in the heart of Manhattan. She imagined she would hear some noise from the street below, like the sound of traffic along Park Avenue, the odd siren, or people walking by. But Sylvie didn't hear a peep as she snuggled under the Egyptian cotton sheets.

'Bliss.' Sylvie exhaled. It had been quite a day. She had taken her first long-haul flight and been whisked to the hotel expecting to go on the show tonight, only to discover they had postponed it. If it weren't for that, she would have dined much earlier and missed bumping into Bertram and his family in the restaurant. It was such a large hotel she wouldn't be surprised if she'd gone through her entire stay without realising they were here. Sylvie was so glad that hadn't turned out the case.

She was delighted when an envelope appeared under her door later that evening, with an invitation to the engagement party inside. The party coincided with her trip to New York. Sylvie couldn't resist writing all about it in her blog. She didn't intend to write while she was away. She thought there wouldn't be time. But she had brought her notebook, just in case. She was glad she did. Now all the events since her arrival had been written in her blog – along with an announcement, for the benefit of her British readers, that she was appearing on that show. It was going to be broadcast live in England too.

Sylvie wondered what her readers' reaction would be when they discovered who she was and how she had been deceiving them, writing all about the supposed benefits of living apart together.

She had been laying there fretting over what she would write for the magazine, once her column ended, when something occurred to her: why would anybody want to read another word written by Love on the Rooftop when they found out the truth about her experiences of living apart together with John?

For now, Sylvie wouldn't worry about that. She'd had a long day – an extra five hours accounting for the time difference between London and New York. When the plane landed, she had been delighted to put her watch back five hours, which meant she still had plenty of the day left to unpack, relax and dine in the hotel restaurant. Now she felt dog-tired and exhausted. For once, she was getting an early night so that she could make the most of her first full day in New York tomorrow.

Sylvie rolled over in bed, getting herself comfortable. There was so much room she thought she could roll over at least twice more without falling out of bed. Sylvie felt very childish, but she gave it a try. The pillows on the other side weren't as comfortable, so Sylvie rolled back, snuggled under the covers once more and felt herself drifting off into the land of nod, grateful for such a comfortable quiet—

'What in heaven's name!' Sylvie's hand shot out from under the bed covers towards the bedside table, feeling for the light switch. She pulled the eye mask up on to her forehead as she switched the lamp on. Sylvie sat bolt upright in bed and stared at the ceiling. 'You have got to be kidding me!' She had been drifting off to sleep, with everything so quiet that she almost imagined she was the only guest in the hotel. She was just thinking what a fantastic stay she was going to have in New York when the music started. It sounded like someone was having a party upstairs.

She leaned her head back on the headboard and grimaced at the ceiling. Worse still, it was coming from the suite above her. Sylvie didn't think that Bertram would allow this sort of behaviour in one of his hotels. She certainly didn't feel it was acceptable for some inconsiderate guest to have a party in their hotel room at – she glanced at the digital clock on her bedside table – 'Eleven o'clock!' Sylvie didn't realise how long she had been sitting in bed writing her blog before she turned in.

Sylvie gave them the benefit of the doubt, so she waited a moment or two to see if the person in the suite above her turned the music down. Five minutes later, she couldn't stand it any longer. She threw off the covers and clambered out of bed. Sylvie flung open her hotel room door to discover she wasn't the only one woken by the racket on the next floor. Other guests, up and down the corridor, had opened their doors bleary-eyed, wondering what was going on.

Sylvie spotted a porter making his way along the corridor carrying a suitcase for a late-night arrival.

'Excuse me!' called Sylvie as he neared. 'Do you know what's going on up there?' She pointed at the ceiling.

'Rumour has it,' said the porter, 'there's a celebrity in the suite upstairs.'

'A celebrity?' Sylvie bristled. 'Well, that's no excuse!'

The porter shrugged as though he'd seen this behaviour countless times before, and it was just one of those things.

Sylvie watched the porter continue on his way down the corridor. She glanced at the middle-aged man standing in the doorway across the hall from her room, yawning and shaking his head. 'I'm going to phone the night manager,' he said. 'This is out of line.'

'I quite agree.' Sylvie empathised. 'This sort of behaviour is unacceptable. They will get a piece of my mind, I can tell you,' Sylvie said to her neighbour before he closed his door.

Sylvie whipped back inside her room and found her room

key, put on her slippers and stepped out into the corridor. She wasn't waiting for the night manager to do something about it. She couldn't call on Bertram to sort it out, because she had no clue what his room number was. Besides which, he might be one of the lucky ones tucked up fast asleep right now in a suite far away from the inconsiderate guest on the next floor.

Sylvie marched along the corridor. The loud thumping music was still playing full throttle above her head. As she made her way to the elevator, the other guests on her floor were closing their doors and returning to bed. Nobody else was marching to the lift, intending to have it out with the person upstairs. But the thought of someone being so inconsiderate made Sylvie's hackles rise.

She knew why she was super-sensitive to the selfish person on the next floor. Sylvie bet her neighbours along the corridor had not experienced this at home. It reminded her of that phase John went through when he was throwing parties upstairs, disturbing her sleep week after week just because she wouldn't move out of the garden apartment so he could rent it out.

When Sylvie still refused to move out, even after she found out about their dire financial situation, that's when John started throwing those godawful parties. He didn't even like parties with loud music. He was more of a dinner party type of person who preferred a small gathering and some classical music playing softly in the background. That's why Sylvie knew he was doing it on purpose just to get back at her.

Sylvie stepped into the elevator and pressed the button for the next floor. Although this was different – she didn't have to get up and go to work the following day – she was not putting up with it.

John thought he heard someone knocking on his door. He wasn't sure because the music in his room was so loud. Trouble was, John was a bit drunk. Unfortunately, he had picked up what he thought were the television controls and had accidentally switched on some music system he didn't even know was in the room. He had no idea how to turn the damn thing off.

John fiddled with the controls. Pressing the buttons at random, he inadvertently turned the volume up even louder. The rap music was giving him a thumping headache. John tossed the controls across the room and made his way to the bedroom to phone the night manager. John was so drunk he was having trouble using the phone. The numbers on the phone were swimming in front of him. John couldn't even remember what number he dialled for the reception. He got through to another guest's hotel room instead.

'Oops, sorry.' John put the phone down and stumbled back into the lounge. Now he could clearly hear someone knocking on his door – banging more like. John raised an eyebrow and glared at the door. 'How rude!' He stepped forward, grasped the door handle and yanked open the door.

'I'm sorry sir, but we've had complaints.'

'Complaints?' John stared at the concierge.

'Yes, sir.' The concierge looked past John into his hotel room. 'Are you having a party in your room?'

'Party?'

'I must insist that you turn the music down.'

'Ah yes – the music.' That reminded John why he was trying to phone reception. 'I can't turn it off.'

'Turn off what, sir?'

'That damn racket!'

The concierge looked John up and down with disdain. He did not appreciate being bombarded with phone calls from irate guests over yet another celebrity who decided to get drunk, or high, on his watch. The concierge sighed. 'May I come in?'

John stepped out of the doorway and with a grandiose wave of his hand ushered the concierge into his room.

The concierge walked into John's suite and rolled his eyes at the state of the room.

John stood in the doorway with his hands over his ears trying to block out that godawful din. A few seconds later everything went deathly quiet. John lowered his hands and sighed in relief.

The concierge appeared by John's side. 'Will there be anything else, sir?'

John shook his head in embarrassment and closed the door, leaving the concierge standing on the other side.

The concierge tutted at the door and turned to leave. He frowned when he spotted a hotel guest marching along the corridor. She was wearing pink pyjamas, and she was walking at such a pace that her silk dressing gown was billowing behind her. She was also wearing pink fluffy slippers, and she had an eye mask on her forehead.

He sighed heavily when he realised she was heading straight for him with a disgruntled look on her face. 'What now?' he whispered under his breath.

Sylvie had spotted the concierge as soon as she stepped out of the elevator. When the elevator doors opened, Sylvie was surprised to discover there was no loud music coming from one of the rooms on this floor. Everything was quiet. As soon as she spied the concierge emerging from the suite at the end of the corridor, she guessed he had beaten her to it and already had words with the guest staying in that suite. Sylvie still wanted to check that the inconsiderate guest had got the message, and it wouldn't happen again. 'Have you put a stop to the party?' Sylvie said to the concierge.

'Party?'

'I heard loud music coming from the room above me.'

'Oh, we have everything under control, madam.'

Sylvie frowned at the door.

'I can assure you,' continued the concierge, 'that there wasn't a party.' The concierge recalled the state of the room and thought there might as well have been. 'The hotel guest had a little problem with the controls to the stereo system. It won't happen again.'

'I see.' Sylvie wasn't sure whether she believed him or he was just covering for his celebrity guest.

'Will there be anything else, madam?'

'No.'

'Well then, I bid you goodnight.' He took his leave.

Sylvie watched him stride down the corridor. She turned back to the door. All was quiet. There wasn't a sound coming from inside that suite. No television. No sound of anybody moving around behind that door. She wondered if the occupant had gone to bed. Sylvie had half a mind to knock on their door anyway just to be sure it wouldn't happen again. If she wasn't standing there in her pyjamas, she might well have.

Sylvie looked down at her fluffy pink slippers. In the heat of the moment, Sylvie didn't think twice about marching out of her hotel room in only her sleepwear. Now she was standing outside some stranger's door she was suddenly feeling self-conscious. Besides, she didn't know who was behind that door. Sylvie was just turning on her heel to leave when something entered her head which swiftly changed her mind. It was the thought of John and those wretched parties.

'Right, that's it!' Sylvie was determined that her week in New York was not going to be spoiled by the inconsiderate guest behind that door. Sylvie wanted to make sure it wouldn't happen again. Celebrity or not, whoever he was, he was going to get a piece of her mind. Sylvie could well imagine the concierge hadn't told them off. He probably asked him, oh so nicely if you please, to turn the music down. And then added in his gracious tone, *will there be anything else, sir?*

Sylvie raised her hand and knocked loudly on the door.

John was spread-eagled face down on his bed when he heard someone knocking again. He turned his head and grimaced. 'What now?' He had just made it from the door to his bedroom, which seemed to take an age. Why did American hotel suites have to be so darn large? John had cursed under his breath forgetting that a few hours ago when he first arrived, he had been over the moon at the size of his suite.

When John finally made it into the bedroom, after the concierge turned the music off, he had stood at the foot of his bed and literally fallen face first on to the bed where he intended to slip away into a drink-induced coma. Unfortunately, he couldn't get off to sleep. The loud knocking was like someone with a chisel and hammer pounding on his brain. John tried putting a pillow over his head. That didn't work.

'Go away!' John shouted although he was aware that whoever was knocking would not hear him from the door.

'Oh, for goodness' sake!' If he wanted them to stop, he would have to answer that door.

Somehow John found himself back at the door to his suite. He opened the door and blinked in surprise. There was nobody there.

John poked his head around the doorframe. The corridor was empty apart from a woman walking down the hall towards the elevator. Although she was quite a distance away, John was pretty sure she was only wearing her night garments.

'Americans!' He tutted. 'You'd never see us wandering around hotel corridors, in the dead of night, in our PJ's and fluffy pink slippers.' We British are far too reserved, thought John as he closed the door.

10

John crawled out of bed and groaned when he caught sight of the empty bottles of booze littering the floor by the minibar, and almost slipped on one as he stumbled into the bathroom. He ran the tap and sluiced his face with cold water.

'What a way to start my first day in New York.' He stood there staring at his reflection in the mirror. 'I look like crap.' John had a hangover.

He emerged from the bathroom some forty-five minutes later, having showered and changed out of the clothes he'd slept in. At least he looked a bit more presentable, even though he was still feeling the after-effects of cleaning out the minibar.

John stood in the doorway to the lounge and groaned. He didn't know what he'd got up to last night. Fortunately, the amount of booze he'd consumed meant he couldn't remember. Although going by the state of his suite, it was apparent he'd done more than raid the minibar. His hotel suite looked like a tip.

'Good grief.' John couldn't get over the state of it.

He walked over and stared at the coffee table littered with small white boxes. He picked one up and glanced inside. 'Ugh!' It was the remnants of a cold Chinese takeaway. John raised an eyebrow. At some point last night, he must have ordered takeout. He didn't remember doing that, although it would explain the greasy brown stain down his new designer shirt.

His eyes drifted to a huge cardboard pizza box. 'What's this?' He bent down and opened the lid. Inside there was a massive pizza, the largest he had ever seen in his life, with only one slice missing. John couldn't believe he'd ordered a pizza, too. He'd also ordered room service, as there were plates with half-eaten sandwiches and nibbles among the leftover Chinese takeaway.

'Why did I order so much food?' John couldn't believe how wasteful he had been. For a split second, he was worried about the hotel bill until he remembered it was an all-expenses-paid trip. Even so, that didn't excuse all this. Maybe he'd had company, he thought. John scratched his head and whipped into his bedroom to check. The bed was empty. He breathed a sigh of relief. So was the bathroom. Although he recalled standing at his door late last night – or was it early this morning – watching a woman in her nightwear walking down the corridor.

John stood there concentrating hard, trying to remember whether he had invited someone up to his room last night. Try as he might, he couldn't recall the events of yesterday evening. What he remembered, with awful clarity, was what had led to this episode of binge drinking: he had seen Sylvie with Bertram in the restaurant of this very hotel. Little wonder he had got upset and raided the minibar.

Worse still, it reminded him of those godawful parties he used to throw in his apartment for Barbara and her friends. He turned around and stared at the kitchenette. It was a silly thought, but he half-expected Barbara to emerge wearing his dressing gown and carrying a plate in each hand containing a cooked

English breakfast. John shuddered. He'd always hated those parties. It was a relief when Sylvie came knocking on his door one day to give him a piece of her mind. It had been the wake-up call he needed to get his act together.

However, when he saw Sylvie leaving the house with suitcases packed, soon after he found his Dear John letter, his first thought was to go out and buy a large bottle of Drambuie to drown his sorrows. Somehow, he'd avoided going back down that route. But seeing Sylvie with that Bertram fellow, knowing they must have flown to New York to stay in this hotel together – well, that was the final straw.

John's eyes settled on the two empty bottles of wine sitting on the coffee table. 'That explained a lot.' He glanced at the mini bottles of alcohol littering the floor. Although there were quite a few, he didn't think you could get drunk on the contents of a minibar. He resolved this evening not to find out. John's head was still pounding after last night. Besides, he wanted to make the most of his time in New York.

This was a chance in a lifetime. He didn't know when he would be back, and he wasn't going to throw away this opportunity by spending his nights getting wasted and his days sleeping it off in a hotel room. Fortunately, he hadn't woken up that late. In fact, glancing at his watch, John realised there would be just enough time to grab some breakfast in the restaurant before it closed until lunch.

John grimaced. The thought of food made his stomach churn. So did the possibility of running into Bertram and Sylvie again, having a cosy tête-à-tête in the hotel restaurant. John decided he couldn't stomach breakfast after all. Despite opening a window, the smell of leftover Chinese takeaway was still permeating the room, making him feel queasy.

'I need some fresh air.' John grabbed his coat, his wallet and his room key, and stepped out into the corridor. It smells a hell of a lot better out here than in there, he thought, closing the door behind him.

He took a deep breath and turned around too swiftly. John caught himself in time before he pitched forward. He paused for a moment and waited for the corridor to stop spinning, realising he'd underestimated the effects of all that booze last night. He wasn't a young man of twenty-odd or thirty-odd anymore. At sixty years of age, even he recognised he was too old for binge drinking.

John had always been conservative and couldn't remember a time in his adult life when he had got drunk – until he retired and made one heck of a mess of things. Fancy converting the house into two apartments. Fancy getting them into debt at their time of life because he had underestimated the cost of the conversion. Fancy losing his wife into the bargain. John rolled his eyes. *What was I thinking?*

He sighed heavily and made his way to the elevator. John exited the lift along with a large group of hotel guests animatedly chatting about the day ahead of them, sightseeing in New York. John wished they weren't quite so loud. He rubbed his temple and held back until there was a sufficient distance between them.

John was shuffling through the hotel lobby, nursing a hangover, and made the mistake of glancing in the restaurant as he passed by. It was later in the morning, and there were very few guests still having breakfast. John spotted them almost immediately. Sylvie and Bertram looked as though they were just finishing a leisurely meal together. At least they were deep in conversation and didn't look over in his direction as he passed by. If they had, they would have seen his miserable face staring back at them.

John walked past reception and managed a smile for the concierge. 'Good morning.'

'Good morning, sir.' The concierge couldn't summon up a smile for the inconsiderate guest who was drunk last night. He pitied the maid who was going to clean up the mess in his room.

John couldn't fail to notice his frosty exterior. Perhaps he wasn't a morning person, thought John, dismissing the grumpy concierge as he approached the doors that led outside.

The doorman opened the door to the guest.

'Good morning, sir. How are you this morning?'

'Very well, thank you,' John lied.

'Have a nice day.'

'Oh, I intend to,' John replied. He stepped out into the bright sunlight. John winced and held a hand over his eyes. 'Why does it have to be so bright?'

'Pardon, sir?'

John turned around to the doorman and smiled weakly. 'Nothing.'

'Can I get you a taxi?'

'No, thank you. I'd like to take a walk.'

He lowered his hand from his eyes and spotted two black limos parked at the kerb. John grimaced. The shrill sound of the phone on his bedside table right ringing insistently had woken him up this morning from his drink-induced coma.

John thought he'd missed the show last night until he remembered they had rescheduled it – thank god. It was the assistant editor in London on the line telling him to get ready for his tour of New York, courtesy of the show's producers. John recalled that early morning wake-up call with distaste as he eyed the stretch limos. He didn't know who the other was for, but he knew one was for him. He might have been tempted if it was the same bubbly young woman who had driven him from the airport yesterday, but that wasn't the case.

'Mr Dear John?' asked one driver through the open window. He had spotted the man in his sixties that fitted the description, leaving the hotel.

'Nope, that's not me,' said John, shaking his head vigorously as he quickly walked by, down the street, heading nowhere in particular. He always wanted to ride in an official New York yellow taxicab. However, it wasn't going by the limo that really bothered him. The real reason he wasn't so keen on the sightseeing tour the producers at the show had arranged was that he had a good idea where they would take him.

It's not that he didn't want to see the view from the Empire State Building or walk over the Brooklyn Bridge, or visit Wall Street and pay his respects at the Twin Towers Memorial. He wanted to do all those things, and more besides. It's just that he always imagined doing them with Sylvie.

John continued walking down Park Avenue. He glanced up at the blanket of clouds above and felt the wind picking up. John guessed a downpour was imminent. He wished he'd brought an umbrella. He'd stepped off his flight yesterday expecting to see snow, but there wasn't a snowflake in sight.

It was December and John had expected he would see New York as it appeared on television in the run-up to Christmas with snow. But it was not to be. It was disappointing; it reminded him of a wet December back in Blighty. John couldn't complain. At least the upshot was that he could get out and about rather than being holed up in his hotel.

John had seen the weather in New York on the news when their winters were ferocious, and they experienced blizzard conditions. The only thing he was experiencing right now was the wind picking up with the promise of rain. A few raindrops fell. Once again John wished he had brought his brolly. He intended to walk the few blocks to Central Park, but if this kept up, then he was going to get soaked.

He was just doing an about-turn, intending to head back to the hotel, when he spotted a yellow taxicab coming down the road in his direction. John stood at the kerb and held out his hand. A boyish smile played on his lips. He'd always wanted to hail a cab in New York.

The taxi driver spotted a man standing at the kerb theatrically waving his hand in the air. Unsure whether he was hailing a cab, the driver pulled over anyway and wound his window down. 'Do you need a cab, sir?'

'Absolutely.' John smiled at the driver and climbed into the back of the cab just as it started to pour.

The driver turned in his seat and eyed his passenger, who sounded British. 'Where to?'

'Now that's a good question.' John shrugged. 'I must confess that when it rained, I just decided to go for a ride in a New York City taxicab. It's always been on my bucket list.'

'Okay.' The taxi driver sighed. 'You're not the first tourist and won't be the last whose come all the way to New York to ride in the back of a yellow cab. But don't you want to see any sights?'

John scratched his chin. There was plenty he wanted to see, just not on his own. Not without—

'There's the Empire State Building. I could drop you off there, and you could see the views from the top.'

John shook his head from side to side.

The taxi driver saw John shaking his head in the rear-view mirror. 'Okay, how about…' He reeled off all the tourist destinations John was familiar with that were also on his bucket list to see in New York.

Once again, John sat there, shaking his head. Then he had a thought. John leaned forward in his seat. 'Can you take me to somewhere a bit off the tourist map, so to speak?'

'Off the tourist map? Did you have anywhere in mind?'

'Nope. Why don't you surprise me?'

'You like surprises?'

John grimaced. 'Not particularly. Let's just say I've grown accustomed to them over the last few months.'

The taxi driver checked John out in the rear-view mirror and caught his sour expression. 'I'll tell you what – how about I surprise you in a nice way?'

John managed a smile. 'How would you like to be my driver for the day?' John hastily added, 'Can I do that? Can I hire a New York City taxi for an entire day?'

'Yes, you can do that. The question is, have you got the dough?'

'Pardon me?'

'We're on the meter, so what I'm asking is have you got enough money to—'

'Ah, right you are,' said John, catching his meaning. He opened his wallet. Inside was a wad of cash in American bills that had been left for him in an envelope at the hotel reception. It was his spending money for the entire week.

'How much would it cost for the day?' He had read somewhere that New York cabbies could earn upwards of one thousand dollars a week. John counted out a thousand dollars, saw the contents of the envelope shrink considerably, and thought, *what the heck*. He could spend the money how he wished. That's why it was called *spending* money.

John thrust his hand over the front seat and waved the wad of cash at the cabby. 'Here. There's plenty more where that came from.' John glanced at the envelope and frowned; that statement wasn't entirely accurate. In fact, at this rate he would run out of cash before the day was out. He didn't know why he said *there's plenty more where that came from*. On second thought, John did. He'd always wanted to utter those words.

The driver turned around in his seat and eyed his naïve passenger. Flashing cash like that was an open invitation to get ripped off. The driver glanced at his meter. One might be tempted to switch it off and relieve the British tourist of a good proportion of that money by charging an extortionate amount. The cabbie glanced at the cash. 'You've just hired yourself a New York City cab for the day.'

John smiled and waved the cash for the cabbie to take.

'Why don't you keep hold of that and settle up at the end. If you want to call it a day at any time, you can just pay me the fare on the meter.' He pointed at the small black box mounted on the dashboard. 'That way, if it gets too expensive…' He trailed off.

John caught his drift; meaning if he ran out of money. He didn't know how much it would rack up to for an entire day, but he thought that sounded fair. 'All right.' Besides, John didn't know yet whether he was going to like any of the places the driver might take him to. Hiring the taxi for the day might not turn out the pleasant surprise the cabbie had promised him. At least this way he could opt out of the arrangement with no hard feelings.

John stuffed the wad of cash back in the envelope and glanced at the cabbie. 'So where are we heading first?'

'It's a surprise!'

John frowned at him and thought it better be a nice surprise.

The cab driver did a U-turn in the street and headed back the way he'd come, passing the hotel. The timing couldn't have been worse; John saw Sylvie and Bertram walk out of the hotel together, arm in arm, towards the waiting limo. John hunkered down in his seat, in case they spotted him as the yellow cab passed by the hotel. He turned to watch them from the rear window. He had half a mind to ask the cabbie to turn around and follow them. John sighed. What was the point? She'd packed her suitcases and walked out into the arms of Bertram what's-his-face.

John forced himself to turn away and face the front. There was no use looking back; there was nothing there for him now but a reminder of what might have been if only he hadn't messed everything up.

Sylvie stepped out of the hotel with Bertram and spotted the she saw them.

'What's the matter, Sylvie?'

Sylvie frowned. She knew one was for her. Marcia Hunt, her editor back in England, had phoned last night and told Sylvie that the show was treating their star guest to a whirlwind all-expenses-paid sightseeing trip around New York City. It wasn't that Sylvie didn't want to see all the sights. Of course she did. The problem was that she had always imagined seeing New York with *the one*. Sylvie glanced at Bertram by her side. Was he *the one?*

'Are you all right?' asked Bertram, his face full of concern.

Sylvie pointed at the limos. 'I think one of those is for me. I'm meant to go on a tour of New York that was arranged by the show.'

'You don't sound too happy about it,' observed Bertram. 'Don't you want to see the sights now you've got some free time?'

'Well, yes. But—'

'I've got an idea, Sylvie. Why don't you let *me* take you on a tour of New York?'

Sylvie thought of the letter from Bertram that he had asked their mutual friend, Julia, to pass on to her. She *still* hadn't opened the envelope. He hadn't brought it up, so Sylvie didn't mention that she hadn't read it yet. Although she didn't know what Bertram had written in the letter, this only confirmed Sylvie's suspicions – Bertram wanted to resume seeing her. She looked him over. Perhaps this was meant. Maybe Julia was right, and he was the one.

Bertram was still waiting for an answer.

One of the limo drivers saw the couple standing outside the entrance to the hotel. He stepped forward. 'Er excuse me, are you the writer, Love on the Rooftop?'

Sylvie turned to the limo driver in his smart black suit. She wouldn't ordinarily lie. Sylvie hesitated.

Bertram stepped in. 'Sorry – not today.' He smiled at Sylvie and whispered, 'I know you're in New York for that show, but how about a day off work, eh?'

Sylvie returned his smile. 'I'll be plain old Sylvie today.'

'Not plain or old,' commented Bertram, holding out the crook of his arm.

Sylvie looked up at him and blushed. He just reminded her why she had agreed to join him at his table on The Rooftop Café all those weeks ago; because out of a room full of people, Bertram had noticed *her*. That was some compliment at her age.

'Where shall we go?' asked Sylvie, taking his arm.

'Let's make sure we ditch the corporate tour.' Bertram nodded in the direction of the limos parked outside the hotel. 'I want to show you the real New York.'

'The *real* New York?'

'Yes. The one you rarely see in the glossy brochures and tourist guidebooks.'

Intrigued, Sylvie said, 'Where do we start?'

'We start by travelling like most New Yorkers when they're not using their feet.'

'By New York taxi,' said Sylvie, watching a bright yellow New York taxicab pass by. For a split second, she could have sworn that was John sitting in the back. Sylvie shook her head. What a silly thought. She turned to Bertram. 'I've always fancied riding in one of those. Like in the movies.'

'Sure – maybe later. What I had in mind is elevated.'

'Elevated?'

Bertram nodded. 'But first, we need to find a subway station.'

Sylvie came to an abrupt halt.

Bertram carried on walking several paces before he realised Sylvie no longer had hold of his arm. He looked about him and discovered he'd left her behind. He doubled back. 'What's the matter now?'

Sylvie stood there, frowning. She knew what a subway was.

'Bertram – I don't go on the London Underground at home, so I am certainly *not* going on the sub—'

'You won't travel on the London underground?'

Sylvie gave him an apologetic look.

'Ever?'

'Uh-uh.'

'Oh.'

'That's going to be a problem in New York – isn't it.'

'Well...er...no,' Bertram lied.

Sylvie looked at Bertram. 'I've ruined your plans, haven't I.'

Bertram gave Sylvie a reassuring smile. 'No, you haven't. I was only using the subway because it was the quickest way to get to a particular destination. Spending the day underground was the furthest thing from my mind. In fact, it was quite the opposite.'

Sylvie remembered him using the word, 'Elevated?'

'Exactly. Come on.' He stepped towards the kerb and held out his hand.

A bright yellow taxicab came to a screeching halt in front of them.

Bertram smiled as he opened the car door. 'Sylvie, you have your wish – a New York taxicab it is.'

11

After several minutes of uncomfortable silence, the cabbie introduced himself to his quiet fare in the back. 'I'm Angelo.'

John turned from the window. 'I'm John. From England.'

'No kidding,' said Angelo, smiling at John in the rearview mirror. 'Which part?'

'London.'

'Ah. I've always wanted to visit London.'

John studied the cabbie's profile. Angelo's dark eyes and olive skin tone suggested he was of Mediterranean descent. With his craggy features and somewhat portly physique, John thought Angelo was around his age, perhaps older. He would hazard a guess that he was nearing retirement. His full head of hair, although peppered grey, harked back to his youth in the seventies when hairstyles for men were layered but longer.

'London is on my bucket list when I retire.'

'Are you retiring soon?' John asked, hoping he wasn't being forward.

Angelo chuckled. 'I should have retired three years ago. My wife keeps on at me about when I will pack it in. But I guess I love my job too much, driving around New York and getting paid for it.'

John stared at him and wondered if there was more to it than that. Perhaps Angelo didn't fancy being stuck at home all day with nothing to do and nowhere to go, and no reason to get up in the morning.

John was thinking of his own experiences when he lost his job. Unlike most people's perceptions of retirement – and by most people, he meant the younger generation who were still working towards their idyllic retirement fantasy – John was under no illusions that it wasn't the bed of roses everyone seemed to think it was. Perhaps Angelo already knew this. Maybe that's why he'd rather stay at work. John would be the first to congratulate him on a wise decision.

Angelo rolled his eyes. 'My wife, she says to me, "Don't come crying to me if you retire and then drop down dead." I told her that's not going to happen. I'll leave next year.'

John couldn't resist a smile at that last comment. He got the impression that Angelo had no intention of retiring soon.

'So… Angelo…. what's the first stop on the tour?'

'It's a—'

'—Surprise.' John heaved a sigh as he looked out the window. He didn't have a clue where they were going, so he thought he might as well just sit back and enjoy the ride – or try to.

John perked up when he recognised a New York landmark. He leaned forward in his seat. 'Is that the Brooklyn Bridge?'

'Oh yes.'

'Are we going over the bridge?'

'That we are.'

'So, we're going to Brooklyn.' John was getting excited.

In the front seat, Angelo smiled. 'And before you ask, all I'm going to tell you is that I can guarantee no tourist would have stepped foot where I'm about to take you.'

John raised an eyebrow. Now he was intrigued. He sat back in his seat as Angelo joined a queue of slow-moving traffic. Once on the bridge, John stared out of the car window and saw tourists walking along the Brooklyn Bridge. They were taking photos and drinking in the views. He wanted to get out of the cab and join them, but he couldn't see anywhere for cars to pull over.

John made a mental note to add a walk along the Brooklyn Bridge to his list of things he would have done if he had been here with Sylvie. He stared glumly out the window as he caught sight of couples holding hands, taking photos, and sharing this special moment before strolling over the bridge together.

'Look, there's the water taxi crossing the East River from Manhattan to Dumbo.'

John looked at Angelo. 'Dumbo?'

Angelo nodded. 'It's an acronym which stands for Down Under the Manhattan Brooklyn Overpass. It's a small neighbourhood in Brooklyn, the first one you come to after crossing the bridge. Most tourists head straight for the Brooklyn Bridge Park along the waterfront where there are splendid views of the Manhattan skyline. You'll catch a glimpse of the park when we exit the bridge into Brooklyn.'

John unbuckled his seatbelt and slid across the back seat to look out the side window on the right-hand side, so he could see the waterfront park.

'There it is!' exclaimed John. The park was bigger than he imagined, with its large waterfront promenade and long tree-lined pathways. John gazed at the sparkling East River down below and glanced out the rear window just before the cab exited the Brooklyn Bridge. That's when he saw the view of the Lower Manhattan skyline for the first time. John sat there transfixed. He'd never seen so many skyscrapers; the old Art Deco style skyscrapers sitting cheek by jowl with their much taller contemporary neighbours.

John had seen images of the Manhattan skyline – who hadn't. But nothing compared to seeing it for real. He recalled that the pictures of Manhattan in magazines were taken in perfect weather, with clear blue skies and sunshine. He didn't think it looked any less impressive on a grey, drizzly day. 'Wow!'

'If you think that's something,' said Angelo, 'you should see the view from Brooklyn at night when Lower Manhattan is lit up.'

'I'd like to see that.' John had also seen a picture of the very same. Once again he made a mental note, hoping that by some miracle he might return here and do all those touristy things with Sylvie by his side.

John sat staring out the window. He spotted people walking along the promenade as Angelo drove the cab into the neighbourhood by the name of Dumbo. Until Angelo told him it was an acronym, John thought he was talking about the animated elephant with the oversized ears.

'Angelo, can we stop at Dumbo?' John fancied getting out at the park and wandering up and down the promenade.

'No,' replied Angelo.

'Why not?'

'Because I thought you wanted a tour off the tourist map?' Angelo glanced at his passenger in the rear-view mirror.

'Well, yes, but—' That was before he saw some of New York.

All he had seen since he had arrived yesterday was the inside of the hotel, and the inside of the minibar. John rubbed his forehead. The headache was better, but he could still do with some fresh air.

Dumbo looked just the place for a quiet, leisurely stroll and the views weren't half-bad either. John was fast changing his mind about a tour off the tourist map. There was a reason tourists visited the same places because they were the highlights of the city; that's why they were in all the guidebooks. What's the betting, thought John, that Angelo was about to take him to some places that would never see the inside of a guidebook?

'Look, Angelo, I think I've changed my—'

Angelo held up his hand. 'I know what you're going to say, but before you change your mind, just let me take you to this one place. I promise you will see something you won't find in a guidebook.'

That's what John was afraid of. However, he had little choice; the waterfront park, with the amazing views, was already fading into the distance. John heaved a sigh. 'Oh, all right.'

'You won't regret it.'

John already was. He glanced out of the rear window and caught one last glimpse of the Lower Manhattan skyline before they turned a corner and headed away from the waterfront.

'The best way to get to Dumbo,' said Angelo conversationally as they sat in traffic in Brooklyn, 'is to take the water taxi from Pier 11 in downtown Manhattan.'

John nodded, although what he really wanted was to see Dumbo right now.

'On a nice day, the city suits have lunch on the promenade along the waterfront.'

'There's a promenade on the other side too?'

'Oh yes. If you take the subway to Lower Manhattan and walk down Wall Street, cross over the main road and keep heading towards the East River, you will come to the promenade. If you walk along the promenade over there, you can see some magnificent views of Brooklyn before taking the water taxi to Dumbo.'

John cheered up – sort of. It was just another thing to add to the list of things he wasn't going to do with Sylvie in New York. John frowned as he recalled Sylvie and Bertram walking out of the hotel towards the waiting limo. Trust Bertram to hire a limo to impress her, thought John miserably.

Thinking of Sylvie in New York made him wonder what she was up to right now...

Sylvie was smiling from ear to ear. She still couldn't quite believe she was here in America, sitting in the back seat of a New York taxicab. And she had Bertram to thank for that.

Bertram leaned forward in his seat and whispered their destination to the cabbie. Then they set off. He turned to look at Sylvie. 'I'm afraid on this tour there is going to be one section of New York's train line you can't avoid.'

Sylvie's face fell. 'But—'

'Trust me. It will be an experience you won't forget.'

'I bet,' said Sylvie glumly, not at all sure it was an experience she wanted to have.

'Are we there yet?' John asked Angelo irritably. He wanted a ride in a New York taxicab but didn't fancy spending all day in one.

'You sound just like one of my grandkids,' commented Angelo. He glanced at John's sour expression in the rearview mirror. 'It won't be long now, and we'll reach our first stop on the tour. So why don't you sit back, relax and enjoy the ride.'

John stared out the window as they left the Brooklyn Bridge behind and turned down a leafy suburban street into a neighbourhood of Brooklyn he hadn't seen in the guidebooks. He was trying to enjoy the drive, but all he could think about was Bertram taking Sylvie out for the day in a limo. John frowned. He had a limo. He could have taken her out in one. John frowned some more at the thought of the limo driver this morning, calling him *Dear John*. That meant he would have to explain to Sylvie just what he was doing in New York. He shuddered at the reflection.

He was still in her bad books over that unfortunate incident with Gertie. It didn't bear thinking about what her reaction would be when she discovered who he had been writing about in his blog and column. She would soon find out when he exposed his real identity on American TV, and everyone found out the woman in question was Sylvie Baxter. Apparently, that show was going to be broadcast live across the pond on English television too. John hoped that Sylvie and Bertram were on a flight home when that happened, although he had no idea how long they were staying in New York. When he agreed to come to take the trip, he assumed there would be the entire Atlantic Ocean between them. Now he was lucky if there were several floors. John didn't know where Sylvie's hotel room was. That was another delicate subject he did not want to think about. Did she even have her own room or were Bertram and Sylvie—

John grimaced. He didn't want to think about that. The only way he would know for sure whether they were sharing a room was to follow them after dinner one evening and find out. It was taking a huge risk. He'd have to wear some sort of disguise. But he was considering it. The only thing that put him off was the thought of his worst fears being realised; that Sylvie had crossed the point of no return – she had forsaken their marriage vows and slept with Bertram. John couldn't decide which was worse: the knowing or the not knowing.

'... Victorian houses as you can see.'

John looked up. 'I'm sorry – what?' He hadn't been listening to Angelo's commentary as they drove through Brooklyn.

'I said that we're now entering Flatbush, where you'll notice some excellent examples of Victorian architecture.'

'Flatbush?' repeated John. 'I've never heard of it.'

'Ah-ha!' Angelo smiled. 'That's good to hear because this is my first surprise.'

John stared out of the window at the neighbourhood of Flatbush. He rather liked Angelo's first surprise. 'Is this what you meant by *off the beaten track*?'

'Yep.'

'Well, this is a surprise.' All thoughts of Sylvie and Bertram were swept aside as John sat there admiring the detached Victorian houses set in long, wide, tree-lined avenues. 'The funny thing is Angelo, when I think of New York, all that comes to mind is Manhattan across the river. I didn't take on board there's so much more to New York than the city.'

'Uh-huh.' Angelo nodded. 'Most tourists head for Manhattan. I don't think they have the time or inclination to explore the other boroughs like The Bronx, Queens or Staten Island. A lot of tourists will cross The Brooklyn Bridge to see the views of Manhattan from the other side, but how many venture further into Brooklyn to see this borough? Few, I guess.'

John was enjoying the scenic drive around Flatbush. 'I like it. This should be in a guidebook.'

'I like it too,' said Angelo, although he wasn't sure he'd want to see Flatbush overrun with tourists. Angelo kept that thought to himself. 'There are a dozen neighbourhoods in what is known as Victorian Flatbush. I'm taking you to the Ditmas Park Historic District.'

'Historic District?' John liked the sound of that too.

'Yes, you will see street after street where no two houses are alike.' Angelo made a right turn down another wide, tree-lined avenue. 'This is Ditmas Avenue.'

John gazed out the window, admiring the large, detached houses as they passed by.

Angelo continued his commentary on the area. 'There's quite a variety of architecture here. There's Queen Anne, Colonial Revival, Neo-Tudor, Spanish Mission and Georgian.'

John nodded, even though he wasn't familiar with most of those house styles. He guessed that some were uniquely American. All he knew was the difference between the Victorian and Georgian properties that abound in London. Even so, he was enjoying this immensely, seeing the different architectural styles. Angelo was right: no two houses were alike.

John marvelled at the turrets and ornate stained glass, at the porches and the deep bay windows. Unlike London, where entire streets were characterised by the same style properties, John had never seen such a variety of house types in a single road.

'When this area was first developed, back in the early twentieth century, they called it "The Village in the City". I still think that description is fitting today.'

John agreed. 'You wouldn't believe you were in New York.' The city seemed like a world away from this tranquil suburb. John had a thought. 'If I didn't know any better, I could almost believe you'd transported me to some other part of the country – like New England, perhaps.'

'Hmm, that is true. However, I think you'd be surprised to learn that there are more Victorian-era houses here than anywhere else in the country.'

'Is that a fact?'

'Uh-huh.'

John gazed out the window as Angelo continued down Ditmas Avenue. He appreciated the tour of Victorian Flatbush and the chance to see the three-storey houses with their colourful facades, gables and porches. But he rather wished Angelo would pull over so he could get out and take a closer look.

John had an idea. 'Angelo, didn't you say this was a historic district?'

Angelo nodded his head.

'Well, I was wondering whether one house was open to the public – like a museum. I'd love to see inside one.'

Angelo shook his head. 'They are all private residences. There is the Victorian Flatbush House Tour though.'

'House tour?'

'Uh-huh. Some owners of these houses allow tours of their homes.'

'Really? Which ones?' John asked, leaning forward in his seat.

'I'm not sure. But the thing is, they only open their doors to the public once a year. I believe it's around June time.'

'Oh.' John frowned. He rather fancied having a look around one of the Flatbush houses. 'Ah well, nevermind.' John slumped back in his seat, feeling disappointed. 'Where to next?'

Angelo pulled the cab over to a stop at the kerb outside a three-storey Victorian detached property.

John glanced out the window. 'Why are we stopping?'

Angelo turned in his seat and grinned. 'Do I have a surprise for you!'

12

John scrambled out of the back of the car feeling for all the world like an excited child. He stood on the pavement; it's a *sidewalk*, John thought to himself as he gazed up at the Victorian property – the first stop on Angelo's tour off the beaten track in New York. Although there were plenty of Victorian properties in England, none of them quite compared to the ones in Flatbush. Up close they were even more impressive – and bigger.

John took in the cream clapboard exterior, beige tiled roof and neat veranda which ran the width of the property. Then something occurred to him. 'I thought you said none of the homes were open to the public this time of year?'

Angelo was already heading up the front path. He glanced over his shoulder. 'Are you coming?'

'Absolutely.' John darted forward through the gap in the white picket fence where Angelo had left the gate ajar. He walked along the short pathway and followed Angelo up the five wooden steps on to the veranda.

John looked up and down the veranda. It was wider than it appeared from the street. John smiled at the swing seat for two under the bay window. The numerous potted plants gave the veranda a splash of colour. Sylvie would have loved this outside space.

It brought to mind the wooden bench that used to be at the bottom of the garden back home until he threw it out, along with all Sylvie's plants and flowers she'd spent years cultivating. He'd replaced Sylvie's wild garden with a square lawn and small borders. John regretted that. He regretted a lot of things. But standing there staring at the swing seat for two, what he regretted the most was never once – in all the years they had lived in that house – taking the time to sit with Sylvie together at the end of the garden.

He recalled she always sat on that bench all alone because he preferred his comfy chair on the patio outside the kitchen door where he could listen to the radio and nip inside for a snack. It didn't seem to bother him that they never sat together in their garden like couples do, making conversation or just being together in the moment. He never thought about it at the time – the significance. But he was thinking about it now. Now that they had parted ways.

It dawned on John that maybe it wasn't simply the case that they had drifted apart as they got older, and the house conversion had brought things to a head. Perhaps the problems in their marriage had been going on far, far longer than that. Maybe the issue in their marriage was him. If only he hadn't been so inflexible and overbearing and tried to let Sylvie just be herself.

He recalled the times he had been on at her about that go-dawful garden. It resembled a wild garden, and John didn't like it one bit. That's why he had taken the first opportunity to get rid of it when he had the builders in to do the conversion. What he never stopped to consider, John realised belatedly, was that it wasn't all about him. What did Sylvie want? All those plans he had made for their lives together, "they weren't our plans", he recalled Sylvie barking at him one day. It was true. Perhaps if he had sat with her on that bench in the back garden, doing one small thing with Sylvie just to show her how much he loved her, then maybe things would have turned out—

'John? Are you okay?'

'Um, yeah, fine.' John tore his eyes from the swing seat and turned to Angelo with a semblance of a smile, wondering how long he had been standing there staring into space, ruminating about Sylvie.

'Are you sure?'

John nodded theatrically. 'Let's go on this house tour.' He couldn't wait to get inside, away from that swing, and take his mind off his wife. Or soon-to-be ex-wife.

Angelo gave John a sideways glance as he knocked on the door. The look on John's face said he wasn't okay, but Angelo had the good grace not to ask him questions.

'Angelo, can we wander around by ourselves or will someone take us on a guided tour of the rooms?'

'Ah, this isn't a house tour.'

'Oh.' John's face dropped.

'This is something much better – you'll see.'

Perhaps it was a museum after all, thought John. His eyes shifted from the door to the veranda with its abundance of potted plants and hanging baskets. He could just imagine the owners sitting outside on a warm evening waving to people as they passed by. Of course, nobody walked much in America – so he'd read.

John wondered if that was really true, although in all the

time they had been cruising the neighbourhood they hadn't passed a single person out taking a stroll. Not even a dog-walker. John glanced over his shoulder, up and down the deserted street. He'd already commented on this to Angelo, who said that most everyone was at work. It made John wonder who they were visiting. The house didn't look like a museum. It looked like someone's home.

Standing beside Angelo, John turned to him and was about to ask who lived here when the front door opened.

'Angelo – *che sorpresa!*'

John furrowed his brow at the little old lady who'd answered the door. 'What did she just say?'

'Mama – English, please. We have a guest.' Angelo glanced at John. 'It's an Italian expression. She's just surprised to see me. I don't normally pay them a visit during the day when I'm working.'

'I see.'

'John, meet my mother.' Angelo stepped aside.

'Oh, er, pleased...to...meet...you,' said John, making sure he enunciated each word so she would understand.

She frowned at John and turned to her son. 'Why does he speak so slowly?'

Angelo shrugged. 'He's English.'

John looked from Angelo to his mother, who spoke perfect English. John wanted the ground to swallow him up.

'Did you just say he is English?'

Angelo nodded.

Angelo's mother grabbed John by the arm. 'Come in. Come in.'

John felt himself being pulled forward. He glanced back at Angelo.

Angelo smiled. 'Mama has never met an Englishman before.' He followed John inside the house and shut the door.

'This way,' said Angelo's mother, a short, rotund woman who was surprisingly sprightly for one so advanced in years.

John followed her down the hallway. Although the lights were on, his first impression was how gloomy it was inside the house. It took a moment for his eyes to adjust to the poor light. The hallway was elegant and impressive with its dark oak panelling which ran halfway up the walls. For someone who favoured bare, bland magnolia walls, he rather liked the panelling and the dark vintage green walls above covered in framed family photographs.

John glanced at the photos as he passed by and caught glimpses of past generations of Angelo's family hanging along-side pictures of a new generation.

When Angelo's mother stopped to open a door at the end of the hall, John paused behind her, his eyes lingering on a portrait of a young couple and a small boy. The image, in old sepia tones, was different to the others in one striking respect: it wasn't staged as old photos so often were. The couple were looking at each other, smiling, in a relaxed pose. What made the picture so interesting was that it was taken on what appeared to be the wooden deck of an old passenger liner.

'That's me,' said Angelo, pointing at the small boy in the photograph. 'And that's Mama and Papa.'

'Where was it—' John was about to ask where the photo was taken when a gruff voice boomed out, '*Non voglio visitatori!*'

John turned to Angelo in surprise.

'Ah, that will be Papa in the lounge. I think Mama must have told him to expect visitors. He has dementia and can get a little confused, so I guess she's just forewarned him.'

'What did he say?'

'Um, he said he can't wait to meet you.'

John frowned. His tone of voice suggested otherwise. He guessed Angelo's translation wasn't entirely accurate.

Angelo gestured at the door. 'Shall we?'

John walked into the lounge and was greeted by a smiling Mama. Angelo's Papa was sitting with his back to them across the room.

John said, 'If it's not a good time...'

'Nonsense,' said Mama. 'Take a seat.' She motioned at a leather sofa.

John looked at the sofa but remained where he was, hovering by the door, feeling uncomfortable. He watched Mama walk over to the old man sitting by the bay window. He was reading a newspaper.

'Papa, trasformare il vostro apparecchio acustico fino.'

'Mama, English *please*!' Angelo rolled his eyes. 'Sorry, John. Mama just asked Papa to turn his hearing aid up.'

Mama said, 'I know he turns it down when he thinks I'm not looking so he doesn't have to listen to me all day, especially when he wants to read his newspaper in peace.' She turned to her husband and folded her arms in front of her chest.

'Okay, okay,' said Papa, folding his paper. 'I'm turning it up – see!' Papa made a big show of pressing the volume-up key.

Angelo whispered to John, 'I'm not sure how much he takes in what he reads now, but he has a routine.'

John stared at the old couple and smiled. If he and Sylvie had grown old together, perhaps that's what he would do in his eighties: switching his hearing aid off so he could read his morning paper in peace.

'What's going on?' asked Papa. 'I want to read my newspaper.'

Mama frowned at her husband. 'I told you already, we have visitors.'

Papa turned in his seat and looked across the room at John.

John smiled nervously. Perhaps Papa did not appreciate being disturbed by some stranger, and a foreigner at that, invading his home first thing in the morning just because he wanted to get a look inside a Victorian property in Flatbush. John stared at Papa, scrutinizing him from across the room.

'Who are you?'

Angelo stepped forward. 'Papa this is—'

'And shouldn't you be at work?' he added, frowning at his son.

'Papa, I *am* at work. You don't need to check up on me. I'm in my sixties. I'm not a teenager skiving off.'

Papa pointed at John. 'So, who is this?'

John stepped forward. 'I'm John, pleased to make your acquaintance.'

'Ah, you're English.'

John nodded.

Papa got up out of his chair with some difficulty, waving his walking stick at his wife not to help him, and made his way towards John. He held out his hand. 'Well, fancy a real Englishman come to visit us.' He shook John's hand enthusiastically.

John looked at him abashed. Papa made it sound as though royalty had dropped by.

'Here, take a seat.' He turned to look at his wife. 'Maria, fetch our guest some coffee.'

John wouldn't dream of ordering Sylvie around. He looked

at Angelo's mother and caught a conspiratorial look pass between her and Angelo. He guessed Papa may think he was the head of the household, but it was Mama who ruled the roost. Wasn't that true of most marriages thought John? Wives had a way of making their husbands believe they were in charge when, in fact, it was quite the reverse.

John took a seat in one of two matching leather wing-backed chairs on either side of the mahogany fireplace.

Angelo sat down in the other chair.

John glanced around the room as he took his seat. It was much brighter than the gloomy entrance hall. The large bay window let in the light, and the cream coloured walls made the room feel bright and airy. The lounge was large enough to accommodate a piano in one corner, and a tall, chunky grandfather clock. All the furniture appeared to be light solid oak, which gave the room a warm, mellow feel.

Angelo's father sat down on the long leather sofa opposite the fireplace.

John turned to him and said, 'Angelo has been showing me around your neighbourhood.'

Papa leaned forward in his seat. 'Do you like it?'

John nodded his head vigorously. 'I must apologise for the intrusion, though. It's all my fault. I kept on at Angelo about wanting to see inside one of these Victorian properties.'

'Ah, you English. You're famous for apologising.'

'Yes, I suppose we are. But I must apologise all the same for the intrusion.'

Papa laughed and waved his walking stick dismissively. 'No apology necessary. We've never met an Englishman before. It is quite an honour.'

'The honour is all mine, I can assure you.' John glanced around the lounge once more. 'The houses in Flatbush are quite something. How long have you lived here?'

'We moved in when Angelo was five years old.'

John turned to Angelo. 'You grew up here?'

He nodded. 'I don't have many memories of the village where we used to live before Mama and Papa brought us to America.'

'A village in Italy?' ventured John, taking a guess. He thought he recognised the Italian dialect and couldn't fail to spot the Catholic religious pictures and paintings adorning their walls.

'Italian American,' said Angelo.

'My grandchildren are first generation Americans,' said Papa proudly.

Angelo explained. 'My brother and I were born in Italy. However, our children were born here.'

'So, you emigrated from Italy?'

'Sicily back in the early fifties,' said Papa. 'Here, let me show you.'

'Don't get up, Papa.' Angelo walked over to a bookcase and returned with a large photo album.

'Come sit with me.' Papa motioned for John to join him on the leather sofa.

John had just sat down next to him when Angelo's mother walked in carrying a tray. She set the tray down on the coffee table in front of them. 'How do you take your coffee, John?'

'Milk and sugar please.'

Mama poured four cups of coffee from the pot, added milk and sugar, and passed John a cup.

'Thank you.' John could smell the aroma of freshly ground

coffee. He took a sip. 'This is amazing coffee,' exclaimed John. He wasn't exaggerating.

'We have none of that instant rubbish,' Papa remarked.

'Papa!' Angelo said, aghast.

'I quite agree.' John smiled. 'I have no idea why we Brits are so taken by our instant coffee.' He'd read somewhere that during the Second World War the American GI's introduced instant coffee to Britain. 'I blame it on the Americans,' mused John.

The room fell silent. John was just about to apologise – he didn't mean to cause offence – when Papa burst out laughing.

The look on Angelo and Mama's face said they didn't get what was so funny.

Papa said, 'I think our guest is referring to the fact that Americans brought instant coffee with them to England during World War Two.'

John nodded and grinned.

'I never knew that,' said Angelo.

Papa opened the album.

'This is Angelo on the steamer coming over to America.'

'Steamer?'

'Yes, we travelled by steamship on the White Star Line.'

John studied the old black-and-white photo of a young, slim Italian woman holding a small boy in her arms. She was smiling up at her husband standing beside her on the wooden deck. 'Hey, I recognise this photo,' exclaimed John. 'There's a framed picture just like it hanging in your hallway.'

'Is there?' Papa said in surprise.

John heard Mama sighing before she said, 'Papa, it's been there since we moved in. It was the first photograph you had framed and hung on the wall in this house, don't you remember?'

'Of course, I remember,' said Papa irritably.

John wondered if that was true.

Papa returned his attention to the album.

'Angelo must have been three-years-old in this photograph.' Papa remarked.

John tried to read the small caption beneath, but it was in Italian. All he could make out was the year – 1953.

'A horrible, horrible journey,' said Mama. 'Thank the Lord it was only ten days.'

Papa glanced at his wife. 'I remember we were in steerage and you were seasick most of the journey.'

'Steerage – what's that?'

Papa turned the page. John saw photos of a crowded room full of bunk beds rammed together. Some people didn't even have the luxury of a bed and appeared to be sleeping on the floor; anywhere they could find a space.

Papa pointed at the photograph. 'This is steerage. We were poor. That was our only option if we wanted a new life in America.'

John studied the pictures. 'What happened when you arrived in America?'

Papa turned the page to reveal fascinating photos taken from the crowded deck of the ship as it docked in America. 'This is the East River pier,' explained Papa. 'The first and second-class passengers disembarked first. Once they went through customs at the pier, they were free to start their new life in America. Things were different for the rest of us.'

John raised an eyebrow. 'What happened?'

'We had to board another boat. It was a ferry to Ellis Island.'

John looked at Papa in surprise. He'd heard of Ellis Island. It was now a world-famous tourist destination. The descendants of immigrants who had passed through those doors on the way to a new life in America could visit and pay their respects to their forefathers, who had made the journey to secure a better life for themselves and future generations.

John did not expect to meet a family who had gone through that experience over sixty years ago. He looked at Angelo in astonishment. 'You were one of the immigrant families that arrived at Ellis Island?'

'One of the last. It closed its doors in 1954.' Angelo smiled. 'I have taken my children and grandchildren to Ellis Island to show them where our new life in America began.'

John wondered how many, out of the millions of Americans who visited Ellis Island, had the privilege of visiting there with a family member who had passed through its doors all those years ago.

'Look here, John. I have a photograph of Angelo in the Registry Room at Ellis Island.'

John studied the picture. Angelo was sitting atop his father's shoulders, smiling. Papa, a young man in his prime, was looking very solemn.

'We had just got our papers to enter America,' said Mama. 'The relief after such a long journey was indescribable. We were so nervous that they would turn us away.'

Papa nodded his head. 'I might not be smiling in that photo, but if you look closely, you will see tears of joy.'

John glanced at Angelo. 'This is really something.'

Angelo grinned. 'I thought you'd find it interesting.'

Interesting. That was an understatement. 'It's fascinating to hear an immigrant's story first-hand.'

'Would you like another cup of coffee, John?' Mama held up the coffee pot.

'Yes, please. I don't think I'll be touching another jar of instant coffee ever again.'

There were chuckles all around as Mama poured another cup of freshly brewed coffee. She offered John a home-baked American cookie.

Papa turned the page in the photo album. 'This is our first home in America.' He paused and looked at John. 'Tell me if I'm boring you.'

'No. Not at all. Do continue,' John said eagerly. He wanted to find out what became of this young family once they were granted permission to enter the United States.

Angelo chipped in. 'I'm afraid Papa does like to reminisce about the past, given half a chance. We could well be here all day!'

Papa gave Angelo a disapproving look before continuing. 'Here is our first home in America.' He pointed at a photo of the tenement block with dozens of children playing in the street outside. 'That's Angelo.'

Angelo let out a sigh. 'I don't think that was me.'

'Of course it is.'

Mama turned to John and rolled her eyes. 'They have the same argument every time he shows someone that photo. 'What do *you* think?'

John couldn't tell if the little boy in the photo was Angelo. He looked apologetically at Angelo's father, unable to give him an answer.

'See,' said Angelo, quick to take John's silence as an affirmation that he didn't think it was him in the photo.

'Papa shook his head. 'No matter.'

'When did you move into this house?'

Papa looked across at his wife. 'When did we move here?'

'It was soon after you got a promotion to head chef at the restaurant, do you remember?'

Angelo chipped in, 'I think I was eight, Papa, when we moved here.'

'Ah, yes it was 1959.' Papa leafed through his album. 'Here we are.' He pointed at a photo of a dilapidated property.

John raised an eyebrow. 'Is that this house back in the fifties?'

'Yes.'

'It looked as though it needed some work,' observed John.

'Oh, it was a fixer-upper all right. That was the only way we could afford to move into a house in a neighbourhood like this.'

'Hey, I don't remember that photo!' said Angelo in surprise. 'That's me standing on the front porch.'

John smiled at the dark-haired boy dressed in a baseball outfit. His face was a picture of concentration as he stood with a baseball bat, poised as though someone out of camera shot was throwing a ball and he was about to swing the bat.

'We all dreamed we would be baseball stars when we grew up.' Angelo sighed. 'But it wasn't to be.'

'So you became a New York cabbie.'

'Uh-huh.'

John couldn't imagine driving around a city all day. He found it stressful enough taking the car out in London to the local supermarket. 'Do you like driving, Angelo?'

'Not really, but I enjoyed owning a medallion.'

'A medallion?'

'It's quite something to own your own medallion,' said Mama proudly.

John knitted his brows.

Angelo caught John's confused expression.

'You've never heard of the medallion system?'

'Nope.'

'Well, in the thirties the government regulated the New York City taxi industry because there was no limit on the number of taxis in the city. So, they created the medallion system. Taxi drivers must get a special license. Each taxi must have a medallion. Before we leave, I'll show you the metal city permit on the hood of the taxi. That's the medallion I'm talking about. It's illegal to pick up anyone hailing a taxi, like yourself, without one.'

'Are they expensive?'

'Phew, you better believe it. I saved up for years just to put a down payment on one. That was thirty-five years ago. It's like a mortgage. Mind you, I borrowed against it to buy my house. And like other medallion owners, I no longer had to work for a garage. I was in effect working for myself. When I wasn't driving it during the day, I had another driver who paid me to drive my car and pick up fares. It's a win-win situation. Everybody I knew who started out driving a New York taxi cab wanted to be in that elite club of medallion owners.'

'Did it appreciate over time – the medallion?' John thought that if he had taken out a thirty-year loan on something, he'd want it to be in bricks and mortar, or tangible things that appreciated over time.

'That's a good question. I sold my medallion a couple of years back because my wife insisted I retire. I was shocked by what I sold it for. It turned out that I did much better than if I had invested in gold or the property market.'

John was a bit surprised it had taken him ten years just to

save up for a down payment. 'If you don't mind me asking, how much did your licence cost?'

'A lot. We struggled for years, but in the end, it paid off. When I sold the medallion, we paid off the mortgage on the house and walked away pocketing a tidy sum.'

'You call three-quarters of a million dollars just a tidy sum? It's a small fortune.'

'I know that, Mama.'

'Then why aren't you at home with your wife, enjoying your retirement?'

That was a good question, thought John. Angelo had the means to retire. And he was well past retirement age. So why hadn't he just hung up his car keys and called it a day?

'It's sheer lunacy,' chipped in Papa, 'that you're still driving around that taxi, but now you don't even own it. You've got to pay someone else for the privilege.'

'Let's not get into that,' said Angelo.

'But it's true.'

Angelo sighed. 'Yes, I'm back driving the same taxi and paying for the privilege. I have to rent the medallion while I'm driving the cab. It's crazy, I know.'

Mama and Papa were nodding their heads, even though Angelo wasn't talking to them. 'You know, John, I didn't realise how much I would miss my job. I'd only just sold the medallion and retired. Within a week I was moping around the house bored and depressed because I knew this wasn't just a holiday. This was it. I felt there was nothing to get up for in the mornings.'

John remembered that feeling all too well. They forced him out of his job into early retirement. At the time, they were okay financially, but he would have given anything to go back to work.

He wasn't the retiring type. The thought of losing his new job as a writer and columnist when Harriet and her team found out he wouldn't be writing about living apart together anymore was already on his mind.

'You could have taken up a hobby,' said Papa.

'Hobbies are a waste of time,' replied Angelo.

John smiled at that. He recalled saying the same thing to Sylvie when he was at home all day, bored and depressed, and she had suggested taking up a hobby.

'I thought about it, but nothing appeals,' said Angelo. 'I just like being out all day meeting wonderful people.' He gestured at John. 'I not only met a very nice person today, but I brought him home to meet you guys. John probably wishes I hadn't.' Angelo glanced his way.

'Oh no, not at all,' interjected John. 'It has been a pleasure.'

'Likewise,' said Papa. He peered at his son. 'Why did you bring him around?'

'Well, John hailed the taxi and didn't have a particular destination in mind, so I thought I'd take him on an alternative tour of New York that he wouldn't see in a brochure.'

Papa turned to John, sitting beside him on the sofa. 'Are you liking your alternative tour of New York, John?'

John glanced at the photo album and smiled at Angelo's father. 'Oh, very much. I think it's been fascinating to meet you and hear all about your experiences of living in America in the fifties.'

Angelo's father smiled approvingly at his guest and turned another page in the album.

John studied the old black-and-white photos of the neighbourhood where they still lived. It was a world away from the tenement where they had started their new life in America. Flatbush hadn't changed all that much in over fifty years.

Papa turned the page and came to the end of the album. 'Oh dear.' He perked up. 'But there are plenty more.' Papa pointed at the bookcase. 'Angelo, fetch me another one, would you?'

Mama said, 'Stay for lunch, John. Do you like Italian?'

John's face dropped. It wasn't the fact that Mama had asked him to stay for lunch, quite the contrary; he'd love to end his tour here and spend the rest of the day in Flatbush, reminiscing with Angelo's parents. It's just that the mention of Italian cooking brought to mind Sylvie and the scrumptious Italian meals she was so fond of making when they were together. He missed that. He missed *her*.

Once again, John couldn't help thinking about what she was doing in New York at this moment. Knowing Bertram, he had probably taken her to see the top sights in the city, like the views from the Empire State Building and shopping at Macy's, and numerous other things that he wasn't visiting today because, quite irrationally, he was still hoping he might one day see them with Sylvie. John frowned. He bet she was having a whale of a time. He wished she wasn't. John hoped Bertram somehow managed to spoil their day out together in New York.

13

Bertram stole a glance at Sylvie sitting beside him in the taxi. The look on her face said she wasn't enjoying herself. Bertram frowned. He wished he hadn't mentioned the subway. The last thing he wanted to do was spoil their day out together. He turned to look out the window. Despite countless trips to New York, he never tired of the city. He only hoped Sylvie wasn't regretting her decision to spend the day in with him.

Sylvie was trying to enjoy the drive in the taxicab and forget about her impending visit to the subway, but it was impossible. She glanced at Bertram. She was wondering if spending the day in New York with him was a bad idea. The more she thought about it, the more she was convinced that letting Bertram surprise her by choosing how they spent their day together would not end well.

Sylvie surreptitiously glanced his way once more. She got the impression that Bertram knew New York very well. But what if his idea of a great day out wasn't hers? How would he know where she'd like to go or what she would like to see on her tour? It's not as though they knew each other all that well. Sylvie was thinking of the subway station they were on their way to right now. Everybody who knew her was aware that she avoided going on the tube in London. She preferred to take the bus or a taxi. The last thing she would choose to do in New York was to go anywhere underground.

Sylvie was trying to remain positive. If she could just cast aside the thought of taking the subway and think of the tour with Bertram as an opportunity to spend some time together and get to know more about each other. Sylvie knew her best friend, Julia, would look at it that way. She was always a cup-is-half-full kind of person.

Sylvie wasn't like Julia in that respect. She was pessimistic, and always looking for the likelihood that things would go wrong rather than turn out okay. She had got in the New York taxicab, feeling as happy as can be, and now her stomach was churning over where they were headed next. It didn't bode well for what Bertram had in store for the rest of the day.

Sylvie was about to tell Bertram that she had a headache and wanted to be taken back to the hotel when the taxi pulled over at the kerb. The driver said, 'This is the closest I can get you to the entrance.'

Bertram handed over the fare and turned to Sylvie. 'It's just a short walk from here.'

Sylvie opened her mouth but couldn't bring herself to tell a fib. She didn't have a headache. She reluctantly got out of the cab and followed Bertram, dragging her heels until they reached an entrance. They walked in and stopped in front of an escalator. Sylvie pointed at the escalator and looked at Bertram. 'Is that where we're going?'

Bertram nodded.

'But it's going up,' said Sylvie, stating the obvious.

'Indeed it is.' Bertram smiled. 'Didn't I say the keyword in this tour is *elevated*?'

Sylvie looked perplexed. 'But I thought we were taking the subway?'

Bertram shook his head and stepped on to the escalator.

Sylvie followed. 'Is this one of those elevated train lines, like our Docklands Light Railway?' She said to his back. 'I like those. What do the Americans call them – El?'

Bertram turned around to face Sylvie as they rode up on the escalator. 'No, it's not an El. Although…' He raised an eyebrow. 'Now I come to think about it, you may be right.'

Sylvie shook her head in confusion. Bertram wasn't making any sense. 'Are we going on an El or not?'

'Well, yes and no.'

Before Sylvie uttered another word, Bertram held up a finger and whispered, 'It's a surprise!' He grinned at her and turned around to face the direction they were going.

Sylvie stood there, frowning at his back as they rode up the escalator. She wished he hadn't used that word – surprise. After the last few months, living apart together with John – and all the shenanigans he got up to in an attempt to force her to move back upstairs – she'd had her fill of surprises. In fact, the mere thought of one made her hackles rise.

She grudgingly stepped off the escalator and looked at her watch, wondering if she should make up an excuse to cut short Bertram's tour. Sylvie was thinking something along the lines that she had to return to her hotel because she'd forgotten she had a meeting with the producers of the show. The trouble was that everything she thought up involved telling outright lies. Sylvie sighed.

'Well?'

She looked up to find Bertram standing there, staring at her.

'Well, what?' said Sylvie glumly.

Bertram stepped aside. 'What do you think?'

Sylvie looked past Bertram and blinked in surprise.

'Excuse me,' remarked a stranger as they tried to get past Sylvie.

Bertram took her arm and eased her to one side, out of the way of other people stepping off the escalator.

Sylvie was so taken aback by Bertram's surprise she didn't know what to say. 'It's a garden!'

'Ah, it's much, much more than that,' said Bertram, leading her by the hand. 'This is the High Line. It's an elevated public park thirty feet above street level.'

'The High Line,' repeated Sylvie, shaking her head. She'd never heard of it. 'It reminds me of that roof garden at Canary Wharf.' Sylvie clicked her fingers. 'Crumbs, I can't for the life of me remember the name...'

Bertram smiled. 'I think you're referring to the tropical roof garden on top of the new train station at Canary Wharf. Didn't it open last year?'

Sylvie nodded.

'I can see the similarity, except that roof garden has got a roof.'

'Of sorts,' commented Sylvie, thinking of the semi-open lattice roof that was cleverly designed for natural irrigation to let in the light and rain. However, Bertram was right: High Line Park hasn't got a roof.

'But it has something that sets it apart from the roof garden at Canary Wharf.'

Sylvie already had an idea what that was. She was looking right at them.

Bertram followed her gaze. 'This wasn't purpose built. This is different.'

Sylvie nodded and looked up at Bertram. 'Are they old railway tracks?'

'Indeed they are. You are walking along a piece of history. This was an abandoned elevated railway line that used to carry freight above the streets of New York's Meatpacking District. I believe it's one and three-quarter miles long although I have never walked the entire length.'

Sylvie smiled. 'Why don't you make it a first and we walk it together?' Sylvie was pleased that she had worn sensible shoes. She had an idea that her day out in New York might involve a lot of walking. It was a city after all, and that's what you did in cities – walked. However, she had no idea she would be walking in Manhattan thirty feet above street level.

Sylvie grabbed Bertram's hand. 'Come on.'

Bertram reluctantly fell in step. This wasn't quite what he had in mind. His portly physique hinted that he wasn't really a walker. What Bertram had in mind was a leisurely stroll a few hundred yards, then a long sojourn on one of the park benches to take in the fantastic views of Manhattan and the Hudson River. Then an even longer stop for lunch, reminiscent of the two-hour luncheons they had when they first met at The Rooftop Café in London.

Bertram already had somewhere in mind for lunch. He surreptitiously glanced at his watch and wondered how long it would take to walk the entire length of the High Line. He'd never done it before, so he didn't know. Bertram frowned as they set off. He glanced at Sylvie as she took his arm. She was beaming.

'Bertram, this was the best surprise – ever.'

'Do you like it?'

'Do I like it?' repeated Sylvie in mock surprise. 'Of course. What's not to like?'

Bertram looked ahead at the walkway that seemed so very long, and thought of their lunch reservation. He managed not to grimace at the thought of losing their table if they didn't turn up on time. They might miss their lunch, but at least he hadn't spoiled Sylvie's day out in New York. Bertram smiled back at Sylvie and quickened his pace. He wanted Sylvie to walk the entire length, if that's what she wished, but he didn't want to miss the special reservation he had made, either.

Sylvie had no problem keeping pace. She had a spring in her step. She'd almost forgotten about the impending show, and what she was really doing here in New York; that was down to Bertram and his wonderful surprise tour. 'I'm enjoying myself, Bertram. I can't wait to find out what you've got up your sleeve next.'

'Who said I've got anything up my sleeve? I could be taking you straight back to your hotel.' Bertram was smiling from ear to ear.

Sylvie playfully nudged his arm. She knew he was joking.

As they walked along the High Line, Sylvie kept glancing Bertram's way. She felt he would have pushed the boat out and taken her to all the top sights in New York, like the views from the Empire State Building and shopping at Macy's. And he'd have done it VIP style. The mere thought made Sylvie feel uncomfortable. What she hadn't expected was for Bertram to take her to a public park. This was a very pleasant surprise indeed. Perhaps he knows me better than I give him credit for, thought Sylvie as they strolled along the concrete boardwalk with the stunning views of the Hudson River.

'I take it you are enjoying the first stop on my tour of New York?'

'Oh, yes,' she gushed. Sylvie was in her comfort zone. She didn't want to go anywhere fancy, and she certainly didn't want the VIP treatment. That was the whole reason she'd ditched the private tour in the limo. Sylvie wanted something authentic. She wanted to go where ordinary New Yorkers go, and do the sort of things they do, like walking in a public park. She didn't think Bertram would understand that.

'I was quite surprised that the first stop on the tour was a public park. I was expecting...' Sylvie trailed off.

Bertram raised an eyebrow. 'You were expecting...?' he prompted.

'Well, I suppose I thought that you would take me somewhere exclusive.' Sylvie was trying to be tactful. Before they arrived at the park, she assumed Bertram would use his money and status to get them into some places that an ordinary tourist could never venture. Sylvie had no idea where or what those sorts of places would be; she wasn't interested in finding out.

She didn't notice Bertram's face drop at that comment. He was thinking about their lunch reservation. Bertram stared at Sylvie. He knew what she was getting at. He had money no object, and although he wasn't flippant, he could afford to push the boat out. That's what Sylvie expected on their day out together. So far, he hadn't spent a penny, apart from the taxi fare. That had surprised her – in a good way.

It didn't change the fact that he liked the finer things in life.

He rarely visited public parks. This was a novel experience for him. Was he enjoying himself? Surprisingly – yes. But Bertram knew the reason; it was Sylvie's company.

His thoughts drifted back to their lunch reservation. He had been looking forward to it immensely, especially how impressed Sylvie would be when she found out he had secured a table at one of the most exclusive places in town. Now he wasn't convinced she was going to that enamoured when he told her about it.

They stopped at a water fountain. While Sylvie took a closer look at the water feature, and appeared to take a keen interest in the American Prairie themed planting, Bertram took a seat on a bench and sat watching Sylvie.

He was debating whether to forget the reservation and take her somewhere less exclusive. But where? He had visited New York dozens of times but went everywhere by private taxi. It would surprise Sylvie to learn he had never been in a New York taxicab. And he had never ventured far outside Upper Manhattan.

He had never wandered the streets of New York and just happened upon a nice coffee shop, restaurant, or bar. He rarely visited cafés and restaurants back in London unless they were pre-booked. Apart from that one time he was talked into going on a blind date at The Rooftop Café in Hanover Square, the day he met Sylvie. That's why he had no idea what to do if he cancelled their table.

Everything he did and everywhere he went was organised ahead, with reservations made by his private secretary. He moved within a select circle of friends and acquaintances and only ventured to places that were the exclusive preserve of the wealthy elite. He wasn't a celebrity, but he was rich. And he was honest enough to admit he enjoyed being part of an elite club that his wealth and status afforded him. The problem was, Sylvie wasn't part of that club. He was wondering whether she would ever feel comfortable with his lifestyle.

Sylvie joined him on the bench. 'You look lost in thought, Bertram.'

'Oh, do I?' said Bertram, sounding distracted.

'Is anything the matter?'

'Uh, no. I was just thinking about lunch.'

'Me too,' announced Sylvie. 'I can't believe I ate such a hearty breakfast at the hotel, and it's not even midday and I'm thinking about food already. Anyone would think I take after John.'

His name slipped out of her mouth before she had a chance to censor it. She looked at Bertram sheepishly. Sylvie imagined he would not want to discover his date was thinking about her soon-to-be ex-husband. Sylvie couldn't fathom why John had popped into her head. She guessed it had something to do with seeing that taxicab pass by the hotel; for a split second, she thought she saw him sitting in the back.

Sylvie shook her head. What a silly notion. It must have been a case of mistaken identity. John wasn't in New York. He was at home moping about the house because he had lost his grandpa days. Now he had nothing to do and nowhere to go to fill the void that Gertie and Alfie had left. Sylvie had dropped Alfie off at Julia's before heading to the airport.

Bertram furrowed his brow. So, despite packing her bags and walking out – Bertram had a spy in the shape of their mutual friend, Julia, who had told him that she believed Sylvie might take him up on the offer of the apartment, on her return from New York – John was still at the forefront of her mind.

Sylvie caught Bertram's disgruntled expression at the mention of John. She tugged his arm affectionately and steered the conversation back to lunch before he brought up the subject of John. 'So, where have you made a lunch reservation?'

Bertram turned to Sylvie and said playfully, 'Who says I've made a reservation?'

'Come, come. We both know you always make a reservation.'

'Perhaps I might surprise you.'

'You already have,' said Sylvie, glancing around High Line Park. She turned back to Bertram and studied him intently. 'I know what you're thinking?'

'You do?'

'I bet you've made a reservation somewhere fancy and now you're wondering if you have made a mistake.' Sylvie recalled their first evening meal together in London when Bertram had surprised her by booking a table at The Savoy. She still regretted how ungrateful she sounded when she'd told Bertram she wished he had taken her somewhere smaller, more intimate – meaning cheaper. Not that she didn't want to dine at The Savoy. Sylvie had enjoyed her evening. What had disappointed her was that she intended to be very modern and go dutch on the bill, something she couldn't afford back then when she discovered they were dining at such an upmarket restaurant.

Back then, with all the debts and bills to cover on the house, she was lucky if she could go dutch on takeaway fish and chips. But now everything had changed. Today was different. Sylvie was an independent woman with independent means. She wouldn't call herself rich. Sylvie couldn't even begin to fathom how much Bertram was worth. She didn't care. But she did have the means to share the cost of a meal out with Bertram. She bet he remembered that episode outside The Savoy, too. Sylvie smiled at him. 'I can't wait to see where you're taking me for lunch.'

'But—'

'I hope it's somewhere special.'

'Special?'

'It's New York. Let's live a little.'

The look on Bertram's face said he still didn't catch her drift, so Sylvie spelt it out. 'I hope you've booked somewhere absolutely divine for lunch. Remember The Savoy?'

'Of course. I love that hotel.'

'Well, why don't you take me somewhere you would love to dine in New York?'

Bertram's face was a picture. 'Let me just confirm my reservation,' he beamed. While he was at it, Bertram called his driver to pick them up in the limo. He didn't mind the New York taxicab. It was certainly an experience. However, Bertram rather fancied arriving at their lunch venue in style.

He got up from the park bench and offered Sylvie his hand 'Madam, would you like to join me for lunch?'

'Of course, kind sir,' giggled Sylvie, taking his hand.

Together they strolled back along The High Line toward the exit, and Bertram's limo waiting to whisk them off to one of the most exclusive restaurants in town.

14

Angelo stood up. 'We can't stay any longer, Mama. I'm taking John out to lunch.'

John gave Angelo's mother an apologetic look. He would have liked to stay for lunch.

Angelo's father closed the photo album. He looked up at John. 'Will you come again? I have plenty more photographs to show you.'

Angelo shook his head. 'I'm sure he has seen quite enough already.'

'No, no,' interjected John. 'I would love to see more.'

'Perhaps another time,' said Angelo, heading for the door. 'We're still on the meter and times a ticking.'

'Angelo!' Mama scolded him. 'I hope you weren't charging John while he was visiting us.'

'Of course not,' said Angelo sheepishly.

'You stop that meter every time he gets out of your taxi – do you hear?'

'Yes, Mama,' said Angelo with a bowed head.

John tried to suppress a smile. Angelo was in his sixties, and yet his mother still had him quivering in his boots like a small child. Maybe if his own mum were still alive, she would have just the same effect on him.

As John followed Angelo out into the hall, he whispered, 'Were you running the meter while I was visiting your parents?'

Angelo looked at him askance.

'I see.' John took that as a yes. He changed the subject. 'I must admit I'm disappointed we can't stay for lunch.'

'If we stayed for Mama's lunch, we'd be here all afternoon!' Angelo rolled his eyes. 'As an honoured guest, she would cook many dishes.'

That's what John was looking forward to.

'Besides, I'm taking you somewhere special for lunch.'

'Okay.' John tried not to sound disappointed. He turned toward the front door.

'Before we leave, I want to show you something.'

John did an about turn and followed Angelo to the foot of the stairs.

Angelo started up the stairs. He glanced over his shoulder. 'Come on. I think you will find this interesting.'

'Oh, okay.' John followed behind Angelo as they marched up the stairs. They walked along the first-floor landing. John glanced in a couple of rooms as he passed by; one was a large airy bedroom, and the other a family bathroom with an old-fashioned free-standing roll-top bath.

He came to a halt beside Angelo outside the last door along the landing. He glanced out the small oval window that over-looked the front yard below as Angelo opened the door. John followed Angelo inside and was surprised to find there wasn't a room behind that door but another flight of stairs, uncarpeted, with creaky narrow stair treads and a musty smell. John raised an eyebrow. 'Are we going up to the attic?'

Angelo reached the top of the stairs and turned around to watch John follow him up. 'This house doesn't have an attic,' he said before disappearing through the doorway at the top.

John shrugged, walked up the stairs, and followed Angelo through the doorway. As he stepped into the room, he couldn't hide his surprise. 'Good heavens!'

Angelo smiled as he looked around. 'It's still pretty much as we left it.'

John stared at the room in disbelief. It was as though he'd just walked back into the fifties – American-style. On either side of the large dormer window were two narrow single beds under the eaves. The bedspreads were old and faded. There were posters of baseball stars from that era on the wall over each bed. From the ceiling light hung an assortment of wooden toy aeroplanes. John recalled building something similar, when he was a child, from one of those aeroplane model kits that used to be popular in the fifties.

'When my two children were small, they loved using this bedroom when they stayed over at their grandparents. In fact, when my brother's kids came over too, there would be arguments over who was sleeping in this room. Now our grandkids are just the same.'

'May I?' said John, pointing at the baseball glove on the bed.

Angelo nodded. 'Be my guest.'

John picked it up and turned it over. He had seen plenty of baseball gloves on American movies, but he'd never seen a real one, let alone picked one up. He slid his hand into the leather glove.

'Here.' Angelo surprised John by tossing a baseball at him.

John held out the gloved hand. Somehow the ball landed squarely in the centre of his glove. John closed his gloved hand around it and looked over at Angelo, feeling mightily chuffed with himself.

'You're a natural.'

'Oh, you're just being kind,' John replied, with typical English modesty.

He took the ball out of his gloved hand and tossed it into the glove, back and forth, as he walked around the room. The ball made a dull thud every time it hit the glove.

John noticed two bats propped up against the wall in one corner of the room. He could just imagine two Italian American boys racing up those stairs in their baseball outfits and fifties crew cuts, diving into this room to grab their baseball bats before going out to practice with their friends in the middle of the street.

John stopped passing the ball back and forth, and only then noticed there was writing on the ball. 'It's autographed.' He held the ball up for Angelo to see.

'Uh-huh. Keep it.'

'Oh, I couldn't do that.' He was starting to worry that Angelo might expect the mother of all tips after his tour. John took off the glove and tried to hand the baseball back to Angelo. 'It must be worth—'

Angelo refused. 'There comes a point, John, when you get to my age that money isn't all that important anymore. I want you to have it.'

John stared at Angelo. God, how he wished someone had said that to him before he went down the disastrous road of converting the house into two apartments just to make more money. Sylvie might still have left him in the end – conversion or no conversion. However, if he hadn't converted the house, she wouldn't have had the opportunity to move downstairs on her own and find a new life without him. Perhaps they could have done that together – moved on with their lives in retirement without splitting up.

When he was forced into early retirement, Sylvie wanted a change. She was ready to move on and do something different with her life. John wasn't. He was still stuck in the past, rooted in a life that revolved around the house and his job and forty years of a routine that he was comfortable with. He wasn't ready to step out of that comfort zone. Now he understood where Sylvie was coming from, but it was too late.

He'd read an article about how divorce among his generation was on the rise. Boomers were living longer than their parents' generation. Perhaps some of them didn't want to spend their twilight years mowing the lawn or knitting their grandchildren mittens. They were more adventurous than that. They were boomers. There were still things to do and places to be and new experiences to be had. He wished he'd understood that when Sylvie told him she wanted to do other things. But he was too busy converting the house to earn more money. What was the point of more money if they couldn't spend it together?

John glanced at Angelo. He was right: there comes a point in life when there are a darn sight more important things than the pursuit of an extra buck.

It made him wonder how many other couples of his generation were splitting up because they couldn't see a way forward together in retirement. Despite not wanting to follow in their parents' footsteps, John guessed most boomers eventually conformed and hunkered down to join the rat race, with a job and a mortgage, so they could provide for their families. Then, with the children flown the nest and no jobs to tie them down, they were free again.

The problem was that unlike their parents' generation who, in John's experience, had one aspiration – to retire in a little bungalow by the sea – boomers wanted something more. Sylvie certainly wanted something more. John didn't know what exactly she wanted because he was too wrapped up in himself. The fact was he didn't envisage ever retiring until he lost his job and it was forced upon him. For once in his life, he didn't have any plans for their future. But John suspected Sylvie had plans; god knows she had asked him enough times what they were going to do when they retired. But he wasn't interest in talking about it until it was too late.

In hindsight, he wished more than anything that he had listened to what she wanted for a change. But he didn't. And here they were, Sylvie in New York with another man, and John all alone.

'Besides, I've got plenty more where that came from.'

'Huh?' John was so wrapped up in self-recrimination that he'd lost the thread of the conversation.

Angelo beckoned for John to come over and take a look.

He walked over and looked in the drawer that Angelo had opened. 'Ah.' He saw half a dozen signed baseballs along with other baseball paraphernalia. John glanced around the bedroom once more, still feeling as though he'd stepped into a fifties time warp.

Angelo closed the drawer. 'I bet you're wondering how come all this has survived from my childhood?'

John nodded.

'My brother and I enjoyed sharing when we were young boys, but when we were teenagers, we moved into a bedroom each on the floor below. When we left home, Mama and Papa redecorated our bedrooms. One is Mama's craft room, and the other is a spare bedroom. But when it came to this room, well, that was a different story. Papa said to me he missed his two little boys and he couldn't bring himself to dismantle this bedroom and all the treasured memories that went with it.'

John gazed around the room. He could understand that.

Angelo sighed. 'The trouble is I've been on at them for years that the house is too big to manage, and they should move somewhere smaller. But if Papa can't let go of one bedroom, how on earth would he let go of the *entire* house?'

John smiled knowingly. It reminded him of the reason he did the house conversion. Since the girls left home, their four-storey townhouse was too big for just the two of them. In hindsight, he should have let go of his precious house and downsized somewhere smaller. That was easier said than done. Family homes had treasured memories that weren't so easy to leave behind.

'Are you coming?'

John had been standing in the middle of the bedroom, lost in thought. 'Right you are.' He took one last look around the room full of fifties nostalgia before he followed Angelo back down the creaky stairs, along the landing, and down the next flight of stairs to the oak-panelled hall on the ground floor.

Angelo's father was standing in the lounge doorway, leaning heavily on his walking stick. 'Now, you be sure to come again. I still have plenty more photograph albums to show you.'

'I will,' John promised. He didn't think it was likely he'd make a return visit on this trip, although he had every intention of returning to New York in the future.

Papa followed John and Angelo to the front door.

John noticed there was no sign of Angelo's mother. He hoped they hadn't offended her by not staying for lunch.

Angelo opened the front door and glanced back at his father. 'Where's Mama?'

Papa shrugged.

John stepped outside onto the veranda.

Angelo joined John on the veranda and was just saying goodbye to his father when his mother came rushing down the hall. 'Wait!'

Angelo was about to close the door.

She arrived breathless at the front door, and said to Papa, 'I told you not to let them go until I returned.'

'Oh – did you?'

Angelo turned to John and rolled his eyes.

Mama joined them on the veranda.

Not to be left out, Papa stepped outside too and got a stern telling off for his trouble. 'You need to go back inside the house where it's warm.'

Papa ignored his wife and ambled along the veranda, his walking stick making a dull thudding sound on the wooden decking until he arrived at the swing seat for two under the bay window. Papa slowly lowered himself into the seat.

Mama tutted at her husband before turning to John. 'Now, I didn't want you to go before I brought you this.' She held up a large brown paper bag.

'Mama!'

John gave Angelo a sideways glance as he tentatively took the bulging paper bag. He got the impression Angelo knew what was inside.

'As you can't stay for lunch,' said Mama, throwing her son a disapproving glare, 'I packed you a little something for the journey, so you won't go hungry.'

Angelo sighed loudly. 'We're only driving back to Manhattan, Mama. It won't take that long.'

John could smell something delicious wafting from the brown paper bag in his hands. 'Thank you.'

Mama stepped forward and held out her arms.

John bent down so Mama could throw her arms around him. She whispered in his ear, 'Thank you for indulging my husband with the trip down memory lane. I hope he didn't bore you too much.'

'Oh, not at all. It was my pleasure.' John meant it. He'd enjoyed meeting the Italian Americans and hearing their story as immigrants coming to America in the fifties.

'Goodbye, Mama.' Angelo gave her a kiss on the cheek. 'Bye Papa.'

John followed Angelo down the front steps and got in the car. He looked up at the house before they set off and saw Angelo's mother and father sitting together on the seat for two on the veranda.

Angelo was also looking in their direction. 'You know, as far back as I can remember there's been a seat on the veranda under that window.'

John stared at Angelo's parents and imagined a young couple sitting together on that bench, watching their two sons playing baseball on the front lawn back in the fifties.

He was back to thinking about Sylvie's garden bench under

the old oak tree. One of the workmen had taken it home to burn for firewood. He shook his head from side to side. All that remained of the little seating area that she used to love in the back garden was the old oak tree under which the bench used to sit. And that was only because there was a preservation order on the tree and John couldn't touch it.

'It's been a while since I've seen them sitting there together like they used to.'

'Pardon me?' Once again, John was so lost in thought, he didn't catch his drift.

'Papa's got dementia. Mama prefers him not to go out of the house in case he wanders off.'

'Oh, I'd never have thought.'

'Yes, you wouldn't believe it to look at him. When he's reminiscing about the past, his mind is as sharp as anything. But ask him what he had for breakfast…' Angelo trailed off.

'I'm sorry, Angelo.'

Angelo turned in his seat to look at John. 'That's life, I guess. He is almost ninety. It's a rare thing to see them sitting out on the veranda these days. You know they used to sit there watching my brother and I play baseball.'

John guessed as much.

Angelo tooted his horn and waved.

Behind Angelo, John looked out the side window and waved goodbye. He took one last look back at the house before he turned in his seat and said, 'Where next?'

John caught sight of the brown paper bag on the seat next to him. Whatever Angelo's mother had packed in that bag still smelled delicious. He peeked inside and saw two rectangular shaped foil containers.

Angelo heard the rustle of the brown paper bag. 'That's Mama's famous homemade paella. You can heat it up or eat it cold.'

John noticed Angelo didn't answer his question. He tried again. 'Where are we going for lunch?'

Angelo remained silent.

'You're not going to tell me – are you.'

Angelo shook his head. 'You'll see when we get there – it's a surprise. But first, we're going to make a quick detour.'

John rolled his eyes at the word *surprise* and glanced at the brown paper bag with Mama's delicious smelling paella inside. His mouth watered. 'Do we have to make a detour? I'm hungry.'

'Trust me – you won't want to miss this.'

15

John tossed the baseball into the glove several times. He paused. John looked to his left, then to his right, before pulling his arm back and throwing the ball as hard as he could across the field.

Angelo hit the ball, dropped the baseball bat, and started jogging towards first base.

John started after the ball, holding out a gloved hand as the ball fell to earth. *Thud.* He was so surprised when it landed in the middle of his gloved hand that he'd forgotten what happens next.

'Well done, John!' exclaimed Angelo, as he jogged to second base. 'Remember, you've got to strike me out.'

'Oh, right you are.' John started for third base. He was gaining on Angelo fast. All that dog walking had paid off. Not that long ago he wouldn't have been able to jog even a short distance, let alone a good few hundred yards.

John picked up his pace, landed on third base well before Angelo, and bounced the ball on the small, hard surface. He grinned at Angelo triumphantly.

Angelo came to a halt and walked the rest of the way to third base. He came up to John and patted him on the back. 'Did you enjoy that?'

'I'll say.' John turned full circle and looked around the empty stadium, imagining a cheering crowd. It was quite something to stand in the middle of the baseball field in Yankee Stadium. It was a lot bigger on the ground than it appeared when he'd first seen the stadium from a window in the museum. That's where Angelo had started the tour of Yankee Stadium. The first stop was the museum, where John had wandered around, taking in various baseball memorabilia, before purchasing a child's baseball bat, glove and ball in the gift shop. John was rather hoping he could interest Gertie in a game when he was allowed to see her again.

Angelo waved at an old man making his way along the terrace, sweeping in between the chairs. It was the janitor – one of Angelo's childhood friends – who had let them on to the field. Angelo turned around and said to John, 'Over there,' he pointed towards the edge of the field, 'that's where we used to walk along and exit the stadium through the main doors. Of course, no one does that anymore. It's tight security now. They wouldn't let anybody on the field after a game. Actually, they don't let anybody on the field – period. Unless you join a guided tour.'

'A guided tour?' John's smile faded. He hoped they weren't going to get into trouble. His eyes darted around the stadium, imagining two burly security guards heading in their direction.

Angelo caught John's frown. 'Don't worry. I've brought my kids and grandkids out here and never had any—'

'Hey – you!'

Angelo and John turned around simultaneously at the sound of a raised voice on the pitch.

John's eyes went wide at the sight of two security guards heading in their direction.

One of them shouted out, 'What do you think you're doing out here?'

John turned to Angelo and happened to glance over at the stadium seating. In the distance, he noticed Angelo's so-called friend with the broom had turned tail and was heading in the other direction. He cast a furtive glance over his shoulder at John.

John looked at Angelo. 'I don't suppose those two,' John flicked a finger over his shoulder at the security guards, 'are friends of yours?'

Angelo smiled nervously at John. 'Run!'

'Pardon me?'

'I said – *run*. Unless you want to finish the tour seeing the inside of New York's finest police cells.'

Bloody hell. He picked up the ball and started running. 'Where to?' John shouted at Angelo.

Angelo pointed to the far corner of the field.

John nodded and overtook Angelo. He stole a quick glance behind him at their pursuers. Although they were several decades younger, the two security guards didn't look as though they exercised much – if at all. They were very overweight. By the time John and Angelo had reached the other side of the pitch, the two security guards had stopped their pursuit and were bent over – wheezing. However, they were soon on the move again.

John followed Angelo through a gap in the stadium seating and down a wide sloping corridor towards a door at the end from which, John guessed, the baseball players entered the centre field. He came to a halt behind Angelo. 'What's the matter?'

Angelo turned around. 'The door is locked.'

John raised his eyebrows. 'Now what?' He glanced over his shoulder. Any minute the security guards would come running down that slope. He could already hear them approaching. Then he heard something else. He turned around and stared at the door. Was that the sound of a key in the lock?

The door opened. To John's surprise and relief there was the janitor who, not less than five minutes ago, had high-tailed it out of there as though Angelo and John on the pitch had nothing to do with him.

The janitor beckoned them inside and swiftly closed the door behind them, locking it shut.

'Whoo-eee!' exclaimed the janitor, slapping his thigh. 'I haven't had this much excitement in years.'

'Open this door at once!' shouted one of the security guards, banging on the door.

Angelo turned to John. 'That was exhilarating. I felt like a kid again being chased off the pitch.'

'I'm not sure I wanted quite that much excitement.' Still, he couldn't help but grin. 'Although I have to say, it certainly got the blood pumping.' John had never, ever done anything close to breaking the rules before. He'd assumed Angelo had sought permission to go out on to the baseball pitch. He raised an eyebrow. Evidently not.

'This way,' said the janitor.

John followed Angelo and his friend through a door, which turned out to be the players' entrance to the stadium. Once they were all outside, the janitor said, 'I better get back to work.'

John shook hands with the janitor. 'Thank you.'

'It's been a riot,' he said, shaking John's hand enthusiastically.

'Well, I think we brightened up his day,' observed Angelo, watching his friend making his way towards the main entrance. 'Come on, John, I'm starved.'

'Me too.' All that exercise had worked up an appetite. John followed Angelo back to the taxi. 'So, where did you say we were having lunch?'

Angelo gave him a sideways glance. 'I didn't.'

John looked at Angelo expectantly, but he said nothing more as he climbed into the taxi. John sat in the back and glanced at his watch as they set off. It surprised him to discover it was almost three o'clock, way past his lunch hour. If he were in England, it would be time for afternoon tea.

'I hope it's not far,' said John, sounding grumpy. He was so hungry he felt like eating some of Mama's paella. The mouth-watering smell inside the cab from the paella wasn't helping. He was just reaching for the brown paper bag when Angelo said, 'You will spoil your lunch.'

John frowned at Angelo as he slid the paper bag along the back seat, out of reach. He folded his arms and looked out the cab window, hoping this next surprise was as good as the last two. Despite the frown because his stomach was growling, he was enjoying his day immensely. So far, he'd been across the Brooklyn Bridge to meet Angelo's parents in Victorian Flatbush and then to The Bronx to see Yankee Stadium. Now he was intrigued by where they were heading next. John spotted a street sign. They appeared to be travelling back to Lower Manhattan.

John was rather hoping lunch wouldn't turn out to be the end of the tour. He did a quick mental calculation and realised he had hailed Angelo's taxi at nine o'clock this morning. It was now three o'clock in the afternoon. Six hours had passed by in a flash.

John suddenly remembered he had to pay for all this. What if he didn't have enough money to settle his fare? For the first time since he got in the taxi, John checked the meter.

'Angelo, I think your meter has stopped working.'

'It's fine.'

John sat on the edge of his seat to take a closer look. They were driving, albeit slowly, in traffic, but the meter was not clocking up.

Angelo came to a halt in traffic and glanced over his shoulder. 'I switched it off.'

John raised a perplexed eyebrow. 'How come?'

'Well, I can't have you running out of money before the end of the tour.' He grinned. 'To tell you the truth, John, I haven't had this much fun in ages.'

John smiled. 'Me neither.'

'You see, me and my wife, well things haven't been…' Angelo trailed off. 'What I'm trying to say is that since I reached retirement age, things haven't been great at home. That's why I ran back to work.'

'Tell me about it!' John empathised. 'I'll tell you this – retirement is not for the faint-hearted.'

Angelo burst out laughing. 'Ain't that the truth. My god if we'd known how tough it would be, being around each other 24/7 with nothing to do all day but read the daily newspaper and potter in the back yard…'

John nodded. He understood perfectly.

'We never used to argue, but now we bicker like an old married couple.' Angelo paused. 'Hey – we *are* an old married couple!'

John guffawed.

Angelo continued. 'I've seen adverts on television about our generation going on cruises and having the time of their lives. But what happens when you get home? Back to the boredom and the never-ending days that follow the same routine; you get up – together. You eat – together. You do the chores – together. You shop – together. Eventually, you're sick of the sight of each other. And then at the end of a day you've got nothing interesting to talk about because you've been virtually joined at the hip since breakfast.'

John wasn't smiling anymore. 'My wife solved that problem.'

'She did?' Angelo had come to a halt in traffic. He turned in his seat and looked at John. 'Well? Don't keep me in suspense. How did she do it? How did you survive retirement?'

John bit his lower lip. 'We split up.'

Angelo's face fell. 'Oh.'

'Yes – oh. It's not what I wanted, Angelo. Not at all. But there you have it. We started living apart together and then—'

'Living apart together?' Angelo looked at John blankly.

'Yeah. Well, it started when my wife moved into the spare bedroom. Then I stupidly converted the house into two apartments, to rent one out. Next thing I know, she moves into the rental apartment downstairs. I didn't see that coming. Now she's moved out altogether. Out of the house. She's left me.'

Angelo was noticeably quiet. He said in barely a whisper, 'My wife moved into the spare bedroom last week. She said she wanted some space.'

John slowly shook his head from side to side. He recalled Sylvie saying the same thing. Then those words: *I want a break – from us.* John didn't expect that break to be permanent.

'I'm worried about where it's leading,' admitted Angelo. 'Do you know how many of my friends are getting divorced at our age – who would have thought?'

'Are you that surprised?' John didn't mean to sound cynical. 'Nobody realises that retirement isn't exactly a walk in the park. I think we all look at it as some sort of panacea, the prize at the end of all those years of hard work. Then when you finally arrive... Well, when I arrived, I thought: what is the point of it? What's the point of retiring – essentially, doing nothing? It felt like I was retiring from life. Do you know what I mean?'

Angelo thought about it. 'Yes, I do.' He stared at John. 'But what am I going to do about my wife?'

John knitted his brow. 'A word of advice: don't whatever you do convert your house into two apartments.' John wasn't joking.

Angelo stared at John, waiting for something more.

John shrugged. 'I'm not the person who can answer that, Angelo. Look at me. I lost my wife. You don't want any advice from me, I can tell you.' John thought about how he'd tried to get Sylvie to move back in with him over the last few months. He had tried every which way to get her back, but all he seemed to do was drive an even bigger wedge between them.

John stared at Angelo's large brown pleading eyes and said, 'There is one thing…'

'Yes?'

It was something John had thought about – a lot – since they started living apart together. It was something he wished he'd acted on from the very beginning before it all got so out of hand and he lost her for good.

'Well?' Angelo prompted.

'I did something for Sylvie. Something she'd always wanted. It was going to be a surprise. I hadn't done anything like that, surprised her, since before we were married…' John trailed off, deep in thought.

'What was it?' asked Angelo, intrigued.

'It's not important. Besides, it's too late now. She's gone.'

'Can't you, you know, surprise her anyway with whatever it was?'

'Perhaps you'll get another opportunity?'

An image of Sylvie walking out of the hotel, arm-in-arm with Bertram, and climbing into a waiting limo flashed across John's mind. 'I don't think so.' John didn't want to talk about it. He wished he'd never brought it up. The only reason he had was to make a point. 'Look, what I'm trying to say is that you know your wife. Is there something special – meaningful to her – that perhaps you could do to surprise her, like when you were courting?'

'Ah-ha!' Angelo pointed at John. 'I get it. Do something un-expected to show her I still love her – is that it?'

John nodded.

A car horn sounded behind them, making John jump.

Angelo turned around in his seat. The cars ahead of them had gone, leaving Angelo's taxi holding up the traffic. Angelo put his foot down, pinning John to the back seat. 'I think it's time we had lunch.'

'Oh yes.' John was famished.

'And over lunch, you can tell me what I can do to surprise my wife.'

'Oh, no.' John was thinking of his brother, Dave. He knew from past experience that asking someone else to help you get your wife back was a terrible idea.

John heaved a sigh. 'That, my friend, you will have to figure out for yourself. My only advice is to do it now before it's too late.' John was thinking of his wife, who was with another man somewhere in New York at this moment.

16

'Now remember the keyword regarding my personalised tour of New York.'

Of course, Sylvie remembered. After their spectacular lunch, how could she forget?

Bertram raised an eyebrow as if to say, *you haven't forgotten already – have you?*

Sylvie smiled at Bertram. 'I haven't forgotten. The word *elevated* sums up the tour so far.'

'I take it you enjoyed lunch?'

'You know I did!' Sylvie had oohed and aahed throughout lunch. In fact, Bertram had to keep reminding her about the plate of food in front of her. Sylvie had acted like a child who was so excited she couldn't sit still. She was talking about their reservation a full hour after they had finished and left for the next stop on the tour.

Little wonder Sylvie couldn't stop talking about the aptly named restaurant called The View. Situated on the forty-eighth floor of the New York Marriott Marquis Hotel, The View was unique in New York because it was the only revolving rooftop restaurant in the city. Every time Bertram had visited New York, he'd tried to get a reservation, but it was always booked up weeks in advance. Imagine his surprise when he'd rang on the off chance, and he was in luck; his call coincided with a cancellation.

However, once he had made the reservation, he was concerned that eating and rotating 360 degrees at the same time might not make for particularly good dining bedfellows. He was worried they would come over queasy and it would ruin their lunch. Bertram recalled he had been to one of these revolving restaurants before – The Skylon Tower in Niagara Falls. He didn't remember feeling queasy there. But that had been many years ago and one of those episodes in his life he'd rather forget; he was there with his wife.

Once they arrived at The View, Bertram soon discovered he had worried out of hand. The revolving restaurant turned very slowly indeed, almost imperceptibly so. Bertram timed it and found it took an hour for it to turn a full 360 degrees to see the views from all directions.

They were enjoying the views so much that their lunch hour became a leisurely affair lasting two hours. Sylvie was so mesmerised by the view that Bertram didn't think she hardly noticed the elegant interior of the restaurant with its linen-topped tables and contemporary décor.

It was Bertram who had studied the extensive menu and ordered for both, but he wasn't put out – not at all. He was pleased that another stop on his tour had gone down a treat with Sylvie. In fact, considering he hadn't planned on a day out together in New York, everything was working out surprisingly well. He hoped the other things he had in store were to her liking.

Here goes, thought Bertram, as he asked his driver to pull the limo over at the kerb.

'Where to now?' asked Sylvie as she climbed out of the limo. She still couldn't believe she had started off the morning thinking that she had made a huge mistake spending the day with Bertram. Now that thought was furthest from her mind. She was looking forward to her next surprise.

Ten minutes later she was holding on to Bertram's hand for dear life.

Bertram turned to Sylvie. 'Relax. There is nothing to worry about.'

'Are you sure?' Sylvie asked, glancing out the window and making the mistake of looking down. Now she wished she hadn't been so enthusiastic about Bertram's idea of doing a tour of New York, encapsulating the word elevated. Right now, she would much rather have her feet planted on terra firma.

Bertram patted her hand affectionately.

'Believe me, these are perfectly safe.'

Sylvie smiled nervously. She had never been in a cable car before. She had seen them on the television, but for some reason every time there was one featured in an old black and white movie, they always seemed to get stuck, suspended in mid-air in some precarious fashion. It didn't fill her with much confidence.

Sylvie didn't fancy their cable car grinding to a halt before they reached their destination. She turned to Bertram. 'How long before—?'

Bertram had anticipated her question. 'Only five more minutes, so enjoy the views because we will be there very soon.'

'Oh, okay.' She looked straight ahead and could see the end of the line coming into view. Sylvie relaxed.

'Look.' Bertram pointed. 'There's Roosevelt Island.' Although it was a nice place to visit – Bertram had been before

and enjoyed a stroll along the riverside walk with views of
Manhattan's Upper East Side – there wasn't an awful lot to do
there. His reason for bringing Sylvie to Roosevelt Island, apart
from a pleasant stroll after lunch, was the chance to make the trip
to the island on The Roosevelt Island Tramway Car. It was the
only one of its kind in New York and not to be missed.

He glanced at Sylvie. Her grip on his hand had relaxed
considerably. A moment later, she let go of his hand. Sylvie got
her camera out and stood taking pictures. Bertram smiled and
confidently consigned this next leg on his tour as a success.

'We are getting the tram back, aren't we?' Sylvie asked,
hoping they were because she rather fancied doing it again now
she had got over her initial wobble.

'Of course we are.' Bertram glanced at his watch. After a
leisurely lunch, they had arrived at Roosevelt Island at almost
three in the afternoon. Bertram had organised another special
surprise for Sylvie – a tour of the Big Apple by helicopter later in
the afternoon. However, after her initial reaction when they took
the cable car, he was reconsidering whether the helicopter ride
was a good idea. He had to concede he still didn't know Sylvie as
well as he'd like.

Bertram decided to ditch the helicopter tour and go for the
safer bet. He settled on taking her to some of the more familiar
touristy destinations that almost everybody does when they visit
New York. However, he intended to stick to the elevated theme.

He made a mental list of all the places he could think of to
take Sylvie for the rest of the afternoon, like the Empire State
Building for one. Once they had knocked off some of the sights,
he had something special arranged for their evening meal
together. It would be the perfect surprise and the highlight of the

tour. He smiled at Sylvie. He couldn't wait to see the look on her face when she found out what he had organised. The only thing he hoped was that she wouldn't be too disappointed that on this occasion it wouldn't be anything elevated.

He was sure that would be more than made up for when she discovered they'd be rounding off their day together on The Hudson River – on a boat.

17

'Where did you say we were having lunch?'

Angelo put the handbrake on and switched off the car engine. He turned in his seat to look at John. 'Nice try.'

John shrugged. He knew full well Angelo hadn't told him where they were having lunch. He had made several unsuccessful attempts to find out what was so special about the next surprise on Angelo's tour of New York – their lunch venue. John's stomach was growling. He glanced at his watch. He was worrying that they had missed lunch, and the restaurant was now closed until the evening.

Angelo opened the car door.

John exited the taxi and followed Angelo, keeping pace with him as they negotiated crossing a busy road. He glanced down a side road as they passed by and saw a street sign – Wall Street. 'Is that the Wall Street,' asked John as they carried on walking.

'Yep.'

For some reason, he didn't expect Angelo to take him to Lower Manhattan, in the heart of the financial district, for a meal. He rather fancied an old-fashioned all-American Mom and Pop diner than some swanky restaurant.

Although Angelo hadn't given anything away when John asked him where they were going, what he did reveal was that it was his regular haunt for lunch. John knew it was condescending of him to even think it, but he was wondering what a taxi driver was doing coming to a place like this to dine, with all the suits. Perhaps he was hoping to catch a fare after lunch. A city professional with deep pockets who might give a generous tip. Even so, didn't Angelo feel somewhat out of place dining among all these white-collar workers?

John looked down at his chinos. Although he wasn't wearing jeans, and he had a blazer, he could pop over his jumper to smarten himself, John still couldn't hide the fact that he was dressed in casual attire. He was already feeling out of place among the office workers. And that was before he took a seat in some fancy restaurant.

John spotted a hot-dog stand. He'd noticed a lot of street vendors selling a variety of hot and cold food. John turned to Angelo. 'I rather fancy a hot dog.'

'I know you're hungry, John, but if you can hang on its only two more blocks.'

'Yes, but—'

A short distance further on, Angelo came to a halt.

John was so busy eyeing a street vendor that he walked straight past Angelo.

'Where are you going?'

John glanced over his shoulder and turned around. He retraced his steps to join Angelo outside what, at first glance, appeared to be an old-fashioned shop front.

Angelo opened the door.

'Is this where we're having lunch?' asked John in surprise.

'Yes. Welcome to the best restaurant in town,' said Angelo as he ushered John inside. The tinkle of the bell above the door announced their presence as they stepped inside.

John looked about him. It was just what he imagined an old-fashioned all-American Mom and Pop diner to look like. He didn't expect to find one in the heart of the financial district, amidst all the trendy bars and restaurants catering to the Wall Street movers and shakers.

Angelo pointed at a booth. 'Please take a seat, John,'

John slid into the booth and took a seat opposite Angelo. He glanced around the diner. It was heaving. 'We were lucky to get a table,' commented John.

'Not really. I always come here for lunch. I guess this has sort of become my table.' Angelo passed John a menu.

John picked up the menu and studied the name on the front – Morelli's. The name sounded familiar. He couldn't recall where he'd heard it before. John shrugged, thinking that he must have read it somewhere. It sounded Italian.

John glanced around the diner as he opened the menu. His first impression, as he stepped inside, was right on the money. He almost imagined a little old man, going by the affectionate moniker, *Pop*, coming over to take his order. John wouldn't be surprised if it was a family concern with the owner's wife in the kitchen preparing the food. 'Does the owner still work here?'

Angelo shook his head. 'The Morelli's are one of the great immigrant success stories. They've got restaurants and shops all down the east coast. You wouldn't find Mr Morelli working in his restaurants.' Angelo tapped the table with his forefinger. 'But this was where it all began. This was the first diner Mr Morelli opened back in the fifties.' Angelo pointed at a faded black and white framed photograph hanging on the wall above their table.

John studied the photograph of a handsome young Italian proudly standing outside his first diner. He shifted his attention to gaze around the room. That wasn't the only picture on the wall. There were framed photos of people who had visited the diner over the years. Some of the old black and white images were taken with Mr Morelli. John didn't recognise anybody, although he guessed, from some of the signed autographs, they must have been celebrities back in the day.

Angelo smiled fondly as he glanced around the diner. 'Impressive isn't it.'

John nodded. The décor added to the charm. A dado rail separated the oak wood panelling on the lower half of the walls from the retro-green flowered print above.

'Over the years they've kept it as it was when it first opened,' continued Angelo. 'The owner's kids and his grandkids spent their vacations from college working here, getting to know the family business from the roots up. I think this restaurant must hold a special place in the family's hearts.'

John had to lean to his left to see Angelo past the low hung ceiling lights which were above each booth.

'So, what do you fancy to eat, John?'

John looked down at the menu in his hands. The ceiling lights must have contained the lowest wattage bulbs he had ever come across because he could barely see the menu, let alone read the faded words inside when he opened it.

A young waitress appeared at their table and was quick to recommend the special of the day.

John was still scrutinising the menu. It was no good. He would have to go with her suggestion. The trouble was that the waitress had such a thick New York accent he didn't quite catch what she had just said. Too polite to ask her to repeat herself, he merely nodded. 'Sounds great.' John was so hungry he'd eat anything.

She scribbled down his order on a small notepad and turned to Angelo.

Angelo peered at the waitress and frowned. 'Are you new here?'

'Yes. I'm Gina.' She pointed at the name badge pinned to her shirt.

John put the menu to one side and looked up at the young woman standing beside their table. He did a double take. She could be his daughter Jess' doppelgänger, with her light olive skin tone, dark brown almond-shaped eyes and long wavy black hair. The resemblance was remarkable.

Angelo glanced at the photograph of Mr Morelli on the wall. 'Gina Morelli?'

'How did you know?'

'There's no mistaking the family resemblance.' Angelo pointed at the photo. 'You have your grandfather's eyes.'

'Great-grandfather,' Gina corrected him.

'God alive!' exclaimed Angelo. 'Where do the years go?'

'Tell me about it,' said John, staring at Gina and thinking of Jess. It seemed like only yesterday that his middle daughter had dropped out of university and gone travelling. That was eighteen years and a lifetime ago.

'I'm only working here during my vacations,' said Gina. 'I started college in the fall.'

John remembered that phone call from Jess saying she'd resumed her education in Australia and wasn't coming home.

Angelo said, 'I was just telling my friend here about Mr Morelli and this diner where his business empire began.'

Gina glanced at the picture on the wall. 'I wanted to spend some time working here like my mom used to when she went to college. It's kind of become a family tradition, like a rite of passage. I guess it reminds us of our roots and all the hard work he put in to create a family business that's given us the start in life he never had. Do you know he came to New York with nothing but the shirt on his back?'

Angelo nodded. Although he'd heard this story countless times before, he never tired of listening to an Italian immigrant success story. Angelo recalled something else about Mr Morelli he'd picked up. 'Didn't he immigrate here by way of England?'

'Yes – so the story goes. Apparently, he was a prisoner of war in England before he came to America.'

Angelo looked in John's direction. 'My friend here is English.'

John stared at Gina and felt oddly compelled to apologise for her great-grandfather's imprisonment at the hands of the British.

'Hey, there's no need to apologise. It wasn't your fault.'

John smiled at the young woman, who reminded him of Jess. 'Do you know what part of England he was...er...sent to?' asked John, interested to know.

'He wouldn't talk about it. He didn't have a bad experience – nothing like that,' Gina quickly added. 'In fact, he once said he was treated very well. He just preferred that the family didn't bring it up. My Mom thinks he wanted to put the past behind him. America was a fresh opportunity. A chance to start over.'

'That's understandable.' John glanced around the packed diner. 'It looks like he did very well for himself. He certainly put his past behind him and moved on.'

Gina's face dropped. 'I guess, kind of.'

'Kind of?' Angelo prompted, studying her thoughtfully.

'Well, you know he passed away recently…'

Angelo nodded his head solemnly.

'There was something in his will, something from his past that—'

'Hey, you! Can we get some service over here?'

John turned in his seat at the gruff voice behind him. 'Can we have some manners first?' John shot back at the rude interruption from the young man seated behind him.

'Are you British?' asked the woman sitting next to the recalcitrant young man. 'I just lurve your accent.' She grinned at John. 'Say something else.'

John bit his tongue and turned around in his seat.

Gina looked at John and Angelo apologetically. 'Sorry guys, but as you can see, I've got a room full of customers. Look, it was great meeting you. Your order will be coming right up.' She moved on to the next table.

John glanced at the photograph on the wall of Mr Morelli. 'I wonder what she was going to say about his past...?'

18

Angelo was just about to pull over and park outside the hotel when John spotted them. 'Crikey!' John exclaimed in surprise. He shouted at Angelo, 'No, don't stop!'

'But we've arrived at your hotel.'

'I don't care – just drive!'

Angelo slammed his foot on the accelerator. The cab lurched forward, sailing past the hotel where John was supposed to be alighting. As he drove past, Angelo noted a man and woman getting out of a limo parked outside the hotel. He caught John in his rear-view mirror, hunkering down as though he was trying to avoid someone. Angelo raised an eyebrow, wondering what on earth had got into him.

John turned in his seat, which wasn't that easy from his position, almost on his knees in the footwell. He raised his head to look out the rear window. He caught sight of Sylvie skipping up the hotel steps, looking as though she'd had a good time. Bertram followed, also with a spring in his step. 'Dammit!' muttered John.

Angelo saw John reappear in his rear-view mirror.

'Are you avoiding someone?'

John breathed heavily. 'Yes, as it happens. I'm avoiding my wife.'

'Your wife! She's in New York too? I thought you were separated?'

'We are,' said John glumly. 'And we didn't come to New York together, Angelo, if that's what you're thinking.'

That's exactly what Angelo was thinking. His first thought was that they had taken a break together in a last-ditch attempt to save their marriage. That's what Angelo would have done. In fact, that had just given him an idea: Angelo was thinking about surprising his wife with a European tour. They had never been abroad before, but he recalled she once talked about going travelling when they retired.

'She's here with someone else. I couldn't believe it when I discovered they were in New York, too,' continued John. 'And worse still, they're staying in the same hotel.'

Angelo's eyes went wide. 'You've got to be kidding.'

'Nope. I said to myself, of all the hotels in all the world why do they have to be staying in this one?'

Angelo nodded his head in sympathy.

John added, 'Perhaps the fact that Bertram what's-his-face the second owns the damn hotel might have something to do with it.'

'Who?'

'Bertram Wyndom—'

'Price – the second,' Angelo cut in.

John looked at him in surprise. 'You know him?'

'Not personally. But I know of him. Everyone does.'

John rolled his eyes. 'Well, I'm not surprised. It seems that anybody who is wealthy, is famous. I have no idea why.'

'It's nothing to do with his wealth or the fact that he owns a string of hotels. There are plenty of wealthy people in New York going about their daily lives with nobody having the first clue who they are.'

John arched an eyebrow. 'So, what makes Bertram so different?'

Angelo had just finished circling the block. He pulled the car up outside the hotel where the limo had been parked five minutes ago. Angelo switched off the car engine and turned in his seat to look at John. Angelo pursed his lips. 'Mr Price's wife disappeared under mysterious circumstances.'

'Disappeared?'

'You didn't know?'

'Of course not.'

'Guess it wasn't big news on your side of the pond, but over here a very wealthy businessman's wife goes missing, and it's big news all right.'

John turned to look up at the hotel.

Angelo followed his gaze. 'We're going back a ways, mind you. It must be almost twenty years ago now, but did you know he was arrested?'

'What for?'

Angelo looked at John askance. 'My, you have led a sheltered life.'

'I'm English.'

Angelo smiled at his English friend. 'He was brought in for questioning over his wife's disappearance. You know the spiel to do with helping police with their inquiries, which really means he's a suspect.'

'A suspect?'

Angelo nodded. 'He was suspected of being involved in her disappearance somehow.'

John furrowed his brow. He didn't like the sound of that. John leaned forward in his seat. 'Did they ever find her – his wife?'

A loud knock on the cab window startled John and Angelo.

Standing beside Angelo's cab was a New York City police officer.

Angelo wound his window down.

'You can't park here. This is a drop-off zone only. Please move on.'

'Sure, officer. I was just dropping off my fare.'

'Well, hurry up about it. There's a queue.' He gestured behind him to a line of taxis waiting to drop off hotel guests.

John hurriedly opened his wallet and handed Angelo all his cash.

Angelo shook his head. 'Keep it.'

'I can't do that!' protested John.

'Yes, you can. And you will. I insist, as a friend. Besides, I think you've earned your free ride by giving me that one piece of advice I needed to hear right now?'

John looked up. He didn't recall giving Angelo any advice.

Angelo took in John's confused expression. 'Remember I told you my wife moved into the spare bedroom last week. She said she wanted some space.'

'Ah yes.' John remembered all right. 'I said whatever you do, don't convert your house into two apartments.'

Angelo frowned. 'No, that's not what I was talking about. Why would I do that?'

Why indeed? John pursed his lips.

Angelo continued. 'You said that you had done something special for your wife. You wouldn't tell me what it was you did for her, just that I had to figure it out for myself – what I could do for my wife to show her how much I still loved her.'

John nodded.

'I think I figured out what I'm going to do.' Angelo glanced up at the hotel. 'Whatever it was you did for your wife, can't you find a way to tell her about it in New York, before it's too late?'

John followed Angelo's gaze. He stared up at the five-star hotel. What he'd done for Sylvie was small fry compared to this. How could he compete now she was with Bertram? As far as John was concerned, it was already too late.

He turned back to Angelo. 'I lost my moment, Angelo. Don't lose yours.'

John unlocked the door to his room and slipped inside. He had almost sprinted through the hotel foyer towards the lifts, afraid he might bump into Sylvie and Bertram. But they were nowhere to be seen.

He frowned when he remembered what Angelo had said about Bertram's wife disappearing. Although it was many years ago, and he didn't know the full story, it still made him feel uneasy. It reminded him that he didn't know that much about Bertram Wyndom-Price, apart from the fact that he owned a bunch of hotels around the world and had his sights set on someone else's wife. John sighed. He was just relieved he had seen Sylvie return to the hotel safe and sound.

John did his best to put all thoughts of Sylvie and Bertram aside. Instead, he focused on a new idea for his column, Dear

John. He was considering writing an article called "An Immigrant's Story". The story of Gina's great-grandfather, Mr Morelli, had piqued John's interest, not least because of the time he'd spent in England as a prisoner of war.

John hadn't broached the subject of his new article with the magazine yet. He hadn't plucked up the courage to tell Harriet that he wasn't writing about living apart together anymore because that episode in his life was over. They would soon find out when he appeared on the show. Still, he wasn't going to think about that. Or his wife having a good time in New York with another man.

John strode across the room towards the desk by the window. He couldn't resist straightening the cushions on the sofa as he passed by. Before he took a seat at the desk, he glanced around his hotel suite. He cringed when he recalled the empty bottles of booze from the minibar strewn on the floor, along with the boxes of half-eaten takeaway food. And the plates of stale sandwiches; John discovered he'd ordered room service, too.

The state of his hotel room, before the maid worked her magic, brought to mind Chloe, his youngest daughter. He knew why thoughts of his suite after his party-of-one last night made him think of Chloe. The empty bottles of booze and discarded takeaway boxes were reminiscent of the state of Chloe's place after her nights out clubbing with friends. Even though her student days were well behind her – Chloe had just turned thirty and bought a house with her fiancé, Declan – John knew she hadn't changed a bit.

But she had settled down. John knew there must be something different about Declan for Chloe to give up her place and move in with him. She had moved in with other boyfriends in the past, but she had never made a commitment to sell her flat and buy a place together. What made Declan so special? John smiled as he sat down at the desk. It didn't take a genius to figure that out: Chloe had fallen in love.

John was still smiling at the thought that he had nothing to worry about. At least that was one less thing on his mind, apart from the possibility that she had forgotten to pop in and feed his pet cat, Mouse. John's smile faded. Wouldn't that be just like Chloe? After all, he didn't have to remind himself that she rarely did someone a favour unless there was something in it for her.

John had been taken aback when Chloe offered to keep an eye on the house and pop into his apartment every day to feed Mouse — assuming she had remembered. He sighed as he switched on his laptop. There wasn't a lot he could do about it from several thousand miles away.

John opened a new word document and typed everything he could remember about his visit to Morelli's and the little he knew about the man behind the restaurant empire — Mr Morelli. He wasn't typing for long when his thoughts drifted back to Chloe; John was still wondering if she had remembered to feed his cat. He stopped typing. John saved what little he had written and got out of his chair. A moment later, he perched on the edge of the bed and picked up the phone. If he was honest, he wasn't just calling about the cat; John was feeling a little homesick and was phoning on a pretext because he fancied a chat.

John had just dialled his home number when he remembered he was on New York time. It would be ten o'clock at night in Blighty. If Chloe had popped in to feed Mouse today, she wouldn't still be there that late in the evening. John put the phone down and went to find Chloe's mobile phone number.

19

Chloe picked up the phone, but whoever had called put the phone down almost immediately. She shrugged and walked back to the sofa. She sat down and reached for her mobile. It took a moment to find it among the discarded boxes of Chinese takeaway. She'd been very naughty and had takeout three nights on the trot and hadn't bothered to clear away the remnants littering the coffee table.

Chloe found her phone but accidentally knocked her wine-glass on the floor. 'Oh, crap!' She bent down and picked up the glass. Fortunately, it was empty. Chloe didn't fancy trying to get a red wine stain out of a cream carpet. She put the glass on the table and sunk back into the cushions. Chloe always had her mobile to hand, so she could catch up with friends on social media, even though she saw them most weekends when she was out clubbing.

She was just scrolling through her texts to see if she had any messages when her phone rang. Chloe didn't recognise the number. She answered it anyway. 'Hello?'

'Chloe – it's Dad.'

'Hi, Dad. How's it going in New York?'

'Fine. I know it's a bit late. I haven't disturbed you and Declan have I?'

Chloe bit her lower lip. 'No, I'm still awake.' She was in her PJ's and was nestled on the sofa, intending to watch a late-night movie on the television, when the phone rang. Chloe's job, working from home as a freelance computer software engineer, meant she could work the hours she wanted. This also meant she could indulge her night owl and stay up late in the evenings, knowing she didn't have to get up early for work the next morning. The late-night phone call on a weekday didn't bother her in the least. But something else did.

'So ... Dad... when are you coming home?'

'Ah well, the thing is they postponed the show, so I've had to spend an extra few days in New York.'

Chloe grinned. 'That's fantastic news – for you, I mean.' Chloe put her feet up on the coffee table and smiled at her new pink fluffy slippers. She'd bought them at Camden Market when she went shopping with Julia the other day.

'Are you having a good time in New York, Dad?'

There was a pause on the end of the line.

'Dad?'

'I'm having a great time.'

Chloe frowned. She could tell by his tone of voice that he wasn't being honest with her.

'Tell you the truth, Chloe, I'm feeling homesick. Look, the reason I called—'

'Meow.'

'What was that sound?'

'What sound?' Chloe looked about her and discovered the cat standing on the back of the sofa, looking over her shoulder.

Chloe held a finger to her lips in a shushing motion.

'I thought I heard a cat. Have you and Declan bought a pet?'

'Oh, Daddy, don't be so silly. You know Declan is allergic to cats.'

'I didn't know that.'

'Neither did I,' Chloe said in exasperation, 'until we moved in together.'

'But I thought I heard—'

'Must have been the television,' Chloe said, telling an outright lie as she watched the cat jump down on to the sofa beside her. Chloe smiled as Mouse nuzzled her soft, furry cheek against her hand. The cat then settled herself on Chloe's lap and started purring. Chloe moved the phone to her other ear and reached for John's television controls. She turned the volume up.

'So ... Dad, when did you say you were coming home?'

'Well, that's the reason for my call. Because I'm going to be away longer than expected, I wanted to make sure you had remembered to keep an eye on the house while I was away...'

Chloe glanced at her overnight bag in the corner of John's lounge. 'Don't worry, I've been keeping a close eye on the place.'

'That's good. And did you remember to feed Mouse? The thing is she has a habit of disappearing. Sometimes she doesn't reappear for days.'

'Oh, you don't have to worry about that. She's right here. Um... what I meant was, she was right there when I popped in.' Chloe rolled her eyes at her gaffe.

'Great. Well, I guess I'd better sign off.'

'There is one thing, Daddy.'

'Yes, Chloe?'

Chloe bit her lower lip. She really didn't want to worry him but, 'It's Mum. I haven't seen her in the apartment downstairs for a while.'

There was a long pause at the end of the line.

'Daddy, are you still there?'

'Your mother started a new job. I don't know if she told you. That's why you've missed her when you drop by the house during the day.'

Chloe fell silent. How could she explain to Daddy that Mum wasn't just absent during the day? As far as she was aware, her mother hadn't stepped foot in the house for the last few nights, either. After the first night sleeping upstairs in John's apartment with no sign of Mum in the flat below, Chloe had got straight on the phone to the one person who would know where her mum was – Julia. Besides, Chloe reasoned that someone had to be looking after Alfie while her mum was away.

Chloe was relieved to discover that Auntie Julia knew where her mum was. She just wouldn't tell her. All she said was that Sylvie had gone on a trip. Chloe's first thought was that Julia refused to give her any details because she had a reputation in family circles for not being able to keep secrets.

Chloe hoped that Dad had told Mum about his trip to New York and she had flown there to surprise him. That was the big secret. Then the two of them would patch things up. That hadn't happened, and now Chloe was back to wondering why Julia had been so vague. It wasn't like her to keep secrets. If Mum wasn't flying to New York to meet Daddy, then why was Julia covering for her? Unless—

Chloe's hand closed tightly around her mobile phone. She didn't want to think about the other possibility, but it was staring her in the face.

'Chloe – are you still there?'

She frowned. Perhaps he knew, and he didn't want to tell her over the phone, when he was thousands of miles away, that Mum had met someone else and they were splitting up for good.

'Chloe – are you okay?'

Chloe's face crumpled as the tears rolled down her cheeks. She wanted to say *no, I'm not okay, Daddy*. For starters, she was still reeling from the thought that Mum had moved out of the family home without telling her or Harriet, or Jess, and had left Dad for another man. What other reason could there be for Julia to keep secrets from her?

She felt that as long as her parents were living under the same roof, even though they were living apart, there was always the chance they would get back together. But if one of them moved out...

'Chloe?'

'I'm fine, Daddy,' Chloe lied as she wiped a tear from her cheek. She couldn't tell him what was on her mind. What if he had no inkling that she hadn't just started a new job, but quite possibly a new relationship, too? How could she tell him that over the phone?

And then there was the other thing. She glanced around Dad's apartment. It had been spotless when she first walked in a few days ago. Now it looked... Chloe shook her head. She had certainly made herself at home. There was mess. There was clutter. If she were at home right now, Declan would hound her to clear it up because, in his own words, *I don't want to live in a pigsty*. Chloe rolled her eyes. Why did he always make such a big deal over nothing? It got on her nerves. Why did he have to be so petty?

Chloe eyed her stuff. She had brought various belongings, mainly clothes and, of course, the computer equipment she used for work, along with a lot of other things she probably didn't need for just a few days away. But Chloe didn't know how long she'd be gone. Or indeed if she was ever going back to the house she and Declan shared; that was the other thing.

Chloe decided she'd better end the call before she told Daddy *everything*. How Mum was no longer downstairs, and his daughter was now living upstairs because things weren't working out with Declan. And how Daddy might just return from New York to find he had a permanent house guest.

'Dad, I've got to go.' Chloe had to get off the phone before she spilled the beans.

'Oh, all right. But you won't forget to look in on Mouse, will you?'

Chloe looked down at the cat purring softly on her lap and smiled at her new flatmate. She was adorable. And infinitely preferable to Declan at the moment.

'Chloe?'

Chloe sighed. 'Daddy, I won't forget Mouse.'

'I'll see you in a few days, sweetheart.'

She put her phone on the coffee table, wishing she could tell Daddy what she had been up to since he left for New York. However, she knew he'd go ballistic if he found out that she had used the situation and gone behind his back, with every intention of staying in the apartment without asking his permission. Even though she had a very good reason: Chloe was trying to save her relationship. She frowned. The problem was Declan didn't see it that way. Chloe recalled the events after she had left Dad at the airport to catch his flight to New York. She had been toying with an idea ever since she and Declan had bought their first house and moved in together.

Unexpectedly, being asked to look after Daddy's apartment while he went on a trip was like fate had stepped in and given her an opportunity to try out the idea that had been germinating for months. Unfortunately, Declan didn't see it quite the same way when she told him what she had in mind…

'You want to do *what?*'

Chloe stared at Declan. By the look on his face, you'd have thought she just told him she wanted to climb Kilimanjaro or something, not try out living apart together.

'But what does that even mean?'

Chloe cocked her head to one side and frowned at her fiancé. Now he was being awkward. 'You know what that means. It's obvious, isn't it?' She enunciated the words, 'Living. Apart. Together. It means we're still together; we just live in separate—'

'Yeah. Right!' Declan scoffed. 'Like that's gonna work.'

'Why not?'

Declan shook his head. 'Where on earth has this come from? One minute we were planning our wedding, the next minute you're talking about splitting up!'

'I'm not talking about splitting up.'

'Oh, really? Sure sounds like it to me.'

'Just moving out.'

'Je-sus!' Declan wiped his brow. 'What has got into you?' He paused. 'Hold on a minute. Talking of weddings…' He pointed at Chloe. 'You paid a visit to Julia the other day. Isn't she meant to be planning our wedding reception?'

'Yeah – so?'

Declan eyed her for a full minute and then raised his eyebrows.

'It's Julia, isn't it? She's put you up to this.'

'I don't know what you're talking about.'

'I knew it! She's a bad influence.'

'Ex-cuse me?' Chloe bristled at that comment. It was something she'd heard often enough growing up, coming from Dad, whenever she'd visited Julia – which was a lot. Chloe loved getting away from her mum and dad, and her two big sisters, and spending time at Julia's place across London. She couldn't see the harm. All she did was go shopping with her Auntie Julia at Camden Market and making clothes on her old Singer sewing machine.

She never understood what was wrong with that. It was only when she grew up that she realised it wasn't the activities they did together, but Julia's lifestyle that her dad didn't agree with. Julia liked to party. She wanted to have fun. She had never settled down, got married, and lived a conventional lifestyle like her mum and dad. Perhaps that's what Chloe loved about her. Bohemian, eccentric Julia was all the things her parents weren't, creative, carefree – and happy. She always wanted to be like Julia when she grew up.

'Well?' Declan cut across her thoughts. 'Have you seen her?'

Chloe glared at Declan. She could feel this building up into an almighty row. She didn't criticise Declan's friends. Besides, Julia wasn't just a friend. She was practically family. Chloe had known her all her life. She was her auntie in all but name. Although she had three real aunts on her mother's side, her mum never got on with her older siblings, and so Julia was the only auntie she had ever known.

Declan put his hands on his hips, waiting for an answer.

Chloe shrugged. It was true. A few days before she found herself with the keys to her dad's apartment, Chloe had paid a visit to Julia's houseboat – the home she had retired to on Regent's Canal.

Despite several relationships, she still lived alone with Holly, her tan cocker spaniel. But she never seemed unhappy – far from it. Before she moved, Chloe recalled she loved living in her flat, throwing parties, and enjoying her life.

As far as her relationships went, Chloe always assumed that the reason she refused to give up her own place and move in with someone was that she had never met the one. She had simply never fallen in love. That's what Chloe believed until something quite extraordinary happened. Julia moved to Little Venice and met someone who had the same dream as her – to live on a houseboat in London. After all these years Julia had finally met her soul mate.

But it wasn't the fact that Julia had fallen in love at the tender age of sixty that surprised Chloe; Chloe believed age wasn't a barrier to romance, to love. It was what they did next that astonished her. Instead of moving in together, because that's what couples do – that's what she and Declan did – Tom shifted his mooring, so their houseboats sat next to each other on Regent's Canal. They were together, living apart.

Chloe smiled. Not only had Julia fallen in love, but she had found her perfect partner – someone who didn't want to give up their own place, their independence either. Someone who also thought you could have it all; be in a loving, committed relationship and still live apart.

Chloe frowned at Declan across the room. She wished she

hadn't told him all this when she had come home from Julia's the other day on a high over her discovery.

Chloe had even researched living apart together on the internet. In fact, unbeknown to Declan, LAT living had become an obsession. All Chloe's fears and anxieties over what was wrong with her that she couldn't commit – not even to the man she wanted to spend the rest of her life with – fell away the instant she realised there was nothing wrong with Julia and Tom's living arrangements.

There was no moral or universal law that said people who love each other, who wanted to be in a committed, stable relationship, had to live together 24/7. Where was the relationship rule book that said you couldn't live your life differently? Why couldn't she love someone, commit to them for the rest of her life, marry – and still live apart? People did. Lots of people from all walks of life, from all over the world, were doing just that – living apart together. She stared at Declan. Why couldn't the two of them?

That's what she'd been thinking since visiting Julia. However, she still couldn't pluck up the courage to tell him what she had in mind until she found herself with the keys to an empty apartment. Her dad would only be gone a few days. This was her chance to try LAT living for real.

She didn't expect Declan to be so dead set against the idea when they hadn't even tried it. This was just what she was afraid of. Fearful that he wasn't like Tom. Worried that he wouldn't feel the same way.

'Please, Declan. I want to do this. I want to give LAT living a try for a few days.'

'I don't believe this. I bet you've been reading that stupid, idiotic writer and her rubbish articles all about it.'

Chloe looked at him in surprise. 'You've read *Love on the Rooftop?*'

'No, I haven't read it. But I know all about it. Who doesn't?' he added sarcastically. 'That writer is everywhere. On the radio. Posters on the tube. Why are women buying into that crap that living apart works?'

Chloe's bottom lip quivered. 'Well, I for one don't think those articles are stupid at all!' shouted Chloe, realising too late *that* was an admission she had been reading *Love on the Rooftop*.

'Fine! But I think she paints a very rosy picture of living apart together – *too* rosy.'

'What are you saying – that the writer is making it all up?'

'Maybe. It's all just too – perfect. Don't you think?'

'I don't know what you're talking about.'

'Why do you think she refuses to reveal her identity?'

'How do I know? Perhaps she doesn't want the media attention. Maybe she's a very private person.'

'Uh-huh. Or maybe she's some divorcee living on her own who was playing around with a blog, writing about a fantasy that wasn't her life, and suddenly it went viral. Then things take off, and she earns good money for writing a pack of lies in a magazine column that, for some bizarre reason, people are buying into.'

Chloe folded her arms. 'Who cares. There's still Julia and Tom. What about them?'

'What about them?' Declan threw back. 'I think they're just weird. I mean – who *really* does LAT living?'

'Plenty of people,' said Chloe matter-of-factly, thinking of the research she had done on the internet.

'Oh right. And it works for all those people does it?'

'Yes, I think it does.'

'Fine! Well, let me show you something.' Declan turned around and grabbed his laptop off the kitchen table. He typed something on the keyboard and then turned it around to show Chloe. 'Let me introduce you to the real world of what happens to a relationship when you live apart together.' He thrust the laptop at her. 'Read that!'

Chloe looked at him in bemusement.

'Here – take it.'

Chloe took the laptop and sat down at the table. She started to read.

Hovering behind her, reading over her shoulder, Declan said, 'You know, the funny thing is that Dear John column sounds just like your parents.'

Chloe turned around and looked at Declan.

'Well, go on read it.'

Chloe sighed. So this was her Dad's column. Dad had told her all about it on the way to the airport. Chloe hadn't bothered to read his column. She didn't have to; she wasn't a stranger to what had been going on with Mum and Dad over the last few months – and now neither was the whole world. Fortunately, Dad had the foresight not to use Mum's real name in the blog, otherwise Declan would have a lot more ammunition to throw at her.

Chloe put the laptop to one side without bothering to read it.

'Aren't you going to read it?'

'I don't have to. I'm aware of Dear John.' Chloe was also well aware that Mum and Dad weren't exactly the poster-children for living apart together. That didn't mean it had to be ruled out for other people – for them.

Declan pointed at his laptop. 'Well?'

'Well, what? I'm not changing my mind, Declan, if that's what you're thinking.'

'Are you serious? You still want to go through with it?'

'Look, just humour me, will you? We won't get another opportunity like this.'

'But I don't want this opportunity, as you call it.'

Chloe ignored him and continued. 'It's not like I can rent somewhere for a few days, and staying in a hotel won't be the same. It has to feel as though we're really living in separate places.'

Declan sighed. 'You're serious about this, aren't you?' He was still taken aback by this bizarre turn of events. They were supposed to be getting married. They had bought a house together. Now she wanted to move out – why?

'I know you 're dead set against the idea, but what's the harm?'

Declan thought there was plenty of harm, like how they felt they could maintain a relationship not living together. Surely that wasn't normal.

Declan rubbed his forehead and took a seat at the kitchen table opposite Chloe. He wasn't angry, just anxious about where all this was leading. He'd met the love of his life. He wanted to spend the rest of his life with her. However, now wedding bells were in the air she was having second thoughts. If she didn't really want to live with him, then perhaps this was a sign she didn't feel the same way about him. Maybe living apart together was Chloe's way of backing out of the relationship.

No matter what Chloe called it – living apart together or taking a break – she needed some space before she fully committed to the relationship. Perhaps now, before they tied the knot, was the right time after all. Something wasn't working for her. If she didn't come back, at least he had his answer.

Declan reached across the table and took her hand. 'Are you sure John is okay with this?'

'Of course,' said Chloe, not looking him in the eye. She knew full well that if Daddy had any inkling of her intentions when he handed over the keys, there was no way he would have left her in charge of his apartment. It wasn't just the fact that she wouldn't leave his place as she found it – clean and tidy – it was the living apart together bit. Dear John would be the last person to advocate LAT living – Chloe knew that.

'When are you leaving?'

Chloe bounced out of her seat and threw her arms around Declan's neck. 'Tonight,' she whispered in his ear. 'I'm so excited.'

Declan sighed again. Unfortunately, he didn't feel the same way. He thought of Dear John's blog – Declan had read the last entry all about the writer receiving his Dear John letter. Declan closed his eyes. He wished to hell he hadn't fallen in love with a woman who was about to break his heart.

20

Chloe eyed the mess on the coffee table and made a mental note to clear it up tomorrow and then go out and buy some air-freshener. The place smelt like the inside of a Chinese takeaway. Her dad would throw a fit if he could see it now.

She smiled down at Mouse, who was still curled up on her lap, purring softly. Chloe stroked her soft fur. She was thinking about that last conversation with Declan when he had shown her Daddy's blog, *Dear John*. Chloe didn't have any plans for this evening. She looked at Mouse. 'I've got an idea.' Chloe scooped up John's moggy and put her on the sofa.

Mouse let out a disgruntled *meow* and swiped Chloe's hand with her paw.

'Hey!' Chloe rubbed her hand where Mouse had scratched her. She pointed at the cat. 'That wasn't very nice.'

Mouse lifted her head up high, turned around, and pounced off the sofa. She walked around the coffee table and jumped up on to one of John's armchairs, curling herself into a soft furball. Mouse fell asleep.

Chloe stared at Mouse across the room. They'd had their first spat. She was getting the impression that her new feline flatmate was going to be a complicated character to live with, unlike her mum's pet dog, Alfie.

Chloe stood up and walked across the living room into John's study. She had already decided that when she moved in, she would not treat it as a holiday. Chloe intended to stick to her normal routine, which meant she had to do some work. Her dad had a study where she could set up a home office.

John's tidy desk, where there used to be one laptop and a stationary organiser, was now covered in Chloe's work paraphernalia. Chloe unplugged one of her laptops and carried it into the lounge. She sat down on the sofa and surfed the internet to find Dear John. Mission accomplished, she put her feet up on John's couch and reached for the packet of prawn crackers that had come with her Chinese takeaway. Popping a cracker in her mouth, she scrolled through the blog to the very beginning. Chloe started to read.

Several times she nearly choked on a prawn cracker when she read the antics John and Uncle Dave had got up to, trying to get Mum to move out of the apartment downstairs. It was so funny that at one point she was doubled up on the sofa in hysterics.

Chloe continued to read. She never knew her dad could write, and it was so entertaining. 'This is *so* good,' said Chloe, smiling. She was enjoying Dear John's account of Mum and Dad living apart together – until she started the last post. Chloe knitted her brow. Her smile faded rapidly. She was reading about Dear John discovering his wife loading her suitcases into the back of a London taxicab. Then there was the note he had found outside the door to his apartment which began, *Dear John...*

He didn't elaborate on the contents, but then he didn't have to. Everyone knew what a *Dear John* letter was. He even said in his blog that this was where he envisaged living apart together would lead. To one of them walking out that door – for good.

Now Chloe had an answer to her question: did Dad know that Mum was no longer downstairs? Chloe looked across the room at Mouse. 'He knows about Mum,' she told the cat.

Mouse opened an eye and yawned before settling down to sleep once more.

Chloe read on about how he had screwed up that note and tossed it over the banister.

'It landed outside her apartment door…' read Chloe. She stared at her laptop. Was that the screwed-up piece of paper she had found on the floor outside the door to Mum's apartment when she was waiting to take Dad to the airport?

She recalled picking it up from the floor and Dad rushing down the stairs towards her and snatching it out of her hand. She recalled that his behaviour was a bit odd. But then she thought nothing more about it, too consumed with the idea of moving into his apartment for a few days. Now she knew why he didn't want her to read that note. He didn't want her to find out that Mum and Dad were splitting up.

Chloe put her laptop to one side and sat there, staring off into space. Then a thought occurred to her. She lunged forward, grabbed her mobile, and started punching in a number. She was going to phone Julia and demand to know where her mum had gone. Chloe was probably less concerned about her whereabouts. What she wanted to know was if it was true – her mum had left Dad for good this time. If anybody would know, it would be Julia. Was this the secret she had been keeping? That her mum had met somebody else?

Julia didn't answer.

Chloe threw her phone across the room in frustration. It landed on the floor beside the armchair where Mouse was sleeping. The cat was woken with a start by a loud thud. She leapt off the armchair in fright and landed on the coffee table in front of Chloe. Mouse meowed at her.

'What?' Chloe said crossly.

Mouse turned her back on Chloe as if to say we're not friends anymore.

Chloe sat watching the catwalk up the stairs to the bedrooms on the next floor before she went to retrieve her phone. These few days were meant to be about her and Declan. She thought she'd enjoy staying at Dad's apartment while she figured things out and waited to see whether Declan would come around to the idea of living apart together. Now all she was consumed by were thoughts of Mum and Dad and if this was it – they were getting a divorce.

She put her head in her hands and stared despondently at her dad's cream carpet. Despite loving the idea of LAT living, Chloe was starting to wonder if Declan was right: this wouldn't spell a new beginning in their relationship if the only place it led was to them splitting up.

Chloe sat down on the sofa once more and toyed with the mobile phone in her hands. She had her mum's number. She could ring her. Chloe frowned. She didn't want to talk to her mum right now if it was true – if she had left Dad. Chloe wiped a tear from her eye and started dialling the one person she always turned to if she was in trouble. Except this time, it wasn't her that was in trouble. It was Mum and Dad. For once, Chloe was putting her own issues aside to focus on a bigger problem – how could she get her parents back together?

Chloe punched in the number and sat biting her fingernail. She didn't know what time it was in Australia. She didn't care. All Chloe wanted to do was talk to her big sister, Jess. She'd know what to do.

21

John opened his eyes. For a moment he'd forgotten where he was and thought he was back home in his apartment in Holland Park. He sat up in bed, looked around his hotel room, yawned and stretched. He'd had a restless night. John put it down to the most peculiar dream. John raised an eyebrow. 'Perhaps I should call it a nightmare.'

He frowned. It was all coming back to him now. After that phone call to Chloe last night, to check that she'd remembered to stop by the house to feed his cat, he'd dreamt she'd done more than just feed the cat; John imagined Chloe had moved in.

'What a silly thought,' John uttered as he climbed out of bed. He pulled the blinds at the windows in the lounge. The street below was already busy with cars and pedestrians, even though it was early. John stared at the street scene four storeys below.

Although he was used to living in a city, their street in Holland Park wasn't on a busy thoroughfare. John wasn't used to the noise of cars and people that went on until the early hours. He guessed that might have something to do with his disturbed night's sleep.

He turned from the window and spotted the breakfast menu

on the coffee table. One quick shower and a clean set of clothes later, he stepped out of his suite into the hall. He intended to go down to the restaurant for breakfast when he had a thought. John stopped short. He reluctantly did an about turn and walked back into his suite. He closed the door behind him and sighed.

Fifteen minutes later, there was a knock on the door.

John opened it and ushered in one of the hotel staff. He was pushing a trolley.

'Would sir like me to lay out your breakfast?'

John looked at the spread on the trolley. He didn't want to eat breakfast in his room when there was a lovely restaurant downstairs, but he couldn't risk it. He bet Bertram and Sylvie were having a nice long drawn-out breakfast in the restaurant this morning after their fantastic day out together yesterday.

'Sir?'

'Oh. Right. The breakfast.' John had been standing there, staring at the trolley, lost in thought.

'Do you want me to—?'

'No, no. That's fine. I can take it from here.'

John showed the young man to the door.

He hovered there in the doorway.

An uncomfortable silence followed until John remembered the tip. John took out his wallet and handed him the first bill that came to hand without bothering to look.

'Gee – thanks,' said the young man, frowning at the dollar bill.

'You're welcome,' said John absently. He closed the door and stood there, looking into his empty hotel suite. Having breakfast alone brought back unhappy memories of losing Gertie and finding himself at home all day with nothing to do but stare at four walls. He had his blog; that's what had kept him sane. He missed the walks in the park, the trips to the library and meeting Sayid, the stay-at-home-dad, in the swing-park. He even missed his four-legged friend, Sylvie's pet dog Alfie, who he used to look after during the day while Sylvie was at work.

John pushed the trolley towards the table and returned to the bedroom to retrieve his laptop before he sat down for breakfast. Thoughts of his blog brought to mind the article he'd started writing last night before he got side-tracked with that phone call to Chloe. He plugged the laptop in and set it up on the table. John then tucked a napkin into his shirt collar and ate a delicious breakfast while he watched the laptop boot up. The hot breakfast of waffles, fried eggs and French toast was delicious.

John buttered himself a slice of white toast, slathered it with plum jam and sat reading the article he had written last night. One paragraph in and his article came to an abrupt halt. John re-read it. It was good. It had the makings of an interesting topic. But that's all it had – the makings. It was by no means complete.

John finished his toast and licked his fingers. 'I want to find out more about this immigrant success story, Mr Morelli,' John announced. Perhaps that's how I should spend the next two days before the show, thought John. He intended to do some more research. As he poured himself a cup of coffee, John decided his first port of call was to pay another visit to Mr Morelli's restaurant and hope Gina, the owner's great-granddaughter, was working today. He was looking forward to finding out more about her great-grandfather.

John stared at the last thing he'd typed on his laptop yester-day evening. *There was something in his will. Something from his past that—*

John re-read that line. Those were the last words Gina had said before a rude diner cut her off mid-flow. John raised an eyebrow. He was still wondering what she was about to divulge about his past.

He finished his cup of coffee, looked at the bagel and was tempted, then removed the napkin and threw it on the trolley. John knew could sit here all morning reading through the newspaper that had been delivered with his breakfast. But he had a story to write.

John left the table and strode purposefully towards the door. On the way out, he made a detour into his bedroom to collect a notebook, pen and his blazer. He was attempting to put the small notebook in his blazer pocket when he discovered a screwed-up piece of paper. John frowned, wondering what it was. He took it out and then remembered. He also recalled that Chloe had nearly read it when she found it in his hallway.

Fortunately, he got to it in time. The last thing John wanted was Chloe and her sisters, Harriet and Jess, finding out Mum and Dad were splitting up before he had a chance to ease them in gently to the new reality that their parents were no longer together. Besides, knowing the three of them, he would never surprise him if they devised some cockamamie plan in the misguided belief that they could get Mum and Dad back together.

'Well, that won't happen in a month of Sundays,' said John, toying with the crumpled-up ball of paper in his hand as he closed the hotel room door and walked to the elevator. He would have liked nothing more than to throw his Dear John letter away, but he couldn't bring himself to litter the pristine corridor. He reluctantly stuffed it back in his blazer pocket and stepped inside the lift.

John was still thinking about that Dear John letter when the elevator doors opened on the ground floor. He was about to step out when he heard a familiar voice. John did a double take when he saw Sylvie and Bertram standing outside. They were too busy talking to one another and hadn't noticed the doors had opened.

John frantically looked at the four corners of the elevator. He was trapped. His only exit was past Bertram and Sylvie. John stared at them wide-eyed. Any second now, they were going to turn around and step inside. He had nowhere to hide. His only option was to be extremely rude and barge right past them, hoping he could keep his head down and go unrecognised. He was about to do just that when a large group of new arrivals, Japanese tourists by the looks of them, appeared outside the lift.

Bertram and Sylvie turned in their direction and were propelled backwards by the crowd. They were forced to step back into the elevator. After much shoving and pushing, as people crammed into the lift, John found himself wedged at the back with Sylvie and Bertram right in front of him. John broke out in a sweat. *This was ridiculous. Now what am I going to do?*

His next thought was that he had no chance of exiting the elevator before them. If they were returning to their suite, which he guessed was on the top floor, then he would have to wait. The worst-case scenario was that all the new guests got out on the lower floors, leaving him alone with Sylvie and Bertram.

John inwardly groaned. He did not fancy explaining to Sylvie, in front of Bertram, what he was doing in New York. John managed to reach up and undo the top button of his shirt. He was feeling mighty hot and bothered.

In front of him, Sylvie took an involuntary step back as the elevator jolted and accidentally stepped on John's toe.

John bit his lip to catch the *yeow*!

In front of him, Sylvie started to turn around.

Fortunately for John, the lack of space meant all she could do was glance over her shoulder to apologise. 'I'm so sorry.'

John kept his head down and said, 'That's no problem, Lady.' He winced at his poor excuse for an American accent. The last thing he wanted was for Bertram and Sylvie to think he was a fellow Brit, otherwise they might feel inclined to strike up a conversation.

John overheard Bertram whisper, 'Sylvie, how many times do I have to apologise for last night?'

Last night? John looked from Bertram to Sylvie and back again.

Sylvie didn't answer.

Bertram leaned in and whispered, 'How was I to know you don't like boats?'

Boats? John stared at the back of Sylvie's head, waiting to hear what she had to say.

Sylvie replied in a hushed voice, 'Anybody who knows me, bloody well knows I don't like boats.'

John couldn't help but overhear every word. He nodded. It was true. Sylvie had an aversion to boats which, by the sound of things, Bertram knew nothing about. John raised an eyebrow at Sylvie's choice of words. Not one to swear, something had happened last night that had put her in a foul mood. Had Bertram done the unthinkable and taken Sylvie on a boat? John couldn't resist a smile. If anything could kill their fabulous day out together, it would be just that. John hoped it was true.

'I thought it was the perfect way to round off the day together in New York,' continued Bertram.

'Well, it wasn't!' hissed Sylvie.

'I know that now. But when I came up with the idea, I thought you'd enjoy having an evening meal while sailing down the Hudson River, seeing the Manhattan shoreline lit up.'

John's lip curled into a grin. *Whoops. Bertram had really screwed up.* John took great delight in finding out that not only had he taken her on a boat, but to make matters worse he'd taken her to a floating restaurant. John bet that combination made Sylvie green.

Bertram tried another apology. 'I'm so sorry. Let me make it up to you.'

Sylvie didn't answer.

Good, thought John.

The elevator doors opened on the floor below John's suite. He was surprised when Sylvie said, 'Excuse me,' as she made her way to the front of the elevator. John furrowed his brow. He'd assumed the most expensive, luxurious, and largest suites would be on the top floor, reserved for the most important guests, like the owner, for instance – Bertram.

Bertram followed Sylvie.

She glanced over her shoulder.

For a moment, John thought he'd been spotted until he realised she was frowning at Bertram.

'Bertram, what are you doing?'

'I'm coming with you.'

'I don't need you to walk me to my room.'

My room? John's eyebrows shot up. It never occurred to him that Bertram might be a perfect gentleman, and thus far, they hadn't—

John tried to brush that thought aside. How would he know

whether Sylvie had broken her wedding vows? But the fact remained Sylvie and Bertram were not shacked up in his hotel suite. At least that was good news. John was elated.

'May I call on you later?'

Before Sylvie had a chance to answer, the elevator doors closed with Sylvie on the other side.

John saw Bertram shake his head, push the button for the top floor, and then stuff his hands in his pockets in a gesture of frustration. He stood there at the front of the elevator, staring at his shoes in sombre contemplation.

On the next floor, the crowd of Japanese tourists started exiting the elevator. John saw his chance. He had no reason to get off on this floor, but if he didn't, he would be left alone in the elevator with Bertram. John moved with the crowd towards the front. He kept a close eye on Bertram, who was still staring at his shoes as he passed by. John stepped out into the corridor.

The elevator doors were just closing when Bertram looked up. Was that a flicker of recognition that crossed his face, thought John as the lift doors closed? He hoped not. John imagined Bertram was so preoccupied with how he'd ruined a perfectly good day out with Sylvie that he wouldn't have registered it was John Baxter, Sylvie's husband.

John walked along the hotel corridor and found the stairs down to the ground floor. He had a renewed spring in his step as he gleefully mulled over the conversation he'd overheard, which ended with Sylvie returning to her hotel room – alone. John was delighted for all of five seconds until he remembered the Dear John letter burning a hole in his pocket. Shoulders slumped, he reached the hotel lobby and walked straight into a commotion.

'I do beg your pardon,' the hotel concierge said as he barged past John. John halted. He saw the hotel staff running around the expansive lobby. They were trying to catch an excitable Labrador puppy. John watched in amusement as the puppy darted between their legs, yapping in excitement.

John ambled over to the empty hotel reception desk and looked at the soft jelly sweets in a glass bowl. He picked one up. John knelt, held out his hand with the sweet and called out, 'Here, boy,' as the dog raced past.

The Labrador pup skidded to a halt on the smooth tiled floor, turned around, and sniffed the air. He raced over, wagging his tail furiously, and launched himself at the sweet in John's hand.

'Good boy,' said John, giving him a fuss as the dog ate his treat. 'Where did you come from?' He noted the puppy had a collar. John took a closer look. Hanging from the collar was a gold name tag engraved with the word *Monte*.

The Labrador puppy sat obediently at John's feet, waiting for another treat.

The concierge wiped his brow as he approached. 'Thank the Lord.'

John looked up. 'Where did the little fella come from?' He didn't think such an upmarket hotel would allow guests to bring their pets.

The concierge rolled his eyes. 'As if I haven't got enough to do, the owner of this hotel decides, out of the blue, to get a hotel dog.'

John looked confused. 'What's a hotel dog?'

'Your guess is as good as mine. He turned up this morning with a doghouse.' The concierge pointed at a wooden kennel in the corner of the hotel lobby. 'Oh, and these...' The concierge held up a ball in one hand and a dog leash in the other. He looked down at the puppy, still sitting at John's feet. 'As you clearly have a knack with dogs, would you mind?' The concierge held out the leash to John.

John took the leash and attached it to the puppy's collar.

'I don't why the owner would do such a thing. As far as I'm aware, he doesn't allow animals in any of his other hotels.' The concierge shook his head at the Labrador puppy. 'What was he thinking?'

John had a good idea what Bertram was thinking. He was trying to make up for last night. Perhaps he thought he could win Sylvie over with a cute puppy. John rolled his eyes and held out the leash to the concierge.

The concierge didn't make a move to take it. 'The problem is that someone has to walk him. We don't have the time. I don't think the owner of the hotel has the first clue about pets.'

John thought back to Bertram meeting Sylvie's dog. John was fairly sure Bertram had never had a pet of his own. He doubted he even liked dogs. John glanced at Monte. A hotel dog. It was a stupid idea. He imagined it was a spur-of-the-moment thing – buying a puppy. He wouldn't be surprised if Sylvie got cross with him when she found out he'd bought one with no thought as to the practicalities of who would look after the dog.

John felt sorry for the concierge. It was very wrong of Bertram to land him with a responsibility like this on a whim. 'I'll walk him.'

'Seriously?'

'Yes. It's no problem.' John looked down at Monte. He didn't mind walking the dog. It solved his problem of what to do with himself this morning. He knew he could do some more sightseeing on his last free day in New York, but John had had such a good time with Angelo yesterday that seeing the sights on his own would be a bit of an anti-climax. Besides, he rather fancied a stroll in Central Park. According to the hotel literature, it was but a short walk away.

'Can you just point me in the direction of Central Park?'

The concierge didn't need to be asked twice. He gave John a small plastic bag for collecting the spoils and dumping them, and accompanied him through the lobby and out on to the street. He pointed towards the park. 'Continue along Park Avenue and take your next left, then cross Madison Avenue and continue straight on until you reach 5th Avenue. The park entrance will be a little way along on your left. Oh, I nearly forgot.' The concierge handed John a ball.

'Come on, Monte,' John said to the Labrador at his heels.

'Oh, Mr Baxter.'

John turned around.

'The dog isn't called Monte.'

John frowned. 'But that's what it says on his dog collar.'

'Yes, I know. Apparently, it was shortened because they couldn't fit all the letters on the name disc. But don't tell Mr Wyndom-Price that.'

'So, what is his name?'

The concierge pointed at the door to the hotel. 'He is named after the hotel.' The concierge smiled at John and said, 'His name is Montgomery.'

'Of course it is.' John rolled his eyes. A pompous pet name for a pompous owner.

When the concierge was out of earshot, John looked down at the puppy and said, 'I am not calling you Montgomery.' He couldn't imagine calling out that name in public. He'd be a laughing stock. 'Today, you are Monte.'

Monte barked at John.

'Good, we agree then.' John smiled at his walking companion, guessing Monte was about four or five months old. He was still a puppy, but he wasn't pulling on the leash. The pup was walking beside John sedately, making for a pleasant stroll along Park Avenue.

To John's surprise, Monte even sat on his rump when they stopped at the kerb to cross the road. 'My word you are a well-behaved dog.' He glanced down at the yellow Lab, wondering if Monte had had some training. Or was it simply the case that Labradors were better behaved than cocker spaniels? John was thinking about the first time he walked Sylvie's dog. Alfie had pulled on the leash, ran off in the park, chased other dogs, and was a general nuisance until John had trained him to be an obedient dog.

John smiled at Monte. This reminded him of taking Alfie for his daily walks in Holland Park, except this time he was in the Big Apple and he was about to step foot in Central Park. *The* Central Park.

22

John walked through the park entrance, and only then did Monte pull on the leash.

'You've been here before,' observed John. He debated whether he should let Monte off the leash; the last thing John wanted was for him to run off. There was no way he could return to the hotel, minus the dog that the concierge had entrusted to him. It might cost the young man his job. John continued walking along the mall with Monte still on the leash.

He couldn't let Monte run free here, even if he wanted to. People were taking a leisurely stroll along the wide promenade and wouldn't appreciate an excitable Labrador running amok. John had seen photos of the mall. It lived up to his expectations. The tree-lined promenade had ornate iron benches and Victorian lamps standing sentry along the route. He could imagine strolling along here with Sylvie. John dismissed that thought and tried to concentrate on enjoying his walk with Monte.

At the end of the promenade, John chose a path at random and was pleasantly surprised to find himself at a place called Mineral Springs. A sign pointed towards the Mineral Springs building, where he hoped he could stop for a cup of coffee. He was getting fed up with Monte pulling on the leash. Even though the dog was nowhere near fully grown, he was much bigger than Alfie, and it was hard work keeping a tight hold of him.

'Monte!' John growled, giving his leash a yank in exasperation.

Monte cowered below John's stern gaze, sensing he'd done something wrong.

John stared at the sweet Labrador puppy and swiftly reconsidered his position on letting Monte off the leash. He knelt and gave him an affectionate pat on the head. 'I didn't mean to snap at you.'

Monte wagged his tail and jumped up at John to lick his face.

'Okay, okay. I think you've won.' John undid the leash from his collar and stood up.

Monte was still sitting at his feet.

'Ah.' John remembered the ball in his hand. He held it up. 'Do you want to play ball?'

Monte barked, stood up, and spun around three times in a circle in front of John.

'Alrighty then.' John stepped forward and threw the ball.

Monte shot off across the grass to fetch it.

John strolled along the grassy path toward the building in the distance. He continued to throw the ball, safe in the knowledge that Monte would return with the ball. As they neared the Mineral Springs building, he absently threw it one last time. A minute later, John looked about him. Monte hadn't returned. John frowned. Perhaps he'd thrown the ball into a thicket, and Monte couldn't get to it?

John shouted out, 'Monte!' as he continued walking toward the building.

Monte didn't appear.

Now what? John glanced at the building, where he could see a café sign and tables outside. He raised an eyebrow. Was that Monte sitting by a table? What was he doing over there? John knew what a greedy Lab was doing at the café: begging for a treat.

John marched over, preparing an apology. Two women were sitting at the table where Monte was waiting patiently for a treat. He also saw a child in a buggy.

Monte started sniffing the child in the buggy.

John quickened his pace. Suddenly, he slowed to a dead halt. 'You have got to be kidding me!' One of the women seated at the table was Sylvie.

He must be mistaken. He'd seen Sylvie exit the elevator to go to her room. What was she doing here? Then John remembered he had travelled two floors up, then got out of the elevator and taken the stairs down to the ground floor. It was just possible that in those few extra minutes Sylvie had grabbed her coat and left the hotel, missing the commotion downstairs when Monte had made an appearance.

She couldn't very well miss Monte now, thought John when he realised it was Sylvie sitting there at the café with a young woman he didn't recognise. Perhaps she'd seen the child in the buggy and struck up a conversation with his mother? John didn't waste any more time thinking about that. What he needed to figure out was how on earth he was going to get Monte back.

Sylvie and the young woman started looking about them, presumably for the dog owner. They turned in their seats and glanced in his direction.

John ducked behind a tree and hoped to goodness they hadn't spotted him.

'I can't see anybody calling out for a lost dog – can you?' asked Sylvie, turning in her seat to look at Amy.

Amy shook her head. 'Me neither.'

They both looked at the yellow Lab, nudging Rory's hand.

Rory giggled and patted the top of the puppy's head.

'He doesn't seem that old,' observed Amy.

Sylvie called to the Labrador, 'Here, boy.'

Monte turned around and padded over. He sat at her feet and placed his muzzle on her lap.

'Aren't you adorable,' said Sylvie, making a fuss of him.

'He's so sweet.' Amy noticed he had a collar. 'Sylvie, can you see a name tag on the collar?'

'Good thinking, Amy.' Sylvie examined the collar and found a small round gold disc on the collar under the dog's chin. 'There's something etched on it.' Sylvie reached into her bag and found her glasses. She slipped them on and then peered at the little round disc. 'Monte.'

Monte barked.

Sylvie smiled at the dog. 'Hello, Monte.'

Amy leaned forward in her seat. 'Is there anything else?'

Sylvie flipped the disc to look on the back. She glanced at Amy. 'There's an address on the back. But the writing is so small I don't think I can…'

'Here, let me see.'

Sylvie let go of Monte's collar.

Amy patted her knee. 'Monte – here boy.'

The yellow Lab scooted over to Amy.

'Good dog,' Amy said, stroking his head as she took hold of the collar. She studied the writing etched on the golden disc. 'You're right, Sylvie, it is very small. I can't read it either.'

'Oh, that's a shame.'

'Hold on. I've got an idea.' Amy rummaged in a bag hanging on the back of Rory's buggy.

'What's that?' asked Sylvie, watching Amy lift out a small plastic container.

'It's Rory's mini-beast pack.' Amy opened it. 'Ah, that's what I was looking for.'

Sylvie laughed when she saw what Amy had in her hand. 'It's a dinky little magnifying glass.'

'Yep. Cute, isn't it? Rory uses it to hunt in the grass for minibeasts.'

'How wonderful.' Sylvie made a mental note to buy one for Gertie so they could have fun learning about minibeasts when she was allowed to see her again. Sylvie pursed her lips and tried not to think about that.

Amy held up the little plastic magnifying glass. 'Right, Monte, let's see where you live.'

Sylvie watched with interest as Amy leaned forward and looked through the magnifying glass at the golden disc on Monte's collar. Amy frowned. 'That's strange.'

'What is it?'

'Well, that can't be right.' Amy looked across the table at Sylvie. 'The address is The Montgomery Hotel, Park Avenue, New York.'

'Are you sure?'

Monte sat obediently in front of Amy as she peered through the magnifying glass once more. 'Yes, that's what it says all right.' She put the magnifying glass back in Rory's mini-beast pack.

They both looked at the Labrador puppy.

'That *is* strange,' mused Sylvie. 'A dog living in a hotel. I've never heard of anything so ridiculous.'

'Me neither,' commented Amy. 'Maybe he belongs to one of the staff. I'm sure Dad will have something to say on the matter. There's no way he'd let a dog stay in one of his hotels. He doesn't even like dogs.'

'He doesn't like dogs?' Sylvie said coolly. Bertram never mentioned he wasn't a dog lover.

'I, on the other hand, adore them. Especially cutey-pies like Monte.' Amy leaned over and gave him a big fuss.

Sylvie smiled at the dog. 'Well, I guess we better make a move.' She glanced at Rory. He'd fallen asleep in his buggy.

What a stroke of good luck that she had bumped into Amy on her way out of the hotel this morning. After leaving Bertram in the elevator, she'd stormed into her room, grabbed her coat and bag, and left the hotel. Sylvie didn't fancy running into Bertram again.

She had avoided him at breakfast by getting down there super early, only to bump into him as she left the restaurant. He then followed her to the elevator, apologising for yesterday evening.

She cast her mind back to that evening when Bertram had ruined a wonderful day out in New York together. He said he'd saved the best till last. Sylvie rolled her eyes. She recalled with toe-curling clarity that disastrous evening she would never forget in a hurry...

'The day isn't over yet, Sylvie. I've got one more surprise.'

Sylvie was about to find out that one of Bertram's passions was boats. He loved being on the water and assumed Sylvie would, too.

'Where are we going?'

The taxi stopped at a place in Manhattan called South Street Seaport. Bertram turned to Sylvie. 'I'm afraid we walk from here.'

'Oh, okay.' Sylvie had enjoyed herself thus far, so she had no qualms about going along with Bertram's next surprise. She eagerly followed him.

Bertram came to a halt. 'Sylvie, can I ask you to do one thing for me?'

Sylvie smiled at her companion. 'Of course, what do you want me to do?'

'Close your eyes.'

'Why?'

Bertram smiled at her. 'It's a surprise.'

Sylvie returned Bertram's smile. 'All right.' She felt a little foolish, but closed her eyes, anyway.

Bertram took her hand. He pulled her gently forward and placed a guiding hand on the small of her back.

'Where are we going?' whispered Sylvie.

'It's a—'

'—Surprise,' Sylvie interrupted with a smile.

Walking along, she felt the ground underfoot change from a concrete path to some sort of wooden decking. Sylvie resisted stealing a glance at her feet. Then suddenly she felt unsteady on her feet. 'That's odd.'

'There's nothing to worry about,' Bertram reassured her, gripping her hand. 'We're nearly there.'

'Where?'

'You can open your eyes now.'

Sylvie slowly opened her eyes and looked around. She appeared to be in a small, snug restaurant. It would have been lovely if it wasn't for the fact that, strangely, Sylvie still felt very unsteady on her feet as though she were about to lose her balance. 'I think I need to sit down.'

'Yes, of course. Let's take a seat.' Bertram pulled out a chair for Sylvie.

Sylvie couldn't help but smile. It reminded her of the first time they met at The Rooftop Café in London. They were both dining alone, so he had asked her to join him. The first thing he did was pull out a chair before she sat down.

Sylvie took her seat and continued to smile at him across the table. She just wished she hadn't come over feeling queasy. Sylvie spotted a jug of water on the table. She poured herself a glass and took a couple of sips while she looked about her. The blinds at all the windows were down, which was odd, but she thought nothing more of it. The tables were all set for a meal by candle-light. Although small, the place had atmosphere.

Sylvie didn't know Bertram had booked a table at a restaurant for an evening meal. 'This is a lovely surprise, Bertram.' She lowered her voice and whispered, 'Are we too early?'

'Too early?'

Sylvie looked around at the empty tables.

'There aren't any other diners.'

'I know. Don't get cross but I booked the entire place.'

'Oh Bertram, you didn't have to do that on my account.'

'I wanted to.'

Sylvie could feel herself blushing. 'Well, you shouldn't have,' she admonished him with a playful smile. 'But it's still a lovely surprise.'

Bertram beamed at her. 'Oh, you haven't had the surprise yet.'

'Haven't I?' Sylvie eyed him, wondering what he was up to. She took a few more sips of water to settle her stomach and glanced at the blinds. It puzzled Sylvie why they were all closed; perhaps that had something to do with the surprise. 'Can I open the blind – are there views?'

'Oh yes, there are views all right. The best in the city.'

Sylvie couldn't imagine what would be better than the views they'd had from the revolving restaurant where they had stopped for lunch that afternoon.

'It's a little different this time,' added Bertram.

'Different – how?' Sylvie suddenly found herself leaning to one side. She righted herself and looked at Bertram in surprise. 'That's weird. I feel as though we're moving.'

Bertram grinned. He motioned for the waiter. 'You can open the blinds now.' An electric motor whirred in the background as all the blinds went up. That's when the apologies began...

'Sylvie, I'm so sorry.'

Sylvie was sitting in the back of a taxi on the way to the hotel, and she was not enjoying the ride. She was still feeling queasy.

'I had no idea...' Bertram continued, holding out a placating hand.

'I wished you'd asked me first.' Sylvie didn't turn in her seat to look at Bertram. She still couldn't look him in the eye. She was too embarrassed about throwing up in the middle of the restaurant with all the ship's crew watching and spending the rest of the time retching in the toilet until the sailing boat docked.

'Anyone who knows me is aware I don't do boats!' Sylvie would not say another word on the matter as she continued to gaze out of the taxi window. She knew Bertram's heart was in the right place. She guessed seeing Manhattan lit up at night on a cruise down the Hudson River would be amazing if your name wasn't Sylvie Baxter.

Sylvie fished in her purse and left some dollar bills on the table for their coffee and croissants. She didn't know why she was thinking about that episode on the boat last night. Perhaps it was finding out that Bertram didn't like dogs; another reminder that she didn't know him all that well.

What other secrets was he keeping from her? Sylvie raised her eyebrows. What a silly thought. She knew she was being paranoid. The real reason she was avoiding Bertram was because she was still embarrassed about the fact that he had followed her into the boat's washroom and found her on her hands and knees retching in the toilet bowl.

Sylvie stood up and gathered up her coat.

Amy said, 'What are we going to do about Monte?'

Sylvie debated whether to hand him over to the staff at the café. After all, Monte had got lost in the park. It wasn't their responsibility to find his owner. She looked down at the sweet Labrador puppy and couldn't imagine leaving him behind without knowing they had returned him to his owner safe and sound.

Sylvie took one last look around. There was nobody in the café searching for a lost dog, and she couldn't see anybody in the distance calling his name.

She turned to Amy. 'I think we should take him back to the hotel with us and then see from there.'

Amy agreed. She glanced at Rory, still sound asleep in his buggy, and was about to set off when she realised there was a problem with their plan. 'How are we going to take Monte back with us, without a leash?'

Sylvie followed her gaze to Monte, already on his feet. 'Good question.' She pondered this for a moment. 'Ah, I have an idea.' Sylvie unfurled the linen scarf from around her neck.

'You can't use that, Sylvie. It will get ruined.'

'Don't worry. I have plenty of these. I don't mind.' Sylvie looped the linen scarf through Monte's collar, tied it in a small knot, and held up the end. '*Voila!*'

Amy smiled. 'Right, what say we go straight back to the hotel and find out which silly person thinks it's a good idea to have a dog living in Daddy's hotel?'

A young couple eyed John suspiciously as they passed by.

John was too busy peeping out from behind the tree trunk, watching Sylvie. He hadn't noticed the young couple approaching. John waved and said, 'Hello,' when they came into view. Then he dropped to the floor, pretending to do up his shoelace in case Sylvie glanced his way.

The young couple exchanged a nervous glance and gave him a wide berth.

John watched them fade into the distance and then resumed spying on Sylvie. She was talking to the young woman. They had both got up from the table. It appeared they were leaving. Thank goodness. Once they went, he could fetch the dog.

John started sprinting from one tree trunk to the next, making his way toward the café, while keeping a close eye on Sylvie, so he wasn't spotted. He was standing at the last tree trunk when Sylvie and the young woman left the café. Walking beside Sylvie was Monte. Sylvie had made a makeshift leash out of her scarf. They were leaving with the dog.

John muttered under his breath, 'You have got to be kidding me!' He started following them at a discreet distance until he ran into a group of school children. By the time he waited for them to pass by, Sylvie and Monte were nowhere in sight; he'd lost them. John slapped his forehead. How was he going to explain to the concierge, when he returned to the hotel, that he'd lost the hotel dog? There was only one thing for it: John decided the best course of action was to avoid the hotel for the rest of the day. He'd just have to cross that bridge later when he got back.

He slumped down on a park bench. After a few minutes people-watching, John was bored. He didn't have a newspaper or a novel to read, so he fished in his pocket and found his note-book. He was flicking through the pages, reading the brief notes he had made yesterday at Morelli's after that interesting chat with Gina, when he had an idea.

John looked at his watch. He hadn't had a morning cup of coffee yet. He could return to the café now Sylvie had gone, but he didn't fancy hanging around in the park, reminding him of the dog he'd managed to lose. John stood up. He decided to pay another visit to Morelli's for a coffee and a bagel. While he was there, he was hoping to catch up with Gina and find out more about her great-grandfather.

John closed the notebook, slipped it back in his pocket and headed down the mall, retracing his route towards the park entrance. He didn't notice two women ahead of him, one pushing a buggy and the other with a dog, crossing the road as he hailed a taxi.

The taxi driver wound his window down. 'Where to?'

Disappointingly, it wasn't Angelo driving the New York taxi-cab.

'Have you heard of Morelli's, the Italian restaurant?' John asked.

'Sure, who hasn't? You want me to take you there?'

'Absolutely.' John climbed into the back of the taxi and tried not to think about abandoning Monte in Central Park.

23

'Ah, Montgomery,' exclaimed the concierge. 'There you are. I was beginning to worry.'

Monte slipped his makeshift leash and ran through the hotel lobby towards the concierge.

The concierge gave him a pat on the head. 'Now, why couldn't you come when I asked this morning?'

'Oh Rory, you're all sticky.' Amy turned to Sylvie. 'Look, he's had ice cream all down his front. I knew I shouldn't have stopped to get him one on the way out of the park. I better take him up to the hotel room to change.'

'Okay.'

'I'll see you this evening, Sylvie.' Amy glanced at the concierge, making a fuss of the Labrador. 'He obviously knows Monte. I wonder if the dog belongs to him.'

Sylvie leaned towards Amy and said, 'Don't you worry, I'll find out what irresponsible person left him in the park.'

'All right. Bye Sylvie.' Amy glanced at Rory in the buggy. 'Say bye-bye to Sylvie.'

Rory let out a yell.

Sylvie nodded knowingly at Amy.

They both said in unison, 'Overtired.'

Amy pushed the buggy toward the elevators while Sylvie made her way across the hotel lobby.

Monte spotted Sylvie and rushed back to her side.

The concierge shouted, 'Monte – no!'

Sylvie picked up the end of her linen scarf trailing on the floor behind him and noted the dirt and frayed edges that weren't there before. 'I think I need a new scarf,' commented Sylvie as she walked over to the concierge with Monte.

'I'm so sorry, madam. I hope Monte isn't being a nuisance.' The concierge only then noticed the scarf attached to his collar. He looked up at Sylvie. 'Where's his leash?'

Sylvie shrugged her shoulders dismissively. 'How do I know? We found him in the park.'

'Oh.'

'He's yours, I presume,' said Sylvie, handing him the make-shift leash.

The concierge took Sylvie's scarf and looked down at Monte. 'Not exactly.'

Sylvie furrowed her brow. 'Not exactly? Who does he belong to then because as a responsible dog owner myself, I am not impressed by—'

'It's not my fault,' the concierge swiftly cut in. 'Please don't tell the owner. It was a guest who—'

'Oh, so Monte belongs to one of the hotel guests.'

'Yes – no. Look, he belongs to the owner.'

Sylvie looked at him blankly. She was starting to wonder if they were talking at cross-purposes.

'The owner of the hotel,' explained the concierge, throwing his hand in the air to indicate the hotel.

'The owner of the hotel?' She looked at him in surprise. 'Are you telling me that Bertram...er, I mean Mr Wyndom-Price bought a puppy?'

The concierge nodded. He looked anxiously at Sylvie when he realised she was an acquaintance of the hotel owner. The concierge put his finger down his collar and gave it a nudge. He was starting to sweat. 'Look, I should have walked him myself. I know that now. It's just that I've got enough to do without having to walk the hotel dog.'

Sylvie stopped. 'Did you just say *hotel dog*?'

'Yes, crazy, isn't it? That's why he's called Montgomery – after the hotel.'

Sylvie looked at poor Monte. *Montgomery? What sort of name was that to call a dog?*

The concierge pointed at a wooden doghouse in the corner of the lobby. 'There – see!'

Sylvie stared at the doghouse in surprise. Above the apex roof was a sign that said: *Montgomery lives here*. Sylvie hadn't noticed it before. She turned to the concierge. 'How long has Monte, er, I mean Montgomery, been here?'

'He only arrived this morning. It was quite a surprise, I can tell you.'

'I'll bet,' said Sylvie, guessing he was not referring to the surprise in a good way.

'Pardon me for speaking my mind, madam, but everyone knows Mr Wyndom-Price doesn't have a fondness for dogs. I've never known pets being allowed in any of his hotels before. This is unprecedented. I wonder if he is considering whether to allow guests to bring their pets.'

Sylvie glanced at Monte and narrowed her eyes. She doubted

it. This was all for her benefit. After last night, he was trying to make it up to her. Sylvie glanced at the adorable puppy. This was not the way to go about it.

She couldn't believe Bertram had been so irresponsible, buying a puppy on a whim just because he could. A hotel was no place for a puppy. They needed a home with daily routines. They needed someone with time on their hands to look after them, not busy hotel staff who had enough to do without catering to the whims of a silly man with more money than sense. Little wonder she'd found Monte lost and alone over the park. It was bound to happen sooner or later. Sylvie was glad she was the one who had found him.

Sylvie intended to straighten this out. Monte was not staying in the hotel. 'I'm going to talk to Mr Wyndom-Price about this.'

'Oh, please don't do that.' The concierge started wringing his hands. 'It wasn't me. I didn't leave him in the park. It was a hotel guest, I swear.'

Sylvie looked at him in surprise. Then the penny dropped: he was worried about his job. Sylvie placed a hand on his arm. 'Don't worry. I won't mention your name. Although I wouldn't mind knowing which irresponsible guest abandoned him in Central Park.' Sylvie folded her arms and stared at the concierge.

The concierge bit his bottom lip. He wasn't in the habit of giving out personal information on hotel guests, but he got the message: this was tit for tat. If she wasn't going to rat on him, then he needed to give her something in return.

Sylvie studied him thoughtfully. 'I understand your reluctance to give me the name of another guest.' Sylvie leaned in close. 'What about a room number?' She stared at the Concierge waiting for a reply.

The concierge looked around the lobby, decided the coast was clear, and whispered, 'Room 223.'

Sylvie nodded. She just had one more question. 'Are they in their room right now?'

The concierge glanced at the reception and noted the room key still hanging from the little hook below the number. All guests left their keys with reception when they went out.

Sylvie followed his gaze and spotted the key. Now she knew how she would find out when the occupant of Room 223 had returned to the hotel: the key would be missing from the hook.

Sylvie smiled at the concierge. After she dealt with Bertram, the next irresponsible person who was going to get a piece of her mind was the guest in room 223. She was looking forward to it.

John sat in the same booth in Morelli's he and Angelo had sat in only yesterday. He sipped his cappuccino and stared at the empty plate on the table in front of him. The bagel was delicious. He was contemplating whether to have another when the waitress came along carrying a freshly brewed jug of coffee. She stopped at John's booth and offered him a refill.

'That's kind of you, but no thank you.' He picked up his empty plate. 'I wouldn't mind another bagel, though.'

'Sure.' The young waitress smiled at John and took his plate.

John watched her weave between tables as she disappeared through the double doors at the back of the restaurant.

It wasn't long before she returned with his bagel. She set the plate down on the table. 'You're the Brit, aren't you?'

John looked up from his notebook. 'The Brit?'

'Yes, Gina was talking all about the Englishman who came in yesterday and sat with Angelo here in this booth. She thinks you're a writer.'

John looked down at his notebook on the table. He recalled getting it out yesterday and writing a few notes when Gina was talking about her great-grandfather, Mr Morelli. He guessed she wasn't at work today, otherwise this nice young lady wouldn't be serving him.

She peered at John. 'Are you a writer?'

He didn't see any reason to lie. 'Yes.'

'What do you write?'

John glanced at the photo of Mr Morelli on the wall by his booth. He turned back to the waitress standing by his table. 'I'm a columnist. I'm doing some research for an article on Italian immigrants coming to America. I was interested in Mr Morelli's experiences as an Italian immigrant in the fifties.' John absently tapped his pen on the notebook in front of him. 'I don't suppose there's anything you can tell me about Mr Morelli?'

'What do you want to know?'

John cut to the chase. 'The last time I spoke to Gina, she mentioned that her great-grandfather had recently died. Unfortunately, she was cut short by some rather rude customers.'

The waitress grimaced. 'I'm afraid not all our customers are as polite as you.'

'I'm of the opinion that there's no excuse for bad manners.'

'I agree,' she said forthrightly. She looked about her. There were hardly any customers this time in the morning, so she put the pencil and notepad in the pocket of her dress and slipped into the booth opposite John. She leaned across the table and lowered her voice. 'Now don't quote me on this, but there's a rumour that when her great-grandfather died, the family discovered he had a property somewhere abroad that nobody knew about.'

'That's interesting.' John started writing. He liked the idea of a bit of family intrigue thrown into the mix. 'Do you know where this property is?'

The young waitress tapped her temple. 'Hmm. Now, what was it people have been saying? The place began with a C…' She gazed at John. 'It sounded like corn something or other.'

John looked up. 'Corn…?'

'Yes.' She shook her head. 'It will probably come back to me when I'm not—'

'It wouldn't be Cornwall by any chance?' John suggested.

Her face lit up. 'That's it! I'm sure of it.'

So was John. He'd put two and two together. He'd been flicking through his notebook and re-read the part about Gina's great-grandfather, who had been a prisoner of war in Cornwall, of all places. John furrowed his brow. Why would he return to England to buy a property there? Cornwall was a beautiful part of the world, but perhaps not a place you would want to revisit if you had been a POW there. It didn't make sense. Especially the part about keeping the property a secret from his family.

John wrote that down and then sat there staring at the new entry in his notebook. 'It doesn't make any sense.'

'Yeah – weird, huh,' agreed the waitress. 'Why would he keep the property a secret?'

'Why indeed,' said John thoughtfully.

'I'd better get back to work.'

'Oh yes, of course. Well, thank you for sharing what you know about Mr Morelli.'

'You're welcome.' She slipped out of the booth. 'Hey, have you been to Ellis Island?'

'Ellis Island?'

'It's where millions of immigrants first set foot on American soil.'

'I've heard of it.' John recalled his visit to meet Angelo's parents in Flatbush yesterday. Angelo and his parents were among the last immigrants to be processed on Ellis Island before it closed.

'You can visit the Ellis Island Immigration Museum,' said the waitress. 'I think you might find it useful research for your article.' She pointed at the old photograph of Mr Morelli in his prime. 'That's where his story began in America.'

John smiled at the young woman. 'Why, thank you. You've been most helpful. I think that's where I'm now headed.' He quickly finished his coffee.

'What about your bagel?'

John looked at the bagel. 'Can I get that to go?'

'Sure.'

John stepped out of Morellis with a brown paper bag, or doggy bag, as the Americans called it, containing his bagel. He wasn't the only one leaving the restaurant with a doggy bag. John raised an eyebrow at the other diners carrying similar bags. It seemed to be acceptable to take your leftovers with you, whereas he wouldn't dream of doing it in Blighty even if he wanted to. It just wasn't the done thing.

John took off down the street. The helpful waitress had given him directions to get to Ellis Island. He was looking forward to following in the footsteps of Mr Morelli when he first landed in America.

For some reason, the eventful start to his day when he nearly ran into Sylvie in Central Park crossed his mind. John smiled knowingly. If there was one place he could guarantee he wouldn't bump into Sylvie in New York, it would be on an island surrounded by water that required a journey by boat to get to. After the previous evening, the last place Bertram would take Sylvie to see was Ellis Island.

24

Sylvie knocked on the door. She couldn't wait to have words about Monte. She was preparing to give the occupant a piece of her mind when the door opened. Sylvie stepped back in surprise. 'What are you doing here?'

'Hi, Sylvie. Do you want to speak to Bertram?'

'Yes, please, Amy.' Sylvie followed Amy inside Bertram's suite. She hadn't been in his suite before. He had asked her if she would join him for a nightcap last night, but that was before the godawful episode on the boat when Sylvie couldn't stop throwing up. After that, a drink in his hotel suite was out of the question. Her stomach had settled by the time they reached the hotel, but Sylvie was still so embarrassed by the thought of Bertram seeing her on all fours retching in the boat's toilet she could barely look him in the eye.

'I left Rory with my fiancé while Daddy and I were going over the last details of the engagement party tonight,' Amy was saying as she led Sylvie down the hall to a set of double doors at the end.

Sylvie was marvelling at the size and grandeur of Bertram's suite when Amy stopped abruptly and turned around.

Sylvie came to a halt in front of her. 'What's the matter?'

'You're not here to tell Daddy you can't come to the party, are you?'

Sylvie stared at Amy. She'd forgotten all about her engagement party tonight. She was meant to be going with Bertram. Sylvie said, 'Of course I'm coming.' But not with Bertram. Sylvie decided she would have to make alternative arrangements to get there.

'Oh, thank goodness.' Amy breathed a sigh of relief. 'I hardly know anybody who is going to the party. It was Daddy's idea. He wanted to throw us an engagement party, so I just went along with his plans. He has arranged everything *and* invited all these people I don't know.'

Amy lowered her voice. 'To tell you the truth, I'm not looking forward to it.' Amy took Sylvie's hand and gave it an affectionate squeeze. 'But having you there will make all the difference.'

Sylvie managed a smile, despite feeling guilty for even considering backing out.

'Sylvie?'

Amy turned around at the sound of her father's voice. 'Oh, there you are.'

'I was just in the kitchen making coffee.' 'Will you join us, Sylvie?'

Amy looked from her father to Sylvie and back again. 'Well, I think I'll leave you two lovebirds alone.'

Sylvie shot Bertram a look, wondering what on earth he had been saying.

Amy headed towards the door. She paused before leaving. 'Sylvie,' she called out.

Sylvie was just following Bertram into the lounge. She paused at the door and looked at Amy.

'Did you find out who that dog belonged to?'

Sylvie nodded.

'Was it a hotel guest?'

She glanced at Bertram, who had joined her in the doorway. 'You could say that.'

Amy glanced at her father. 'Daddy, we found a lost dog in Central Park, and it had the address of this hotel on its name tag, as though it lives here. How daft is that – a dog living in a hotel?'

Sylvie wholeheartedly agreed.

'I don't think it's daft at all,' said Bertram, as he made his way down the hall towards Amy. He gave her a fatherly hug and ushered her out the door. 'I'll see you this evening.'

'Okay. Bye Sylvie.'

Bertram shut the door and turned around. 'Right, how about that cup of coffee?'

Sylvie was still standing in the doorway. She eyed him coolly. Either he wasn't listening, or he wasn't at all perturbed that someone had taken Monte out and lost him.

When Sylvie didn't respond to his offer of a cup of coffee, he said, 'Would you prefer tea?'

Sylvie folded her arms.

Bertram offered a nervous smile. 'Why don't we take a seat in the lounge?' He ushered her inside.

She perched on the leather sofa.

Bertram sat down in an upholstered chair opposite. 'Look, about last night…'

Sylvie rolled her eyes. 'I'm not here to talk about that.'

'Good.' Bertram clapped his hands together. 'I'm glad we've

moved on. So, about tomorrow evening. I've arranged a limo to pick us up at—'

'I'm not here about that, either. I want to talk about Monte.'

'Monte?'

Bertram raised his eyebrows.

'Who's Monte?'

'I meant Montgomery.'

Bertram was still looking confused.

'The hotel dog...'

'Ah. Yes. Montgomery.' He chuckled. 'I'd forgotten about that.'

The look on Sylvie's face said he'd better backtrack on that last comment – and fast. 'What I meant to say was—'

Sylvie held up her hand – *save it*. 'Honestly, Bertram, how could you buy a puppy on a whim *and* bring him here to live in a hotel? I know what you're up to...' Sylvie wagged her finger at Bertram. 'You thought he would make the perfect ice-breaker after last night.'

Bertram didn't deny it. He looked sheepishly at Sylvie. 'You probably miss your dog, and I thought having Montgomery around would, you know...'

'No, I don't know.'

'Well, I thought you might fancy taking him for a walk or whatever it is you do with a pet dog.'

'Whatever it is you do with a pet dog,' repeated Sylvie. She shook her head. 'You haven't a clue, have you?'

Bertram looked at Sylvie. 'I'm guessing you didn't think it was a good idea.'

'Of course it wasn't a good idea. What were you thinking? Monte, I mean Montgomery, needs a home, routines, a family who will look after of him and won't lose him over the park.'

'I didn't do that,' Bertram said defensively.

'But that's the point, Bertram. You haven't got time to look after a puppy. You can't just land this sort of responsibility on your staff. Something is going to go wrong. Something already has. It was just lucky it was me and Amy who found him. He could have run out of the park into the path of a car.'

'I'm sorry, Sylvie. I didn't think.'

'No, you didn't.'

Bertram looked across at Sylvie. 'I want to make things right. What can I do to make it up to you?'

'Well, for starters, Montgomery can't live in a hotel. He deserves a *proper* home.'

Bertram nodded. 'I can do that. I can find him a home.'

'Good.'

There was a pause. Bertram regarded her thoughtfully. 'Look, no more surprises – I promise.'

'All right,' Sylvie said slowly.

'But I still want to make it up to you.'

Sylvie stood up. 'Just sort out a home for Montgomery – that's all I ask.'

Bertram rose from his chair. 'Can't you give me one last chance?'

'A chance for what?'

'To get to know you better, renew our friendship.'

Sylvie wavered.

He held out a placating hand and glanced at his watch. 'The day is still young. Let's go out somewhere. No surprises this time. You choose. What do you say?'

Sylvie regarded him. 'There is one place I'd love to see.'

'Fantastic – what is it?'

They both took their seats once more as Sylvie explained, 'I'm thinking of writing an article for my column about something related to New York…'

'Go on,' prompted Bertram.

'I was interested in doing some research to find out more about the experiences of Italian immigrants who came to America in the fifties.'

'Hmm sounds interesting.'

Sylvie caught Bertram's bored expression. 'You don't have to tag along. I can go out today on my own. I don't need a chaperone.'

'I wouldn't hear of it. Sorry if I came over preoccupied, it's just that I've got the engagement party on my mind. It was my idea to hold the party in New York. I hope it goes well. I don't want anything to spoil Amy's big day.'

Sylvie looked at Bertram. 'I'm sure the party will be wonderful.'

'I hope so. I've pulled out all the stops and invited as many VIPs as I could think of to make it a grand affair.'

Sylvie tried not to think about the look of relief on Amy's face when she confirmed she would be there. It didn't sound as though Amy knew any of the guests who were coming. She hoped Bertram had asked his daughter if she wanted an engagement party here in New York rather than steamrolling her into it.

'Where did you come up with the idea for your article, if you don't mind me asking?'

'Not at all.' Sylvie was pleased that he was taking an interest. 'Do you recall I took my mother's ashes to scatter them in Cornwall?'

Bertram sat forward in his chair. 'Yes, I remember. How did that work out?'

'Well, that's the thing. She left specific instructions that she wanted her ashes scattered in the garden of a cottage she once owned many years ago.'

'Did you find the cottage?'

'Yes, but that's when things got complicated. It's a holiday home, and the owner lives abroad. The agent, who looks after the place in his absence, offered to drive me there and turn a blind eye while I scattered my mother's ashes in the garden.'

'What did you do?'

'I couldn't do that, Bertram. So, I wrote the owner a letter instead. I wanted to ask their permission first. It just felt like the right thing to do.'

'I agree.'

Sylvie smiled at him. She recalled John's reaction when he discovered she had written to the owner. John couldn't understand why she hadn't just gone ahead and scattered her mother's ashes.

'Did you hear back?'

'Not yet. The owner lives in America. We found out through word of mouth in the village that he is an Italian American. The agent gave me his name – Paolo Morelli.'

'Ah, so that sparked your interest in writing an article for your column.'

'Yes, that and my daughters' rather active imaginations.'

Bertram raised an eyebrow.

Sylvie explained. 'When I returned from Cornwall, the girls did some research on the internet and found out there was a Mr Morelli who was a prisoner of war in Cornwall. They couldn't find out anything more, but they came up with this outlandish notion that he was the person who owned the cottage, and some years after immigrating to America he returned to Cornwall and bought that cottage.' Sylvie shook her head. 'I think it would be too much of a coincidence if they were the same person.'

Bertram nodded. 'It seems a bit of a stretch to think someone who has started a new life in America would want to return to a place where they were a prisoner of war and buy a holiday home.'

'Yes. My thoughts exactly. Although Cornwall is a lovely part of the world, I imagine that was an episode in their past they wouldn't want to revisit.'

'Unless they had a particularly good reason.'

Sylvie stopped short. 'What do you mean?'

'I don't know, Sylvie.' Bertram shrugged. 'Perhaps someone or something made him want to return. Anyway, this is all conjecture. You said yourself it was unlikely to be the same person.'

'That's true.'

'But this Italian American, Morelli...' continued Bertram.

'Do you want to find out more about immigrants like Morelli and their experiences coming to America?'

'Yes. But I don't know where to start.' Sylvie creased her brow, deep in thought.

'What about starting at the beginning?' suggested Bertram.

'How do you mean?'

'You could start with the place where they first set foot on American soil.'

Sylvie stared at Bertram. 'What a brilliant idea. I imagine they came by boat and landed in New York – but where?' Sylvie stood up. 'I need to return to my room and fetch my laptop, so I can go on the internet and find out.'

'No need. I know exactly where their story begins.'

'You do?'

'Oh yes. I haven't been there in a while. It's one of the most visited tourist attractions in New York. You've probably heard of it, Sylvie. Ellis Island?'

'Oh yes,' Sylvie nodded. She recognised the name.

'From what I recall there's an informative Museum of Immigration there too.'

'Great. Then that's where I want to spend to the day.' Sylvie strode to the door. She paused and turned around when she realised Bertram wasn't in tow. To her surprise, Bertram had not got up from his seat. Sylvie frowned at him. 'Don't you want to come after all?'

'Of course I want to come with you, Sylvie. It's just... there's a problem.'

Sylvie's shoulders sagged.

'It's closed today – isn't it.'

'No, that's not it.'

Sylvie was getting impatient.

'Well, what's the problem?'

Bertram now regretted suggesting it. He'd forgotten about last night. He looked sheepishly in her direction. 'Ellis Island is, well, an island.'

'Okay.' Sylvie still didn't see what the problem was.

Bertram sighed. 'It's surrounded by water. You can only get there by boat.'

Sylvie's face fell. The penny dropped. She groaned as she sat back down on the sofa. Sylvie was about to abandon the idea when she had a thought. 'We'll go by helicopter.'

Bertram looked at her in surprise. 'Pardon me?'

'You're bound to have one. Or at least I bet you can get hold of one. You can make arrangements for us to be flown there by helicopter.' Sylvie caught Bertram's amused expression. 'What?'

'Helicopters and pilots don't just grow on trees, you know. It's not like hiring a car and a driver. Besides, you've always baulked at me using my money and privilege just to impress you.'

Sylvie rolled her eyes. 'I know. It's true. But this is different. I *want* you to impress me. You have my permission to roll out the red carpet and take me there in style.'

Bertram laughed. 'I would if I could, Sylvie. For all I know there may be a helipad to land on. But Ellis Island is a national monument. They won't let anyone just land there.'

'But you're not just *anyone*.'

'Even my money and influence wouldn't get you a helicopter ride there. I'm afraid this time we have to do what every other tourist does, and that's get the ferry boat to Ellis Island. Unless you want to swim,' joked Bertram.

Sylvie looked at him sharply. 'That's not funny.'

'I know it isn't, Sylvie. I'm just saying that if it's *that* important to you, you will just have to get over your fear of boats and make the crossing.'

Sylvie slumped down on the sofa. 'That's just it – I can't.'

'I've got an idea.' Bertram reached for the phone and called the concierge. 'Hello, it's Mr Wyndom-Price. Can someone bring me some motion sickness tablets?'

Sylvie threw up her hands. When Bertram got off the phone, she said, 'You think travel sweets are going to help me get over my fear of boats?'

'No, but I believe seasickness is not helping matters.' Bertram rose from his chair and disappeared along the corridor.

When he returned with his coat, there was a knock on the door. He went over to answer it. 'Thank you.' Bertram turned around with a small paper bag in his hand. He peered inside. 'Ah, Stugeron. Apparently, they're highly effective.' He looked up. 'Well, what are we waiting for?'

Sylvie refused to budge from the sofa. 'You know very well I am *not* getting on a boat.'

'Then we're not going,' said Bertram, shutting the door. He walked over to Sylvie. 'Just think of all the things you'll be missing,' Bertram teased her. 'For example, did you know the main building that still stands on the Island was the immigration station that millions passed through on their way to a new life in America? Just think you can walk in their footsteps.'

'Stop it,' said Sylvie glumly. She knew what he was doing.

Bertram grinned. 'Oh, and then there's the Ellis Island Immigration Museum. And let's not forget the American Immigrant Wall of Honour.'

'What's the Wall of Honour?'

'Outside the main building, there's a wall inscribed with thousands of names of American immigrants. Who knows, perhaps your Mr Morelli, who owns that cottage in Cornwall, is one of them? Oh, but we're not going to find out because—'

'All right!' said Sylvie, gritting her teeth. 'You win.' She couldn't believe what she was about to do. 'Let's get the ferry boat to Ellis Island.'

25

John stepped off the ferry on to Ellis Island. In front of him was the impressive main building where the National Museum of Immigration was housed. He paused for a moment, wondering how it would have felt to be an immigrant stepping off the boat on to American soil for the very first time.

He'd done some research on the internet beforehand. John discovered that reaching Ellis Island didn't guarantee entry into America. Some two percent of immigrants were turned away, forced to make the long, arduous journey back to where they came from. Little wonder Ellis Island was sometimes referred to as The Island of Tears, thought John.

He moved forward with the crowd of tourists who had disembarked from the ferry and entered the impressive building. Everybody was aiming for the Registry Room on the second floor, where the new immigrants arrived to be processed.

The room was so vast that the crowd of people quickly dispersed because of the sheer scale of the place. John gazed around the grand area, trying to imagine what it would have been like back in the nineteenth and early twentieth century when thousands of people passed through the Registry Room every single day in the heyday of immigration to America. He'd seen some of the old black and white photographs online that showed this room full of people waiting anxiously for their fate to be determined.

John had remembered to collect the audio guide. He was looking forward to following the audio tour. It was included in his ferry ticket. The aim of the tour was for visitors to gain an insight into the immigrant experience by imagining they were a new arrival.

John turned on the audio guide and listened. As he followed the tour he thought of Angelo, a three-year-old boy back in 1953, who was carried in his father's arms as they entered the Registry Room, and Gina's great-grandfather, Mr Morelli, arriving on Ellis Island with little more than the shirt on his back. They had both arrived here the same year, thought John. They could even have been standing in this very room on the same day.

When the tour was over, John handed the audio guide back, and made his way to the museum to find out more about the poignant stories of some of the twelve million immigrants who passed through Ellis Island. It surprised him to learn that a staggering forty percent of the American population can trace their roots back to an ancestor who passed through this very building.

John was two hours in the museum. It held the fascinating new gallery called the Peopling of America Center. He enjoyed finding out about the immigrant experience before Ellis Island opened its doors in 1892. And then what became of the island once it closed as an immigration centre in 1954. It was a year after a three-year-old Italian boy called Angelo along with his family, and a young man named Mr Morelli, passed through on their way to the land of opportunity. John made a quick pit stop in the shop where he bought a baseball cap, with the words *Ellis Island* emblazoned on the front, for his brother, Dave.

He was just leaving the shop when he spotted the name *Sylvie* on the handle of a souvenir mug. John picked it up. He didn't intend to buy her a memento from New York. She was in New York; she could buy something herself.

John held the mug in his hands. He was drawn to the picture on the front depicting the Registry Room with the words, *Ellis Island: the Front Doors of Freedom*. He turned the mug over. On the back was a brief history of the Ellis Island Immigration Centre.

John kept hold of the mug and walked back to the counter where he had paid for the cap. 'Excuse me, would you have one of these with the name *John*?'

'I'll have a look for you, sir.'

He waited for the shop assistant to return. She was carrying a mug identical to the one John had picked up on his way out of the shop, except this one had his name on the handle. He watched the shop assistant wrap the mug in tissue paper.

'Would you like this one too?' she said, picking up the other mug.

John had no idea why he said yes, but the shop assistant was already wrapping it in tissue paper before he changed his mind.

'That will be twenty dollars.'

John handed over the cash and slipped the two souvenir mugs into the plastic bag with the baseball cap. Once outside, he retraced his steps to catch the ferry back to Manhattan. He groaned when he saw how many people were already in the queue. John glanced at the bag in his hand. Inside was a souvenir guidebook about Ellis Island that he had also bought in the shop.

He took it out of the bag and flicked through the pages while he waited.

It wasn't long before the ferry from Manhattan docked. John looked up and glanced at the passengers disembarking. He closed the book and was just slipping it back in the bag when he froze. John's mouth dropped open. It wasn't possible. There was no way she would—

I must have been mistaken, thought John as he searched the orderly line of people making their way past the long queue he was standing in for the return journey. John's eyebrows shot up when he saw them. It was Sylvie. He thought he'd seen her, and in a matter of seconds, she would see him. John delved into his plastic bag, grabbed the baseball cap and put it on, pulling it low on his forehead. Then he opened the guidebook and held it up in front of his face.

'Now, the first thing I want to do is look at the Wall of Honor and see if his name is etched on one of the panels...' Sylvie was saying as she passed within inches of John.

John slowly lowered the guidebook as they walked by and stared at Sylvie. His first thought was how, in heaven's name, had she made the journey to Ellis Island without walking off the boat a quivering wreck? She didn't do boats. Everyone knew that. It made her ill just at the thought of going somewhere by boat. And yet, from what he'd witnessed, she looked as right as rain. How was that possible?

John's next thought was what, in heaven's name, was the Wall of Honor? He flicked through the pages of his guidebook and found it. 'Oh.' John realised he'd missed one of the must-see attractions on the island – The American Immigrant Wall of Honor. He hadn't exactly missed it. John had been swept along with the crowd into the main building and passed it by without stopping to take a look.

'Damn!' he muttered under his breath. He didn't realise it contained the names of over seven hundred thousand immigrants, a good proportion of whom had passed through Ellis Island.

John closed the guidebook and slipped it into the plastic bag. The queue of people was now moving forward, boarding the ferry for the return journey. John glanced over his shoulder. He wanted to go back and see if he could find Mr Morelli's name on one of the panels. He knew he had the time. There would be another ferry back to Manhattan. John frowned. There was just one problem: Sylvie.

John dithered as he moved ever closer to boarding the ferry. From what he'd overhead as Sylvie passed by, her first port of call was the panels, too. He raised an eyebrow, wondering who Sylvie was looking for on the Wall of Honor. As far as he was aware, she didn't have any American friends or relations who might have had a descendant's name inscribed on a panel.

John looked over his shoulder once more. He could avoid them. The island wasn't small. Besides, as soon as she finished with the panels, and moved into the main building to see the Registry Room, then he would have his chance.

John continued to move forward as those at the head of the queue boarded the ferry. The problem wasn't bumping into Sylvie and Bertram on the island, John realised, but how to avoid them on the journey back to Manhattan if they ended up on the same boat. He'd already had a close shave. The chances of bumping into them on a ferry were far higher.

John took off the baseball cap and put it back in the plastic bag as he boarded the ferry. He found a spot on the open deck and thought about Sylvie as he stood watching Ellis Island fade into the distance. The gulf between them was wider than ever. John frowned and turned around to find a place inside. He took a seat inside the warm cabin, got out his notepad, and jotted down some notes for his article to take his mind off Sylvie and Bertram. It wasn't working. He put the notebook away. Everywhere he looked were couples of various ages enjoying their trip together.

John's thoughts returned to another couple who were enjoying their trip to Ellis Island together. They'd obviously patched things up. *Damn!* John shook his head in dismay. Bertram must be doing something right, because nobody had ever managed to get Sylvie to overcome her phobia of boats – until now.

26

John walked into the hotel and breathed a sigh of relief when he saw Monte chewing on a bone outside the doghouse in the corner of the lobby. He kept his head down and quickly sidled past the concierge, who was busy talking to another guest. John didn't fancy explaining how it came to be that he hadn't returned with Monte to the hotel this morning. However, he couldn't resist pausing to stroke the dog on his way to the elevator. 'Good boy.'

Monte stopped chewing the bone and licked John's hand.

John made a mental note to wash his hands as soon as he got back to his suite. Out of curiosity, he peered at the small gold disc attached to Monte's collar. The address of the hotel had been engraved in very tiny writing. He could just about make out the words: *The Montgomery*.

'So that's why Sylvie brought you home,' said John under his breath. 'Now that little mystery is solved, I'll leave you to your bone.' He patted the dog's head and stood up. He glanced over his shoulder and saw the concierge standing at his desk, throwing a black look at his least favourite guest.

John walked over to the elevator, hoping the concierge didn't come over and have words with him about abandoning Monte in Central Park. He breathed a sigh of relief when the elevator doors opened. He was about to step inside when he encountered a young woman pushing a buggy towards him.

'Oh, pardon me,' said John, stepping back to allow her to pass.

'Thank you,' said the young woman in an unmistakable English accent.

John glanced at the little boy in the buggy and smiled at him as she strode past. He stepped into the elevator and turned around. Just before the doors closed, the young woman glanced his way. Their eyes met. A flash of recognition crossed both their faces.

John stood there, frowning. He was positive he'd seen her somewhere before. And the little boy in the buggy. But where? He racked his brain until it came to him. In Central Park, Sylvie had been sitting with a young woman who had a child in a buggy. Perhaps that's where he'd seen her before.

John wasn't convinced. From that distance, he had recognised Sylvie sitting in the café. That wasn't a surprise. They'd been married for decades; he'd recognise her anywhere. But the same couldn't be said for the young woman. He thought she had short blonde hair like that young woman, but he hadn't taken a lot of notice. His focus of attention had been on Sylvie. Even if it was the same young woman who was with Sylvie in Central Park, John was still convinced he'd seen her somewhere before. He knew this for a fact because he recognised the little boy.

The woman sounded British. Perhaps it was during Grandpa Duty back home in Blighty, thought John. He used to take Gertie to the swing park most days, and then there were the parent and toddler sessions at the library every week – or in his case, grandparent and toddler sessions. John raised an eyebrow. Perhaps he'd seen her there. John nodded his head. That had to be it. He'd seen that flash of recognition cross her face; she definitely seemed to recognise him. John still couldn't picture where it was he'd seen them. He blamed it on his age; the memory was not as sharp as it once was.

As the elevator doors opened on the fourth floor, he was about to step outside when he realised he'd forgotten something. He turned around and pressed the button for the ground floor. In his haste to avoid the concierge, he'd neglected to collect his room key from the front desk.

John stood there, watching the numbers count down to the ground floor. When the elevator doors opened, he paused before stepping outside. He was checking the coast was clear; he didn't fancy a run in with the concierge over Monte. Across the lobby, the concierge was nowhere to be seen. John scooted over towards the front desk.

The young woman with the child in the buggy was handing over her room key to one of the staff on reception.

John came to a sudden halt in the middle of the lobby. It suddenly hit him where he had seen them before. John gaped at her. It was the day he played detectives and took Gertie to Hanover Square to spy on Sylvie and this Bertram fellow who she was meeting for lunch at The Rooftop Café. It was after their lunch date, when they went their separate ways, that John had followed Bertram back to a hotel near the café. Gertie had chosen that moment to need a wee.

Gertie had just finished using the hotel facilities when John had heard a commotion in the lobby. John recalled seeing this young woman with her child standing at the reception, demanding to see Bertram. And he recalled inadvertently calling attention to himself as he carried Gertie outside when she spotted the little boy in the buggy and shouted out, boy! The young woman had turned around and stared at John as he made a hasty retreat out of the hotel.

John narrowed his eyes. That's why the young woman had recognised him. He was sure of it. She might not have been able to place where she'd seen him before, but she remembered his face, nevertheless.

John stared at her as she handed over the room key on her way out of the hotel. He was stunned to see her here. 'That two-timing scoundrel!' John said under his breath. Evidently, Sylvie wasn't the only woman in Bertram's life. Did Sylvie know about this other woman? John couldn't imagine that she did. There was no way Sylvie would have anything to do with Bertram if she knew.

John had tried to tell her what he'd seen at the hotel in London – but Sylvie wouldn't listen. She was livid when she found out he had been following her. John shook his head when he recalled seeing them sitting together, chatting amiably in the café in Central Park. Good grief. If only Sylvie realised what was going on.

John's eyes followed the young woman as she pushed the buggy out the door of the hotel. He grinned as a glorious thought occurred to him. It was time to confront Sylvie over Bertram's past indiscretions. Screw the show. He was past caring about how he would explain what he was doing in New York when Sylvie discovered he'd been right here, in this hotel, all along. He didn't give a jot about the production or his writing career at this moment. All he cared about was straightening things out with his wife before she returned from New York and made a massive mistake moving in with Bertram.

Someone tapped John on the shoulder, making him jump. He turned around to find the concierge standing behind him.

John stepped back in surprise.

The concierge gave John a disarming smile before he held out a dog's leash. 'Now, I think you still owe me – or should I say Monte – a walk.'

'Look, about that. Monte ran off and—'

'And I expect you're looking forward to walking him again.'

John glanced at Monte, sitting by the concierge's feet, wagging his tail. John didn't mind walking the dog – not at all. It's just that he had something pressing he needed to do, namely, to straighten things out with his wife.

He looked at the concierge apologetically. 'I'd love to walk Monte, but the thing is, I had something I needed to—'

'I'm sure it can wait until later.' The concierge put the leash in John's hand.

'Yes, I suppose it can.' John shrugged as he made his way across the lobby with an excitable Labrador puppy at his heels. He glanced at Monte as they walked out of the hotel. Although John would like nothing more than to see Sylvie right now and set the record straight regarding Bertram's past indiscretions, there was no chance he would bump into Sylvie in Central Park this time around. She was probably still on Ellis Island. And when she returned, he couldn't exactly pop up to her room. He knew what floor she was on, but that was it. He didn't know her room number.

John was quite sure the concierge would not divulge her

room number, even if he offered to walk the dog every day until he left. His only option was to come down to the hotel restaurant for dinner and wait for Sylvie and Bertram to turn up. Wouldn't they both be in for a surprise when they saw him sitting at a table? John was looking forward to it.

27

Sylvie approached the hotel reception for her room key. 'Thank you,' she said when they passed her the key.

'Can I help you with anything else, madam?'

Sylvie felt her face flush in embarrassment. They had caught her lingering at the desk, trying to find out whether a certain guest had returned to the hotel and collected their room key. Sylvie spied the key hanging on the hook of room number 223.

'No, that's all,' answered Sylvie, disappointed that she still hadn't had an opportunity to have it out with the occupant of that room over abandoning Monte in Central Park. Thinking of Monte, Sylvie walked across the lobby towards the elevator, hoping to say hello to the sweet Labrador puppy. She was aware Bertram was looking for a suitable home for Monte, but for now, the puppy's home was still The Montgomery.

Sylvie stopped at the doghouse and looked inside. Monte wasn't there. Sylvie was disappointed. She wouldn't have minded taking Monte for a walk. She missed her dog, Alfie. Sylvie was already feeling homesick, and she'd only been gone a matter of days.

'Sylvie?'

She turned around and smiled at Bertram. He was waiting by the elevator for her. They rode up together, and Sylvie alighted on her floor.

'I'll meet you in the restaurant downstairs at seven,' Bertram said, before the elevator doors closed.

Sylvie nodded an affirmative.

'Oh, and well done for getting on that ferry today.'

Sylvie smiled at him. 'That was all down to you, Bertram. Thank you for the—'

The doors closed. Sylvie reached inside her pocket and got out the packet of motion sickness pills. She turned them over in her hand. How silly that after all these years her phobia of boats, which made her feel physically sick, wasn't a phobia at all and could be cured by simply popping a pill.

Sylvie put the pills back in her pocket and made her way along the corridor to her room. She was intending to spend the next few hours before meeting up with Bertram in the restaurant, typing up her notes in preparation for the article she was submitting to her editor, Marcia, for her column, *Love on the Rooftop*. Something was troubling Sylvie. She was worried about how the article would be received by her readers and her editor.

Sylvie knew this would be the first time she deviated from her normal subject – living apart together. She still wanted to write her column, but the question remained: would Marcia keep her on when she found out her star writer wasn't intending to write about LAT living anymore?

Sylvie was done with living apart together. That's what she had come to New York to tell her readers. She never expected that her column would become so ridiculously popular. It was all built on a lie. She wasn't living in bliss with her husband as a consequence of living apart together. Far from it. Unbeknown to her readers, living apart together had quite the opposite effect. She was here in New York waiting to appear on a live chat show to set the record straight.

The peculiar thing was, Sylvie was looking forward to it. How long could she keep living a lie? Her family had no idea she was the writer, Love on the Rooftop. How could they? Her daughters knew very well that since the house conversion, when their mother moved downstairs, things had gone from bad to worse regarding their parents' marriage. It was a very different story to that which Sylvie had depicted in her column. Her readers, however, lapped it up. What they didn't realise was that it was all a fiction of epic proportions.

Sylvie put her notebook down and sat there staring into space. How had she let things get so out of hand? Her popularity continued to soar to new heights with each article on the romantic goings-on of the Baxters living apart together in Holland Park. But things had come to a head. She couldn't hide behind her anonymity any longer. People were clamouring to meet the writer behind the column. And now they would get their wish – on live television, no less.

There were only two people who knew the truth: her best friend Julia and her editor, Marcia. It was Julia who had encouraged her to stretch the truth. Outright lie if that's what it took to sell her articles and make money. It was at a time when they were in dire financial straits financial straits because John had underestimated the final cost of the conversion.

Sylvie had two choices: to move back in with John or remain living on her own. She chose the latter. But it came at a price. She had to earn money – and fast. If that meant writing a load of baloney about how living apart together had brought romance back into their lives after forty years of marriage, then so be it. But that was back then before the writer, Love on the Rooftop, got herself in a bind by writing about living apart together and becoming a minor celebrity in the process.

Once again Sylvie was back to thinking how on earth she had let things get so out of hand. It should have made her feel better that her editor was in on it. Sylvie didn't know this to begin with, but it turned out that Marcia had known for some time her star writer had been spinning lies for the sake of her readers and that things were not anywhere near the romantic idyll she was portraying in her column.

It wasn't the case that something, in particular, had alerted Marcia to this. On the contrary, through all the money worries and shenanigans with John at home, when he had tried every which way to get her to move back in with him, she'd shown the utmost professionalism regarding her new career. She always turned up at the office and worked just as hard as her fellow journalists. But that was her downfall.

Marcia had finally questioned why, if Sylvie had such a wonderful relationship with her husband, did she find any excuse to work at the office rather than working from home and spending time with her spouse? Something didn't add up. Then, to cap it all, there was that one time Sylvie had spent two hours on a lunch break with another man – it was the day she had met Bertram at The Rooftop Café in Hanover Square.

Sylvie couldn't hide behind her column after that. She admitted to Marcia what she had suspected all along – that living apart together wasn't the panacea her star writer was depicting.

Sylvie thought Marcia would fire her after that. But she didn't. What she wanted was for Sylvie to continue with the lie.

Sylvie wasn't at all surprised. Marcia's magazine had gone from a little-known women's monthly to one of the most popular bestselling titles, all thanks to Love on the Rooftop. Sylvie's column was pulling in readers in droves. To Sylvie's knowledge, only one other writer had the same effect on the magazine they were writing for – Dear John.

Sylvie would never admit to another living soul that his articles about living apart together were a lot closer to the truth than hers. Living apart together doesn't work. At least not in her experience, and by the sounds of it, not in Dear John's experience either. The difference was he had written the truth, and she had not.

Sylvie sighed. Marcia didn't realise her star writer was intending to go on that show and tell the world she was a liar and a fraud. Sylvie knew she shouldn't worry about how her next article would be received, because she most likely wouldn't have a job after the show. She couldn't imagine Marcia would keep her on after this. But the fact remained, there was only so long she could keep her identity under wraps before somebody found out the truth.

All this was at the forefront of her mind because it was now a matter of hours before she was due to appear on the show. Sylvie glanced at her watch – twenty-four hours, to be precise. The show was tomorrow afternoon, and Sylvie was feeling nervous.

She didn't have to tell the whole truth if she didn't want to. Everyone would eventually find out who Love on the Rooftop was – a sixty-year-old former secretary from Holland Park W1 who dreamed of becoming a writer. But they didn't have to know all about the web of lies she'd been spinning about living apart together – not yet, anyway. It wasn't as though John would be there to refute her little charade.

It wasn't Sylvie's intention to continue the lie. But the thought of standing in front of that studio audience, with all those cameras focused on her broadcasting around the world, made her wonder whether she might bottle out of telling the truth about her alter-ego.

Sylvie tried not to think about it. She switched on her laptop and began to write her article entitled New York: An Italian Immigrant's story, which most likely would never be published. It didn't stop Sylvie thinking about further lines of inquiry to find out more about Mr Morelli, who may or may not be the former POW in Cornwall that her daughters had discovered on the internet. Sylvie smiled. Published or not, it wouldn't stop her writing.

Sylvie was back to thinking about the show. She was going to have her five minutes of fame before disappearing into obscurity. She didn't want her new career as a writer to end, but there was a new kid on the block – Dear John – and he was going to have a lot more credibility as a writer when Love on the Rooftop outed herself for the fraud she was.

Sylvie didn't want to think about the show or that other anonymous writer out there. Her nemesis, writing under the pseudonym Dear John. Instead, she focused on typing up the research she'd gathered today from her trip to Ellis Island, reminding herself that she had a lovely evening to look forward to with Bertram. Sylvie was determined that nothing would spoil what remained of her free time in New York.

28

John stopped typing up his notes from his trip to Ellis Island earlier in the day and glanced at his watch. The hotel restaurant was now open for dinner. He wondered what time Sylvie and Bertram would arrive at the restaurant for their evening meal. Since he'd discovered Sylvie wasn't the only woman in Bertram's life – there was the young woman with the child that he recognised from the hotel in London – John was set on confronting that two-timing scoundrel. He was going to do it this evening, at the house restaurant, in front of Sylvie.

John didn't know how he was going to explain his presence in New York. He decided he would cross that bridge when he came to it. Besides, he didn't think that was important. What was important was that Sylvie knew what was going on right under her nose before things went too far. Thank god he had found out, quite by chance, that Sylvie and Bertram were staying in separate hotel suites. How long that would last was anybody's guess. He was determined to put a stop to this. Bertram might be fooling his wife, but he wasn't fooling anybody else, least of all John.

John cast his mind back to the young woman with the child in the buggy. He'd recognised her, all right. She was most definitely the person he'd spotted arguing with the hotel receptionist in London, demanding to see Bertram. John knew he wasn't mistaken because she recognised him. He could see it written all over her face – that look indicating she had seen him somewhere before, although she couldn't put her finger on where.

After finding out she had a room at this hotel, he was looking forward to introducing Sylvie to the real Bertram who was two-timing her.

John had been sitting at a table in the middle of the restaurant for the last hour, nicely positioned to see them walk through the door. He'd eaten a starter, polished off the main course, and was now studying the sweet menu while keeping an eye out for Sylvie and Bertram.

This was the only time he had eaten in the restaurant. John recalled the first time he stepped foot in the restaurant on the day he arrived. He got the shock of his life when he spotted Sylvie and Bertram dining together and discovered that, by some insane coincidence, Sylvie was in New York staying at the same hotel. When John found out Bertram owned the hotel, it was all too apparent what Sylvie was doing here – Bertram had whisked her away to New York for a romantic break.

John thought back to a few days ago before he found out he was being sent on an all-expenses-paid trip to New York to meet his nemesis, Love on the Rooftop. He remembered with sickening clarity getting the shock of his life when he discovered Sylvie had left him a Dear John letter before she had departed in a taxi. John recalled standing at the window, wondering where she was going with her suitcases. Now he knew. She had gone to

New York with Bertram. The question on John's mind was what would happen on her return?

John felt it was unlikely she would return to Holland Park and simply pick up where they left off – living in separate apartments under the same roof. He had his Dear John letter. She'd left him, and that was that. But if Bertram thought that when they returned to London, she was going to move in with him instead, then he could think again. That's what he was here to put a stop to.

He couldn't force Sylvie to move back in with him, even if he begged her to move back into the garden apartment downstairs. John would have had her back any which way he could, even if it meant they were still living apart together. However, he could put a stop to Sylvie moving in with Bertram. At least that was something.

John put the sweet menu down on the table. He was getting restless. Another fifteen minutes had passed, and they hadn't arrived. He was wondering if they had gone out for an evening meal instead.

When the waiter came over to take his dessert order, John said, 'I believe Mr Wyndom-Price and a lady friend were due to dine here this evening. I wonder if you could tell me when you are expecting them.' John added, 'I'm a friend of theirs, and I was hoping to join them,' telling an outright lie.

'I will find out for you, sir.'

John nodded his appreciation.

'In the meantime, would sir like something from the sweet menu?'

John declined. The food was delicious, but he already felt he needed to loosen his belt a notch – or two.

'Very good, sir.' The waiter took his menu.

John watched him walk over to the maître d' and have a word.

The maître d' looked over in John's direction as he listened to the waiter's request from one of the diners. A moment later, the maître d' made his way to John's table. 'Good evening, Sir. I understand you are looking for Mr Wyndom-Price?'

John nodded. 'Yes.' He glanced toward the restaurant entrance.

'I'm afraid they have gone out for the evening.'

'Gone out?' John barked. 'Where?' he demanded, although he didn't really expect the maître d' to tell him where the hotel owner had gone to dinner.

The maître d' looked at John askance. 'I thought everyone knew about the engagement party?'

'Engagement party?' said John in surprise.

'What engagement party?'

'They announced it in the newspapers.'

John looked at the maître d' agog. He couldn't believe what he was hearing. *Good god, they hadn't even signed the divorce papers and Sylvie was getting engaged?*

John had to put a stop to this. 'Where is the engagement party – I demand to know!' exclaimed John, slamming his fist down on the table and attracting surprised stares from diners at the surrounding tables.

'Now there's no need for that, sir.' The maître d' smiled nervously. 'It's no secret. I can tell you about the venue. But without an invitation...' he trailed off.

'Let me worry about that,' John said, his fist still clenched on the table.

The maître d' shrugged. 'Okay. Would sir like me to arrange a taxi to take you to the party?'

John stood up. 'Yes – you do that.' He threw the fancy white napkin on the table. 'I'm finished,' John announced.

'Very good, sir. I'll see to it that the concierge arranges a taxi.'

'Good.' John strode out of the room leaving behind a very relieved maître d' glancing around the restaurant hoping the nutjob who was sitting at table four hadn't upset the other guests.

John shot up to his room and promptly changed into a clean pair of slacks, crisp white shirt and a navy blue blazer – the smart set of clothes he was saving to wear on the show tomorrow.

On his way out of the hotel, he stopped at the small boutique shop in the lobby to buy a bottle of bubbly. The price was extortionate. He didn't think twice about handing over almost all that remained of his spending money. If he was going to attempt to blag entry and come up with some bullshit line about losing his invitation, then he better look the part. John didn't think he'd have a problem gate-crashing the party – after all, he was British!

29

'Holy crap!' exclaimed John as he stared out of the taxi window.

The taxicab driver glanced in his rear-view mirror at the passenger in the back. 'Is everything okay?'

John turned from the window and looked wide-eyed at the driver. 'Are you sure this is the right address?'

'Yes. It's the address the concierge gave me, buddy.'

They were driving slowly up a long gravel drive, behind a queue of black limousines, approaching a 1930s style mansion straight out of an F. Scott Fitzgerald novel. John was thinking of *The Great Gatsby*. Or better still, those mansions on Rhode Island. He'd never seen anything like it outside of a Hollywood movie.

The taxi came to a halt. The driver glanced at the meter on his dashboard and turned in his seat. 'That will be one hundred and fifty dollars.'

John gulped. It had taken near on ninety minutes to get here. He had no idea where he was going and hadn't accounted for the cost of coming all this distance by taxi.

He opened his wallet, hoping he had enough money to cover the fare, something he hadn't thought about when he was paying three hundred dollars for the bottle of bubbly. John breathed a sigh of relief when he spotted the last two one-hundred-dollar bills inside. 'Here – keep the change.'

'Are you sure?' The taxi driver wasn't used to getting a fifty-dollar tip. Then again, it wasn't every day that he drove someone all the way from Manhattan to The Hamptons.

'Yes.' John's wallet was now empty. But it wasn't as though he needed any more spending money. The show was tomorrow afternoon, so all he would have to do in the morning was to walk Monte. That wouldn't cost him anything. Then he had one more night in the hotel after the show, and he was catching his flight home.

John stepped out of the taxi and watched it depart, only then realising he didn't have a dime in his wallet, let alone the hundred and fifty dollars, to get a taxi back to the hotel. 'Oh, crap.'

He shrugged. 'Guess I'll have to blag my way into staying the night.' He gazed up at the mansion and could only imagine how many rooms were inside. Perhaps there was a reason Bertram was holding the party here; maybe some guests had travelled a distance and were stopping over. If that was the case, he wondered if there was a spare bedroom available. Failing that, he could bed down on a sofa somewhere and hitch a ride back to New York in the morning with one of the other guests. John hoped so.

As he walked along the gravel drive towards the mansion, he couldn't get over the sheer size of the place. John scowled. Trust Bertram to be so extravagant and hire an estate in The Hamp-tons for their engagement party.

John looked about him. More guests were still arriving. He glanced at the couples alighting from the stretch limos and Mercedes parked in the driveway. The guests making their way to the house were the same generation as Sylvie and Bertram. He noticed their evening attire. John was feeling under-dressed.

Now he wished he'd thought to bring a tie in his luggage. He knew why he hadn't. The days of wearing a suit and tie to the office were long gone. John reminded himself he wasn't an accountant anymore, he was a writer, and writers didn't wear ties – not this writer at any rate. From what he was seeing, he realised a tuxedo wouldn't have gone amiss. Now John was anxious he wouldn't be able to blag entry after all, let alone ask if he could crash on their couch tonight.

If he did gain entry to the party, now would be a good time to find out who owned the sprawling, ivy-clad 1930s mansion, so he could inquire if there was a possibility he could stay the night.

'Good evening, sir.' An old gentleman in a black suit bowed in front of John, just like he had for all the other guests who passed through the double doors into the marble entrance hall.

'Good evening.' John paused, waiting for him to ask to see his invitation. He didn't.

'This way if you please.' With a wave of the hand, he indicated for John to enter.

John saw his chance. 'I'd like to book a room for the night.' He didn't have any cash, but he did have his bank card, so at least he could offer to pay for bed and board.

'This isn't a hotel.'

John was aware of that. He didn't see a hotel sign when he arrived. That's why he guessed Bertram had hired the mansion as the venue for the party.

'I'd like to speak to the owner of this...er...house.' John wanted to ask if he could stay the night.

'All in due course. He is otherwise engaged.'

'I see.' John didn't budge. He was holding up other guests waiting to enter the house. 'Look, can you tell me if he will be at the party because I'd like to —'

'Didn't you read your invitation?' interrupted the old man at the door. 'It's the owner of this house that's throwing the party – Mr Wyndom-Price.'

'Bertram!' John took an involuntary step back in surprise and backed straight into the person queuing behind him.

'So sorry,' said John, glancing over his shoulder at the disgruntled guest.

'This is Mr Wyndom-Price's private residence in New York. It's quite a privilege to be invited to attend a function at his home. This way if you please…' The old man showed John through the door into the house.

John stepped into the massive marble foyer and stood there with the other guests looking around Bertram's opulent New York home. He felt his stomach twisting in a knot. Why was he holding the engagement party here? Was this where Sylvie was going to live with Bertram, in his mansion in The Hamptons?

John thought of their house in Holland Park, now divided into two apartments. Did he really think, after all this, Sylvie would return home to live with him in a two-bedroomed apartment, with tenants living below them?

He turned full circle, taking in the sweeping staircase. The inside of the sprawling mansion looked like something out of Gone with the Wind. John never imagined Bertram was this well off. Even if he told Sylvie all about that young woman he'd seen in the hotel, would she give up all this – for him? John inwardly groaned. He wished he'd never gate-crashed the party, only to find out he didn't have a hope.

He was about to leave when the music started. John stood there in the giant marble entrance hall, with the other guests looking about him, wondering where the distinctive sound of jazz was coming from. It sounded like a live jazz band. John found himself tapping his foot to the rhythm of the beat. He stopped that immediately and frowned. He wasn't here to enjoy himself. John was about to go when he caught sight of the double doors at the far end of the hall slowly opening.

John was swept along with the crowd as everyone surged forward through the doors into a large reception room. The room was even more palatial than the entrance hall. He was right: there was a live band. John counted four band members – a jazz quartet – all dressed in white tuxedos. One was seated at a piano, and they were playing their musical instruments with such aplomb that John was transfixed. He'd never seen or heard a live jazz band before. Now he felt like he'd stepped into an F. Scott Fitzgerald novel.

Once again, John found his foot tapping on the marble floor to the rhythm of the beat. He was nodding his head in time to the music when the band switched gear and abandoned the jazz for something altogether different, more mellow and slow. They were playing some classical music. John wasn't enjoying it any less. In fact, more so.

Although he didn't recognise the artist, the music took him back to a simpler time when he and Sylvie were still together, and they had their routines. He used to like nothing more than to wake up to the Beeb playing classical music on BBC Radio 2 while he waited for Sylvie to bring up his morning cuppa and newspaper. John always read the paper and drank his cup of tea while Sylvie prepared the breakfast. That seemed a lifetime ago.

The music reminded him of home, but a home that no longer existed. A life together he had destroyed by stupidly converting the house into two apartments, not expecting his wife to decamp downstairs – permanently.

Permanently? John raised an eyebrow. He wished she *had* moved downstairs for good. At least she'd be there when he got back. At least they'd still be together, in a manner of speaking, if you called living apart together *still* together. John grimaced. *What a thought*. But even so, he'd still have preferred she hadn't packed her suitcases and walked out into the arms of another man with a mansion in The Hamp—

A sudden round of applause rudely interrupted John's thoughts. The band hadn't stopped playing, which left John looking about him in bewilderment. He was standing by the door behind a group of people, so at first, he couldn't see what they were applauding. John bobbed his head this way and that until he saw them. In the centre of the vast reception room, lined with guests around the periphery, were two people dancing the waltz.

John watched with fascination as they whirled around the room. They could have been professional dancers if it wasn't for their age; he guessed they must be retired because they appeared to be the same generation as most of the guests here – in their sixties. They were damn good together. He was enjoying the show until they whirled over to his side of the room. John recognised them in an instant. His breath caught in his throat. Bertram and Sylvie looked like the perfect dance partners. This was just another nail in the coffin of their marriage, thought John miserably.

His first reaction was to march across the dance floor and cut in. But him and Sylvie, they had never danced like that. John frowned. In fact, they had never once danced together in all the years he'd known her, despite Sylvie telling him on numerous occasions that before she met him, she loved to go dancing. John raised his eyebrows in consternation. *If only I'd listened.*

John spotted a waiter weaving his way through the throng of people. He reached out and took a glass of bubbly from the tray as he walked by. Other couples joined Sylvie and Bertram on the dance floor. John turned around with the glass in his hand and walked out of the room, gulping the drink down in three large swallows. When he'd finished, he turned around to hand the glass back but discovered someone had closed the double doors from the inside.

John stood there in the deserted hall with the empty glass and the expensive bottle of bubbly he'd bought from the hotel. He looked from one to the other and decided to put two and two together. John looked about him and wondered where he could go and drown his sorrows. He glanced up the staircase from John didn't know what to say.

and settled to find himself a room for the night.

He was just starting up the stairs when he heard voices coming from above. John spotted two people, a man and a woman, walking along the upper landing. He backed down the stairs and swiftly turned around, intending to head for the main entrance. The last thing he wanted right now was for someone to question what he was doing here without an invitation. John headed to the door, only to find it was locked.

He did an about-turn and spotted another door ajar at the far end of the hall. He was hot-footing it past the stairs when he overhead a snippet of the couple's conversation.

'Why don't you tell him?' the young man asked.

'I can't do that – not now.'

'But if he loves you, I'm sure he'll understand—'

John was just closing the glass door behind him when he glanced into the hall and did a double take. It was the young woman from the hotel. He couldn't believe she was here in his house in The Hamptons. Now John saw his opportunity to march back in there and expose Bertram for the scumbag he was – in front of Sylvie and all those people.

30

John remained where he was, rooted to the spot behind the glass door, staring into Bertram's house in The Hamptons. John couldn't do it. He couldn't bring himself to confront Bertram. It wasn't that he was past caring. He was tired. Tired of trying every which way to get his wife back.

He closed the door behind him and stepped on to the lawn. Although it was growing dark, a soft glow of yellow light partially illuminated the garden; it was coming from the room where the party was in full swing. The band had resumed playing jazz. The upbeat music did not match John's mood.

John wandered across the grounds looking for somewhere to sit so he could open the bottle of bubbly, get mighty drunk, and perhaps pass out on the lawn.

'Now that sounds like a plan,' John said out loud.

He was walking along, not venturing too far from the house, when he thought he heard something. John paused to listen. It sounded like someone crying. Then the wind changed direction, and he heard nothing more. He raised an eyebrow, thinking that perhaps he'd imagined it.

John continued walking. He passed the room where the party

was in full swing, willing himself not to glance through the window and glimpse his wife, stunning in a strapless ball gown, in the arms of another man. Instead, he abruptly changed direction. Turning his back on the house, he strode across the lawn, the garden dissolving into shadows as dusk fell. That's when he saw her, sitting alone on a garden bench at the end of a short gravel path. John hesitated. Did he turn around and return to the house or announce his presence?

'Who's there?' a woman's voice called out.

John stepped out of the shadows on to the gravel path. 'Bride or groom?' John blurted, for want of something to say.

She hesitated long enough for John to guess the truth. 'Me neither,' John added.

'Pardon?'

'The engagement party – I'm neither with the bride nor the groom.' John looked about him, stepped closer and whispered, 'I gate-crashed the party.'

The woman regarded John for a long moment. 'So, what are you doing here?'

John looked at the woman and thought he might ask her the same question. But he didn't. Instead, he said simply, 'I came to confront my wife. She's with another man.'

'And did you – confront your wife?'

John shook his head and looked at his shoes. 'I bottled out.'

'Me too.'

John looked up and furrowed his brow at the woman with the tear-stained face. She could have been in her thirties or well in her forties; it was hard to tell in the fading light.

John drew closer. 'You gate-crashed the party to confront someone too?'

She nodded. 'I couldn't do it either. I found out about the party through an announcement in the newspaper. I knew I shouldn't have come.'

They stared at each other; both taking in the other's pained expression.

'May I?' John asked, indicating a spot on the bench next to her.

She nodded.

John took a seat next to the woman who, on closer inspection, appeared to be in her mid-forties. He saw the fine lines around her mouth and eyes, and whispers of grey streaking her long blonde hair. John looked away, in case she thought he was staring, and remembered the bottle in his hand. He held it up. 'Would you like a drink?'

The woman shook her head – no.

John looked at the bottle. The urge to get plastered had dissipated, which was just as well; he knew he couldn't hold his liquor. If he got drunk, he was liable to do something very foolish, like march back into the party and announce that Bertram was a right royal shit. That wasn't a bad idea in itself, it's just that he was worried what Sylvie would think of him stumbling into their party blind drunk, not to mention what he was doing in New York.

He put the bottle and glass on the seat next to him and turned his attention to his new acquaintance. He held out his hand. 'I'm John, by the way.'

'You're British,' she said as she took his hand.

'What gave me away?'

She wiped her eyes dry and smiled at his British sense of humour. 'I'm Amelia.'

John returned her smile. 'You're American.'

'How did you know?' she said, feigning surprise.

John laughed at that.

They both fell silent and sat there listening to the sound of the jazz band coming from the house. John was still preoccupied with thoughts of Sylvie with that scumbag. Thinking of scumbags, he wondered about the woman sitting next to him. He glanced her way. John was dying to ask what she was doing here – or more specifically, who she'd come here to confront. He didn't know any of the guests at the party, so it would be of no consequence if she gave him their name. But it still didn't stop John speculating. Maybe she was here to confront a husband or boyfriend who had left her for somebody else.

It was now almost pitch dark. John was about to suggest they make their way back to the house when Amelia broke the silence. 'I bet you're dying to ask me what I'm doing here or, more to the point, who I came here to confront.'

John shook his head vigorously, adding a little fib. 'The thought hadn't even crossed my mind.' There was just enough light for him to catch a look on her face that said: Don't lie.

'Oh, all right,' John admitted. 'Yes, I am intrigued. I was only at the party for a few minutes, but I didn't see anybody around your age. They were all in their sixties. Apart from a young woman who—'

'Her name is Amy.'

John looked at her in surprise. 'You know her?'

'Yes. She's my daughter.'

'Ah.' John was getting the picture. This woman had found out her daughter was carrying on with someone who was old enough to be her father, and she was here to put a stop to it.

'I wanted to see her before the wedding…'

John hoped it was to talk some sense into her daughter and tell her she had to break things off with Bertram.

'But then I caught sight of Bertram and I… I couldn't go through with it.'

John could feel his hackles rise. 'It's Bertram who is in the wrong here. How old is your daughter?'

'She's almost twenty-one.'

'A young woman having an affair with a man in his sixties…' John shook his head. 'Money is obviously the attraction. But he shouldn't abuse his position by taking advantage of a young, gullible—'

'What are you talking about?'

'Bertram carrying on with a much younger woman – with Amy.'

Amelia stared at John.

John felt uncomfortable under her gaze. 'What is it?'

'Bertram may well have dated younger women. In fact, I'm pretty sure he has, but Amy isn't one of them.'

'Why do you say that?'

She looked at him askance. 'You don't know Bertram all that well, do you?'

'I don't know him at all. I told you, I gate-crashed the party. It was my wife I really came here to see.'

'Then you don't know that Bertram has a daughter.'

John raised his eyebrows; that was news to him.

'It's Amy.'

Amy? John's eyebrows shot up. Now it all made sense. The young woman, with the child in the buggy, he'd seen in the foyer of a hotel in London. She wasn't there, demanding to meet the father of her child. She was there to see her own father. They had obviously had a falling out over something. Whatever the case, she was now staying in his hotel in New York, and he had invited her to the engagement party. They'd clearly patched things up since John last set eyes on her in London.

It dawned on him what a fool he would have been if he'd confronted Bertram in front of Sylvie, and all the guests at the party over a relationship that turned out to be not at all what he thought. John cringed. He couldn't believe he had jumped to conclusions before finding out the facts. That wasn't like him. John knew why he had. He wanted it to be true because he had to find something that would tarnish Bertram's reputation in Sylvie's eyes.

He still couldn't get his head around the fact that he'd got it so wrong. John almost had to hear it again. He turned to Amelia and said, 'Amy is Bertram's daughter?' as if to say, are you sure?

She nodded. 'And mine.'

'Pardon me?'

'I know what you're thinking: after all these years how could I crawl out of the woodwork and assume I had any right to turn up at my daughter's engagement party and—'

'Wait!' John held up his hand. 'Did you just say this is your daughter's engagement party?'

'Yes, of course. Why – whose party did you think it was?'

'Oh, er nevermind.' John rolled his eyes. It all made sense now. He'd seen Sylvie and the young woman together in Central Park. Sylvie knew Bertram's daughter, Amy. Perhaps she had even helped Amy plan her engagement party.

'Now you can see why I bottled out and couldn't go through with it.'

John had completely lost the thread. He focused on Amelia. 'Is it because of Bertram?' he ventured. 'Didn't he want Amy to invite you to her engagement party?'

'Oh, if it were that simple.' She sighed heavily and then burst into tears.

John's eyes went wide in surprise. He didn't know what to do. He reached into his pocket and found a clean handkerchief, which he awkwardly dangled in front of her.

Amelia looked up at John as she reached for the handkerchief. 'I did a terrible thing.'

'I'm sure it can't be as bad as all that,' John said in a soothing tone.

She shook her head, wiped her nose, and turned to John. 'I'm afraid it is.'

John eyed her thoughtfully. A conversation he'd had with Angelo came to mind. They were parked outside the hotel when Angelo told John something about the hotel owner that he wasn't aware of. Some years ago, Bertram's wife had disappeared under mysterious circumstances. John looked at the woman he had met in the grounds of Bertram's mansion. 'Do you want to talk about it?'

She swallowed hard, looked into John's blue-grey eyes, and told him her story. Twenty years ago, she was a student from a privileged background. She had begged her parents to let her study in London. When she arrived, she wanted to immerse herself in the whole student experience. She tried to act just like her peers, who were working part-time jobs to fund their studies. Amelia didn't need the money, but she started a part-time job just for the hell of it. That job would change her life.

She worked as a waitress in a hotel restaurant. That's where she met Bertram. He was twenty years her senior. Bertram had just turned forty, but despite the age difference, Amelia was instantly attracted to him. He was serious, driven and nothing like the young men from old money who she had dated back home. They were boys compared. Boys with no vision, no motivation, and no charisma. Bertram, by comparison, was someone she could fall in love with. Someone she did fall in love with.

Contrary to what some may think, it was she who had chased after him and badgered him to go out on a date with her, not the other way around. At first, he refused. She had never met anyone before who had rejected her advances. Her persistence paid off, and he relented. And the rest was history. After a brief courtship, they were married before her first trip home from college to visit her parents.

Her parents were horrified that she had returned with a ring on her finger. Worse still, she had married a man twice her age who had not even bothered to visit America with his wife to meet her family. She had explained he was a terribly busy man, building his hotel empire. They weren't impressed. As far as they were concerned, he had taken advantage of their daughter, which couldn't have been further from the truth.

They lived together in marital bliss, and travelled the world as he built his business, until their daughter, Amy, came along. Amelia hadn't been ready for motherhood. She loved visiting exotic places and living out of a suitcase in hotels. Bertram wanted a family and a wife who would stay at home and look after the children while he was away on extended business trips. She missed staying in hotels and seeing the exotic places she could no longer travel to because he wanted her to stay home with their child.

'I was young and selfish and never knew I had it so good,' confessed Amelia. 'I had a lovely home in a leafy part of London, a beautiful baby daughter, and a husband who doted on me – when he was around. But it wasn't enough. I didn't want to be a stay-at-home mom. I wanted adventure.' She paused. 'That's when I made the worst decision of my life. I have regretted it ever since.'

'What did you do?'

'I left our daughter with the nanny one morning, walked out the door and never came back.'

John didn't know what to say.

'There, you see. I told you I did something terrible.'

John *still* didn't know what to say. He couldn't imagine walking out on his children. 'Didn't you try to contact Amy before now?'

'Yes, on many, many occasions. It was only a few months later, when I was on the road travelling through India with a group of backpackers, that I saw a mother with a small boy drawing water from a well. It was a scene I'd encountered many times before, but for some reason, on that day, the enormity of what I'd done, leaving my child and the man I loved – hit me. I was young, foolish, and impetuous. I had no business being a wife and a mother – at least that's what I thought. But somewhere along that road to Delhi, bumping along a dirt track in the back of an old bus, I grew up. And I wanted my old life back.'

John said softly, 'But that didn't happen.'

She shook her head. 'He had me declared an unfit mother in my absence. I wasn't unfit. I just made a foolish, selfish decision to leave them because I was young and naïve. He was hurt. I understand that. I hurt them both, but I wanted to come back. It was Bertram's stubborn refusal to forgive me...'

'Did you try to see your daughter?' John ventured.

'Of course. I wrote letters. I telephoned. I turned up at his address in London. In the end, I returned to America to fight him through the courts to get access, but I had no money. My parents refused to support me and help me out financially. Their attitude was that I'd made my bed and... well... I got what I deserved.'

'That's harsh.'

'Is it? Eventually, I came around to believing they were right. After walking out on them, I didn't deserve to see my daughter. The only glimmer of hope was when I received a notification that he was filing for divorce. I knew we'd have to start communicating again, even if it was through lawyers. But the divorce papers never came.'

'You're still married to Bertram?' said John in surprise.

She nodded. 'Weird – huh? We've been married for over twenty years, and I haven't seen him in all that time. I've had relationships since, but nothing ever led to re-marrying, which was just as well, I guess.'

'How could someone forget to file for divorce?' John was thinking aloud. He looked at Amelia.

She just shrugged.

John narrowed his eyes in quiet contemplation. This was an interesting turn of events. Why, in all these years, hadn't Bertram filed a petition for divorce? John was quite sure, under the circumstances, it would have been granted. So why didn't he? Was it simply the case that he had forgotten, however unlikely that may seem? Or was it something else?

John stared at the woman sitting next to him. Could it be

that Bertram was still in love with his wife, he just hadn't acknowledged that fact? And what about Amelia? In all these years, why hadn't she severed all ties with Bertram permanently, by filing for a divorce herself?

She caught him staring at her. 'What is it – what are you thinking?'

John selfishly thought that if he could get these two back together, then perhaps he might still be in for a chance with Sylvie. John did not speak his mind. Instead, he said, 'Does Amy know you're here?'

She shook her head. 'I came here to see my daughter, but when I saw Bertram, I was afraid he'd stop me before I had a chance to talk to her.'

'What do you think he told Amy, over the years, about her mother – about you?'

'That's just it – I don't know. I sent letters, birthday cards, and Christmas cards but I heard nothing back. I suspect she never received them.'

It struck John what a world of grief we create for ourselves when we stop listening to the ones we love and let the lines of communication breakdown. It didn't have to be that way. John was thinking about Sylvie. Despite his Dear John letter, he resolved to talk to her before he left New York – come what may. But he had to concede that this was neither the time nor the place. It was Amy's engagement party, and the last thing he wanted to do was reach out to Sylvie and risk ruining Amy's party if it all went horribly wrong. John winced. He knew only too well from past experience things didn't always go according to plan.

Amelia got up from the bench.

John looked up. 'Where are you going?'

'I'm leaving.'

'Wait!' John stood up. It might be too late for him and Sylvie, it might be too late for Amelia and Bertram, but as a father, he couldn't watch her leave without at least knowing she had tried to reconcile with her daughter. 'Go see your daughter first. You might not get another chance.'

She paused.

'Don't for god's sake leave it and gate-crash the wedding instead.' John wasn't joking. 'Do it now. You're her mother. What if she's been looking for you? I bet she would love to know that you want to be in her life.'

'After all these years – are you certain?'

John wasn't sure of anything. All he knew was that if he had the opportunity to make it up to his daughter, Harriet, in any way he could, then that's what he would do. She still wasn't speaking to him after that debacle over Gertie. It was just unfortunate that his son-in-law, Dominic, had unexpectedly turned up to collect Gertie early. If it weren't for that, they wouldn't have found out he'd left her for a couple of hours with a trusted friend without their permission.

It was even more unfortunate that as a consequence of banning both grandparents from seeing Gertie, he had called his parents down from up North to stay over and help out with Gertie for the time being. John rolled his eyes. He knew why it hadn't all blown over, and Harriet still wasn't speaking to him. She had the in-laws living with her, no doubt driving her crazy. They never got on.

John was thinking of Gertie when he casually said, 'Besides, now Amy is a mother I'm sure she'd want you in her life.'

'She's a mother?'

'Oh.' John looked at her, aghast.

'I have a grandchild?'

'A boy,' said John slowly.

She burst into tears.

John put a tentative arm around her shoulders. 'I had no idea you didn't know.'

'It's all right.' She found John's handkerchief in her pocket and wiped her eyes. 'I think I've made up my mind.'

John released her and stepped back.

'I'm going to find my daughter,' she said forthrightly.

John nodded. 'I'll just hang back here while you—'

Amelia was already striding purposefully up the path towards the house.

John watched her cross the lawn and enter the house. 'Good luck,' he whispered.

He sat down on the bench once more and wondered how they were going to react when she made an appearance...

31

'To the happy couple,' said Bertram, raising his glass to toast his daughter and future son-in-law. He winked affectionately at Amy, who was standing to his left, and then glanced around the crowd of friends and acquaintances gathered before them.

Bertram had just raised the glass of champagne to his lips when a woman stepped forward. A woman Bertram would recognise anywhere. His heart skipped a beat.

Amy had just finished her glass of champagne when she glanced at her father and saw his glass suspended in mid-air, his face ashen. 'Daddy, what's wrong?'

The jazz band resumed, and the crowd dispersed, oblivious to the drama that was about to unfold.

The woman stepped closer. 'Hello, Bertram.'

Amy looked from her father to the woman standing in front of them. 'Who are you?'

The woman turned her head and stared at Amy. 'You're all grown up. And you are so beautiful.'

Amy said, 'Do I know you?'

'I'm... I'm your mother.'

Amy shook her head and glared at the woman. 'I don't know

what your game is. My mother is dead.'

Amelia's eyes went wide. Her bottom lip quivered. She turned to Bertram. 'Is that what you told her?'

'You shouldn't be here,' Bertram hissed. 'I didn't invite you.'

Amy looked at her father sharply. 'Who is she?'

'I want you to leave,' said Bertram, ignoring Amy.

'Daddy, who is she?'

Bertram heaved a great sigh and turned to Amy. 'Look, I can explain…'

Amy stepped back and felt her fiancé's hand reach for hers. She clutched Ralph's hand as the woman walked over and stood beside her father.

'Oh my god!' Amy's eyes flickered between her father and her mother. 'Oh. My. God.' She turned on her father. 'How could you lie to me all these years?'

Bertram reached out a consoling hand. 'Look, I was trying to protect you. She left us. I didn't want her to hurt us again.'

Amy narrowed her eyes. 'Were you thinking of me when you cut her out of my life or were you thinking of yourself?'

Amelia turned to look at Bertram. 'Is it true, you couldn't see me because you were afraid I would…' she felt a lump in her throat, 'break your heart again?'

'And you!' Amy rounded on her mother. 'You left me when I was a baby. How could you?'

'I tried to see you.'

'Well, you didn't try hard enough – did you?'

'I'm sorry,' Amelia said in a small voice.

'Amy…' Ralph cut in, 'perhaps we should all calm down—'

'You mean, I should calm down!' Amy let go of his hand and pointed at the two of them. 'You've ruined my party – both of you.' Amy looked at her parents and burst into tears. What she meant was they'd ruined her life.

All she wanted growing up was to be part of a family. Her dad bought her everything money could buy, clothes, exotic vacations, an expensive education. However, he couldn't give her the one thing she thought she'd never have – a mum of her own. And now she discovered he had it in his power to do just that. He had connections. He could have found her. But for his own selfish reasons, he chose not to.

'I hate you!' Amy shouted and ran out of the room.

Amelia and Bertram exchanged a glance, wondering which of them that comment was directed at.

John was walking up the garden towards the house, with his bottle of champagne still unopened and an empty wine glass in his hand, when he saw a young woman streak past him. John turned to see who it was and thought he recognised Amy. He turned back to the house and almost ran straight into Bertram, who passed John in a hair's breadth, calling out, 'Amy, please stop. I'm sorry...'

Next up was Sylvie. John stepped back in surprise and watched her pass by, taking no notice of the man standing in the middle of the lawn holding a wine bottle and a glass.

'Bertram – wait!' she called out.

Bertram came to a halt. He bent over double, holding his sides and panting.

John looked back at the house, wondering whether anyone else was going to make the sprint down the garden. Sure enough, a young man appeared at the back door. He paused for a moment, as if looking for someone, then darted out the door. He sprinted past John.

As he legged it down the garden, passing Sylvie and Bertram, he glanced over his shoulder and shouted, 'Bertram, you're an idiot!'

John raised his empty glass. 'I'll drink to that.' He guessed that was the fiancé. He was also guessing that whatever had gone on in there when Amelia made her presence known, Bertram was not in anyone's good books. John smiled at the thought. He would love to linger and find out what happened next, but he knew he had better return to the house before someone realised it was John Baxter, standing in the middle of the lawn. He was about to do just that when he heard Sylvie's voice...

'I can't believe you told her she was dead!'

John turned around and sidestepped to his left, hiding in the shadows of an American sycamore tree.

'Well, I hardly expected her to show up at the engagement party,' replied Bertram, sounding breathless. 'I didn't invite her. Hell, I didn't even know where she was.'

'What kind of excuse is that?'

John was still smiling. He could tell by the tone of her voice that Bertram was in trouble. He was about to leave the safe haven of the sycamore tree when he spotted Amy and her fiancé striding back up the lawn in their direction.

The first thing out of Amy's mouth was, 'The wedding is off.'

John's smile faded. He was thinking what a shame if Amy had been put off getting married because of her parents' mistakes.

Bertram said, 'Amy, you can't call the wedding off because of us.'

'Who said anything about calling off the wedding?'

'But you just said—'

'I'm not getting married here, in New York. That's what I meant. We're going home. I'm having my own ceremony back in England, just me, my fiancé, his parents, and some close friends. And you aren't invited, neither of you. Oh, I don't mean you, Sylvie. You're still invited. I meant my... *that* woman.' Amy looked about her. 'Where is she, anyway?'

Everyone looked about them.

John slunk further into the shadows under the great sycamore tree.

Bertram said, 'Amy, please reconsider. I have spent a small fortune on—'

'For god's sake!' Amy stamped her foot. 'You don't get it, do you? I don't need the glitz and the glamour. I don't want all this. I just want a simple affair. I was only doing this for you, Daddy, because it's what you want. But if the engagement party is anything to go by, then I dread to think what you've got planned for the wedding.'

Bertram grimaced. 'What does that mean?'

'Everything with you is grand gestures.' Amy threw her arms wide.

'I just want the best for you.'

'Well, sometimes the best doesn't have to cost the earth.'

John nodded his head in agreement.

Bertram fell silent.

'Look, Daddy, I don't know any of these people and I didn't want them at my engagement party, and I bloody well don't want them at my wedding. I want my friends, and the people I know like my good neighbours in the little terraced street where I live to be at my wedding. Not all these fancy people.'

'But I did all this for you, Amy.'

Amy sighed so loudly John could hear her from where he was standing fifty yards away.

'Why can't you just be normal like my fiancé's mum and dad?'

John edged out of the shadows of the sycamore tree to risk a glance at Bertram. He was wearing an expensive tuxedo. With his shock of white hair and deep tan, he wouldn't have been out of place in an episode of *Dynasty*. In fact, that's what the whole bash reminded him of. It was a bit surreal, like he'd just stepped into some eighties American soap.

'I suppose it could have been worse.'

John jumped at the sound of a voice right behind him. It was Amelia. She'd joined him under the sycamore tree.

John turned to face her. He had to ask, 'Just how could it have been any worse?'

'I don't know. I just said it to make me feel better.' She glanced toward her husband and daughter arguing on the lawn. 'You heard what happened then?'

'I guess things didn't go according to plan.' John sighed. 'I have a confession to make. That tends to happen when I'm around. I have a habit of screwing things up.'

'It's not your fault, John. Don't blame yourself.'

'But I do. I'm so sorry. I should never have encouraged you to go in there and—'

'It wasn't your doing. After all, that's what I came here to do. It's just that I lost my nerve until...'

'I showed up,' said John, groaning loudly. 'I can be quite the idiot sometimes, I can tell you.'

'I'm sure that's not true.'

'Oh, you don't know the half of it.' He thought of Harriet storming off the way Amy had not a minute ago. It reminded him of that awful day Harriet and Dominic took Gertie away. John didn't want to think about that. He hoped to goodness it had all blown over by the time he returned home. He missed his granddaughter like the blazes.

She touched his arm. 'Are you all right?'

John turned to look at her. 'It's me who should ask you that question, not the other way around.'

'I guess we've all got our crosses to bear.'

John nodded. 'I guess so.' He looked over at the house. 'Are you staying in a hotel hereabouts? Can I get you a taxi?' John was fishing in his pocket for his mobile phone when his hand alighted on his wallet. John rolled his eyes when he remembered he didn't have any money to pay for a taxi. Still, that didn't stop him from calling one for her. He'd just have to make do with sleeping on the garden bench until first light. Then he'd have to hitchhike back to New York City.

'I don't want to be alone tonight.'

That stopped John in his tracks. He looked at her in surprise. 'Excuse me?'

'I guess you're staying in a hotel. I could sleep on your couch if you have one. I won't be any bother. You won't even know I'm there. I just don't want to be alone tonight.'

John felt somehow responsible. If he hadn't happened along, then perhaps she wouldn't have gate-crashed the party after all and got everyone in such a pickle. John glanced at Bertram and Amy. Bertram was holding out pleading hands, to no avail. Amy and her fiancé stormed off down the garden.

John turned to Amelia and said, 'Of course you can sleep

with me tonight. Oh. Goodness. Did I just say that? What I meant was—'

'It's all right, John.' She linked her arm in his. 'I know you'll be the perfect gentleman.'

John smiled at her. 'And I know you'll be the perfect lady.'

'How can you be so sure?' she said, teasing him.

John laughed. He liked that through it all, she could still keep a sense of humour. 'I better call for a cab.' John just hoped she wouldn't think him any less a gentleman when he couldn't pay for the taxi fare.

'I came in my car. I could drive us back to your hotel?'

He didn't need to be asked twice. If she were staying overnight in his hotel room, he would insist on taking the couch, but it was a darn sight preferable to sleeping on a garden bench.

Down the garden, John could hear Bertram calling after Amy, beseeching her to stay in New York for the wedding.

He turned his head in their direction. 'Come on, we better get going before they see us.'

She nodded at John and fell in step with as they started for the house. 'Do you think he's going to be okay?'

'Who – Bertram?' He looked at Amelia, surprised by her apparent concern. John wasn't feeling in the slightest bit sympathetic towards Bertram and his current predicament. He'd lied to his daughter all these years. He was an idiot, simple as that.

John caught Amelia staring at him, still waiting for an answer to her question. 'Is he going to be okay, do you think?'

John furrowed his brow. Something occurred to him that was, on the face of it, a ridiculous thought: was it possible that after all these years, despite what Bertram had done, she was still in love with him?

32

'If she thinks that after all these years she can just walk back into my life and everything will be fine, she can think again,' said Amy haughtily. 'And as for Dad...' She was so angry with him she couldn't even put into words how she was feeling about him right now.

Sylvie understood Amy was upset. 'Amy, have you spoken to your father since the party last night?'

'No, and I don't intend to.'

Amy's fiancé walked across the lobby towards them and perched on the arm of the leather high-backed chair where she was sitting. He looked down at Rory, fidgeting on Amy's lap, and reached over to brush a lock of hair out of his eyes. He said to Amy, 'I've ordered a taxi for the airport.'

'Good.'

Sylvie stood there staring at all their luggage piled up, ready to be loaded into a taxi. 'Do you have to leave?'

'I want to go home, Sylvie.'

Sylvie looked at Ralph. 'Can't you at least speak to Bertram before you go?'

He shook his head. 'I'm sorry, Sylvie. I'm with Amy on this

one. This is the last straw. How did he think it was okay to keep something like this from her for all these years? Her mother is alive, for goodness' sake.'

Sylvie shook her head from side to side. Bertram was an idiot. She told him that in no uncertain terms on the way back from the party in the limo. What was he thinking? That the truth would never come out? In Sylvie's experience – she was thinking of John trying to conceal the financial mess he had got them into because of the house conversion – one way or another the truth will out, as they say.

Sylvie thought about that tense journey back to the hotel last night. Just the two of them in his limo. She knew that after the party, when the guests left, Bertram's idea was that they all stayed the night. Rory was already asleep upstairs. In fact, it sounded as though Bertram wanted his family to move out of the hotel and stay in the Hamptons until the wedding. His plans were scuppered when Amy took Rory from his bed – still in his pyjamas – and left with her fiancé in a taxi.

Amy wasn't the only one not speaking to Bertram. By the time the limo arrived at the hotel late last night, Sylvie wasn't talking to him either. She still couldn't believe he had told Amy her mother was dead.

'As far as I was concerned, she was dead,' Bertram had said, as if that made it perfectly acceptable to lie to his daughter.

Sylvie couldn't accept what she was hearing. 'What sort of excuse is that?' Sylvie had retorted. 'To do that to Amy, deny her access to her mother is just plain wrong. I understand that she was the one who left you, Bertram, but couldn't you swallow your pride for the sake of your child?'

Bertram had turned away in that moment and spent the rest

of the ninety-minute journey staring glumly out of the window into the black night.

Sylvie remembered sitting in the back of the limo staring at Bertram, until something occurred to her that was, on the face of it, a ridiculous thought: was it possible that after all these years he was still in love with her?

The concierge crossed the lobby and came to a halt in front of the pile of luggage. 'Your taxi has arrived, sir.' He picked up a suitcase and motioned for another member of staff to help with the luggage.

Amy passed Rory to her fiancé and stood up. She turned to Sylvie.

Sylvie opened her arms and stepped forward to give her a hug. 'I'm going to miss you.' Sylvie released her. 'All of you.'

Amy's fiancé smiled at Sylvie. 'Likewise.' He glanced at Amy before he added, 'When we've sorted out the details, we're going to send you an invitation to our wedding.'

Amy nodded. 'You will come, won't you?'

'Of course I will.' Sylvie didn't bother asking if Bertram and her mother were getting an invitation.

Ralph said to Rory, 'Say bye bye to Sylvie.'

He waved a podgy little hand at Sylvie. 'Ba-ba.'

Sylvie took one look at Rory and was quite overcome. 'I think I'm going to cry.'

Amy found a tissue for Sylvie. 'We'll keep in touch I promise.'

By the time they had said their goodbyes, they had loaded the luggage into the taxi. Sylvie glanced around the lobby. To her surprise, Bertram hadn't appeared to talk them out of leaving.

Sylvie walked with them to the door of the hotel and watched Amy's fiancé carry Rory outside to the waiting taxi.

Amy lingered by the door. She cast a look back at the lobby, as though she was searching for something – or someone.

Sylvie watched her and inwardly groaned. She knew who Amy was looking out for. Bertram had an opportunity right here, right now, to tell Amy the truth: why he had to cut Amelia out of his life and, as a result, out of hers. It was obvious – she'd broken his heart.

She followed Amy's gaze to the empty lobby and shook her head sadly when she realised Bertram wasn't coming. Sylvie turned back to Amy. She saw her shoulders sag as a look of utter disappointment swept across her face; she knew it, too.

'Well, this is it,' said Amy. 'It's time I left.'

'I know.' Sylvie sighed. 'You can't hang on any longer.'

A knowing look passed between them.

Amy stepped outside and waved goodbye.

Standing by the hotel entrance watching them get ready to leave, Sylvie felt terribly homesick, missing her family dreadfully. She thought *to hell with the show*. Sylvie had the sudden impulse to run out to the taxi before it departed and go with them to the airport in the hope she could catch a flight home today. Sylvie had her handbag with her passport inside. She'd just have to get her luggage sent on.

Sylvie stood there, procrastinating until it was too late. The taxi moved off into the morning traffic and sped down Park Avenue in the direction of the airport. She stood there watching the taxi fade into the distance with a mixture of regret, disappointment, and frustration. Regret that she hadn't said to hell with it and gone with them to the airport. Disappointment that they were no longer here in New York, new friends and familiar faces she had grown accustomed to seeing every day.

Frustration that after everything she'd done to help Bertram mend his relationship with his daughter, he'd blown it. Sylvie heaved a sigh and stepped back into the hotel lobby.

She was heading to the restaurant for some breakfast when she passed by the reception desk, and something caught her eye; the key to room 223 wasn't hanging on the hook. That meant the irresponsible person who had taken Monte for a walk and abandoned him in Central Park was in their bedroom. Sylvie scowled. She was in such a foul mood that this wasn't the right time to confront them. Or perhaps it was. Sylvie stormed off toward the elevator.

As she passed by the restaurant, she stopped abruptly and back-tracked. She stood there looking through the glass doors at a man seated alone at a table. He was eating a croissant. *You idiot!* Sylvie couldn't believe Bertram had been in the restaurant this whole time. She narrowed her eyes. If he was waiting for her to join him, then he would have a long wait. She had no intention of having breakfast with him after this. Besides, she didn't even know if she had time to grab a bite to eat this morning. Sylvie was running out of time to make it to the show. She hadn't factored in meeting Amy in the hotel lobby to see her off. Even though the show didn't air until the afternoon, it wouldn't be long before the limo arrived to take her to the studio. She had to be there several hours before the cameras rolled for hair, makeup, rehearsals and so forth.

Sylvie glanced at her watch as she stepped into the elevator. She didn't have time for breakfast and barely had time to get ready. But if there was one thing she was going to do before she left, it was to confront the person in room number 223. Sylvie was looking forward to it.

'John, shall I get that?' Amelia called out when she heard someone knocking on his bedroom door. She didn't catch his response, but she heard the sound of the shower coming from the en suite bathroom in his bedroom.

On her way to answer the door, she glanced at the sofa where he'd slept last night. The blanket and bed sheet were neatly folded and left on the armrest. He'd also arranged the cushions back on the sofa; she had tossed them off last night when she was helping him make up the sofa bed. He'd even cleared away all the empty little bottles of booze they had consumed after raiding the minibar last night, along with the dirty plates and dishes that were left on the coffee table when she eventually went to bed. After consuming the booze, they had ordered some food, courtesy of room service, and then stayed awake into the early hours chatting about their lives.

She enjoyed listening to John. He was easy-going, amiable and very funny. She laughed out loud when he talked about some of the antics and mishaps that had happened in his house in London when John and his wife started living apart together.

Living apart together. She'd heard of that arrangement whereby couples in a relationship decide to live apart. She had two friends, both divorcees in their forties, who preferred to stay living in their own homes rather than move in together. As far as she could tell, it hadn't affected their relationship – far from it. It was something that she wouldn't rule out if she met someone else.

She wanted to be in a loving relationship like her friends. She just couldn't imagine giving up her personal space. Perhaps that's why, in all these years, she hadn't been in a long-lasting relationship. She didn't want to look after someone. Ironing their shirts, cooking their evening meals, and shopping at the supermarket together; all the boring drudgery that was bad enough when you were on your own, let alone living with someone else.

Amelia knew deep down that she needed to maintain her independence and suspected it had something to do with her work. She was an artist and spent long periods alone painting. When she was working, she locked herself away in her studio for hours at a time, preparing for her exhibitions in New York. Amelia couldn't bear being interrupted.

Her thoughts returned to John. Unlike her friends, John and his wife hadn't chosen this living arrangement. By the sound of it, they had fallen into living apart together because of the house conversion. Despite putting on a brave face, she could tell he wasn't happy about it. Although his British sense of humour meant he could laugh about it — he had her in fits of laughter — she was aware it wasn't really a joking matter; he confided that they were heading for a divorce. The sad part was that although he didn't come right out and say it, she suspected he was still in love with his wife.

A loud, insistent knocking interrupted her reverie. She'd forgotten there was someone at the door. Amelia was still feeling a little worse for wear after staying up, drinking into the early hours. She caught sight of herself in the mirror. Yesterday she had gone to town to make herself look presentable for the party. She knew it would be a big affair. Bertram was hosting the party, and he never did things by halves.

Now she was makeup free and her hair, which had been styled by a hairdresser, was falling about her shoulders in a dishevelled mess. She'd had such a dreadful night, tossing and turning over meeting Amy and all the things she wanted to say to her daughter but never got a chance, that her hair looked as though someone had back-combed it. It was that bad. On top of which, she hadn't bothered to run a brush through it since she got out of bed. As she approached the door, she glanced down at her bare legs; she was still wearing one of John's shirts he'd given her to sleep in.

'Amelia, would you mind answering that?'

She glanced over her shoulder at the sound of John's voice. He must have stepped out of the shower and heard someone knocking on the door. Although she felt embarrassed over her appearance, she was wondering if he had ordered room service and it was the hotel porter delivering breakfast. She bet they had seen a lot worse than this; Amelia was almost unrecognisable from the woman who had confronted Bertram and Amy at the party. Which was just as well because when she opened the door, she instantly recognised the woman standing before her. It was the woman who had been standing next to Bertram when she confronted him last night. Amelia didn't know whether she was just another guest or – something more.

'Well, it's about time. I've been standing out here for ages.'

Amelia gawped at her. Her first thought was that Bertram had sent her. Her next thought was, how did he know she was staying at this hotel? Amelia stood there staring dumbly at the woman until she realised no flash of recognition crossed the woman's face when she answered the door. Amelia concluded she did not recognise her from the party last night. She breathed a sigh of relief and said, 'Can I help you?'

Amelia watched the woman fold her arms in a confrontational gesture. 'I want to have words with you about Monte…'

John walked into the lounge feeling refreshed after that invigorating shower. There was nothing like an American power shower to wash away the cobwebs, he thought. He was just doing up the top button of his shirt when he was surprised to find Amelia standing at the door, talking to the person who had knocked. And she was still wearing his shirt from last night.

He was trying to avert his eyes from staring at her long bare legs when he heard her say, 'Look, I told you before, I have no idea what you're talking about. I didn't take Monte, or whatever the dog's name is, for a walk yesterday.'

John stopped dead when he heard the person on the other side of the door reply, 'I know for a fact it was someone staying in this room. If it wasn't you, then I want to speak to the irresponsible occupant who left Monte in Central Park yesterday.'

Oh god! It was Sylvie. And by the tone of her voice, she was spoiling for an argument. Fortunately, Amelia was sufficiently tall and broad-shouldered to block Sylvie's view into the hotel suite. Otherwise she would have spotted her husband backing up towards the bedroom door, looking as guilty as hell.

Amelia glanced over her shoulder at that moment and caught John backing out of the room.

John stopped dead like a rabbit caught in headlights. He furiously shook his head and motioned for her to shut the door.

She frowned at John. Amelia turned back to the woman at the door. 'Sorry, can you give me a minute?' She didn't wait for an answer before pushing the door shut. Amelia glared at John and held up her hands as if to say *what's your problem?* She waved at him to get over here and deal with this.

319

John took another step back and shook his head.

Amelia strode across the room and stopped in front of him. She whispered, 'What's the problem?'

John whispered back, 'I can't come to the door.'

'Why not?'

John stared at Amelia, wearing nothing but his shirt.

'It's complicated.'

'She seems very cross. What did you do? Is it about Monte?'

'Er – not exactly.'

'What's going on in there?' Sylvie's voice could be heard from behind the door. 'I can hear you whispering…'

They both looked over at the door.

John turned back to Amelia and cupped his hands together in a pleading gesture. 'Please – you *have* to get rid of her.'

Amelia narrowed her eyes. She slowly turned her head toward the door. When she turned back to look at John, what she was thinking was written all over her face – *you know her.*

John smiled nervously.

'Who is she?'

John hesitated. 'She's my wife.'

'Your wife!' Amelia said in surprise. Then she looked down at John's shirt she was wearing. 'Oh.'

John whispered, 'Exactly!'

'I thought you came to New York alone?'

John sighed. 'It's a long story.'

Amelia looked up at John, raising her eyebrows at him to spill the beans and tell her what was going on.

John glanced anxiously at the door. 'On top of which she doesn't exactly know I'm here, in New York. It's a—'

'—Long story.' She eyed John. 'Okay, leave it with me.'

John breathed a sigh of relief and ran into the bedroom. He hid behind the door and heard Amelia say to Sylvie, 'Look, my husband apologises about Monte, but he can't come to the door right now because he is only in his underpants.'

John clamped a hand to his mouth to stop the sudden urge to laugh.

'Well, um in that case,' said Sylvie, sounding flustered, 'I hope he realises he was lucky that I found Monte and brought him back to the hotel.'

'I'll be sure to tell him.'

'He should think twice before he gets a pet of his own. You can't just abandon them, you know.'

'I will tell him that too.'

When John heard the door to his hotel room click shut, he breathed an enormous sigh of relief.

Amelia popped her head around the door. 'She's gone.'

'Thank god.' John collapsed on the sofa in relief. All he could think about was Sylvie finding him in a hotel room with a woman twenty years his junior, wearing nothing but his shirt. Would she believe him when he told her it was as innocent as the day is young and he had slept on the couch? He doubted it.

'John, can I ask you a question?'

'Of course.'

'Bertram and your wife...' began Amelia.

John looked up. He had an idea what was on her mind. 'You saw them at the party together, didn't you?'

'Yes.'

'Are they *together*?'

He sat there, rubbing his temples. 'Honestly, I don't know what the nature of their relationship is.'

'Is that what you're here to find out?'

'Not exactly. It's a—'

She cocked her head to one side.

'Sorry,' John apologised. 'But it is a long story.'

Talking of long stories brought to mind his column, Dear John, and why he was here in New York. He glanced at his watch. He'd all but forgotten about the show this afternoon. At least the limo wasn't picking him up until mid-morning, which meant he had time for a relaxing breakfast.

Not that he imagined he'd eat much. John felt absurdly nervous about the show this afternoon and meeting his nemesis on live television.

Amelia slumped down on the sofa next to John, looking miserable.

He took in her grim expression. 'Look, if it's any consolation, I know for a fact they are staying in separate hotel rooms.'

'Really?'

'Yes.' John paused. 'You still love him – don't you.'

A single tear rolled down her cheek. 'I can't believe, after all these years, he's still the love of my life. That's crazy, isn't it?'

'Not at all.' John smiled at her, trying not to think of the love of his life sitting down and writing him that Dear John letter before packing her suitcases and moving out. His smile faded. 'You know I keep telling you it's a long story.'

She wiped the tear from her cheek and nodded.

'Well, I'll tell you something: it all began when we stopped communicating. It seems simple enough now. All we had to do was sit down and talk things through before one thing led to another and... well, here we are.'

She sat nodding her head. 'I should have told him how I was

feeling all those years ago but instead, I just walked out, and as you say: here we are.'

They both sat in silence for some minutes.

Amelia suddenly stood up. 'Let's get out of here. Come to mine for breakfast.'

John looked up at her. 'Yours?'

'Sure. I live in Greenwich Village. I'll cook us an all-American breakfast. Eggs, bacon, ham, hash browns – the works.'

John was about to say yes when he remembered he had somewhere to be. He glanced at his watch.

She noticed John checking the time. 'Greenwich Village isn't that far. We won't be long.'

John smiled at her. 'Why not. I'll just grab my coat.' John bounced off the sofa and headed for the door.

'Er... John.'

John was putting on his coat. He turned around.

'I need to change out of your shirt before we go.'

33

John opened the door a fraction and peeked outside.

'Is the coast clear?'

He checked up and down the hallway. 'I think so,' he replied, glancing over his shoulder at Amelia.

It hadn't taken her long to freshen up. She'd changed out of his shirt and put her party clothes back on, as that was all she had with her. The biggest change was her hair. When John first saw her this morning, she looked as though she'd had a rough night, which didn't surprise him after the events at the party. Her hair was a tangled mess. Now she looked much better. She'd taken a quick shower and brushed her long blonde hair, leaving it to dry naturally. She'd also applied some makeup, not much but enough to highlight her eyes and add some colour to her cheeks.

John eyed Amelia and checked one last time that Sylvie wasn't marching up the hallway towards his room. He wouldn't put it past her to make a return visit in order to speak to Amelia's so-called husband about Monte. He didn't fancy the thought of trying to explain to Sylvie what he was doing, stepping out of a hotel room with a young lady who happened to be Bertram's wife. Never mind what he was doing in New York.

The coast was still clear. They both stepped outside. John closed the door behind them. He just hoped he didn't see Sylvie in the elevator like last time. He was about to suggest they take the stairs when he saw Amelia slip on her heels. John glanced at her high heels and decided against the stairs.

Fortunately, they rode down to the ground floor alone. When the elevator doors opened, John made sure the coast was clear before they stepped out into the lobby. The first thing he did on their way out was introduce Amelia to Monte.

She bent down, gave Monte a brief pat on the head, and looked apologetically at John. 'I'm not really a dog kind of person.'

He smiled. 'They grow on you, you'd be surprised.'

'I'll take your word for it.' Her hand was wet where the puppy had licked her. She grimaced.

John found a clean tissue in his pocket. 'Here.'

'Thanks.'

They were just passing the restaurant on their way out when Amelia came to an abrupt halt.

John made his way across the lobby, preoccupied with thoughts of Sylvie spotting him in the hotel. He'd just reached the door and was about to step outside when he realised Amelia was no longer with him. John looked around and spotted her. He walked back toward the elevators and stopped beside her, wondering what had caught her attention. She was standing outside the restaurant staring at something – or someone.

'Would you prefer breakfast in the hotel, after all?'

She shook her head.

John followed her gaze. There in the middle of the dining room was Bertram, sitting at a table. John noticed there were no tell-tale signs of other plates or cutlery on the table, apart from his own, suggesting he was breakfasting alone. Clearly, he was still not in Sylvie's good books after she found out he had lied to his daughter all these years.

John wasn't surprised. He knew if there was one thing Sylvie abhorred, it was lies. She always told the truth, no matter what, and expected other people to do the same. It seemed that people had a habit of disappointing her. John wasn't just thinking of Bertram, he included himself, too.

He turned to Amelia. 'You should talk to him.'

She shook her head. 'He won't want that.'

'How do you know? Besides, what have you got to lose?'

She turned to face John. 'But what about that breakfast I promised you?'

'Rain check?' said John, just being polite. This was his last day in New York. He was leaving first thing tomorrow morning for the airport.

Amelia walked over to the restaurant door and paused. She turned to look at John as if to say: *are you sure I'm doing the right thing?*

He offered an encouraging smile. 'Just tell him how you feel.'

She nodded.

John turned to go.

'John!'

He turned back. 'Yes?'

'Perhaps you should take your own advice.'

'Huh?'

'Speak to your wife. Tell her how you feel. What have you got to lose?' She gave him a tentative smile before opening the door to the restaurant. She paused a moment, as if summoning up the courage to take the next step, then she walked inside.

John hung back, taking a risk that Bertram might spot him if he glanced this way. He watched with trepidation as she approached his table. He saw Bertram look up. John held his breath. It seemed like an eternity; Bertram sitting at the table, Amelia standing there opposite him, their eyes locked on each other. He guessed they were both unsure how to proceed.

Bertram pushed his chair back and stood up.

John's eyebrows shot up. This was just what he was afraid of: Bertram, like the fool he was, would throw away his one opportunity to make things right.

John knew what he'd do if Bertram came storming out. He'd give him what for and send him back to talk to her, if not for her sake, then for the sake of their daughter, Amy. John hoped it wouldn't come to that, but if he had to reveal he was here in New York, then so be it.

John watched with interest as Bertram stood there at the table. He wasn't storming out of the restaurant, as John had expected. A smile crept to his lips when he saw Bertram skirt the table and pull out the chair opposite him for her to join him. Bertram's hand brushed her shoulder as she sat down. He then resumed his seat and called over to the waiter.

John was about to leave when Amelia looked in his direction. She mouthed thank you.

When Bertram turned in his seat to see who had caught her attention, no one was there.

John was crossing the lobby, aiming for he knew not where, when the concierge ran up behind him and tapped him on the shoulder.

He turned around and found himself holding the dog's leash.

John shook his head. 'I haven't got time for—'

'Oh, but you owe me one.'

John furrowed his brow. 'What are you talking about? I walked Monte yesterday, remember?'

When he realised there was no one else to walk the dog, John relented. 'Oh, all right. I'll just have to make the time.'

The concierge grinned at John. 'You're fast becoming my favourite hotel guest.'

'Is that a fact?' John looked down at the Labrador. 'Come on, Monte. How about a walk in Central Park?'

'Remember to bring him back, won't you?'

John gave the concierge a black look. He was thinking about Sylvie knocking on his door this morning and wondering how she had got hold of his room number.

'Mr Baxter, what happened to your British sense of humour? I was only joking.'

John rolled his eyes at the concierge and left the hotel. He walked briskly along Park Avenue with a bouncy Labrador puppy raring to go. Monte was pulling on the leash. John didn't admonish him. All he needed was a good run in the park.

John's stomach rumbled as he walked into the park, reminding him he hadn't eaten breakfast. Thirty minutes later, after Monte had run off some energy, John stopped at the café in the Mineral Springs. He made doubly sure Sylvie and Amy weren't anywhere to be seen before he took a seat at a table outside. He ordered a bagel smothered in cream cheese and a strong black coffee for breakfast.

It wasn't the all-American breakfast he had been looking forward to at Amelia's place in Greenwich Village, but he wasn't complaining. He was beyond pleased that it appeared things were

working out for her. To what degree, John would have been
interested to find out. If Amelia and Bertram got back together,
then that meant Bertram was out of the picture, as far as Sylvie
was concerned.

John sat eating his bagel, thinking about what Amelia had
said about taking his own advice. He knew what she meant: he
needed to sit down and talk things through with his wife.

John wiped his mouth with the paper napkin and polished
off his cup of coffee. He glanced at the yellow Labrador lying by
his feet. 'Come on, Monte, there's something I need to do.'

John sat in one of the leather wing-backed chairs in the hotel
lobby, waiting for Sylvie. He glanced at the puppy asleep in his
doghouse. Monte didn't seem to mind that his walk was cut short.
John wanted to return to the hotel and catch Sylvie before he left
for the show. He knew that at some point she would pass
through the lobby on her way out of the hotel. Lucky for him, he
also knew Sylvie wasn't an early riser. He'd already looked in the
restaurant, on his return, hoping to find her sitting there having
breakfast, but there was no sign of her.

'Excuse me, sir.'

John looked up to find one of the hotel receptionists standing by his chair. 'Yes?'

'Are you John Baxter?'

'Yes.'

'There's a limousine waiting for you outside.'

'Already?' John checked his watch.

'Shall I tell the driver you're coming?'

John shook his head yes, then no.

'Which is it, sir?'

John glanced around the hotel lobby. It was almost lunchtime, but there was still no sign of Sylvie. He had been diligently keeping an eye out. Then it dawned on him that she might have slipped out before he returned from Central Park with Monte. Damn.

'Sir?' The receptionist was waiting for an answer.

John sat there in a world of indecision over whether he should take the limo to the show or wait, however long it took, for her to return.

The hotel receptionist was getting impatient. 'Sir?'

34

When John gave Chloe the keys to his apartment at the airport before he left to catch his flight, she had resisted the urge to punch the air with a fist and shout out, 'Yes!'

Chloe had been hoping Mum would hurry up and vacate the garden apartment, and move back in with Dad, so she had a place to stay in order to try out living apart together. The last thing she expected was a phone call from her dad to tell her he was off to New York, leaving her in charge of his flat while he was away.

Chloe didn't know what had stunned her the most: the fact that Dad had trusted her with his apartment or the reason he was going to New York. On the way to the airport, he'd told her everything: all about his blog, the column he now wrote called *Dear John*, and his trip to meet the enemy. That's what he called this other writer, his arch-rival, whom he would encounter for the first time in New York on a live American chat show.

Chloe had already scanned the television listings in the newspaper and circled the programme in red felt-tip pen. She couldn't wait to see her dad on television, and find out how he faces off the enemy, this mystery woman who wrote the column,

Love on the Rooftop. Chloe was also dying to find out who this mystery writer was because she adored *Love on the Rooftop*; Chloe read her column avidly and loved the idea that two people could live in separate apartments and still have a successful relationship together.

Chloe wasn't the only one sitting in John's apartment on his sofa in front of the television, eagerly awaiting the start of the American chat show. When Harriet found out Chloe was 'looking after' Dad's apartment while he was away, she packed an overnight bag and moved in too. Harriet was royally sick of her in-laws. She'd had a huge row with Dominic, issuing an ultimatum – either they go, or I go – and had decamped to John's apartment.

And then their sister Jess arrived.

Chloe had lost count of the number of long-distance calls she had made, keeping Jess updated with the family saga; John's phone bill would be astronomical. For the second time in as many months, Jess returned home from Australia, worried about her parents. This time she intended to talk some sense into them because nobody else could. But she had arrived too late; Dad had gone to New York, and Mum was nowhere to be found. Jess decided to stay until their return in John's apartment.

Just before the show was due to air, the girls changed into their PJ's. They microwaved some popcorn, or rather over-microwaved it, making a mess in John's kitchen, and then opened a bottle of wine. Chloe accidentally spilt some wine on his sofa as they poured themselves a glass. All three girls did their best, albeit unintentionally, to mess up John's tidy apartment.

Chloe, Harriet, and Jess were all sitting comfortably on the sofa. They couldn't wait to see their dad and the mystery writer on live television. Their only regret was that Mum wasn't here to see this. Even though Chloe had already told Jess and Harriet that Mum wasn't at home – according to Julia she was on a trip – they still ventured downstairs to the garden apartment and knocked on her door, just on the off chance she'd returned. Harriet even tried calling her number downstairs, to no avail.

None of them knew her whereabouts. It was out of character and worrying that she hadn't told either one of them where she was. She must have switched her mobile phone off because it went straight to voicemail when Jess tried to call.

Harriet said, 'The only other explanation is that she is staying with Julia for a few days.'

Chloe rolled her eyes at her sister. 'I told you that I've already spoken to Julia and she won't tell me where Mum is.'

Jess chipped in, 'Perhaps Mum wants some time on her own, and she thinks that if we know where she is, we might tell Dad.'

Harriet nodded in agreement. 'That's quite plausible considering Mum and Dad's major falling out over Gertie.' Harriet remembered their almighty row after she told them they couldn't see Gertie. Harriet recalled that she could still hear them arguing when she walked out of the house and down the street.

'When *are* you going to let them see Gertie?'

Harriet glared at Chloe. 'I don't want to get into that right now if you don't mind.'

'Touchy, aren't we!'

Sitting in between her sisters on the sofa, Jess let out a sigh. It seemed that being the middle sister meant she always acted as the go-between. Over the years, this never changed. Perhaps it was because they were so alike, thought Jess, looking from Harriet to Chloe; they argued constantly when they were together.

'Can we get back to the matter at hand, you two?'

Harriet said, 'So we think she's staying with Julia at the moment.' She looked from Jess to Chloe. The three of them sat there mulling this over, aware that there was one huge problem with that scenario. If it weren't for the fact that Julia now lived on a boat, they would have been quite happy to leave it at that. But anyone who knew their mother knew there was no way in hell she was staying on a boat.

'I'm giving Julia a call,' announced Harriet.

'There's no point phoning Julia,' Chloe said in exasperation. 'I told you I did that already.'

Harriet grinned at her little sister. 'But you have a reputation for not being able to keep a secret. Maybe she'll talk to me.' Harriet got up from the sofa.

Chloe pulled a face at Harriet's back and mimed, maybe she'll talk to me, giving her sister a black look. She caught Jess staring at her with a bemused expression. Chloe studied her fingernails. 'I expect you're going to tell me to grow up.'

Jess shook her head. She glanced Harriet's way. 'I'd forgotten how haughty she can sometimes be.'

Jess and Chloe exchanged a smile while their haughty sister disappeared into John's study to phone Julia.

Harriet returned to the lounge with a sullen face.

'I take it she didn't tell you either,' said Chloe, relishing being right for a change.

Harriet slumped down on the sofa next to Jess. 'All she said was that there's nothing to be concerned about. Mum's fine. And we're not to worry.'

'Well, if Julia knows where she is, did you ask her to get in touch with Mum and tell her to switch on the television?'

Harriet gave Jess a blank look.

'The show, Harriet. Mum could still catch the show and see Dad on television.'

'Oh crumbs, I forgot all about it.'

'Here.' Chloe handed Harriet her mobile phone, with Julia's number on speed dial.

'Hi Julia, it's me again.' Harriet glanced at her sisters. 'Look, I know you won't tell me where Mum is, but can you at least give her a message... You will? Great. As soon as I get off the phone, can you call her straightaway and tell her to switch on the television?' Harriet paused as a thought occurred to her. 'She does have a television where she is, doesn't she?'

Jess and Chloe leaned closer, trying to overhear Julia's reply.

Harriet nodded her head and mouthed yes to her sisters when Julia replied.

'Great. You must tell Mum to switch on the television right now and watch *The Who's Who Show*. It's a live show in New York, and Dad is going to be on it, not just in the audience, one of the actual guests. Can you believe it? Mum can't miss this!'

'What are you talking about, Harriet darling?' said Julia over the phone. Of course Julia had heard of the show; that's why she was sitting in her houseboat on the sofa in front of the television, eagerly awaiting the start of *The Who's Who Show*. She couldn't wait to see the writer, Love on the Rooftop, who was none other than her best friend Sylvie, appear as the guest on the show.

'I'm talking about my dad,' said Harriet. 'When I found out, through the grapevine, that the anonymous writer – Love on the Rooftop – was appearing on that chat show, it was my idea to get the two columnists together for the first time, face-to-face, on live television.'

Chloe turned wide-eyed towards her sister, interrupting her phone conversation. 'Wait! Are you saying Daddy works for your magazine? You hired him? You knew he was Dear John all along?'

'Shhh! Pipe down,' said Harriet. 'Julia, are you still there?'

Julia hadn't really been paying attention. She was distracted by the television. The show was about to start any minute. Julia didn't want to miss a thing. She was leaning forward on the sofa in anticipation, her finger on the remote control in readiness to turn the volume up as soon as it started. And she was recording the show, so she and Sylvie could have a girl's night in and enjoy watching it together when she got back.

'Julia – are you still there?'

'Uh yes, sorry,' Julia said absently. 'I don't understand, Harriet. Who is it you want to get together on live television?'

'The two writers, Dear John and Love on the Rooftop. I discussed it with my editorial team at work, and we came up with this brilliant idea: what if we could get the two mystery writers together for the first time on live television? The writer, Love on the Rooftop, assumes she is the only guest and has no idea that the writer, Dear John, will be there on the show to surprise her.' Harriet paused. 'You have heard of Dear John, haven't you?'

'Of course I've heard of Dear John,' replied Julia. She enjoyed reading Dear John's column almost as much as she enjoyed reading Sylvie's column, but she wouldn't dare tell Sylvie that. Reading both columns over the last few weeks, Julia had detected something she couldn't put her finger on, as though these two rival writers were building up quite a rapport with each other. But she wouldn't dare tell Sylvie that, either.

Julia scratched her head. 'I'm sorry, Harriet, I still don't see what this has to do with your dad.'

'Because Dad is Dear John!'

Julia didn't take in what Harriet just said over the phone because her attention was momentarily diverted by the television. The evening news had just finished. The show was about to start. 'Harriet, can we talk about this later? I'm tied up at the minute. I have to go.'

'Didn't you hear what I just said? My dad, he's the writer of the blog and column, *Dear John*.'

Julia was pointing the remote control at the television, about to turn up the volume, when she froze. 'What did you just say?'

'I said that my Dad – John – is Dear John…'

Julia's eyes went wide.

Harriet finally had her full attention.

'And we've sent him to New York to surprise—'

'Bloody hell!' Julia dropped the remote control. 'I don't believe it!' She jumped out of her seat with such a start that anybody watching would have thought she had just been prodded with a hot poker.

'Yes, incredible isn't it,' continued Harriet, registering her surprise. 'Even I couldn't quite believe it when Dad first came into my office and told me he was the writer, Dear John. I never knew he could write. You sound just as surprised as I was.'

'You have no idea,' said Julia, speaking into the phone, now wedged under her chin. Julia was frantically rummaging in her handbag to retrieve her mobile phone. She found it – thank goodness! 'Look, I've got to go.' Julia dropped the phone from under her chin and let it fall to the floor. She didn't bother to pick up the receiver and put it back on the hook to disconnect the call. She quickly scrolled through the saved numbers on her phone, trying to find Sylvie's new mobile number.

Harriet was still on the end of the line. 'Julia? Are you still there?'

Chloe turned to her sister. 'Harriet, get off the phone! The show has started. Love on the Rooftop is about to walk out on stage any minute!'

Harriet shrugged her shoulders and handed Chloe her phone. They all sat staring avidly at the screen.

Jess helped herself to some popcorn from the large bowl balanced on her lap. She glanced at her sisters sitting either side of her.

'The suspense is killing me,' said Chloe, absently dunking her hand in the bowl of popcorn and retrieving a huge handful. 'I've got butterflies in my stomach. I can't wait to see Dad. I wonder if he'll look different on TV.'

'Shh!' said Harriet, dipping her hand in the bowl of popcorn on Jess's lap.

'You are recording this, aren't you?' Jess asked Chloe. 'Just in case Mum doesn't see Dad's big moment.'

'Shh!' hissed Harriet.

'Look,' said Chloe, pointing at the television and sending a spray of popcorn all over the coffee table in front of them. 'I think she's coming out!'

They all sat forward on the sofa as the host said, 'Now, let's give a warm welcome to the woman behind the very successful blog and column called *Love on the Rooftop*!'

A round of applause went up from the studio audience as the first guest walked across the stage.

Jess didn't notice the bowl of popcorn slide off her lap on to John's carpet. 'Mum?'

'Oh. My. God!' cried Chloe, jumping up and rushing over to

the television just to make sure she wasn't seeing things. 'I don't believe it! It's Mum!'

She turned around and stared wide-eyed at her sisters. 'Mum writes *Love on the Rooftop*, can you believe it? She's like a celebrity! Our mum is bloody *famous*!' Chloe rushed back to the sofa and sat down next to Jess. All three of them sat there staring dumbfounded at the television screen.

'Why didn't she tell us?' Harriet said slowly.

Chloe frowned. 'Oh, do be quiet, Harriet. I want to hear what she has to say.'

'But I don't understand why she didn't tell us?'

Chloe turned to Harriet. 'You're just pissed off because she didn't choose to write for *your* magazine.'

'Well, I've got a right to be angry; she stole my freelance work from right under me.'

Jess rolled her eyes. 'Will you two stop bickering so we can at least hear what she has to say?'

'I don't know what you're moaning about,' said Chloe, who always had to have the last word. 'At least you got Dear John.'

Harriet and Chloe looked at each other and said in unison, 'Dad!' With the shock of finding out their mother was none other than the writer, Love on the Rooftop, Harriet had forgotten all about the little surprise she had in store for said writer when she appeared on the show.

'I think Mum is in for quite a surprise,' commented Chloe.

'A shock – more like,' added Harriet.

They all exchanged glances. Jess asked Harriet, 'Are you sure Mum doesn't know the identity of the writer, Dear John? Are you sure she doesn't know it's Dad?'

'I'm positive,' said Harriet. She knew why John wanted to

keep his identity a secret, because he had been writing all about their personal lives. Which begged the question – what had Mum been writing about? Harriet raised her eyebrows. It was obvious. Unbeknown to her readers, the articles by Love on the Rooftop were complete fiction. Little wonder she wanted to keep her identity under wraps.

Chloe turned to Harriet. 'What about Dad? Do you think he knows the writer, Love on the Rooftop, is Mum?'

Harriet shook her head and thought of the lies Mum had been spinning in her blog and column. 'Absolutely not.'

They all sat there staring at the screen wondering how on earth this was going to play out when Mum and Dad, Love on the Rooftop and Dear John, finally came face-to-face with the truth.

On a houseboat in Little Venice, Julia found Sylvie's number in her list of contacts. She pressed the *call* button and glanced at the television. The show had started, and a very nervous-looking Sylvie was just walking across the stage. The show's host held out his hand and guided her to a chair.

Julia looked at her phone. The word *call* flashed up on the screen. A moment later she heard a mobile phone; it was coming from the television...

Chloe watched her mum on the show sit down in the chair opposite the host. She was just turning the volume up on the TV when she heard a mobile phone ringing. Chloe turned to look at her sisters sitting beside her on the sofa. 'Oh, for goodness' sake, whose phone is that?' They all looked at their phones, including Chloe.

'Not mine,' said Harriet.

'Me neither,' added Jess.

Chloe said, 'It's coming from the television.'

They all turned in unison to watch their mum rummage in her purse for her mobile phone. Her face was a deep shade of crimson as her first words on live television in front of the studio audience were, 'I'm so sorry, I forgot to switch my phone off.'

The host said jokingly, 'Aren't you going to answer that?'

'Oh, I'm sure it can wait until later.' Sylvie looked at her mobile live on air, realised it was Julia phoning from home, and said, 'It's only my best friend calling for a natter, but I think I'm a bit busy to take this call – don't you?'

The studio audience and the host laughed uproariously, as though Sylvie had just told a hilarious joke. She even got a round of applause.

Chloe said, 'How funny, Mum forgot to turn off her mobile phone.'

Harriet narrowed her eyes. She had a good idea why Julia was phoning her mum. 'Julia knows.'

Jess and Chloe turned to look at their sister.

'She's known all along,' continued Harriet, 'about Mum and her secret – Love on the Rooftop.'

'Why do you say that?' asked Jess.

'Isn't it obvious? I just phoned Julia a moment ago and told her that Dad is Dear John, and he's appearing on the show. Then suddenly Julia is on the phone to Mum. Bit of a coincidence – don't you think?'

Jess cottoned on. 'So that's why Julia is calling, to warn her that Dad is about to appear on the show.'

'Precisely.'

Chloe said, 'Julia knew how worried we were about Mum's whereabouts. I don't understand why she wouldn't tell us Mum was in New York. Didn't she think we'd want to see Mum on live television?'

They glanced at the television. The host was flapping his arms, gesturing at the studio audience to quieten down. The round of applause died down.

Harriet eyed her little sister. 'Chloe, I get the feeling Julia didn't have a choice. I think Mum didn't want us to find out – not yet anyway.'

Chloe frowned. 'Why ever not?'

Harriet sighed. 'Have you read *Love on the Rooftop*, Chloe?'

'Of course I have. It's great.'

'It is if you enjoy reading a work of fiction every week. It's not real, Chloe. You realise that, don't you, now you know it's Mum whose been writing about living apart together?'

Chloe stared at her sister. For once, she didn't have a sarcastic retort or make any attempt to get the last word in. Her bottom lip quivered at the thought that the whole reason she was here, in Daddy's apartment, was because she believed Love on the Rooftop's experiences of LAT living were true.

Jess caught her little sister's expression and put a comforting arm around her shoulders.

Harriet pointed at the television. 'You can see now why Mum didn't want us to find out she was Love on the Rooftop from a chat show before she had a chance to tell us herself just what she'd been up to.'

From a houseboat in Little Venice, Julia was sitting on her sofa shouting at the television screen, 'No. No. Nooooo!' as she watched Sylvie switch off her phone and put it back in her purse.

Julia was still holding her mobile phone to her ear. She heard Sylvie's phone go straight to voicemail as soon as she switched it off. Julia didn't bother leaving a message; it was too late for that now. It was too late to warn her just what was about to happen next.

35

Sylvie stole a glance at the studio audience and was just thankful they, and the show's host, were good-humoured about the phone call. She silently scolded herself for not remembering to switch off her mobile phone before appearing on the show. She'd already made a fool of herself, and she hadn't even been on the show five minutes.

What an embarrassing entrance, thought Sylvie. And what was so urgent that Julia had to call her right now? She tried to keep a smile on her face in front of the host. Julia knew all about her trip to New York. She even said she was going to stay up late and watch the show. So why on earth was she trying to contact her?

'Tell us about the writer, Love on the Rooftop.'

Sylvie looked nervously at the host sitting at the table in front of her and tried to focus her attention on him. She was trying not to think about all those people sitting just a few feet away, making up the live studio audience, not to mention all those cameras pointing right at her for the benefit of the viewers watching at home. It wasn't easy.

'What do you want to know?' Sylvie asked.

He smiled at the anonymous writer who had been hiding behind her pseudonym all this time. 'How about your name, for a start?'

The audience offered a friendly laugh.

'My name is Sylvia Baxter, but my friends and family call me Sylvie.'

'Sylvie, welcome to the show.'

The studio audience clapped.

Sylvie returned his smile and relaxed a little. She listened intently as he prepared to ask her another question. She felt as though she was sitting in a job interview.

'You've kept your identity a secret until now. I understand that was to protect your family from intrusion from the press. I have to say, in hindsight, that was quite an astute decision on your part considering how phenomenally successful your blog and your column has become.'

Sylvie nodded, avoiding eye contact; she knew that was a load of rubbish.

'You have chosen to come forward and reveal your identity – why now?'

Sylvie was about to answer that question when she realised he hadn't finished.

'There has, as you know, been a lot of speculation surrounding your interesting living arrangements. This so-called LAT living was going to end, eventually. There's the expectation that you and your husband would move back in together, which is what we suspect you're here to tell us today.' He glanced at the audience and then looked at Sylvie keenly.

Sylvie smiled nervously. That wasn't what she was here to tell him, or the studio audience, or the folks at home, or all the people who read her blog and weekly column. Sylvie opened her mouth; she was about to spill the beans and tell the truth when the host leaned forward in his chair, and said, 'First, let's go back to the very beginning, to how all this started.'

Sylvie blinked in surprise.

'Please tell us in your own words Sylvie, how you and your husband found yourselves in two separate apartments, living apart together, in the house you once shared as a married couple for almost forty years.'

Sylvie's shoulders sagged. Did she have to? She would much prefer to cut to the chase. However, she'd been warned by Marcia Hunt, her magazine editor, that people were clamouring to know all about the writer Love on the Rooftop, and she had to expect these sorts of questions. The trouble was that with all that had gone on in her life over these past few months, she was having a problem figuring out just where to begin.

Sylvie glanced at the studio audience, still feeling over-whelmed by all this. She couldn't believe she was sitting right here, on the famous Who's Who Show, like some kind of celebrity, with people hanging on her every word. It was making her feel nervous and tongue-tied. The more she thought about it, the more nervous she became.

The host, sensing a dose of stage-fright, came to her rescue. 'Why don't we start with the obvious question: where does the writer, Love on the Rooftop, live? Where is the famous house that has been converted into two apartments?'

That was a nice, straightforward question and a good place for Sylvie to start. 'I live at 67a Penfold Street, Holland Park, London NW1. The house used to be just number 67. It was my husband's idea to number the apartments and create two separate addresses.' The host of the show smiled at Sylvie and glanced at the studio audience, listening with rapt attention.

'We even have our own post boxes now,' continued Sylvie. 'That was the very last thing we did once we completed the conversion.' Sylvie didn't stop there; she talked about her mother passing away and the profound effect it had on her, making her re-evaluate her life's choices. She wasn't getting any younger. It made her stop and think about what she'd done with her life, and what she still wanted to do with the time she had left.

The studio audience were nodding in silent agreement, empathising with the loss of a loved one.

Sylvie told them that's when she left her job to find herself, and how that didn't work out because, shortly afterwards, her husband lost his job and became a royal pain in the behind; he used to follow her around all day like a lost puppy-dog.

The studio audience laughed at that.

Then she told them about this bright idea he had one morning, to convert the house into two separate apartments.

'And... well, the rest is history,' concluded Sylvie. 'That's when my blog, *Love on the Rooftop*, began. So, for any of you who haven't read my blog and need a quick history lesson...?'

The studio audience laughed. They got the joke – everybody in the audience had read her blog. Sylvie got another round of applause.

The host stepped in and asked, 'About your husband, the man behind the grand plan to convert the house. I bet he had no idea where it would lead, to a famous writer living under his roof and a celebrity in the making.'

Sylvie slowly nodded her head, avoiding eye contact.

'What's his name, by the way?'

'John,' said Sylvie in a small voice.

'And what does he think of all this?'

Sylvie hesitated. 'He thinks... he thinks—' Sylvie stopped dead. She looked at her host and then turned her head to gaze at the studio audience. The time had come for Sylvie to do what she came here to do, and that was to tell the truth.

Sylvie turned back to the host and blurted, 'Look, the truth of the matter is he doesn't know. None of my family knows that I am a writer, apart from my best friend, Julia. Hello Julia!' Sylvie waved her hand in front of one of the cameras.

The host looked at Sylvie in surprise. 'Let me get this straight. Are you saying that your husband and your family do not know you are the writer, Love on the Rooftop?'

'That is correct,' said Sylvie, wondering what John's reaction would be when he found out she was the mystery writer behind the phenomenally successful blog, *Love on the Rooftop*.

'Well, he is in for quite the surprise when he finds out. Is he watching the show, do you think? Or will you tell him when you get home?'

Sylvie stared at the host. She didn't even know if she was going home after this, back to her apartment in the house they shared in Holland Park. She had other options and could always move into the flat Bertram had bought her in London. Now Sylvie had got over her fear of boats, she could even stay with Julia for a little while on her houseboat in Little Venice. Julia wouldn't mind.

When Sylvie didn't answer his question, the host changed tack. 'Now, I'm sure you're here to tell us that you and your husband are getting back together, not that anybody is going to be surprised.' He gave a sideways glance to the studio audience.

'We all know that's where your blog and column, *Love on the Rooftop*, is leading. To the end of LAT living.'

A murmur of agreement arose from the audience.

Sylvie sat squirming in her seat. The chat show host was wrong, very wrong; they were in for a surprise when they discovered it was extremely doubtful she would get back together with her husband. Sylvie looked at the studio audience and wondered if she could go through with it; did she have the courage to sit here in front of all these people and tell them the god's honest truth?

'But before you give us all the details of that happy event, we have a surprise for you.'

'Oh, you shouldn't have,' said Sylvie, assuming someone was about to walk out on stage and give her flowers and a box of chocolates. It was a nice thought, but Sylvie really didn't think she deserved any presents. Besides, she didn't want to prolong this any longer than necessary. All she wanted to do was say what she came here to say and get it over with before she bottled out.

The host leaned forward in his chair. 'We had this idea that you and our studio audience, and the viewers at home, might be interested to find out the identity of your rival, the anonymous writer, Dear John.'

'Well, naturally,' said Sylvie, smiling. If she was honest, that writer was furthest from her thoughts right now. She cast a glance around the studio, anticipating that a member of the production crew would walk on stage any minute with the bouquet. Sylvie wished they'd hurry up about it.

The host said to Sylvie, 'What would you say if the rival magazine that published Dear John's column thought it would be a great idea to get these two writers, that's you and him, in the same room together?' Sylvie wasn't saying anything because she was wondering where he was going with this.

'And what would you say if Dear John was right here, at this very moment, sitting somewhere in the studio audience?'

Sylvie went bright crimson at the mere thought. What she would say to that was something they couldn't broadcast on live television. She hoped he was joking.

'You have got to be joking.'

The host shook his head and grinned at Sylvie. 'No joke. He is, in fact, right here as we speak, sitting somewhere in the studio audience.'

There were gasps from the studio audience and plenty of heads in the audience bobbing around as though they might spot him sitting among them.

There were gasps from three young women sitting on Dear John's sofa at home, dying to see her reaction when their dad sitting in the audience stood up and joined his wife, their mum, on the stage in front of the cameras.

There was a gasp from a retired primary school teacher called Julia, sitting with two cocker spaniels on her houseboat in Little Venice, waiting with bated breath for her best friend to get the shock of her life when John stood up and revealed himself as the writer, Dear John.

There was a gasp from Sylvie at the thought that all this time her arch-rival, her nemesis, and a man she hardly knew, but with whom she thought she might be falling in love, had been sitting watching her the whole time.

Sylvie stared at the host in disbelief. She wasn't just surprised; she was downright shocked. How could they do this to her? How could they not at least give her some forewarning that they had also invited Dear John as a guest on their show? She had already made a right fool of herself, leaving her mobile phone switched on. Her next thought was what she had come here to do: tell the audience and all the viewers at home that she was a liar and a fraud and that she was wrong about LAT living; it won't provide the happy ending she had led them to believe. In fact, it was quite the reverse.

Sylvie could do that under the glare of the spotlights, and the cameras, and a live studio audience. But face-to-face with Dear John? That was a whole other ball game. This was not what she had in mind when she divulged the truth. To then have Dear John smugly say to her face, 'I told you so,' gloating that he had been right all along, and she had been wrong. This was meant to be *her* last hurrah – *not his.*

Sylvie had intended to face off her arch-rival, her nemesis, through writing her last column about LAT living and coming clean about the truth of her own situation. She didn't mind that, because writing was her thing. Not public speaking. Not talking to this mystery writer in person and being put on the spot in front of all these people, all these cameras.

Sylvie bristled. This wasn't what she signed up for – no way. *No bloody way.* No matter how much she wanted to meet Dear John in the flesh, she didn't want it to be like this, exposing herself for the fraud she was in front of him, with millions of people watching. She had a good mind to stand up and walk out, but she didn't move a muscle because Sylvie's curiosity got the better of her. Just like everybody else sitting in that studio, she was dying to know the identity of Dear John. Sylvie looked toward the studio audience, but the lights were blinding; all she could make out were dark shadows.

The host said, 'Let's have the studio lights on the audience please.'

Suddenly the bright lights directed towards the stage where Sylvie was seated were gone, casting her in a cool shadow. Sylvie could now see the studio audience for the first time. She felt incredibly self-conscious, naked even, sitting alone on the stage with all these people watching her. Among them the writer, Dear John.

A single spotlight playfully danced around the studio audience, seeking out Dear John.

36

The host stood up and walked across the stage with a hand-held microphone. He stopped at the edge of the stage, in front of the studio audience, and spoke into his mike, 'Dear John, please stand up and reveal yourself.'

Sylvie's eyes were darting around the audience, on the lookout for any movement, watching for the first sign that somebody was rising from their seat.

The host scanned the audience for his second guest. He spoke into his mike once more, 'You're keeping us in suspense, we like that – thank you. But now is the time to reveal yourself, so please stand up.'

Nobody stood up. A low murmur swept through the studio as people looked around them in search of the mystery writer.

The host put his hand to his ear where a small Bluetooth earpiece was concealed and listened to the producer of the show off-camera confirming that their second guest had arrived; he was seated somewhere in the studio audience. The host looked up. 'We know you're here. I promise I won't bite.' He laughed nervously, wondering why his second guest wasn't coming forward.

John sat in his seat, his legs feeling like jelly, his eyes never leaving the woman sitting on the stage. The writer, Love on the Rooftop, was his very own wife, Sylvie. He still couldn't get over the shock of seeing her walk on that stage looking for all the world as though she belonged right there, appearing so professional and sophisticated, and looking like some sort of celebrity.

Bloody hell! This was not what he'd signed up for. He wished he was still sitting in the hotel lobby and hadn't decided, at the last minute, to take the limo to the show instead; all because his curiosity had got the better of him and he wanted to meet Love on the Rooftop.

John continued to stare at Sylvie. She was sitting there, looking radiant. All that time he'd been waiting for her in the hotel lobby, she must have been at the studio already having her hair and makeup done before the show. When John first saw her come out on stage, he didn't recognise her until she uttered her first words to the host. *I'm so sorry, I forgot to switch my phone off.*

While the rest of the audience were laughing at her jokes and enjoying the show, John was shaking his head and muttering, 'Oh my god. Oh. My. God.' Nobody would believe he was the writer, Dear John, least of all his wife. She would assume this was some kind of prank. She was going to think that he had followed her here and was masquerading as Dear John.

'Dear John – where are you?' the host said in a sing-song voice. He listened to the producer through his earpiece for the location of his second guest. Then he stepped down from the stage and walked up the steps among the audience.

As soon as John saw the chat show host heading his way, he

knew the game was up. Slowly, John rose from his seat. He had the impulse to bolt up the steps and try to make a run for it, but he knew there were security guards at every exit and he couldn't get out. They wouldn't let him leave. He was the second guest on their show – their surprise guest – and they wanted to see her reaction when she came face-to-face with Dear John.

John didn't. Not now he knew it was his wife down there. She was going to kill him.

The moment John rose from his seat, the spotlight was on him in an instant.

'Ah, there you are,' said the host, smiling in relief. He thought for a minute he might have to call security to haul him out of his seat.

Sylvie's eyes darted to the man in the audience, enveloped in a bright spotlight. His hand was obscuring his face from the glare of the light.

The host realised the spotlight was too bright, preventing anybody getting a good look at their second guest, the man behind the phenomenon *Dear John*. He made a hand gesture, and suddenly the spotlight was gone. The normal studio lights came up.

Everybody in the audience turned to look at John.

And so did Sylvie. Her jaw dropped open. It can't be. This was some kind of joke. No, it wasn't a joke. She knew exactly what this was; somebody had leaked her identity at the magazine she worked for and flown John out here to surprise her, under the guise that he was the writer, Dear John, who he clearly wasn't.

The host pranced up the steps to where John was standing, staring down at his wife, and asked, 'You are the writer, Dear John, are you not?' He thrust the microphone in John's face.

John looked at the microphone and discovered that when he opened his mouth, no words came out.

The host, used to a healthy dose of stage fright, clapped him on the back which made John splutter, 'Yes, I am.' He kept his eyes fixed on the host standing in front of him.

'No,' said Sylvie under her breath, 'he can't be!'

'As you know, the writer, Love on the Rooftop, has revealed her identity live on air. Now, it's your turn.' The host held the microphone up to John. 'Please, can you tell us your name?'

John shook his head.

The host laughed. 'Ah, good old British humour, we get it, we do,' he lied. 'The clock is ticking, and we don't want to run out of time on air, so please tell us your name.'

The host was right: the clock *was* ticking, and John wanted to get this over with. 'It's John.'

A peal of laughter went up from the studio audience, who assumed he was just messing around.

The host frowned at the audience, switched his microphone off, and turned to his second guest. 'Stop screwing around and just tell us your name. We haven't got all day, for Chrissake!' He switched the microphone back on and managed a pearly white smile for the benefit of the audience.

John spoke into the microphone. 'My name is John. John Baxter.'

The host sighed in relief. 'Welcome to *The Who's Who Show*, John Bax—'

The host stopped mid-flow and raised his eyebrows. 'Did you just say Baxter?' He glanced down at Sylvie, who was now out of her chair and stalking across the stage towards the audience.

Sylvie still thought it was a prank, and any minute the real writer of the phenomenally successful *Dear John* was going to step out on stage and surprise her. It couldn't be her husband. It just couldn't be John because he was an accountant, not a writer. John had never hinted that he had any leanings to a career writing. He even discouraged Harriet from becoming a journalist.

Sylvie's train of thought stopped dead. If John wasn't who he claimed to be, if he wasn't Dear John, then where on earth did he get the money to fly all the way to New York to appear on this show? How did he even get on this show? It's not like you could walk straight into the studio off the street; even the audience was carefully vetted.

There was a simple explanation that Sylvie was having a hard time getting her head around; he really was the writer, Dear John, and the magazine he worked for had sent him on an all-expenses-paid trip to New York.

She still couldn't believe it was true because that would mean John had been working for the same magazine that employed Harriet. And that would mean the editor, her very own daughter, had known about John's new writing career all along. If he was Dear John, then why would they have kept something like that a secret? Sylvie stared at John. She had the answer to that little conundrum. It was for the same reason Sylvie had kept her identity a secret from them; John and Harriet were worried about how she would react when she found out John had put their personal lives out there.

Welcome to my world, thought Sylvie, suddenly having the urge to laugh at the absurdity of the situation; she had been writing about John without his knowledge, and he had been writing about her.

Sylvie stood there, centre stage, staring up at her husband. It all made sense now. The more she thought about what he had written in his *Dear John* blog and magazine column, the more Sylvie could recognise herself in the things he'd been describing. She recalled Dear John's blog starting with a housewarming party to celebrate the completion of the conversion. That's when Dear John's wife demanded the keys to the apartment downstairs and promptly moved in, taking him completely unawares. Then there was the party she threw – a seventies-themed house party. And the puppy a friend gave her as a moving-in present.

Sylvie stared at John. Why hadn't she guessed the truth? Why hadn't it even crossed her mind that her neighbour upstairs had been writing *Dear John* while she was downstairs writing *Love on the Rooftop*? Sylvie knew why she had no inkling it was him, because John had not been completely honest about what was really going on at home with his wife. Dear John had been stretching the truth to the point where he'd veered off into a complete fantasy about how his wife wasn't coping, living on her own without her husband. That wasn't his wife he was writing about, that wasn't Sylvie.

Sylvie smiled at the delicious thought that she wasn't the only one who had been fabricating the truth for the benefit of her readers. John had also been lying in his blog, and his weekly column, about what was really going on at home. That's why she never guessed the truth. Unlike Sylvie, Dear John's fictional creation couldn't cope with living on her own with all the calamities that kept befalling her. On top of which, Dear John neglected to mention the part he played trying to force her to move out by sabotaging her apartment.

And then there was the episode she remembered reading

about when he started referring to his wife as "the neighbour from hell." Apparently, she threw dozens of parties in the middle of the week, without even telling the neighbours, without even telling him. In hindsight, it sounded like something John used to do when he was going through his, *I'm behaving like a child because I'm not getting my own way,* phase because Sylvie was still refusing to vacate the garden apartment so he could rent it out.

And where, pray tell, were the details about Dear John's wife financially supporting the show? Had he mentioned the fact that his wife was working hard to pay off all his debts because he'd been irresponsible and got them into a big financial hole? So big, in fact, that they risked losing the roof over their head? No, not a bit of it. Dear John never mentioned any of that. Dear John made his wife out to be childish, irresponsible, needy, and pathetic. Sylvie was going to kill him.

'Now I know England is a small country...' began the host, 'but what an interesting coincidence that these two writers have the same surname.' The host looked around the audience for their reaction but got a reaction from Sylvie instead.

'John!' barked Sylvie. She was standing at the front of the stage, seething.

John cast his eyes down to the stage where Sylvie was glaring back at him, hands on hips, her posture leaving John in no doubt he was in big trouble.

'Sylvie,' he said in a small voice. 'Look, I can explain...'

The host looked from John to Sylvie in confusion. 'Wait a minute.' He stared at John. 'Do you two know each other?' He put the mike up to John's face.

John mumbled, 'She's my wife.'

'Pardon me? Please speak into the microphone so the studio

audience, and the viewers at home, can hear what you just said.'

'I said she's my wife. Sylvie Baxter is my wife. I had no idea she was the writer, Love on the Rooftop.'

The host stared at John, unsure whether this was true or whether it was just one of those English wind-ups the Brits loved to play on unsuspecting Americans. He intended to find out. He left John standing among the studio audience and raced down the steps to where Sylvie was still standing front and centre on the stage.

'Sylvie, is that your husband standing up there?'

'Unfortunately, yes,' admitted Sylvie, wondering who thought it might be "fun" to get the two rival writers in the same room on live television; it wasn't.

A murmur arose from the studio audience as all eyes were on John.

Standing next to Sylvie, the host put his hand to the small earpiece lodged in his ear, listened to his producer, nodded his head that he understood, and raced back up the stairs to repeat the question that had just been shouted in his earpiece.

Thrusting the microphone in John's face, he asked, 'Are you saying that you have been writing about your relationship with your wife living apart together, and all this time the woman you were writing about, your wife who was living in the garden apartment downstairs, was none other than the writer, Love on the Rooftop?' He pointed at Sylvie, still standing on the stage in front of the studio audience.

The audience was so quiet, so still, that John could almost imagine they had all vanished, leaving him, Sylvie, and the annoying bloke who kept thrusting a microphone in his face, alone in the room together.

'Yes, it's true.'

That annoying bloke repeated the question just to make sure. 'You had absolutely no idea that your wife was the writer of the hugely successful blog and column, *Love on the Rooftop*?'

John shook his head. Staring down at his wife, he was still having a hard time getting his head around the fact that he had no clue. Then suddenly the penny dropped. *Sylvie's blog!*

He recalled that one time he sat alone in Sylvie's kitchen and noticed she had left her laptop switched on. It was during one of his missions to sabotage her apartment in the early days of them living apart together. He had idly glanced at her laptop and seen the icon flashing on the desktop called *Sylvie's blog*. Later he remembered searching the internet and finding nothing remotely going by that name.

He just assumed she'd decided against doing the blog. It never occurred to him that the reason he couldn't find her blog on the internet was not that she didn't have one, but because like John, she too had chosen to remain anonymous. He couldn't find it because her blog wasn't called *Sylvie's blog*; she had changed the name. That's when John had an epiphany; *Love on the Rooftop* was... 'Sylvie's blog!' John shouted out. It all made sense now.

'I'm sorry – what?' said the host, looking confused.

John was no longer speaking to the host. He was not even aware of the host; the only two people in that vast studio were just two writers, him and his wife. 'Sylvie's blog,' John shouted at her.

'What did you say?' Sylvie glared up at him. She shook her head. What on earth was he talking about?

'This all makes perfect sense. I saw the icon on your laptop saying *Sylvie's blog*. I searched for it online but—'

'When were you on my laptop?'

'You know that time I let Dangermouse loose in your kitchen, so you thought you had mice, and I could come to the rescue.'

Sylvie remembered that episode all too well. She thought she had a rat infestation when all it turned out to be was a pet mouse John had borrowed from his brother, Dave.

'Well, after I put some cheese down in his cage, and I was waiting for him to reappear, I was sitting in the kitchen and noticed your laptop was on—'

The host interrupted, 'Please explain to us and the viewers at home, who is this Dangermouse?'

'You were on my laptop?'

'I was bored. I swear I didn't touch anything, Sylvie. But I saw the icon. So, when I went back upstairs with Dangermouse, I searched for it online, but I couldn't find your blog.'

'I don't believe it!' Sylvie exploded. 'You come into my apartment without my knowledge, rigging the electricity so I thought I had a power cut, tampering with my washing machine which flooded my kitchen floor, then making me think I've got a rat infestation. And then you were on my laptop going through my personal stuff?'

'Sylvie, I swear I just saw the icon. I didn't go through your personal stuff.'

The host was listening to what sounded like a married couple about to have a bust-up. He realised this most definitely wasn't some British wind-up. These two really were married.

'This is unbelievable!' said the host as he looked around the studio audience who were just as captivated by the drama unfolding as he was. 'Unbelievable! Are you getting this?' He tapped his earpiece to check his producer was getting this. 'You couldn't make this shit up! Oops, can I use the word shit live on air?'

'You just did – twice!' said the producer in the earpiece.

Larry turned to a television camera, and while Sylvie and John were still arguing in the background, said to the viewers at home, 'As you can see, there's no question that these two are married. Dear John and Love on the Rooftop had no clue they were husband and wife. They had no idea they were living under the same roof writing about each other, living apart together.' He glanced back at them. 'Unbelievable! This is just... fantastic!'

Larry listened into his earpiece as the producer had another question. He left John standing in the audience as he raced down the steps to ask Sylvie a question.

'Sylvie, what's this about John flooding your kitchen floor and switching your electricity off?'

'Ah yes,' said Sylvie, thinking back to that episode. 'You won't find that written anywhere in his blog or his column. You see, Dear John has neglected to mention a few things that have been going on in the Baxter household.'

'Perhaps you'd like to enlighten us?'

'Perhaps I would,' said Sylvie gleefully. 'Shall we start with the fact that he has failed to mention in his blog, or in his column, that his wife – that's me – has been paying all the bills and the mortgage?'

A chorus of disapproval swept through the audience, with some people shouting out, 'Boooo!' at John.

The host looked around at the audience, giving them plenty of time to voice their opinion, before returning his attention to Sylvie. 'Are you saying that John hasn't been completely honest with his readers?'

'You bet I am!' said Sylvie.

Oh boy, thought the host, this just keeps getting better and better. He had followed Dear John's blog and read all his articles. He wasn't surprised the wife of Dear John would not be pleased with some of the things he'd said about her; especially if it turned out they were fabrications.

Larry hot-footed it back up the stairs to get John's reaction. 'What do you say about that? What do you say to your wife's claims that, quite frankly, what you've written about her in *Dear John* is all bullshit!'

John didn't get a chance to utter a single word in his own defence before the host, who had been listening to the producer through his earpiece, suddenly changed tack.

'Let's just step back for a moment and look at the bigger picture before we get into the whys and wherefores of who said what, when, and about whom.'

The host could well imagine there would be enough of that when those two got home. He didn't envy John. If he were in John's shoes, his wife would murder him. Fortunately, he wasn't. But unfortunately for the show, and the studio audience along with all the viewers at home, there just wasn't enough time to air all their dirty laundry on live television; the producer was quite right, he had to cut to the chase and get down to the heart of the matter – living apart together.

The host cut to the chase. 'You both admit in your blogs and magazine columns that you've got very differing views on the subject of LAT living.' He turned to John. 'John, you think it doesn't work. Your view is that you can't have a successful relationship and live apart.' The host turned around to look down at the stage. 'And you, Sylvie, think the opposite.'

John nodded his approval at that assessment, watching Sylvie do the same, wondering where he was going with this.

'Now let's move on from differing views to your personal situation as a couple. I'm confused...' – he glanced at the camera and furrowed his brow – 'and I'm sure our studio audience and the viewers at home are a little confused too.' He turned away from the camera to focus on Dear John. 'John, you said your relationship with your wife is falling apart. Anybody who has been reading your column can see that it's only leading in one direction: straight to the divorce courts.'

John frowned at the host, although he didn't deny it.

'As for you, Sylvie, anyone reading *Love on the Rooftop*... well, it's been non-stop romance – hasn't it. The expectation all along is that you will be moving back in with your husband.'

Down on the stage, Sylvie gave the host a black look but didn't deny it.

The host continued, 'But you can't both be right. You're either splitting up or getting back together. Which means one of you has been, to borrow a British colloquialism, telling pork pies.'

'It's porky pies,' corrected John. 'That's Cockney slang for lies.'

The host repeated, 'One of you has been telling porky pies.' He looked from John to Sylvie. 'Well? Which one of you is it? Which one of you has been stretching the truth, getting creative on your blog, *lying* in your column?'

John and Sylvie stood there in complete silence, both avoiding the host's intent gaze.

Sylvie was studying her fingernails.

John was staring at his shoes.

Sylvie surreptitiously glanced John's way. She had no

intention of owning up to the deceit now. If she did, people might think everything John had written about his wife, about the writer, Love on the Rooftop, was true. Besides, she wasn't the only one telling porky pies. They were both complicit in a deception, giving their readers what they wanted to hear. Sylvie wasn't going to give him the satisfaction of owning up and being the fall guy until John confessed he had also lied. Sylvie kept her mouth firmly shut.

That wasn't the only reason Sylvie had changed her mind about admitting The Big Lie. Because if she did, then it was tantamount to saying that the views and opinions expressed in *Dear John* were correct. LAT living and having a successful relationship just weren't compatible. Sylvie didn't believe that was true for everybody. It just wasn't possible for them.

'Come on, guys, we all want to know which one of you was telling the truth. We all want to find out how the story ends.' Larry turned to John. 'Is Dear John splitting up from his wife – permanently?' He then glanced down at Sylvie. 'Or is Love on the Rooftop moving back in with her husband?'

The host stood there, waiting to see which one of them would answer his question. He had put them both on the spot, in front of a live studio audience, in front of the viewers at home, in front of the whole world. 'Come on, tell us what happens next in the saga of Dear John and Love on the Rooftop living apart together.'

A murmur arose among the studio audience. Somebody from the audience shouted out, 'How does your story end?'

The studio audience chanted, 'Tell us! Tell us! Tell us!'

Sylvie stood there, staring at the audience. This was it. This was what she had been dreading. She had no choice now but to come clean and tell them The Big Lie, that she had misled all her readers; they weren't getting back together. Love on the Rooftop had no happy ending. It meant Dear John had been right all along: LAT living doesn't work, at least not for them.

Sylvie was just about to speak up when she heard John's voice loud and clear in the microphone.

'All right, I'll tell you.'

The host held up his arms for the studio audience to quieten down.

John continued, 'You want to know how our story ends? I can tell you how it ends because I have it right here, in writing, and I'm going to read it to you...'

Sylvie looked up at John in surprise. Had he written his final *Dear John* article and brought it here to share it with the audience on the show before it was published? Sylvie hadn't considered doing that. What a brilliant idea, and a great swansong to do that on live television. She watched John intently, wishing she had thought of that first.

John shoved his hand in his pocket and got out a crumpled, screwed up piece of paper, the note Sylvie had left him that began: *Dear John...* He sighed. It was the Dear John letter he hadn't bothered to read because he knew exactly what it said.

John unfolded the screwed-up piece of paper, smoothing it out as best he could. All this had to end sometime. He glanced around him at the studio audience and thought why not it do here, read them his Dear John letter, so everybody knew, without a shadow of a doubt, how their story ends.

37

John addressed the audience. 'I have here in my hand a Dear John letter. Shall I read it?'

Shouts of *YES!* went up from the audience.

The host held up the microphone.

John coughed into his hand, took a deep breath, and read the first two words, "Dear John." He glanced down at Sylvie standing on the stage before turning his attention back to the note. "I am going away on a brief business trip…"

John paused, a little confused, but continued nonetheless. "Just to let you know I shall be gone for a few days, in case you're wondering where I am and why it's rather quiet downstairs…"

John was still waiting to get to the *Dear John* part. The bit where she tells him that she has found someone else, and she's leaving him for good.

He continued reading the note out loud. "I have left Alfie with Julia while I'm away because you and I both know you don't like dogs…"

John raised his eyebrows and frowned at his wife. 'That's just not true, Sylvie. I like dogs.'

'No, you don't,' retorted Sylvie. 'You said so yourself. You said you didn't want a dog in the house.'

'I did say that, didn't I,' mused John, thinking back to that episode when he first discovered Sylvie had got a dog.

John recalled telling Sylvie you can't have a dog in an apartment, which he knew was a load of baloney; he was just making it up on the spot because back then, before he got to know Alfie, John couldn't abide the thought of an animal in the house. He didn't understand why people wanted pets. Who knew that a few months down the road he would have a pet of his very own?

John looked down at the note; he was nearly at the end. He continued to read out loud, "I left him with Julia because I didn't trust you not to hand Alfie over to a complete stranger while you gallivanted off to god-knows-where—"

John stared at the note. He turned the piece of paper over, but it was blank on the other side. *Was that it!?*

There was nothing more. And not only that, he also couldn't believe she had brought *that* up again. He knew that last comment, about leaving Alfie with a complete stranger, was a sarcastic reference to leaving Gertie with Barbara. John grimaced. Was he never going to hear the end of it?

'Well, that's all very interesting, John,' said the host, glancing at the note, 'but I don't see what that has to do with—'

'That wasn't my fault!' shouted John, ignoring the host and shoving past him as he headed down the steps towards Sylvie. 'If you had kept your bloody promise to look after Gertie that afternoon, then—'

'Oh, we're back to that, are we?' said Sylvie. 'It's my fault, is it?'

'Your darn right it is!' John stepped on to the stage in front of her. '*You* were the one who forgot about her. *You* were the one who neglected to look after your own grandchild!'

Gasps of surprise arose from the studio audience.

'Yes, I forgot. It's true. But I've been busy, John. I've been busy working and paying all the bills while you didn't lift a finger. In fact, you spent your time getting drunk and having house parties…'

John cast his eyes heavenward.

Sylvie was still having a rant, '… and then I find out you've been on my laptop and discovered Sylvie's blog, and you get this splendid idea to write a blog all about your wife…' Sylvie glared at John. 'All about how irresponsible she is, throwing wild parties, and turning into, I quote, "the neighbour from hell." Somehow you forgot to mention that your so-called neighbour from hell has got you out of a financial hole and saved our house from being repossessed.'

'Well, it didn't save our marriage, did it,' John shot back sarcastically. 'What about that? And what about all that malarkey you've been writing in your column, all that crap about how LAT living has put a spark back in your relationship and brought romance back into your life?'

'What about it?' Sylvie wasn't going to deny it. 'It was true once, don't you remember? Or have you forgotten the romantic evenings out when you took me to a restaurant and bought me flowers? Not to mention the fun we had in the taxi on the way home, confusing the taxi driver because we lived at separate addresses under the same roof.'

'Yes, of course I remember,' mumbled John, staring forlornly at the floor. How could he forget the best moments he'd shared with Sylvie in decades?

'And then you went and screwed it all up!' said Sylvie, poking him in the chest.

The host glanced at the audience. They were sitting there in rapt silence. He could tell they were enjoying this outburst immensely, as was the host, especially when he thought about the show's ratings zooming through the roof.

He turned his attention to the two stars. Things were hotting up between them. Tempers were fraying. The host couldn't believe their luck. What a scoop to get these two rival writers in the same room together and watch the sparks fly as they turned out to be a husband and wife at each other's throats.

'You're saying I screwed things up?' said John, raising his voice. 'I screwed up?'

Perhaps things were hotting up a bit too much, thought the host, who was wondering how far this marital spat might go. He watched them nervously as he gave the hand signal to two beefy employees who always stood sentry in the wings, out of camera-shot, in case they had any incidents on stage like guests coming to blows.

The two men stepped forward at his signal.

'Yes, you screwed up,' Sylvie argued, 'because you didn't have the balls to tell me to my face that you had taken one too many financial risks at a time in our life when we could least afford it. And I had to find this out from the postman.'

'The postman shouldn't have given you my letters.'

'Oh, so it's the postman's fault now, is it?'

'Well...no. But if you'd just moved back in with me, then we wouldn't have got into that financial mess in the first place.'

'Oh, so it's my fault. Is that what you're saying?'

'Well... yes,' John said matter-of-factly.

'You're incorrigible!' They were now standing almost nose-to-nose. She added, 'At least I didn't leave my grandchild with a perfect stranger!'

John threw his arms up in the air in frustration. Not that again! He reiterated, 'I did not leave Gertie with a perfect stranger!'

John and Sylvie were so busy arguing, that they had forgotten the row that they originally started in the privacy of their own home, over whose fault it was that they had lost contact with their grandchild, was now being conducted in front of a studio audience, and broadcast around the world on live television. They failed to notice two men striding purposefully across the stage in their direction. Moving toward Sylvie and John, preparing to cart them off the stage.

As Sylvie was suddenly lifted off the floor and John was dragged across the stage – he'd lost his footing when he was grabbed from behind – the studio audience went wild and started clapping and cheering. They even stood up to give them a standing ovation for an exceptionally entertaining performance.

The host looked around the audience in surprise. In all the years he had been hosting this show, the audience had never given any of their guests a standing ovation – until now.

They were still clapping as Sylvie was carried off the stage over one of the burly man's shoulders. Bum in the air, she kicked her legs, losing one of her expensive shoes as it shot across the stage into the audience. This was not the last hurrah Sylvie had been expecting. She thought she just might die of embarrassment.

John tried desperately to get his footing so at least he could walk off the stage with some dignity, but he was being dragged along too fast. He thought he might just die of embarrassment until he glimpsed Sylvie's utterly undignified exit. Now he felt it was far more likely he'd cop it at the hands of the writer, Love on the Rooftop before the day was out – she was going to murder him when all this was over.

The host breathed a sigh of relief as soon as they disappeared from view. He walked down to the stage and turned to look at the studio audience who were just loving it. They broke into another spontaneous chant, 'Tell us how the story ends! Tell us! Tell us!' The host stared at the audience in bemusement. They must all be as thick as two planks. After John and Sylvie's meltdown live on air, wasn't it obvious where that car wreck of a marriage was heading?

He held up his hands, gesturing for the audience to quieten down. Of course, he wouldn't say what he was thinking. 'Well folks, we're almost out of time, so I guess we're going to have to wait for the next instalment of *Dear John* and *Love on the Rooftop* to find out how the story ends.'

Although he had an idea how it all ends, he for one was still going to log on to their blogs and find out for himself. This had been one of the best shows he had ever hosted.

They were the most entertaining and surprising guests he'd ever had the pleasure to meet. He had a feeling that this couple had a few more surprises in store before they called it a day. He hoped so. And he hoped they were prepared for the fall-out of this show. The show's ratings had just rocketed. If those two writers thought they were already well-known as a result of their blogs and their magazine columns, after this performance, their notoriety was about to go stratospheric.

38

Sylvie and John were bundled into the back of a limo; no easy feat considering that as soon as the two men had escorted them outside, they were mobbed by camera crews and journalists. They all wanted to get the reaction of the writers, Dear John and Love on the Rooftop, who had just discovered on live television that they were, in fact, husband and wife.

'John, John!' shouted a journalist. 'What was your first reaction when you discovered that your rival, the writer of the hugely successful *Love on the Rooftop*, was your wife living downstairs?'

'Sylvie, Sylvie!' shouted another. 'Tell us how you felt when you found out your rival, the writer Dear John, was none other than your husband living upstairs?'

Neither Sylvie nor John uttered a word to the press. They sat in the limo as it sped away from the television studio, both completely taken aback by the unexpected media furore their appearance on the show had generated.

Sitting in the back of the limo, all Sylvie could think about was that she was still missing a shoe.

Sitting next to her, all John could think about was his *Dear*

John letter that hadn't turned out to be a *Dear John* letter at all. It didn't mean Sylvie wasn't going to leave him. And if she didn't intend to leave him when she wrote that note, she was most likely considering it now after his appearance on that show.

John stared out of the window. As the limo neared their hotel, he groaned. Outside was the same media frenzy they'd just escaped from when they left the studio. He was guessing someone must have leaked the name of the hotel where they were staying. He leaned forward in his seat to speak to the driver. John was about to ask whether he could drop them off at a back entrance when the limo sailed past their hotel.

Sylvie noticed it, too. 'Excuse me, but you've just passed the hotel where I'm staying.'

John looked at Sylvie and decided now was not a good time to tell her he'd been staying in the same hotel all along.

The driver nodded. 'Your bags are being sent on.'

'What do you mean, *sent on*?' Sylvie said indignantly. 'Sent where?'

'You've been moved to another hotel.'

Sylvie said in surprise, 'By whom?'

'By the hotel owner.'

'Bertram?' said Sylvie and John in unison.

'Mr Price sent the limo to pick you up. He didn't think you'd want all the media attention.'

Sylvie nodded. 'Well, he's right – we don't.' She quickly rephrased, 'I don't. I can't speak for *him!*'

John glanced at Sylvie and saw her finger pointing in his direction. He sighed and looked out the window, thinking how thoughtful of Bertram to go to all the trouble of shifting them. He must have watched the show and realised why the media had descended on his hotel. Then John thought of an altogether different reason Bertram had gone to all the bother of shifting them. John raised a suspicious eyebrow. Could it be that he didn't want the media camped outside his hotel in case some nosy reporter caught a whiff of another story – the reappearance of Bertram's wife – before they reconciled out of the glare of the media? From what Angelo had said about her disappearance, her reappearance would be big news.

Thinking of Bertram and Amelia reconciling, John stole a glance at Sylvie. He was very much hoping that they could talk things through this evening together in the hotel restaurant. John gave Sylvie a sideways glance. He couldn't imagine she'd accept his invitation to dinner if he just came right out with it and asked her; first, he had to break the ice. He didn't know where to start. Perhaps an apology was in order.

'Sylvie I—'

'DON'T!' Sylvie wagged a finger at him. 'Not. Another. Word.'

John rolled his eyes. He didn't think it would be *that* easy. She was still giving him the silent treatment. After his appearance on the show, it wouldn't surprise him if Sylvie never spoke to him again. He stole another glance at her profile. John still couldn't quite believe she was his rival, the writer Love on the Rooftop; the writer with whom he had shared such witty banter. While reading and responding to her magazine column, she had entertained him, often infuriated him, made him laugh, and sometimes made his blood boil. But through it all, what had surprised John was the realisation that he was falling in love with this writer. A woman he thought was a complete stranger. A woman he hoped to meet one day in person.

That's why he wanted to come to New York to meet this exceptional woman who, as it turned out, he'd been married to for the last forty years, and with whom he had fallen madly in love with all over again. Sitting here with Sylvie, he now knew there was so much more to his wife than he ever realised; there was a part of her that had been a stranger, a side to her she had never revealed.

John smiled as a thought occurred to him. It was as though they had bumped into each other all over again – two strangers on a collision course. However, they hadn't bumped into each other this time, not on a street corner like before. It was almost forty years ago when Sylvie, late for work, wasn't looking where she was going and had collided with John on a street corner and changed the course of his life forever.

This time they collided in a virtual world; they were two anonymous writers, just getting on with the business of writing, when Dear John and Love on the Rooftop careered into one another. John supposed it was inevitable that two writers with such opposing views on living apart together should come to each other's attention. Through writing their blogs and magazine columns, they had got to know one another. And John had fallen in love again.

It made him wonder if there was any chance she might have felt the same way about her rival, about Dear John. He tried hard to dismiss that possibility; what did it matter now? Love on the Rooftop wasn't even speaking to Dear John.

John turned from Sylvie to stare out the window. It was pitch dark outside until they drove through Times Square on the way to their hotel. John's attention was drawn to the massive neon signs on enormous billboards everywhere he looked. He turned to Sylvie and was about to say, *Blimey, look at that!* when he caught the look on her face which said, *I'm still not talking to you.*

John slumped back in his seat. He wished they had more time in New York to take in the sights. Then again, he wouldn't want to stay if he couldn't spend the extra time in New York with the woman he loved, with Sylvie. On second thought, John was only too pleased they had booked him on a flight home tomorrow.

Sylvie stole a glance at John. He was staring out of the window. She wondered what he was thinking. She wondered if he was disappointed when he found out that the writer, Love on the Rooftop, wasn't some mysterious, sultry, amazing woman, but only Sylvie – the woman he married.

Sylvie tried to brush that thought aside because although she could have murdered John after what happened on that show, it didn't change the fact that she had fallen in love with the writer, Dear John. She'd known this for some considerable time before her startling discovery that her husband and Dear John were the same person.

Sylvie glanced in his direction once again. She was still mad at him. She still wasn't speaking to him. And she *still* wasn't convinced he was *the one*. It was a ridiculous thought; how could he not be the one she was meant to spend the rest of her life with? How could she even think that after discovering John was Dear John, a writer just like her? Wasn't that a sign? *The* sign?

Despite her best efforts to convince herself otherwise, Sylvie had a feeling it wasn't the sign she was looking for. She knew why she felt this way. It was all because of that bizarre recurring dream, a dream that had inspired Sylvie to call her alter-ego Love on the Rooftop.

When the taxi arrived at the hotel, Sylvie refused John's invitation to join him for dinner in the restaurant. Instead, she ordered room service and retired to her suite for the evening.

That night, in her new hotel room in New York, Sylvie had that dream again in which she found love on a rooftop.

39

'Why is a lawyer demanding to see me?'

It was nine o'clock the following morning and John had just wandered into the hotel lobby, on his way to the restaurant for breakfast, when he thought he heard Sylvie's voice. He spotted her standing at the reception desk. John was pleased to see her because he was rather hoping they might have breakfast together.

'I'm sorry madam, but I can't help you with that.'

John sidled up to Sylvie hoping he got a better reception this morning after getting the cold shoulder in the taxi last night.

John said a tentative, 'Good morning.' He noticed the envelope on the front desk with her name on it and an official letter in her hand.

'Oh, John,' Sylvie turned to face him, looking anxious. 'I came down to the reception desk this morning, to ask where the restaurant was for breakfast, and there was this letter waiting for me.'

'What is it?'

'Well, that's just it,' said Sylvie. 'I'm not sure. A firm of lawyers has summoned me to their office here in New York, and I don't know why.'

'May I?' said John, indicating the letter.

Sylvie handed it to him. 'Go ahead, read it.'

John skimmed the brief letter asking Sylvie to attend a meeting with a lawyer at their office in Manhattan. It was typed on expensive headed paper, and the tone of the letter made it seem very official. Now John was worried too.

'Oh god,' said Sylvie in dismay, 'I think I know what it is. I'm being sued by some disgruntled reader for writing a pack of lies about living apart together in my blog.'

John looked at her askance. 'Can someone do that?'

'Maybe,' said Sylvie.

'This is America. People sue other people all the time, don't they?'

'I don't know about that,' replied John, not convinced. 'What about freedom of speech and all that? I don't think anybody could sue you for just being a bit creative in your blog. I bet some people go online and make things up about themselves all the time – that's their prerogative.'

'That's true,' agreed Sylvie. 'What about my magazine column, though? What about the porky-pies I wrote in that?'

John scratched his head and thought of a much more likely scenario. 'There is another possibility...'

'What's that?' Sylvie asked anxiously.

'Perhaps after our behaviour yesterday, the producers are suing us because things got so heated, they had to remove us from the show.'

Sylvie's face went ashen. 'That's it, isn't it!' She glanced at the letter in John's hand. 'But that doesn't explain why I'm the only one who has been summoned to see a lawyer? Surely, it involves the both of us.'

John thought about it and cocked his head to one side. 'Perhaps they felt you started it?'

'Give me that!' She snatched the letter out of John's hand. 'A fat lot of help you are.' Sylvie turned to the man on the front desk. 'Can you get me a taxi?'

'Of course. When does madam require it?'

'Madam requires it right now!' Sylvie glared at John before turning on her heel and storming off.

'Where are you going?' John followed Sylvie to the ornate double doors that led out the hotel.

'Where do you think?' Sylvie shot back. She came to an abrupt halt in the street outside and held up the letter in front of his face in answer to his question.

'Can I come too? It wasn't just your fault, you know. I'm as much to blame. They should have sent me a letter too.'

Sylvie regarded John for a moment. 'Fine!'

They left the hotel together and got into a waiting taxi. Sylvie gave the taxi driver the address of the lawyers' office and got a titbit of information in return they rather wished they hadn't.

The cab driver commented, 'They are one of the most prestigious and expensive lawyers in Manhattan. Did you know that?'

John whispered to Sylvie, 'I think we're in trouble.'

'No. I am,' mumbled Sylvie, nervously turning over the letter in her hands. When they arrived at the plush offices, they were directed to a reception room. As they sat down together on a comfortable leather sofa to wait for Sylvie to be called for her appointment, the receptionist gave them another titbit of information. They rather wished she hadn't. It turned out Sylvie's appointment was with the most senior partner of the law firm, who was now semi-retired. He rarely ventured into the office, and rarer still did any lawyering, apart from overseeing the most difficult cases.

The receptionist looked at Sylvie gravely before returning to her desk.

John looked down to find Sylvie was holding his hand. He gave her hand a reassuring squeeze, a gesture that said *don't worry, I'm right here.*

'Mr Beauregard will you see you now.'

John and Sylvie looked up to find the receptionist standing over them.

'Already?'

Sylvie gulped and looked at her watch. 'My appointment isn't for another fifteen minutes.'

'This way, please,' she gestured for them to follow.

Sylvie and John exchanged a nervous glance and reluctantly got up from the sofa. They followed the receptionist along a wide corridor, passing by individual offices on either side. They could see the firms' lawyers, busy at work, through floor-to-ceiling glass windows that ran its length.

As they made their way to Mr Beauregard's office, the receptionist gave a potted history of the law firm for want of something to say.

John didn't take a blind bit of notice although he did catch her mention something about the further you walked along the corridor, the more senior the lawyers became – like some sort of hierarchy – until you arrived at the very end of the passage, the very last office; the one with the superb views over Manhattan apparently, and the one belonging to Mr Beauregard, the most senior partner.

John noticed that the further along the corridor they walked, the more attention they were attracting; lawyers busy at work in their glass offices stopped to notice who was on their way to see the most important person in their law firm.

John was feeling more nervous with every step. He knew Sylvie felt the same way because she still had hold of his hand. She was clutching it tightly, making John's hand hurt. He didn't complain though, because this was the first physical contact he'd had with his wife for what seemed like an age. It felt good just simply holding hands.

He wished they were back home in London, holding hands and taking a stroll in Holland Park like they used to. Not walking along a glass corridor in a skyscraper in Manhattan, facing the possibility that despite making a success of their writing careers and staying financially solvent, they were going to be sued and lose it all.

John looked down at Sylvie's hand in his. He no longer cared about losing the house, and all their money, as long as he still had Sylvie.

The smart young receptionist stopped outside the office at the end of the corridor. The name *Mr Beauregard* was etched in gold lettering on the door. She knocked on the door once and opened it wide.

You'd think to look at them that Sylvie and John were walking into a room to face a firing squad, not a kindly round-faced old gentleman sitting behind a giant oak desk.

John peered at the gentleman across the room and raised an eyebrow.

Mr Beauregard stood up as they entered and caught John's expression. He looked down at his clothes and said, 'I must apologise for my attire.' He chuckled amiably. 'I'm never usually in the office at this hour in the morning.' He looked back at John and Sylvie. 'In fact, I'm never usually in the office.' He chuckled again. 'I'm afraid I came straight from the golf course.'

Something caught Mr Beauregard's eye. He suddenly bellowed, 'Marlowe – no!' A large, old yellow Labrador appeared from behind the desk. He spotted Sylvie and John in an instant and came bounding over to say hello, his tail wagging furiously as he nudged John's hand with his nose.

'Sorry, folks,' Mr Beauregard apologised. 'I hope you don't mind dogs.'

'Not at all,' said John, kneeling and giving the friendly Lab a good scratch behind the ears, momentarily forgetting the serious nature of their visit. 'What a good dog,' said John, pleased to meet him.

'Marlowe – come!'

John stood up as the dog bounded back to the desk and sat down, panting.

'Now let's get down to business,' said Mr Beauregard, motioning at the two chairs in front of his desk before he sat down.

John and Sylvie exchanged nervous glances and moved forward as one to take a chair in front of Mr Beauregard.

The lawyer was now seated behind his desk. His demeanour suddenly all business-like. Mr Beauregard laced his fingers together on top of his desk and looked at Sylvie. 'Thank you for coming along at such short notice. I'm sure there are plenty of other places in New York you'd rather see this morning than the inside of my office.' He chuckled.

'You have no idea,' remarked John.

'Although I do have the most spectacular view of Manhattan,' said Mr Beauregard jovially, glancing over his shoulder at the view of the Manhattan skyline from the window behind him.

Sylvie and John glanced at the view. Both nodded in agreement – it was quite stunning – both still wishing they were anywhere else but here marvelling at that view.

They turned their attention back to Mr Beauregard.

'Right, well, let's get on with it, shall we?' He looked across the table at John and Sylvie. 'Let me start by saying that I saw *The Who's Who Show* yesterday evening.'

John groaned.

Sylvie clutched John's hand again. It's just what they had both feared: they were being sued, or at least Sylvie was.

Mr Beauregard continued, 'I loved the fact that neither of you knew what the other one was getting up to, working anonymously for rival magazines, writing about each other, and all the while you were living under the same roof – no less. What a revelation that was on live television!' He shook his head in awe. 'That was one hell of a show, I can tell you.'

John and Sylvie exchanged confused glances; surely, he hadn't brought them here just to tell them that?

'And I'll tell you another thing…' Mr Beauregard leaned forward in his chair. 'It turns out I wasn't the only one watching the show last night.'

John furrowed his brow, wondering what was coming next.

'Our new intern watched the show, too. A dazzling kid. Only started with us last week. I'm surprised she found the time to watch any television, considering her workload. All our new interns start by going over a lot of our cases, taking work home with them to familiarise themselves with what we do.'

John didn't want to think about the kind of work they specialised in – lawsuits, most likely.

'What sort of work do you do?' Sylvie asked.

John rolled his eyes at Sylvie. Wasn't it obvious?

Mr Beauregard replied, 'Family law, mostly. We deal with drawing up wills, managing people's estates when they die, probate, that kind of thing.'

John looked up in surprise. He wished, in hindsight, he'd listened to the receptionist's potted history of the firm. He doubted Sylvie had been listening either; they were both too preoccupied with what was going to happen when they walked through the door at the end of the hall.

'Ah, I can tell you're a little surprised,' said Mr Beauregard. 'I expect you've seen too many of those American legal programmes on the television. I'm afraid we're rather boring. There are no lawsuits and big courtroom dramas for us. We only go to court if a plaintiff is contesting a will.'

Sylvie and John breathed a collective sigh of relief.

John raised a questioning eyebrow. If they weren't being sued, then what were they doing here?

'But I digress. Let's get back to the business at hand. Our intern was watching you on the show last night and put two and two together.'

John had a question.

'Just a moment.' Mr Beauregard held up his hand before John had a chance to ask what this was all about. 'Let's see if our intern is available. Perhaps she might like to tell you herself.'

John and Sylvie looked at each other as Mr Beauregard pressed a button on his phone. 'Please can you send Miss Watts into my office with the file. I have the client here with me now.'

Client? John looked at Sylvie.

There was a knock at the door. John and Sylvie turned in their seats to see a young lady, presumably the intern, entering the room carrying a file.

She walked confidently up to Mr Beauregard's desk. After brief introductions, she opened the file and took out the single sheet of paper. She laid it on the desk in front of Sylvie.

Sylvie recognised her handwriting immediately. 'That's my letter!' said Sylvie in astonishment, picking it up to take a closer look. 'Well, a copy, in any case.' Sylvie showed the letter to John. 'This is a copy of the letter that the estate agent in St. Columb forwarded to the person who owns the cottage in Cornwall.'

John nodded, recalling Sylvie's trip to Cornwall to scatter her mother's ashes in the garden of the cottage by the sea. A handwritten note had been left to Sylvie in her mother's will, detailing her final wish. The trouble was that the owner lived abroad. Sylvie had written that letter some months ago seeking his permission. But as far as John was aware, Sylvie had heard nothing back.

Mr Beauregard explained, 'We open all correspondence on behalf of our clients and take a copy before we forward the original on to them.'

Sylvie stared at Mr Beauregard. 'I knew they sent my letter care of a lawyer in New York, but it never crossed my mind when I was summoned here this morning that you might be the lawyer who had received my letter. I've been waiting for a response for so long, I'd almost given up.'

Sylvie looked from Mr Beauregard to the young intern standing next to his desk. 'What did he say? Did he grant my request?'

Mr Beauregard exchanged a glance with his young intern. 'Ah, this is where it gets tricky. I'm afraid I have some bad news. I'm sorry to tell you that shortly after receiving your letter, Mr Morelli passed away.'

'Oh dear,' said Sylvie, saddened to hear that news.

Morelli? John recognised that name.

'He was one of our oldest clients and a dear friend of mine.'

'I'm so sorry,' said Sylvie.

'Me too,' said John, not sounding quite as sincere as Sylvie, because all he could think about was that her mother's ashes might have to stay in their house forever.

Mr Beauregard continued, 'We have been in the throes of dealing with his will. I must apologise for the fact that we put your letter to one side while we dealt with Mr Morelli's bequests.'

Sylvie understood. 'There really is no need to apologise.' She realised her letter was not a priority under the circumstances. It wasn't as though she was going to get an answer from him now he was dead. Sylvie was disappointed, nonetheless.

'The problem is we have been having some difficulty locating all the beneficiaries of Mr Morelli's will.'

'Please,' interrupted Sylvie, getting up from her chair. 'There's no need to explain. I quite understand.'

'Oh, but I don't think you do,' said Mr Beauregard, motioning for Sylvie to resume her seat. 'Let me hand you over to Miss Watts.' He smiled at the young intern.

Sylvie sat and listened to what the young lady had to say.

'I have been helping with the search for all the beneficiaries of Mr Morelli's will by doing some research into his past. I discovered that during the Second World War he was an Italian prisoner of war in England in a POW camp near a village called St. Columb in Cornwall.'

John sat forward in his seat as he recalled that conversation with Gina about her grandfather – Mr Morelli, the owner of Morelli's in New York – who it turned out had been a POW in Cornwall during the Second World War.

'Really?' said Sylvie. 'Are you sure?' She was thinking about Harriet and Chloe and their research on the internet that uncovered an Italian by the name of Mr Morelli, who had been a POW in a camp near St. Columb. Sylvie dismissed it at the time, thinking it was a bit of a stretch to assume the owner of the cottage in Cornwall could be the same person.

The young intern said, 'It's true.'

Sylvie couldn't wait to tell them they'd been right all along.

'Go on, tell her the rest,' said Mr Beauregard excitedly. 'Tell her how you put two and two together.'

She smiled at her boss and turned to Sylvie. 'After I discovered this about Mr Morelli's past, I recalled seeing a letter sitting in another file sent from St. Columb, Cornwall. That's when I made a connection.'

'That's right,' said Mr Beauregard, nodding his head and taking over from his young intern. 'You see, we didn't find your letter in with his personal papers because it had been put in a separate file. I'm embarrassed to admit it, but your note had completely slipped my mind. I had forgotten all about you, my dear. That's where our young intern came in. She found the missing link; she remembered your letter sitting in another file. Thanks to Miss Watts here, we found the last beneficiary of his will.'

Sylvie looked at him blankly. 'I don't follow...'

'It was stupid of me not to remember,' admitted Mr Beauregard. 'The day my good friend, Mr Morelli, received your letter he called an urgent meeting with one of our lawyers and added a codicil to his will.' He held up his hand. 'Before you ask, let me explain. A codicil is an amendment to the will. In this case, he made an amendment whereby a new beneficiary was added. That beneficiary being you.'

'I'm sorry?' said Sylvie, still having a hard time following all this lawyer-speak.

John had been listening intently to all this, and finally spoke up, 'Are you saying Mr Morelli made my wife one of the beneficiaries of his will?'

'Yes, that is correct. We couldn't believe our luck when we saw you on *The Who's Who Show* right here in New York. I just needed to get you into my office to confirm you were the same Sylvia Baxter who sent that letter.'

Mr Beauregard opened a drawer in his desk and produced an official looking document which he placed in front of him. He turned to Sylvie and started to read, 'To Mrs Sylvia Baxter, I do so bequeath Trevelyan Cottage…'

Miss Watts, the young intern, smiled as Mr Beauregard read the codicil that had been added to Mr Morelli's will. He then passed a sealed envelope across the table with the name and address of the cottage on the front and the words House keys written underneath.

'The cottage in Cornwall is yours to do with as you wish. I think we can safely assume Mr Morelli has granted your request to scatter your mother's ashes in what is now your garden in Cornwall.'

Sylvie stared at the envelope in front of her.

John said, 'Bloody hell! We own a cottage in Cornwall. I don't believe it!' He bounced out of his chair to shake the lawyer's hand, thanking him profusely. He then turned to the young intern, Miss Watts, and did the same. John couldn't get over all this. He'd walked into Mr Beauregard's office thinking they were going to be sued and face financial ruin, and now they were walking out of that office with the keys to a cottage in Cornwall.

Bloody hell! This was not what he was expecting. They knew people who had come into an inheritance, like Sylvie's best friend, Julia, but that was never on the cards for them. To John, this was like winning the lottery.

Sylvie was still sitting in her chair, the keys in the envelope on the desk, untouched. She looked across the table at Mr Beauregard. Sylvie had one question. 'Why?'

John stopped bouncing around and looked at Sylvie.

'Pardon me?' said Mr Beauregard.

'Why did he leave the cottage to me?'

Mr Beauregard picked up the envelope and smiled at Sylvie. He walked around the desk and placed it in her hands. 'I'm afraid I can't answer that question. Perhaps he read your letter and it just seemed the right thing to do.'

Sylvie turned over the envelope in her hand, the outline of the keys protruding from the white paper envelope. 'But to leave a cottage to a complete stranger…?'

Mr Beauregard shrugged. 'Perhaps he knew your mother?'

Sylvie looked up sharply.

John glanced at his watch. 'Oh crumbs! Come on, Sylvie,' John held out his hand, 'we've got a plane to catch.'

Sylvie looked at her watch too. 'Gosh, is that the time?' She stood up and took John's hand.

Mr Beauregard walked them to the door and held it open as

they stepped into the corridor outside. He lingered in the doorway, trying to shake off the feeling that he had neglected to mention something.

He was just about to close the door when he remembered. 'Just one more thing before you go,' he called out.

Sylvie and John stopped and turned around.

'I'm sorry, but in all the excitement, it completely slipped my mind. There was something else bequeathed to you in the will. I'm afraid we don't have it here, and as you're leaving today, there isn't time to locate it in storage for you. I'll get my intern on it straight away and we will mail it. I expect you'll receive it soon.'

He closed the door before Sylvie asked what else she would get from a man she never knew. She stood there, staring at the envelope in her hand.

John looked at his watch. 'Sylvie, I'm afraid we have to go.'

After a quick detour back to their hotel to pick up their luggage, they made their way by taxi to the airport to catch their flight home. In the back of the taxi, Sylvie turned to John with a question. It was a question that had been going through her mind on a continuous loop since she left Mr Beauregard's office. 'I don't understand why Mr Morelli would leave his cottage in Cornwall to a stranger?'

John was still on a high over their apparent good fortune. 'Oh Sylvie, what does it matter? Why can't you just accept how lucky you are? You've just been left a cottage that's got to be worth...' John tried to guess what a cottage in Cornwall might be worth; he couldn't come up with a figure and shrugged. 'Well, it must be worth a lot of money because it's in Cornwall, for goodness' sake. And a stone's throw away from the beach, from what you've told me. Isn't it detached?'

Sylvie nodded absently.

'Goodness, I did not expect to be travelling home from New York with the keys to a cottage in Cornwall!' John was at it again, grinning from ear to ear, unable to believe their luck.

Sylvie wished he'd button it up and stop carrying on about how much money it was worth and how lucky they were. Unlike John, Sylvie was feeling extremely uncomfortable about this strange turn of events. She didn't believe in luck, not that sort of luck, only the kind that came your way when you worked hard and got what you deserved. As far as Sylvie was concerned, she didn't deserve this; inheriting houses, inheriting anything was never on the cards for them, not from family and certainly not from strangers.

Something didn't smell right, and Sylvie was determined to get to the bottom of why a man she had never even met had left her a cottage in his will.

40

Sylvie was standing in Business Class refusing to take her seat.

'I'm sorry, Mrs Baxter, but this is the seat you have been allocated,' the flight attendant said calmly. 'You must sit down and fasten your seatbelt.'

'I'm not sitting next to him!'

The flight attendant glanced at the gentleman sitting in the window seat.

He smiled up at her and offered an apologetic shrug before returning his attention to the newspaper on his lap.

'But that's...er...your husband, Mrs Baxter.'

'I know that!' said Sylvie in exasperation. She looked at John. Sylvie didn't want to sit next to him hearing about that blasted cottage, and their apparent good fortune, for the entire flight home but the flight attendant refused to budge on the issue. She remained where she was, standing in the aisle, waiting for Sylvie to take her seat.

Sylvie glared at the flight attendant, glared at John sitting there reading the newspaper, and then took her seat.

The moment she sat down, he folded the newspaper away and started on again about the cottage.

Sylvie threw her hands up in frustration. She knew it. She just knew it. She was going to have to sit here and listen to him, like a broken record, for the entire flight home from New York.

'Right, that's it!' Sylvie was sick and tired of hearing about their blasted good fortune, and finally flipped. She got out of her seat as soon as the seatbelt sign was switched off, got John out of his seat, and dragged him to the toilets at the end of the aisle. 'Look, John,' she said, trying to poke him in the chest, but having great difficulty at such close quarters. 'For one thing, *we* did not inherit a cottage. *I did.*' She noted his confused expression.

Sylvie wagged a finger at him. 'I have not forgotten about yesterday.' She was still smarting from the surprise encounter with him on *The Who's Who Show*, not to mention the sheer embarrassment at being carted off the stage over someone's shoulder.

'Oh, I see,' mumbled John, trying to look anywhere but at Sylvie, which was difficult standing nose to nose.

'This doesn't change a thing, John.' If he thought he was going to get off that easily, he could think again. Sylvie glared at him before storming out of the toilet and nearly colliding with another passenger waiting to use the facilities.

The passenger was just about to step into what he thought was a vacant toilet when John followed Sylvie out. The passenger stepped back in surprise.

John gestured in Sylvie's direction, shrugged at the young man, and said, 'Mile High Club.'

'Lucky bastard,' said the young man, watching John make his way back to Business Class.

Sylvie sat down in John's seat this time, so she wouldn't have to get up when he returned. She stared out of the cabin window at the blanket of dense white cloud cover beneath them and thought about that cottage by the sea. She was wondering if the lawyer, Mr Beauregard, was right and Mr Morelli had known her mother. Sylvie wouldn't be happy about any of this until she knew the whole story.

Sylvie spent the rest of the flight mulling this over in peace and quiet. John spent the rest of the journey looking subdued after his unexpected trip to the in-flight toilet to be told by Sylvie, in no uncertain terms, that nothing had changed.

Apart from the fact that she wanted to put a stop to his incessant yacking about their perceived good fortune, which was getting on her nerves, Sylvie didn't want to build up any expectations that somehow this sudden windfall, in the shape of a cottage in Cornwall, would change things between them. It didn't mean they were getting back together – not after she had that dream again last night.

'Did you forget to turn out the lights before you left?' Sylvie asked as she stepped out of the taxi and looked up at the house.

John had just paid the taxi fare and was busy unloading their suitcases and bags on to the pavement outside their house. 'I don't think so,' he replied.

He turned around as the taxi departed and looked up at the house. It was almost midnight, and pitch dark outside, but there was a light on in the upstairs apartment. 'Oh, I must have left a light on.' John shrugged. 'Either that or Chloe forgot to switch it off when she popped in to feed Mouse.' Almost as an after-thought, he added, 'I hope she remembered to leave my keys under the doormat for my return.'

Sylvie was about to pick up her suitcase. She stopped and looked at John. 'You gave Chloe the keys to your apartment?'

'Yes.'

Sylvie shook her head, thinking that he might live to regret that. She was surprised to hear Chloe had volunteered to look after John's cat while he was away. She knew her daughter only too well. In her experience, Chloe never went out of her way to do someone a good turn unless there was something in it for her. Sylvie narrowed her eyes and looked up at the window in John's apartment where the light was on. She had no reason to suspect Chloe had moved in while he was away. She couldn't imagine Chloe and her fiancé, Declan, had split up. They'd just bought a house together. They were getting engaged, soon to be wed.

Chloe had never got that far with any of her other boy-friends before. She'd never hung around long enough to make a commitment – until Declan came along. Still, Sylvie couldn't shake the feeling that John was about to discover he had a house guest; it would never surprise her if Chloe had packed her bags and moved right in.

John helped Sylvie carry her suitcase up the garden path and into the house.

Sylvie opened her apartment door and let him carry her bags inside and deposit them in her lounge.

He lingered for a moment in the lounge. 'Well, I guess I better be off upstairs then.' He looked across the room at Sylvie. She was standing by the door.

'I guess so,' said Sylvie.

John reluctantly walked out the door. He did a quick about turn and planted a kiss on Sylvie's cheek before she had time to object. Then he scooted upstairs.

A smile danced on Sylvie's lips as she shut the door. Then the exhaustion of a long-haul flight caught up with her. Not to mention the stress and anxiety of being summoned to a lawyer's office in New York, only to discover the visit had raised more questions than it answered. Sylvie looked at her suitcases. She was too tired to unpack. All she wanted to do was crawl into bed and sleep for a week.

Sylvie's next thought was her blasted dream about finding love on the rooftop; that wiped the smile off her face. She wished Julia had never told her about stupid *signs* and finding *the one*. Then perhaps she would stop reading so much into a dream and focus on the man she had been falling in love with these past weeks – Dear John.

Sylvie was just rummaging through her suitcase, trying to find her toothbrush, when a loud knock on her apartment door startled her.

'Sylvie – it's John.'

'I'm exhausted,' Sylvie called out, yawning heavily as she approached the door. 'Whatever it is, can't it wait until tomorrow?' Sylvie opened the door and told him, 'I just want to get some sleep.'

'Well, so do I!' exclaimed John, standing in her doorway, looking agitated. 'But the girls won't let me into my apartment!'

'Girls?' Sylvie looked past him, up the stairs. 'What are you talking about?'

'Chloe, Harriet and Jess are all upstairs and refuse to let me in.' John knitted his eyebrows. 'Sylvie, what on earth is going on?'

Sylvie put her hand to her mouth.

John studied her. 'Are you finding this funny?'

Sylvie tried to stifle a laugh, but she just couldn't help herself.

She wasn't surprised Chloe was up there, not in the least. But when John told her Harriet was up there too, and Jess was home from Australia, Sylvie had an idea what they were all up to. He had stupidly given Chloe his keys, and now all three of them were in his apartment, refusing to leave, probably thinking they could force their parents back together.

Sylvie smiled at her naïve husband. 'They're staging a sit-in, John.'

'A what?'

'A sit-in. You know, like a protest or—'

'I know what a sit-in is,' John said gruffly, interrupting. He glanced up the stairs and then turned to Sylvie. 'Why?'

'Isn't it obvious?'

'Not to me!' John turned on his heel and marched back up the stairs. He stopped outside his door and demanded, 'Girls, I don't know what you think you're playing at, but I want you to open this door at once!'

'Sorry, Dad, no can do,' said Chloe from behind the door.

Harriet chimed in. 'There's no way, after New York, that you two are going to return to your separate apartments like nothing has happened. You are going to sit down together and sort this out once and for all,' lectured Harriet, sounding very pompous.

'Dad, as you may have gathered, we're staging a sit-in,' added Jess. 'That was my idea, by the way.'

John heaved a sigh and wandered back down the stairs with his shoulders slumped. Short of breaking down the door, he was resigned to the fact that he wasn't sleeping in his apartment tonight.

Sylvie was standing in her doorway. 'Well?'

John looked at her in exasperation. 'I might find this almost comical if it wasn't so late and I wasn't feeling so exhausted.' He gathered up his suitcase.

Sylvie watched John head for the front door. 'Where do you think you're going?'

John shrugged. 'To book into a hotel for the night.'

'Don't be stupid.' Sylvie turned around and walked back into her apartment, leaving her door wide open.

John hesitated. 'Are you asking me to stay the night?'

'Of course I am,' Sylvie called back.

John didn't need to be asked twice. Grinning like a Cheshire cat, he hot-footed it into Sylvie's apartment and closed the door behind him. When he turned around, Sylvie was throwing the cushions off her sofa.

'John, come and help me with this.'

Fifteen minutes later, John had changed into his pyjamas and was lying on the sofa bed in the lounge, under a spare blanket, staring up at the ceiling. He frowned as he reached over and switched off the table lamp beside the sofa. This wasn't exactly what he had in mind when Sylvie asked him to stay the night.

41

John turned over and heard the springs twanging beneath him. The sofa bed was uncomfortable. Not that it mattered. After such an eventful week in New York, and a long-haul flight, he imagined he would go out like a light. He didn't. He turned over in bed and stared up at the ceiling. Despite the exhaustion, he was wide awake. Tossing and turning some more didn't do the trick. Eventually, he threw off the blanket, got up and crept out of the lounge.

John knocked softly on Sylvie's bedroom door. He knew it was late. They were both exhausted. This should wait until later. But there was a reason he couldn't get to sleep; John had a confession to make.

'What is it?' hissed Sylvie.

John opened her bedroom door a crack and whispered, 'Are you awake?'

Sylvie switched her bedside table lamp on. John wasn't the only one having trouble getting off to sleep. Sylvie also had something on her mind: she didn't want to dream that dream again. She hadn't had her recurring dream, where she finds love on a rooftop since Bertram had been reunited with his daughter on The Rooftop Café. Sylvie thought that was it – dream over. Then it returned the night after the show before they left New York. She'd been lying awake, wondering why that dream had started again, wondering what it all meant.

'Did I wake you?' ventured John.

Sylvie propped herself up on one elbow. She looked him up and down as he walked into her bedroom. 'Why are you wearing a coat over your pyjamas? I didn't think it was that cold. Do you want me to put the heating on?'

'No… er, Sylvie, can you do something for me?'

Sylvie sat up in bed. 'Do you want a cup of tea? A milky drink?' Sex, thought Sylvie, raising her eyebrows, wondering why that idea had suddenly popped into her head.

'Er no… um… what I'd like is for you to get out of bed and put a coat on, please.'

Sylvie looked at him askance. 'But it's the middle of the night. What's going on?'

After some persuasion, Sylvie decided to humour him. She was wide awake anyway. It wasn't as though she was going to nod off anytime soon. She got out of bed and slipped on a coat over her nightie.

'You'll need some shoes too.'

Sylvie looked at John. 'Are we going out?'

'Kind of…'

Sylvie walked over to the wardrobe and found her comfortable walking shoes. She put them on and then caught sight of herself in the mirror on the inside of the wardrobe door. She frowned at her reflection. 'What do I look like?' She had a three-quarter-length coat over her flimsy knee-length nightie, bare legs, and walking shoes.

John said, 'You'll do,' when in fact what he thought was that she looked quite sexy.

John led Sylvie downstairs to the basement kitchen and unlocked the french doors to the garden. He took a flashlight from the kitchen drawer, although he knew that wasn't necessary. As soon as they stepped outside, the security light blinked on and threw a sheet of fierce white light across the patio.

Sylvie's teeth chattered.

Standing on the patio just outside the french doors, John motioned for Sylvie to step aside. He then reached up and pulled a chord.

As part of the conversion, they were required by law to have a fire escape fitted on the outside of the house. It was like the ones often found on American apartment buildings. They'd had it fitted so that the first flight of metal steps was suspended above the window, out of sight of the basement kitchen. That was the chord John pulled for the stairs that came floating down in the dark.

'John, what on earth are you doing?' asked Sylvie, standing in the garden in the freezing cold, her teeth still chattering. She stood there looking at that metal staircase she'd forgotten all about until John pulled that chord. What was he up to?

John walked up the first few steps and turned around, holding out his hand. 'Sylvie, take my hand.'

Sylvie hesitated. 'I'm not going up there!'

'There's something I want to show you. Trust me.'

Sylvie raised her head and eyed the metal staircase that led up the back of the house and disappeared into the darkness. She turned her attention to John. He was still standing a short way up the metal staircase, holding out his hand, looking sincere.

Sylvie reached out to grasp his hand. 'This better be good.'

The garden security light over the patio lit most of the way up the metal fire escape until they neared the top, which was obscured in darkness.

They paused while John switched on the flashlight.

'Not far now,' he said, glancing over his shoulder at Sylvie, right behind him.

'What are we doing up here?' said Sylvie, pulling her coat around her and wishing she had thought to slip on a pair of trousers; the wind was whipping around her bare legs, making her shudder with cold. Then again, she didn't know she'd be climbing up the back of their house like bloody Spiderman. This was ridiculous.

Sylvie repeated the question, 'What are we doing up here, John?'

'You'll see,' John shouted over his shoulder. 'We're nearly there.'

'Nearly where?' Sylvie called back. 'We're almost up to the roof!'

'Exactly!' John smiled as he stepped up on to the rooftop. He turned around and held out his hand for Sylvie.

Sylvie hesitated, looked down, thought about turning back, but then countered that thought with the fact that John had the flashlight. Besides, she'd come this far. She might as well find out why he had got it into his head to drag her all the way up to the roof of their four-storey townhouse.

Sylvie took John's hand and stepped up on to the rooftop. 'John, I don't know what we're doing up here...' she began. Something caught her eye. She saw a twinkly light at her feet. It looked like a garden solar light glowing in the dark.

John stepped aside to reveal something he wanted to show her months ago.

Sylvie gasped and turned to look at John, her face a mixture of emotions – surprise, shock, disbelief, amazement. And then a reaction John had not been expecting: Sylvie started to cry.

He stared at her in bewilderment. 'Sylvie, I did it for you. I thought you'd like it.'

Sylvie wiped her eyes dry with the sleeve of her coat. 'Like it?' She stared at her husband in astonishment. 'You daft fool. I don't like it, I love it. I absolutely adore it,' gushed Sylvie, trying to take it all in. The myriad of twinkly solar lights illuminated the rooftop garden she didn't know even existed.

She turned to John. 'Oh John, it's everything I imagined a rooftop garden could be - and more.'

'You said you wanted one once – don't you remember?'

Sylvie remembered, all right. She wanted one from the very beginning, when they first purchased the house back in the seventies. When John started to renovate, Sylvie's first suggestion was a rooftop garden so together they could watch the sunset over London; it would be her dream come true, she told him one day, not long after they had moved into the dilapidated house in a then rundown area full of bedsits called Holland Park. But it wasn't John's dream.

Although Sylvie went along with everything he wanted to do to the house, every time she brought up her idea of a rooftop garden John had a delaying tactic up his sleeve; always finding an excuse to do something else, something he preferred to spend the money on. Until he ran out of excuses. Until there was nothing more to be done to the house. Sylvie had asked one last time if she could have her rooftop garden – John said no.

John stood there, staring at Sylvie. He'd lost count of the number of times she'd asked for a rooftop garden when he was renovating the house all those years ago. He recalled telling her it wasn't practical; it was too expensive and a luxury they couldn't afford. But then so was the kitchen he had installed when he knew he could have found a cheaper alternative, or the under-floor heating that wasn't necessary when the gas fired central heating was more than enough.

The difference between what John wanted and what Sylvie wanted was that he held the purse strings, and Sylvie did not; and he was a selfish git who, if he loved his wife that much, should have given her the one thing she craved. But he didn't. And that turned out to be a lasting regret. One that John finally found a way to rectify when he came up with the idea of converting the house. There was just one problem: he had underestimated the cost of the work to create Sylvie's rooftop terrace garden, and that's when things went wrong.

John knew he should have called a halt to it and scrapped the idea when things got out of hand, but he couldn't do that. This time, come hell or high water, Sylvie was having her rooftop garden – whatever the cost. So he took out a loan, used up his savings, re-mortgaged the house, and got himself in a whole heap of financial trouble into the bargain.

He confessed all this to Sylvie. 'That's how I ended up getting us into such a financial mess,' admitted John, finishing his confession as he followed Sylvie, drinking in her delighted expression as she marvelled at the rooftop garden he had spent a small fortune on.

'Why didn't you tell me about this before?'

He shook his head. 'There just never seemed to be the right

moment to tell you I'd been so stupid. You see, it was never part of the plan. It was so...'

'Spontaneous?'

'Well, yes, but I was going to say reckless. One day I said to the builder, can you create a rooftop terrace garden? I didn't plan for it or budget for it. It was so unlike me. I just wanted you to have one.' John sighed. 'I've been a foolish man, Sylvie. I should have at least thought it through before—?' He didn't manage another word, for suddenly Sylvie's lips were on his.

When they both drew back to catch a breath, all Sylvie said was, 'You may be a foolish man, John Baxter, but you're the one.'

John looked at her, perplexed. 'The one?'

Sylvie gazed around her rooftop garden. She turned to John with tears in her eyes. If he could have done one thing, above all else, to prove how much he still loved her, then this was it. At that moment, she knew this was the sign she'd been looking for. Her dream had come true; Sylvie had found love on the rooftop.

She wiped her eyes dry, then stood on tiptoes and kissed him again, taking him by surprise once more.

'I say,' exclaimed John, holding her in a warm embrace when their lips parted, 'I think I like being the one.'

Sylvie stared into his blue-grey eyes.

'I've got a brilliant idea, John.'

'What is it?'

'In the spirit of doing stupid, crazy things, we're both wide awake so why don't we get some blankets, wrap ourselves up warm, light the garden stove...' – she pointed at the small cast iron multi-fuel wood burner that John had thoughtfully bought for the garden – 'and sit up here on our rooftop garden to watch the sunrise over London?'

John thought that was an excellent idea. In answer to her question, he grinned. 'You wait here, and I'll go and fetch two blankets.' He was already heading back to the fire escape before he finished that sentence.

Sylvie wrapped her coat tightly around her and listened to the sound of her husband clambering down the fire escape. The beam of the flashlight danced and dimmed as he made his descent.

Sylvie was thinking about what her life would have been like if she hadn't met John; she wouldn't have had three wonderful daughters, or a grandchild called Gertie, or even Alfie – her cocker spaniel. Or come home from work one day to see a lovely man, in his early sixties, building a snowman for their grand-daughter and pulling funny faces, making her laugh.

If she hadn't met John, she wouldn't have seen the house they had lived in for most of their married life converted into two apartments. And as a consequence of living apart together, she wouldn't have started a successful career as a writer and columnist or found love again where she least expected it – in the arms of the man she married. If she hadn't met John, she wouldn't be the woman standing here today, realising true happiness.

Sylvie thought back to the first time they met. It was nearly forty years ago, and Sylvie had been walking along a London street during her lunch break from work. She hadn't been watching where she was going, and she'd walked straight into him; a few seconds earlier, a few seconds later, a few inches left or right, and her life would have been a different story.

She'd thought about that moment throughout their married lives, how a chance encounter had brought them together. At the back of her mind, she had always wondered what if...? What if they had never met? Would her life have been different? Would her life have been better somehow? But today she was happy this had been her story. Today, standing in her rooftop garden, she realised he was and always had been *the one*.

The one appeared at the top of the fire escape with two blankets over his arm and a box of matches to light the stove.

Sylvie came over to take a blanket and brushed John's cheek with her hand, leaning forward to share another kiss.

'What on earth did I do to deserve that?' John said playfully, after another show of affection from his wife.

'Oh, nothing in particular – just for being you.'

'Well, I think I can keep that up.' John grinned at his wife. 'I'll light the stove.' He lit a match.

Sylvie looked about her. 'Oh, I think we needed a rug.'

John blew out the match, satisfied the firelighters under the logs would do the rest. He turned around and looked at Sylvie. 'A rug? What for?'

'It's okay, we can sit on one of the blankets and share the other.' Sylvie lay a cover down on the wooden decking.

John walked over and picked it up. 'I think it will be a tad uncomfortable sitting down there, don't you think?'

'But—',

John took her hand and led her over to one side of the wooden, decked terrace. 'Now close your eyes.'

'Close my eyes?'

'Yes, Sylvie.'

Sylvie did as she was asked. 'What are you up to, John?'

'You're not peeking, are you?'

Sylvie shook her head. 'No, John. I'm not peeking.'

John removed a folding natural reed garden screen and stepped aside. 'You can look now.'

Sylvie tentatively opened her eyes.

She was so quiet, John wondered if he'd done the right thing. He hesitated. 'Er... I emailed Declan while I was in New York and asked him to buy one and set it up for when we returned.' John quickly added, 'Not that I was assuming we would...you know...get back together. I just wanted to do this – for you.'

Sylvie still didn't say a word.

'I got the idea when I was in New York,' John said nervously, 'Did I tell you about the taxi driver I hired for the day?'

Sylvie slowly shook her head – no.

'We visited his parents. On their porch – I guess it was more like a veranda – was this wooden garden swing chair for two and well, I thought of you. Actually, if I'm honest, I was thinking about something else.' John took a deep breath. 'Look, I'm really sorry about getting rid of your bench that was in the back garden under the old oak—'

Sylvie turned around, threw her arms around John, and said, 'I love you, John Baxter.'

'Oh,' said John in surprise. 'Does that mean I can join you on the garden seat for two?' He held up the blankets.

Sylvie released John, took a blanket, and walked over to the wooden swing chair. She sat down. It was remarkably similar to the old bench she used to adore, except this one was much, much nicer. Not because it was newer, or that it gently rocked back and forth, or even because of its position next to the warming garden stove, with the views over the London skyline. What made this seat special was something else, something Sylvie had longed for all her married life.

John continued to hover in front of her. He watched her put the blanket around her shoulders. Then she lifted one end and looked at John.

John pointed at his chest silently asking, *you want me to come and sit with you?*

'Only if you want to, John.'

'Of course I want to sit with you.'

And *that* was what Sylvie had longed for all these years; he wanted to sit with her on the garden swing chair for two. He wanted to *be* with her. Not like before, thought Sylvie, when she sat at one end of the garden, on her bench under the old oak tree, and he sat at the other; back then it was more important for him to sit on his comfortable garden chairs near the kitchen, where he could listen to the radio and nip in for a snack if he got peckish.

John sat down next to Sylvie on the garden swing seat for two.

Sylvie passed the other end of the blanket around John's shoulders. They cuddled up together under the rug, warm and cosy despite the chilly night air. Sylvie smiled. What a dramatic change in John that he could do without his creature comforts because it was more important to spend time with his wife.

Almost as soon as John sat down, he was out of his seat again.

'Where are you going?'

John gave Sylvie a mischievous grin. He was up to something, she could tell.

'Just give me two ticks...'

John returned in two ticks and caught the look on Sylvie's face. 'What's the matter?'

Sylvie frowned. 'Is that your radio from the kitchen?'

He looked down at the wireless in his hands. 'Yes.'

'I thought we were just going to sit together and watch the sunrise?' Sylvie grimaced. She imagined the next thing he'd do was produce some snacks, so he didn't get peckish.

'We've still got plenty of time before the sun rises. Before we settle down again, there's something I'd like us to do first.'

Sylvie yawned. The warm blanket around her shoulders and the heat from the garden stove, coupled with the gentle rocking motion of the swing seat, back and forth, back and forth, was making her drowsy. 'I think I'd rather sit here, if you don't mind. Whatever it is, you can do it yourself – can't you?'

John frowned at her. 'Oh, that won't do at all, Sylvie. This has to be done together.'

Sylvie sat up in her seat. 'Did you just say *together*?'

John nodded and smiled. 'Yes – together.'

42

Harriet was woken by the sound of music. She'd been fast asleep in John's bedroom when she was disturbed. Her first thought was that Chloe, who was across the hall, supposedly asleep in John's spare bedroom, was listening to something on her laptop. Harriet got up to investigate, intending to tell Chloe off for waking her up. She'd been looking forward to her first uninterrupted night's sleep since Gertie was born; Gertie still hadn't slept through the night.

Harriet crossed the hall to the second bedroom, but there was no tell-tell sign of a light radiating from beneath the door. Harriet poked her head around the door.

There was a rustle of covers. Chloe was awake, too. She sat up in bed and switched on her side light. 'What's that noise?' asked Chloe, rubbing the sleep out of her eyes. 'Were you woken up too, Harriet?'

Harriet nodded.

'Do you think Jess put the television on downstairs?'

Harriet didn't know, but she was going to find out.

They both crept down the stairs to the lounge to find the television wasn't on. Jess was fast asleep, cocooned in her sleeping bag on John's sofa. Harriet turned to Chloe and put a finger to her lips. She motioned for them both to turn around and go back to bed.

The streetlight outside illuminated the room, casting a subtle glow through the curtains, but not enough to stop Harriet from walking into the side table and stubbing her toe. 'Shit!'

'What's going on?' a muffled voice said from the sofa.

'It's nothing, go back to sleep.'

Jess wriggled out of her sleeping bag. 'Is that music?'

All three girls walked upstairs and stood listening in the hall. Chloe said, 'Do you think it's coming from next door?'

They all stopped and concentrated on the direction of the music. Jess walked past the two bedrooms and stopped outside a door at the far end of the hall. 'Sounds like it's coming from the cupboard.'

'That's odd,' said Chloe, walking up to the door to listen. 'But I think you're right.'

Harriet frowned and walked over. She opened the cupboard door to reveal a hanging rail containing John's old suits he used to wear to work. They all peered inside. The music seemed to come from the back of the cupboard. Harriet swept the clothes aside to reveal another door.

'A hidden door?' exclaimed Harriet in surprise. She turned to look at Chloe and Jess.

'That's strange.'

'It's like we've just stepped into an episode of *The Twilight Zone,'* added Chloe. 'Can you open it?'

Harriet grasped the doorknob. As soon as she opened the door, the music could be heard more clearly than ever.

'What's behind the door?'

Harriet stepped aside for the others to see.

'A staircase?'

Chloe and Jess exchanged confused glances.

Harriet said, 'What on earth has Daddy been up to?'

Jess said, 'Let's find out.' She took the lead, followed by Harriet and Chloe. A gentle glow of light emanated from the top of the stairs, illuminating the way.

'I feel like I'm five again,' said Chloe. 'Remember when we used to play hide and seek around the house?' Chloe saw Jess and Harriet bobbing their heads up down as they climbed the stairs. 'You two always used to trick me and leave me to go hide when all the while you were downstairs in the kitchen helping yourself to ice-cream.' Chloe frowned. 'Sometimes it wasn't much fun being the youngest.'

'Sorry,' said Jess and Harriet in unison, not sounding particularly sorry about playing tricks on their naïve little sister.

As they neared the top of the stairs, they could hear the music distinctly. They stopped to listen.

Jess said, 'I recognise that song, but I can't remember what it's called.'

'*Dancing in the Moonlight*,' said Harriet as she reached the top stair.

'What can you see?' Chloe asked from below.

Harriet giggled. She put her hand to her mouth to stifle a laugh. 'Oh dear.'

Jess crouched beside her on the top step and looked through the panelled glass door to the rooftop garden beyond. Jess turned to Harriet. 'Did you know about the rooftop garden?'

'No, of course not. Wow, look at that…' she pointed.

Chloe chipped in, 'Did you just say *a rooftop garden?*'

Jess looked at where Harriet was pointing. 'Oh goodness, I never knew they could—'

'What is it?' hissed Chloe, dying to get past her sisters and find out what was going on. 'What can you see?'

Grinning, both girls turned around to look at Chloe. 'We can't really explain. I think you'll have to see for yourself.'

Harriet and Jess pressed themselves up against the wall on either side of the stairs and let Chloe squeeze between them. Harriet said, 'Kneel down, so they don't see you.'

Chloe knelt and peered out of the glass-panelled door. She spotted a beautiful rooftop garden illuminated by solar lights. On the decked area was a small table and chairs for alfresco dining. Chloe didn't see any food on the table, just Daddy's old radio cassette player that used to be in the basement kitchen downstairs before the conversion. It was blasting out that song. Chloe could also see a ceramic stove alight with a warming fire.

She knelt up further on the top stair and spotted a garden swing seat for two, still swinging back-and-forth as though someone had just got up. There was a blanket left on the bench.

Then they came into view, her parents dancing in the moonlight. Chloe's mouth dropped open as she watched them, mesmerised. She never knew either of her parents could dance. It wasn't exactly *Strictly Come Dancing*, but what struck Chloe was how well they danced together, as though they had been dancing partners all their lives.

Chloe wiped a tear from her face with the sleeve of her pyjama top before she reached for the door handle to go outside.

Harriet caught her arm. 'Leave them be. Let's go back to bed and get some sleep, eh?' Harriet put an arm around Chloe's shoulder.

Jess added, 'I'm sure we'll hear all about it in the morning. Here...' She offered Chloe a tissue.

Chloe took the tissue and turned back to look through the glass door into the rooftop garden beyond one last time. 'What do you think it means? Do you think they're getting back together?'

Harriet smiled at her sister. 'I think we have our answer – don't you?'

Three pairs of eyes watched them dancing in the moonlight until they kissed. The girls took that as their cue to go back to bed. All three were looking forward to the morning when they could find out all about the magical rooftop garden they never knew existed. And welcome home the two people dancing in the garden who were no longer just Mum and Dad but two famous writers, Dear John and Love on the Rooftop. The girls couldn't have been prouder.

'I didn't know you could dance,' Sylvie said, catching her breath after John had planted his lips on hers as soon as the music stopped. 'You always refused to go dancing with me when we first met. I assumed that was because you didn't know how to dance and didn't want to learn.'

'You assumed right,' said John, leading Sylvie by the hand to the swing seat near the warming stove. He lifted the blanket from the bench. When she sat down, he put it around her shoulders before sitting down next to her. The swing seat gently rocked back-and-forth.

He turned to Sylvie and found her staring at him intently, the surprise still evident in her eyes. John explained about the dancing. 'It all started when I discovered you were seeing Bertram. I thought what's he got that I haven't got?'

'Apart from money and a successful business, and hotels around the world...'

John frowned at Sylvie. 'At first, I wasn't aware he was loaded. But when I found out, I knew you wouldn't be taken in by his money. It had to be something else. I recalled something you said – he took you dancing.'

Sylvie nodded her head.

'I never took you dancing because I couldn't dance. And you're right: I was not inclined to learn.'

John paused to look around the rooftop garden. All these years she'd wanted a rooftop garden, but he selfishly wouldn't even consider it, just because he didn't want one himself; it was the same story with the dancing. He knew she used to go dancing before they met, but John had never considered how much it meant to her – until Bertram came along.

Sylvie and Bertram clearly had a good time. John could tell by the way her face lit up when she talked about their evenings out together, but was it the dancing, or was it Bertram? The only way John could find out was to do something he would never, ever have considered if it wasn't for the fact that he loved his wife and would do anything to get her back.

'I learned to dance for you, Sylvie.'

'You went to dancing lessons – for me?'

'Yes – every Saturday evening. I haven't been doing it for long. I'm sure it shows that I'm just a novice.'

'So that's where you were going every Saturday evening,' mused Sylvie. 'I thought you were seeing a woman.'

John picked up the other blanket and wrapped it around his

shoulders. 'I was. Ten women, in fact.'

'Pardon me?'

'There I was every Saturday evening at the dance academy, just me and ten women. I've never been so popular. I was the only bloke. I had women fighting over me — would you believe? They all wanted to be my dance partner.'

Sylvie laughed at the thought. She was still trying to get her head around the fact that John could dance. The strange part was that although he was just a novice, dancing in John's arms felt so natural. It was as though they had been dancing together for years.

'Once I started to learn, I found I was enjoying myself. Although I must admit I was nervous about dancing with you Sylvie, in case I forgot the steps. But the strange thing is I never danced with any of the other ladies like I did with you tonight. My teacher would have been delighted. With the others, I always felt as though I had two left feet, but with you, it felt so natural. I can't really explain it.'

'I can,' said Sylvie emphatically.

'It's called synergy, John.'

'Synergy,' mused John, nodding his head and staring at his dance partner. 'Yes, we make one hell of a team.'

'That we do,' smiled Sylvie. 'It's just taken us forty years to work that out.'

'But as the saying goes…' John put an arm around Sylvie's shoulders and pulled her close. 'Better late than never.'

Sylvie rested her head on his shoulder; never a truer word was spoken.

John got up and put another log on the stove. 'Warm enough, love?'

'Kind of…' Sylvie was feeling the cold. She stuffed her hands in the pocket of her coat and discovered something she had forgotten all about – Bertram's letter; the one Julia had passed on to her from Bertram. It was when she'd stopped returning his calls after losing contact with her grandchild.

Sylvie took it out of her pocket. The last time she'd found this letter was on the flight to America. It was still unopened. With everything that had gone on during her trip, unexpectedly meeting Bertram in New York, and the discovery that John was Dear John, somehow the letter had languished in her coat pocket, forgotten until now.

'What's that?' John caught Sylvie trying to stuff it back into her pocket before he saw it.

Sylvie showed him the unopened envelope addressed to her.

'It's from Bertram.'

'Oh. I thought things were over between you.'

They had barely begun, but Sylvie had already explained all that to John. Even so, he was looking worried – she could tell.

'Don't open it, Sylvie. Toss it on the fire.'

She looked at the envelope simply addressed, *Dear Sylvie*, and thought about what Julia had said when she handed her the envelope. Julia liked Bertram. She wanted Sylvie to give him another chance if that's what Bertram wanted.

Sylvie had already explained to Julia her doubts over how this relationship could work. It wasn't just about Bertram's wealth or the time they would spend apart; Sylvie had a life here in London, and Bertram's hotel empire took him abroad for a good proportion of the year. The real crux of the matter was that although Sylvie knew Bertram was immensely fond of her, and they got on well together, Sylvie realised she would always play second fiddle to the only woman he had ever loved. The woman with whom he had fathered a child and had subsequently left him almost twenty years ago – his wife.

Sylvie stared at the letter and thought of the woman who had turned up at Amy's engagement party unannounced. She saw the way Bertram looked at her. Even after all these years. Of course, it didn't mean they would resume their relationship where they left off. But for Sylvie, knowing she wasn't the one for him made all the difference.

Sylvie recalled when they first met at The Rooftop Café. He was looking for someone with whom to travel, to go out to restaurants, to have an intimate relationship. Sylvie wanted all those things – and more. She wanted love, and to feel loved in that special kind of way that was only possible with somebody who didn't want to be with anyone else but her. Bertram could never be that person.

That person was sitting right next to her, anxious to hear what was written in that letter. Sylvie knew he had nothing to be worried about; her mind was already made up. It didn't matter if she opened the envelope; nothing inside would change her mind – of that, she was certain.

Sylvie opened the envelope, cleared her throat, and to John's surprise, read aloud…

"Dear Sylvie, thank you for bringing me to my senses over my daughter and grandson. I've been the biggest fool imaginable. You have no idea how grateful I am to you for making me realise what I stood to lose. I have decided to stay in London and get to know my daughter, grandson, and future son-in-law…"

Sylvie paused. 'Obviously, this was written before Bertram flew to New York.'

John grimaced.

Sylvie glanced his way. 'John, whatever is in this letter does not affect us. You do understand that, don't you? That's why I'm reading it out loud. I don't know what's coming next, but I do know that it won't change a thing. Shall I continue?'

John reluctantly nodded his head.

Sylvie resumed reading. "'I've used my resources to find—"' She paused.

'What is it, Sylvie?'

Sylvie turned to look at John. 'Bertram was intending to find his wife.'

'Really?' John's frown lifted in an instant.

Sylvie continued to read the letter, "'I'm sorry, Sylvie, I do like you an awful lot. Perhaps if we'd met when we were young, before I met her..."'

John sat there listening to Sylvie reading the letter and thinking of the day he had bumped into Sylvie on a London street corner, all those years ago. It could have been someone else rounding that corner about to career straight into her; it could have been someone like Bertram.

Sylvie was still reading the letter, "'... seeing my daughter and grandson has made me realise how much I want to find her.'"

John raised his eyebrows. 'I wonder if—'

'He found her, John, if that's what you're wondering.'

John gave her a sideways glance. That wasn't what he was thinking at all. He was several steps ahead of her, wondering how things panned out when Bertram offered her a seat at his table in the hotel restaurant in New York.

Sylvie explained, 'It was at Amy's engagement party in New York that—'

'I know all about what happened at the engagement party.'

Sylvie stopped and turned to look at John.

John sheepishly held her gaze and decided it was the time to spill the beans and fess up about his trip to New York. Until now, he had been rather selective over what he told her he'd got up to in New York. Now he told her everything, starting with the fact that he'd been staying in the same hotel in New York, along with the assumption he'd made when he discovered Sylvie in the hotel restaurant with Bertram. Then there was that excruciating ride up in the elevator, standing right behind them the whole time. And not to mention losing Monte over the park.

'That was you!' Sylvie exclaimed in surprise.

John nodded. 'I didn't exactly lose him. When I saw you in the park I—'

'But it couldn't have been you,' interrupted Sylvie. 'I found out their room number and paid them a visit. A woman answered the door…'

'Oh that.' John's eyes went wide. He'd forgotten all about Bertram's wife staying the night in his hotel room after the party and answering the door the following morning, wearing nothing but his shirt.

'Are you saying that was your hotel room?'

'Now look, Sylvie, I can explain…' The words tumbled out of John's mouth as he told her all about gate-crashing the engagement party and discovering Bertram's wife had done the same. How he'd stupidly encouraged her to speak to Amy at the party, all because he selfishly thought if he could get Bertram and his wife to reconcile; in which case he might be in for a chance to get Sylvie back once Bertram was out of the picture.

Then he told Sylvie how he hid in the shadow of a sycamore

tree, in the grounds of Bertram's mansion, watching the drama unfold. And finally, how he'd felt responsible for the aftermath, so he'd agreed to let Bertram's wife stay in his hotel room because she didn't want to be alone that night.

John took a breath and stole a glance at Sylvie. Worryingly, she hadn't uttered a single word.

'Sylvie, I swear nothing happened in that hotel room. I slept on the couch – it's the god's honest truth.'

Sylvie sat there, staring wide-eyed at John. Suddenly, she burst out laughing.

John looked at her in surprise. That wasn't the reaction he was expecting.

When she had recovered from her fit of laughter, she said, 'And I thought my trip to New York had been eventful!' Sylvie smiled affectionately at her husband. 'Oh John, you do get yourself into the most amusing scrapes – don't you, darling.'

John rolled his eyes. 'I know.'

Sylvie glanced down at the letter in her hands. She was thinking about Bertram's wife and her surprise appearance at the engagement party. She told John, 'The way Bertram avoided talking about her made me suspect that he had buried his head in his career, brought up his daughter, and ignored the real issue: he still loved the woman who had abandoned them all those years ago – I was sure of it. This letter just confirms my suspicions.'

Sylvie slipped the letter back in the envelope. 'Maybe now he knows what happened to her, he can move on with his life.'

John was looking worried again.

'John?'

'What if he they don't get back together? Will he... will you...?'

Sylvie rolled her eyes. She knew what he was getting at. 'You are a daft brush sometimes, John Baxter.'

John raised his eyebrows.

'Bertram and I, we were just good friends. It was never going to turn into something more.'

John said, 'Because of Amelia?'

Sylvie eyed John for a long moment. 'No, darling, because of you.'

'Oh.' John grinned.

'But now she's walked back into his life, I hope they can find a way back to each other.'

'Like you and me?'

'Yes, John, like you and me.' Sylvie smiled. Although they hadn't been separated for the past twenty years, like Bertram and his wife, the way they had drifted apart meant they might as well have been. But now, looking around her rooftop garden, Sylvie knew all that was about to change.

John reached out and took Sylvie's hand. It was times like these that he realised how lucky he was to have serendipity on his side when he bumped into a beautiful young woman who wasn't watching where she was going. He'd seen her up ahead, reading a book as she walked along the street. She could have bumped into any number of people. She could have bumped into nobody and continued on her way. But John made sure she bumped right into him.

Throughout their married lives, he'd often thought about that moment when he had stepped into the path of a beautiful woman; the woman he wanted to spend the rest of his life with. In the intervening years, he'd never regretted that intentional misstep or wavered from that view.

They'd had their ups and downs over the course of forty years together. None more pronounced than just recently, living apart together. But neither of them had chucked in the towel. They might have come close, but Sylvie hadn't walked out the door and left him for good. John squeezed her hand. He was a very lucky man.

That sat together holding hands, watching the sunrise over London, as John finally told Sylvie what his plans would have been with the additional money from renting out the garden apartment.

Sylvie winced at his use of the word *plans* until John explained he had intended to use the money to have the retirement that Sylvie had always dreamed of – doing things together. Travel, perhaps a cruise, restaurant meals, and having fun together spending money on frivolous things they would never dream of doing in the past.

John gave her a sideways glance. 'I've got a small confession to make. I've done it again, Sylvie. I've been a bit reckless – financially.'

'Oh, John, I've just got on top of the bills and paid off our debts.'

'I know and I'm grateful, Sylvie. But I've been saving my pension and... well... we didn't have any time to spend together in New York, just the two of us, without our alter-egos Dear John and Love on the Rooftop getting in the way.'

Sylvie nodded her head in agreement.

'So, I thought we might like to go back there together, just the two of us, and spend some time sightseeing. I've booked the flights to New York, and a hotel so we can spend a few days there after Christmas. It was a spur-of-the-moment thing, but I thought we could see the famous Rockefeller Christmas tree and go ice skating in Central Park and—'

'You're joking.' This was a surprise. Since when did John do anything on the spur of the moment without thinking things through and planning it to distraction? Sylvie caught herself looking around the rooftop garden. She smiled. She guessed all that started right here. Even so, Sylvie couldn't work out how this new impulsive, throw-caution-to-the-wind, John Baxter, found the time to book a break in New York.

'Ah-ha,' said John, reading her expression. 'You're wondering where I found the time to arrange all this.'

Sylvie nodded.

'Remember on the way to the airport, we stopped at the hotel so I could collect our luggage before we left New York? That's when I booked the hotel. The concierge was extremely helpful and booked the flights.'

Sylvie had a question, 'John, how did you know—?'

'—We would return to New York together?' John smiled. 'That's easy. It was when I found out the person I was falling in love with, the writer Love on the Rooftop, was none other than my wife.'

Sylvie smiled at the writer she'd fallen in love with, Dear John, and snuggled up close on the swing seat for two. They sat together, holding hands on the rooftop garden as dawn approached.

It wasn't the spectacular sunrise Sylvie had hoped for; it was grey and dull, and starting to drizzle, but it didn't bother Sylvie. Nothing could dampen her mood. She was here with the man she loved; the man she was going to spend the rest of her life with. Sylvie knew she was a very lucky lady. She turned to John. 'I've got an idea. There's something I'd really like us to do together.'

John grinned at his wife. He liked the sound of that. Except what she had in mind didn't turn out quite as John had hoped; Sylvie wasn't thinking about spending the rest of the day between the sheets but calling a taxi and taking their suitcases, still packed from their trip to New York, to catch the next train to Cornwall with Sylvie's mother – or more precisely, her ashes. John did his best not to groan at the thought.

Sylvie nipped upstairs and slipped a brief note for the girls under John's door just before they left. It was still early. Sylvie didn't hear a peep from inside his apartment.

In the note, she explained that she had been bequeathed the property in Cornwall, and that Mum and Dad had decided to travel down there and spend a few days in the cottage. They wanted to spend some time, just the two of them, getting away from it all to sort things out. Sylvie was sure they'd understand.

She didn't mention in her note just what she intended to sort out: Sylvie wanted to get to the bottom of why Mr Morelli had left her that cottage in his will. Until she did that, she felt unable to carry out her mother's last request and scatter her ashes in the garden of Trevelyan Cottage.

43

A seagull's cry woke Sylvie from a deep sleep. She smiled as soon as she opened her eyes. She was lying in a large comfortable double bed in the main bedroom of Trevelyan Cottage. Bright winter sunshine flooded the room from the two cottage windows looking out to sea. Sylvie could taste the salty sea breeze from the open window.

She cast her eye around the room. Waking up in the large, airy bedroom reminded Sylvie of home. The décor throughout the property was much like Sylvie's apartment in London and made her feel at home the moment she'd stepped inside the cottage. Her thoughts turned to the empty urn she'd left downstairs. She was wondering what to do with it now her mother's final wish was complete; she had scattered her ashes in the cottage garden only yesterday.

Sylvie propped herself up on one elbow and gazed down at John, still fast asleep beside her. She was thinking about the past week they had spent in Cornwall. What an eventful week it had turned out to be. Not only the fact that they were back together, but Sylvie was also thinking about her mother and the secret she'd discovered about her past.

Sylvie had phoned Julia as soon as they arrived in Cornwall because she had to let Julia know she wouldn't be collecting Alfie for a few more days. She couldn't wait to tell her the incredible news about the cottage she'd been left in Mr Morelli's will.

Sylvie told Julia that after Mr Morelli had received her letter asking permission to scatter her mother's ashes in the garden of his holiday home, he amended his will to leave the cottage in Cornwall to Sylvie; the lawyer called it a codicil. Sylvie believed there was more to it than just an incredibly kind and generous gift from a stranger. She needed to know why he would do such a thing. She wanted to find out if Mr Morelli knew her mother.

Julia suggested that Sylvie should try to find somebody in the village who knew her mother all those years ago when she lived in St. Columb. Maybe a friend. Perhaps even a best friend who might recall if Sylvie's mum and Mr Morelli were acquainted, however impossible that may seem, considering she was a fifteen-year-old local lass, and he was a nineteen-year-old POW.

A visit to the local pub to catch up with George, who had helped Sylvie and Jess find the cottage on her last visit to Cornwall, unearthed the name of an old lady, Rose, now living in a local nursing home. She was a friend of her late mother. That's when Sylvie had discovered the truth and the reason Mr Morelli had left her the cottage.

Sylvie climbed out of bed, slipped on her dressing gown, and silently tiptoed out of the bedroom. She slowly closed the latch door behind her. John was still fast asleep. She made her way along the hallway, passing three further bedrooms and a bathroom. Sylvie paused to look at two of the framed paintings of picturesque Cornish coves and fishing villages hanging on the wall before descending the stairs.

At the bottom of the stairs, she stepped down into a small rectangular-shaped entrance hall. She passed the front door leading out into the handy little gabled porch where they had left their raincoats and damp walking shoes. The weather had not been kind this past week; it rained. They didn't mind the wet December weather. Sylvie and John were relishing spending their time just relaxing in the cottage and enjoying each other's company. That's what the week was all about; Dear John and Love on the Rooftop getting re-acquainted.

Sylvie walked across the hall and glanced into the dual aspect sitting room with a bay window on the front and double doors overlooking the garden at the rear, and views of the sea beyond. The room was furnished with an oak sideboard, matching coffee table, and a handy nest of tables. There was a bookcase filled with paperback novels neatly slotted into one alcove next to the fireplace. A single high-backed chair was positioned in the other alcove beside an old tube television.

A large Persian rug, in a strikingly vibrant design Julia would have approved of, covered the wooden floor in front of the fireplace. A contemporary floor lamp with low-wattage bulbs stood behind the high-backed chair, casting a soft, subtle glow in the corner of the room. Sylvie had forgotten to switch it off before they retired last night.

They had spent the wintry evenings relaxing in this cosy room, curled up together on the deep-cushioned chenille sofa in front of the open fire, watching late-night movies and reading old paperback novels, their pages yellowed with age.

Sylvie always associated Cornwall with the summer and thought she might be disappointed returning here in the winter months. But she wasn't – far from it. There was something very romantic, magical even, about being holed up together in a detached cottage with the wind and the rain lashing on the windowpanes and the sound of the waves crashing on the shore below.

Sometimes, when the rain held off, Sylvie would wrap up warm and stroll out into the garden alone to stand by the garden seat where her mother used to sit in the summer sunshine so many years ago. Sylvie would stand there in quiet contemplation, staring at the deserted beach below, with only the blustery wind and the memories of her mother for company.

As dusk crept up on her uninvited one evening, when she was standing alone in the garden, she felt as though she had stepped into a Daphne du Maurier novel. She imagined that at any moment she would spy a line of oil lanterns flickering in the gathering gloom signifying people walking down the lane to the beach, lanterns lighting the way, heading to the shore to plunder a shipwreck that had been run aground. But that was just Sylvie, the writer, letting her imagination run away with her; just like the times she thought she heard her mother's voice calling her to come in for tea, when it was only John calling her back inside for a hot drink and to warm herself by the open fire.

Sylvie used a flashlight to retrace her steps along the cobbled garden path to the stable door at the back of the cottage. With no streetlights or surrounding properties, it was pitch dark. Their nearest neighbours were the farmer and his wife, who lived in the white farmhouse a ten-minute walk away. It was so quiet, so deserted, and so different to what they were used to living in the heart of London, that often it felt as though they were completely cut off from the outside world, marooned together in their little piece of paradise – Trevelyan Cottage.

However, this was far from the case; their private drive led up to a tarmacked road and a short drive to the village. On the day they arrived, through the wind and the rain, a delivery van turned up later that afternoon with their weekly grocery order from the local supermarket. They had everything they needed in the cottage, even sheets and towels – and Wi-Fi internet, although both Sylvie and John agreed they weren't going online to read all about Dear John and Love on the Rooftop's appearance on *The Who's Who Show.*

They had hired a car for the week from a local car hire firm at Newquay train station. It was John's idea to have their shopping delivered so they wouldn't have to waste time visiting the supermarket. Sylvie took some persuading after her last disastrous experience with online shopping until John finally owned up to his part in that fiasco. He hoped his confession didn't spoil their time away together when she found out what he'd been up to.

In hindsight, she wondered why she'd never guessed the truth, especially after that excruciatingly embarrassing shopping trip with John to the supermarket when he kept sneaking things into her trolley.

'All is forgiven,' Sylvie had reassured a very anxious John after his confession.

Sylvie stood at the door to the lounge smiling when she recalled that conversation just the other day; there were no more secrets between them. Her eyes drifted to the open fire and the grate full of cold ashes from the roaring fire they'd had the night before. She debated whether to clear out the grate, but Sylvie decided that could wait until later and settled on making a morning cuppa instead.

Sylvie closed the door to the lounge, turned around and glanced up the stairs, wondering if she should nip back upstairs and see if John was awake. She listened for a moment, but all was quiet in the cottage; there was no sound of creaking floorboards, latch doors opening, or toilets flushing. John was still asleep. She opened the latch door on her right and walked into the kitchen to put the kettle on.

A few minutes later, Sylvie sat down at the small pine table with a cup of tea and looked out of the kitchen window at the garden. She could be forgiven for thinking she was back home in London, sitting at the kitchen table overlooking her garden; the way it used to be before John decided it would be a good idea to get rid of her lovingly cultivated cottage garden and replace it with a turfed lawn. Sylvie didn't mind that now; having a decent-sized lawn was a lot more practical now she had a dog. Besides, Sylvie didn't miss it anymore, not now she had her own cottage garden right here in Cornwall. Her mother would have loved it here. Her mother *did* love it here many years ago.

Sylvie sat staring at the garden, thinking back to the meeting that changed her world. Julia had suggested Sylvie's best course of action was to find somebody from the village who might have known her mother before she moved away to London; perhaps someone she grew up with. Sylvie had been incredibly fortunate to find her mother's best friend alive and still lucid. Her name was Rose, and she revealed a secret that Sylvie's mother had kept from Sylvie her whole life.

Sylvie's mother and Rose had been best friends until the day Sylvie's mother was forced to leave her home in St. Columb to live with her aged aunt in London. Sylvie still had the photograph Rose had given her only yesterday when she tracked her down to a local nursing home. It was an old photograph that her mother had entrusted to Rose for safekeeping.

Sylvie looked at the two black and white photographs she now had of her mother. One was the photograph she'd found amongst her mother's possessions soon after she passed away. It was the photograph of Sylvie and her mother outside the cottage. Written on the back of the photo were the words: *summer 1957*. Sylvie was four years old when that picture was taken.

The other photograph Rose had kept all these years, and given to Sylvie, was one she hadn't seen before. It was a photo of her mother with a young man Sylvie didn't recognise. He had large brown eyes and jet black hair. They were standing arm in arm in the garden outside the back door of the cottage.

She thought back to her visit to the nursing home when Rose handed her the photograph. Sylvie had turned it over and read the date written on the back: *summer 1952*. Sylvie was born the following spring. She sat sipping her tea and mulling over that conversation with Rose.

Rose said, 'Your mother never told you, did she?'

Sylvie shook her head. Although she did recall, 'My mum always said I was special.'

'And now you know why,' Rose said, adding, 'you have your father's eyes.' Rose pointed at the young man in the photograph.

Sylvie listened intently as Rose told her the story of how her mother and father had first met and fallen in love. How they had been separated by her family, and how eventually they had found each other again. Sylvie's mother was only sixteen years old when she fell in love with an Italian prisoner of war billeted to Camp 115, Whitecross, near the town of St. Columb Major, during the Second World War. His name was Paolo Morelli.

When her parents found out, they were furious. They sent Sylvie's mother away to live with her aunt and uncle, who had moved from Cornwall to London. Although Sylvie's mother had fallen in love, she had confided in her best friend Rose that it was all innocent and nothing had happened, not even a kiss. They'd met when Paolo and other prisoners of war started working as farm labourers. She saw him in a field one day when she and Rose were cycling by, and she was smitten. She believed it was love at first sight, and so did he. But her family would rather have risked her life in the bombing raids in London than her honour.

That didn't stop the couple in love making a vow: when the war was over Paolo promised he would wait for her, and Sylvie's mother promised she would return to Cornwall. But the course of true love never runs smoothly; something went wrong with their plan. Not long after Sylvie's mother was sent away to live with her aunt in London, she got a letter from Rose with the news that the Italian prisoners had been moved and German prisoners brought into the camp in their place. Rose and everyone in the village had no idea what had happened to the Italians; it remained a mystery whether they had been sent to another prisoner-of-war camp nearby, or whether they were somewhere else in the country or abroad.

Shortly afterwards, Sylvie's mother received word from her family that they wanted her to return to Cornwall. She knew why they were allowing her to return home – because Paolo was gone. Sylvie's mother refused. Instead, she continued living with her aunt, with whom she had become quite attached. It was 1941. There was no telling when the war would be over. There was no telling where Paolo would be, and if he would still be alive. Then another man walked into her life. Sylvie's mother had listened to her aunt's wise words when she found out a young vicar wanted to court her. He was good-natured, kind, and reasonably good-looking. Her aunt believed he would make a good husband and that love would blossom in time.

Sylvie's mother agreed with her aunt's sentiments. However, she confided in Rose that even though she might grow to love this man, she knew she would never love him in the same way as she loved Paolo. Sylvie's mother married the vicar, making her aunt incredibly happy. They remained in London, taking her aunt, now a widow, with them to live in a large vicarage provided by the church. Although her aunt still owned the cottage in Cornwall that she and her husband had bought many years ago, intending to retire by the sea, she chose to live out the rest of her days with her favourite niece, Sylvie's mother, and her new husband in London.

Soon after they married, four children arrived in quick succession. Four years later, the war was over. By then it was too late for Sylvie's mum to keep her promise to Paolo and return to Cornwall. Rose told Sylvie that her mother tried awfully hard not to regret that decision. She had a loving husband and four beautiful children and accepted she had made her choice. She consoled herself with the thought that her aged aunt was right: Paolo may not have returned to Cornwall either. Perhaps he would have forgotten all about her. Maybe he had died in the war. Sylvie's mother never wanted to find out what happened to Paolo; she felt it was better to let sleeping dogs lie.

As for Rose, she stayed in the small Cornish town where they grew up and married a local boy. She recalled that soon after the war ended, she had been on her way to have a picnic with her beau, riding her bicycle along a country lane, when she spotted a dark-haired young man working with others in a field. She thought he seemed familiar. Was that Paolo? Had he returned for her best friend just as he promised?

Rose had kept in contact with Sylvie's mother in London, sharing all her news, but once the war was over Sylvie's mother had stopped replying to her letters. Rose already knew Sylvie's mother was married with children. What good would it do if she knew he was alive? If she learned he'd come back for her? What good would it do either of them? Rose decided that it was better if she never knew; perhaps ignorance was bliss. It crossed her mind that her best friend had thought that, too. Maybe that was the reason she stayed away from Cornwall and stopped replying to Rose's letters, afraid of what news they might bring.

Rose did not send word that Paolo was alive and well and had returned to the village when the war was over. Rose even debated whether to walk across that field and tell Paolo that it was no use waiting. She would not be coming back. But what if he wanted to see her just one last time? What if he made Rose write and tell her he was here?

Rose told her fiancé about Paolo. His advice was to stay out of it; the Italian would find out eventually – why get involved? They had their own lives, their own future to think about now. So, Rose did not write and tell Sylvie's mother the news that Paolo had returned.

Some years later, Rose got a letter out of the blue from Sylvie's mother. She was returning to Cornwall because her aunt had died and left her a cottage by the sea. Seven years after the war ended, Sylvie's mother returned to Cornwall. She travelled down from London by train to sort out her aunt's affairs, intending to sell the cottage she had inherited.

She didn't sell her inheritance, not then anyway. When Sylvie's mother finally returned to Cornwall, in the early fifties, she discovered that one of the Italian prisoners of war had returned to the village when the war ended, getting work on a farm while he waited for his love to come back to him. His name was Paolo.

Paolo had kept his promise and not only returned to the village but waited seven long years for her. It was 1952. She was married with four children, and she could not bring herself to leave her husband. However, Sylvie's mother did something she knew she would never regret; she spent that summer with Paolo in the cottage. A summer of love. A summer she wished would never end.

She confided in Rose about that summer she'd spent with Paolo and how she wished, with all her heart, that she could freeze that moment in time, so she could live that summer over and over again. She could not bring herself to sell the cottage at the end of the summer, although she was forced to sell ten years later because they were having difficulties making ends meet raising five children on a vicar's salary. But at the time Sylvie's mother could not let go of that cottage; she couldn't let go of that summer spent in Cornwall with Paolo.

She knew there would be no more summers in Cornwall with Paolo. He left for a new life in America. But she did spend subsequent summers in her cottage with their child, Sylvie, who was born the following spring.

44

Sylvie finished her cup of tea. She was still sitting at the kitchen table studying the old black-and-white photograph her mother had entrusted to Rose for safekeeping; the one of her mother and father standing outside this very cottage the summer before she was born.

Sylvie sighed. Everything made sense now. The pieces of the puzzle that were Sylvie's life had finally fallen into place. She stared at the photo of her father, Paolo Morelli. This was the reason Sylvie's mum called her special, and treated her like she was her favourite child, and only took Sylvie with her down to Cornwall to spend the summers in this cottage.

Sylvie felt like an outsider in her family. She always knew she was different. Quieter than her siblings, and more introspective. She was a child who preferred her own company. Sylvie often found it difficult, living in a household full of loud theatrical types, to get a bit of solitude to read her books or write in her diaries without being tormented by the others.

She wondered if Pa, the man she thought was her father, knew the truth. It would explain why he let his wife take only one of their children to Cornwall with her every summer. Perhaps her mum was hoping one summer Paolo would return and he could meet his daughter.

Sylvie cast her gaze around the kitchen with its cream shaker-style cabinets and large black Aga. She still couldn't believe the cottage now belonged to her. She looked at the photo of her father. The burning question she had for Rose was when did Paolo discover Sylvie was his daughter? He must have known she was his daughter; that's why he left her the cottage. This was the last part of the puzzle and Sylvie's biggest regret; she never got to meet the man in the photograph and ask him the question herself.

Sylvie wanted to find out if he'd known about her all along, or whether the letter Sylvie had sent to him concerning her mother's last wish for her ashes to be scattered in the garden, had given him pause for thought?

Rose couldn't answer that question; what she did know was that Sylvie's mother hadn't told him she was pregnant with their child. At the end of that summer they had agreed, for both their sakes, to sever all ties. Paolo sought a new life in America. He left England with no idea that he was leaving behind his child.

Although they might have severed all ties, it was obvious Paolo never forgot Sylvie's mother because some years later he returned to Cornwall – a wealthy restaurant owner and businessman from New York – and bought this cottage; the place where he had many happy memories of his summer of love. A cottage he intended to leave to his daughter – if he could find her.

Sylvie knew all this because it was right here that she found the answer she was looking for. Sylvie had discovered a box; the one now sitting open in front of her on the kitchen table. Inside that box, carefully wrapped in tissue paper, Sylvie found her long-lost diaries; the notebooks she'd written during the summers she spent in this cottage when she was young. Each entry was clearly marked with the date, her name and her age.

Discovering those journals brought back a long-forgotten memory of a child who always left her most treasured possessions – her diaries – behind in the cottage each summer when she returned to London. Otherwise she was afraid her jealous siblings would find them, and she would never see them again. But she lost them anyway when the property was sold because her mother refused to travel to Cornwall to retrieve them for her; she was too heartbroken at having to sell her cottage. Sylvie never saw her diaries again – until now.

If a stranger had happened upon those notebooks, they would have read with interest the accounts of a little girl who spent her summers right here in this cottage in the 1950s. They would no doubt have enjoyed a nostalgic trip down memory lane to a bygone era. But it wasn't just some stranger who had happened upon them; it was Mr Morelli.

He bought the cottage some years later, after it had passed through several hands, and discovered those notebooks under a loose floorboard during renovation work. When he read those diary entries about a little girl and her mother, and their summers in Cornwall, he must have guessed the truth. That's why he hadn't just tossed them out but wrapped them in tissue paper and stored them in a box. He had left a note inside the box too.

Sylvie picked up the yellowed sheet of notepaper and read the note for the umpteenth time... *These diaries belong to Sylvie. I believe she is my daughter. I hope in the years to come I have the good fortune to find her and return them to her.*

That's just what he did, not in person regretfully, but Sylvie was thankful for what she had; thankful she finally had the answers she was looking for. She hoped one day she could meet his family, the Italian American relations she never knew she had.

Mr Beauregard had contacted Sylvie and asked her permission to reveal the identity of the last beneficiary of his will. Nobody in the family even knew he'd purchased a cottage in Cornwall until it came out in the will.

Sylvie had left it to the lawyer to explain her connection with Mr Morelli and by extension the rest of his family. Sylvie had spent her week in Cornwall wondering how they would take the news that their father had an affair with a married woman, and had a child out of wedlock, before he met his future wife, their mother. She'd wondered what their reaction would be when they discovered they had a sister in England they never knew about.

Now Sylvie had their reply, right here in black and white. It was a letter addressed to Sylvie from her American siblings. The letter arrived yesterday morning. Sylvie had opened it with trembling hands when she realised who it was from. The last thing she wanted to do was cause a rift in the family when they found out the truth.

The letter began, *To our dearest sister...*

Sylvie picked up the letter. It still brought a tear to her eye when she discovered she had three half-sisters and a half-brother, and they were all longing to meet her.

Sylvie furtively glanced at the kitchen door as she reached under the table for her travel bag. Inside, unbeknown to John, Sylvie had brought her laptop. They were supposed to leave them at home. They had agreed that their trip to Cornwall was just meant to be about the two of them, with no distractions like

444

work or the internet. But Sylvie couldn't help herself. She was feeling like her youngest daughter, Chloe, who couldn't go anywhere without being 'connected.'

However, Sylvie didn't bring her laptop away with her to surf the internet, or to find out what her readers thought of her appearance on the show in New York. She didn't know why she had brought it with her but was glad she did because in that letter from her newfound siblings was an email address.

She had emailed them as soon as she read their letter, explaining that John, her husband, had booked flights to return to New York after Christmas. Sylvie decided at this point not to muddy the waters and tell her American siblings about their alter-egos Dear John and Love on the Rooftop. Sylvie suggested perhaps they could all meet up on her next trip across the pond.

She had been eagerly awaiting their reply. That's why she was awake far too early this morning. She was dying to get online and find out if they had responded to her email. Sylvie waited impatiently for the laptop to boot up and then launched her email. She had to scroll through dozens of unread emails.

She'd opened one yesterday from her editor, Marcia Hunt, demanding: *Where are you? The whole world wants to know how your story ends!*

Sylvie randomly opened several more, from fans, from the press, from her colleagues at work. From Chloe, who wrote, *Harriet and Jess told me not to email. I know you're having some time together to sort things out, but I was wondering when you will be coming home. Declan and I had a little falling out…*

Sylvie raised her eyebrows at the *little falling out* part; what had Chloe been up to this time? Sylvie had an idea it had something to do with Chloe moving into her father's apartment when she and Declan were meant to plan their wedding. Sylvie suspected Chloe was getting cold feet. Even so, she read on, wondering where this email was leading…

So, I thought it would be a good idea if Declan and I could have some time together to, you know, patch things up. And I couldn't think of a nicer place to do that than in Cornwall… Especially if it was a free holiday in Mum's cottage, thought Sylvie, smiling. Typical Chloe, always thinking what was in it for her.

Sylvie kept scrolling through her emails – more fan mail, more emails from Marcia – until she came across the reply to her email. Sylvie took a deep breath before she opened it. She wanted to meet her American half-siblings on her next trip to New York, but she was also nervous at the prospect. What if they didn't want to meet her after all?

She clicked on the email. It started with an apology. Sylvie's shoulders sagged. From the tone of their letter, she was expecting an altogether different response to her suggestion. Sylvie wished she hadn't sent the email until she read on. She realised she'd jumped to conclusions. They were only apologising because she wouldn't get to meet *all* the family on her next trip. It turned out they had a large extended Italian American family who didn't all live in New York.

Sylvie noticed there were several attachments. As she clicked on each one, she realised word must have spread like wildfire throughout their extended family about the relative in England they never knew they had. Members of the extended family had sent pictures to be included in the email. Sylvie clicked on each attachment with the same caption – *Hi Sylvie* – to look at the photos of the Morelli clan. There were individuals, family groups, young and old, all waving for the camera, waving to her.

Sylvie felt overwhelmed by all this as she moved the cursor over to the last attachment. Sylvie opened it. It was a photograph of four people, a man and three women in their fifties. She stared wide-eyed at the photo. Sylvie took after her father, and so it seemed did her American siblings; the family resemblance between her and the four people in the photograph was unmistakable.

She finished reading the email. They couldn't wait to meet her and John in New York. Sylvie smiled as she shut down the laptop and slipped it back in her bag. She sat staring out the kitchen window, lost in thought.

'Is everything all right, dear?'

Sylvie turned in her seat to find John standing in the doorway. His hair was sticking up in all directions. His pyjama top was askew. John looked as though he had just got out of bed, which she guessed he had.

'Everything is perfect,' said Sylvie, telling a little white lie. Eyeing John reminded her everything was not *perfect*. She wished it was. 'Why don't you go back to bed and I'll bring you up a cuppa.'

John yawned and stretched, nodding his head. 'I'm parched. A cup of tea is a grand idea,' he said, turning on his heel and taking his sleepy head back upstairs.

Sylvie put the kettle on and made a quick phone call while she waited for it to boil.

'Hello, Julia.' Sylvie couldn't wait to let Julia know that her idea of finding an old friend of her mother's had paid off. They both knew it was a long shot, but lady luck was smiling on Sylvie. She told Julia she had met her mother's best friend, Rose, and found out a lot more than she bargained for – in a good way.

'You don't sound too happy about it,' remarked Julia.

'It's not that.' Sylvie groaned. 'It's John.'

'Oh no, what's he done this time?'

'It's not so much what he's done. I can't really explain it. It's just that as the week has gone on, I couldn't help but notice that he's getting increasingly irritated by the least little thing. Sometimes I feel as though everything I say or do is getting on his nerves. I don't know what's up with him.'

'Have you tried asking him what's wrong?'

'Of course I have, but that just makes things worse.'

'Look, Sylvie, you've both been through an awful lot lately. You've had a lot of things to digest. I don't need to remind you that you've made some surprising discoveries about each other…'

Sylvie knew she was referring to Dear John and Love on the Rooftop meeting in person on *The Who's Who Show*.

'Add to that,' Julia continued, 'the unexpected visit to see the lawyer in New York about an inheritance. Not to mention your discovery that Mr Morelli was your father. And then you arrive back from New York to yet another surprise.'

'Yes, that's true.' Sylvie nodded her head, thinking about John surprising her with the rooftop garden.

'You've hardly been home from New York any time at all – you didn't even unpack, for goodness' sake – and the next thing you know, you're high-tailing it down to Cornwall.' Julia paused. 'It's enough to make anybody's head spin.'

Sylvie never thought she would see the day when Julia made excuses for John's behaviour. Since she found out he was Dear John, a writer and columnist, it was as though Julia saw him in a whole new light. Consequently, relations between them had improved dramatically.

Julia suggested, 'Maybe it's time you returned home, and things got back to normal.'

Sylvie had the phone tucked under her chin. She was listening to her best friend while she made John a mug of tea. Sylvie was just getting a pint of milk out of the fridge when Julia made that suggestion about returning home. She put the milk on the kitchen worktop and paused to give Julia her full attention.

'Do you know what, Julia? I think you're right. That's the best bit of advice I've had in ages.'

'Do I take it you're coming home?'

'You bet.' Sylvie had made up her mind. 'I'm going to pack – we're leaving today!'

'Today?' Julia sounded thrilled. Sylvie wasn't surprised. It felt as though they hadn't seen each other in an age. It had only been a fortnight, but they had a lot of catching up to do.

'I'll see you soon, Julia.' Sylvie put the phone down and picked up the milk carton. She poured a splash of milk into John's mug of tea, and then added a teaspoon of sugar.

Sylvie stood there stirring John's tea, thinking about her spur-of-the-moment decision to return home. As much as Sylvie wanted to savour their time together in Cornwall, Sylvie missed her family and desperately wanted to see Jess before she returned to Australia. She missed her grandchild, Gertie, and hoped Harriet would let them see her on their return. She missed her dog, Alfie, and her best friend, Julia. Furthermore, Sylvie missed going into work and seeing her editor, Marcia Hunt, and all her colleagues working at the magazine who had become such an integral part of her life now, almost like a second family.

There was no denying that she loved getting away from it all down in Cornwall, in her cottage by the sea, but she had a life back in London, friends and family she couldn't wait to see, and a home in Holland Park with a rooftop garden. Yes, Sylvie decided, she was ready to go home; she was ready for things to get back to normal.

But she did promise herself one thing: she would return to spend the summer in Cornwall. Sylvie had always dreamed that one day she would write sitting in a cottage by the sea; it was what she loved most when she was a child during the long, hot summers they spent there.

It did not particularly bother her about swimming in the sea or building sandcastles like other children her age; often she could be found sitting on a cushioned window-seat, in a bedroom upstairs, avidly writing her diaries. It was bliss. There were no siblings squabbling in the background, no threat of interruptions, just the sound of the waves gently lapping on the beach below, and the distant cry of a seagull carried through the open window on a cool summer breeze. It was Sylvie's little piece of heaven.

It had been Sylvie's dream to be a writer when she grew up. She thought she would sit and write in the cottage by the sea. By the time she reached adulthood, Sylvie had dismissed that notion as just a foolish childhood fantasy, a dream like winning the lottery that only ever happened to other people. In hindsight, she knew why she let go of her dream. Her childhood fantasy evaporated when her mother sold this cottage. But life, Sylvie realised, had a peculiar way of leading you to where you were meant to be – and who you were meant to be with.

She smiled. It just goes to show that it was never too late to follow your dreams and live the life you had always imagined. She was already looking forward to spending the summer writing in her cottage by the sea. But summer was months away, and Sylvie had things to do and places to be and people she missed. It was time to shut up the cottage for the winter months and return to London.

Sylvie picked up John's mug of tea and took it upstairs to tell him to start packing. They were going home.

45

Sylvie smiled across the table at John. Whatever had been going on with him in Cornwall, he'd more than made up for by surprising her with a romantic meal together at their favourite restaurant on their return.

They had just arrived home and deposited their bags in the hall when John told her he had booked a table at a restaurant and they were going out for a meal that evening. They both agreed it was the perfect way to round off their holiday. Even so, Sylvie had an idea there was more to it than that. This was the moment they had both been waiting for: they were finally going to move back in together. What better way to mark this new beginning than having a celebratory meal on their return from Cornwall.

The problem was that Sylvie didn't feel like celebrating. She wasn't sure why, although she had her suspicions; Sylvie suspected it was because she didn't want to give up her apartment and her newfound independence. Her dilemma was that she didn't want to give up John, either. Sylvie decided not to dwell on that and just enjoy their meal.

Sylvie enjoyed the evening meal at the restaurant. It brought back fond memories of the dinner dates and romantic walks together shortly before it all fell apart when she found out about their dire financial situation. With all that had happened since then, those good times she shared with John when they were living apart together seemed like a lifetime ago.

Now they were both successful writers. And Sylvie had got to the bottom of why John had managed to get them in such a financial fix; it was all because, after forty years of marriage, he still wanted to show his wife just how much he loved her by giving her that rooftop garden – whatever the cost.

Sylvie smiled. She was looking forward to seeing the garden once more. Even more so when she discovered that next time, she would not have to climb the fire escape to reach it. There was a door on to the rooftop garden from the top floor of John's apartment. They didn't have access to that door the first time around because of the girls staging their sit-in.

The girls had received her note about their trip to Cornwall. Satisfied their parents were finally addressing their marital issues, they had vacated John's apartment. Sylvie knew this for a fact, because she'd received a text message from each of her daughters.

Chloe had returned home to the house she shared with Declan, deciding that she too needed to sort things out between them once and for all. Harriet wanted John to resume grandparent duty on his return from Cornwall and had summarily dismissed the in-laws, threatening Dominic with divorce if he didn't get rid of them. Jess had gone to visit some old school friends, promising to return home for a few days before leaving for Australia. John and Sylvie had returned from Cornwall to find, much to their relief, they had the house to themselves.

John paid for the meal and ordered a taxi. They enjoyed

some entertaining banter up the dinner table as they debated tongue-in-cheek whether to take separate taxis home or share one and then decide who should be dropped off first.

Sylvie said, 'Do you remember the first time we shared a taxi home? After you dropped me off, you asked the driver to circle the block?'

'Oh yes,' John grinned. 'How could I forget? You should have seen the look on the taxi driver's face. He thought I was barmy.'

'You are barmy,' replied Sylvie laughing at the memory of John accompanying her to the door and then inexplicably leaving in the cab, only for it to reappear outside their house five minutes later to drop John off.

Their conversation was interrupted by the maître d' informing them, 'Your taxi has arrived.'

John and Sylvie exchanged glances and fell about laughing, leaving the maître d' wondering what was so funny.

They left the restaurant and got into the waiting taxi.

'Where to?' said the taxi driver. He turned in his seat to face them, adding, 'Or should I say, whose place first?' He smiled broadly.

'No way!' said John, recognising a familiar face. 'Not you again!'

Sylvie laughed again, so much so that she had tears in her eyes.

'I wouldn't miss this for the world,' said the driver. 'It's been a while, but as soon as I heard your name, I insisted on taking this fare. You guys are hilarious. When I saw you on *The Who's Who Show*, I couldn't believe it!'

'You saw that show?' John and Sylvie said in surprise.

'Oh yes. I told all my mates at work that I knew Dear John and Love on the Rooftop.'

John and Sylvie smiled as the taxi set off toward their home. They were no longer embarrassed or bothered by the show because a few moments of toe-curling embarrassment had done wonders for their careers. Dear John and Love on the Rooftop were more in demand than ever. And that wasn't all. They were now being talked about as a writing team. There were rumours they were going to collaborate on their next article.

The first thing John and Sylvie knew about it was reading the rumours in a tabloid newspaper on their way home from Cornwall on the train. They'd spent the rest of the journey discussing the idea. It appealed to them both.

They'd been mulling over what they could write about and debating whether to use any of their experiences in New York, when they both discovered they had started researching the same story: immigration to America in the nineteen fifties. Sylvie fancied writing it from a personal angle by telling her father's story – the successful restaurateur and businessman, Paolo Morelli, who came to America in the fifties with nothing but the shirt on his back and realised the American Dream.

John thought that was a marvellous idea until he thought about it some more and warned her that if she told his story, then people might find out the *whole* story. Did she want everyone to know about her past? He glanced at Sylvie sitting beside him holding his hand and recalled her response to that question: "It's bound to come out, eventually. We're in the public eye now. The fact is people want to know who we are – everything. I'd prefer they heard it from me than in some sordid headline in a sensationalist tabloid newspaper."

She was right: there was no denying their lives had changed beyond all recognition. They had started out as just an ordinary couple struggling to find a new direction in life. In some ways, it was an unfortunate consequence of getting older – retirement. No one was really prepared for the reality. John and Sylvie weren't. But the difference between them and the thousands of baby boomers, up and down the country, facing the scary prospect of what lies ahead in their twilight years, was that they started living apart together. It changed them. It made them who they were today: Dear John and Love on the Rooftop.

LAT living had brought with it opportunities John and Sylvie could never have envisaged at their age. John wasn't just thinking about his second career as a successful writer. Although that was a wonderful by-product, what he was really thinking about was the opportunity to find himself as an individual again after years and years of being a husband, a parent, a provider. Perhaps, when all was said and done, that's what retirement was all about: the chance to find yourself freed of the constraints of what society expected of you.

John squeezed Sylvie's hand. The fact that through it all, they'd managed to stay together was quite something. He would have given it all up – his writing career, the money, the cottage in Cornwall – just to be with the woman he loved. However, the question he was asking himself, as they drove inexorably closer to their home in Holland Park, was could he give up his apartment?

The taxi driver interrupted John's reverie.

'My wife can't believe I've met Dear John and Love on the Rooftop. You guys are like celebrities. You're practically famous.'

'Oh, I wouldn't go so far as to say that,' said John, although he wouldn't deny it either.

'I would,' said the taxi driver. 'I watched you on that show and saw how the audience went wild when they found out you were husband and wife, living in the same house, with no clue you were writing about each other.' He shook his head as though he still couldn't quite believe it himself. 'I always knew you two were crazy.' He tapped the side of his temple with a finger and then pulled the car up outside their house in Holland Park. 'Little wonder everyone wants to know how the story ends.'

He switched the car engine off, turned around in his seat, and looked at them expectantly. 'Well? How *does* your story end? Are you guys getting back together – or what?'

John exchanged glances with Sylvie and let go of her hand. He leaned forward in his seat as though he were about to confide in him. 'I'm afraid you will have to find out from the next instalment of *Dear John* and *Love on the Rooftop*, just like everyone else.'

'Pah! I thought we were friends.'

'We *are* friends,' said Sylvie, smiling at him affectionately. 'That's why we're inviting you to a party.' Sylvie looked at John for confirmation the invite was all right with him.

'You're having a party at your house, and you are inviting *me*?' The taxi driver looked positively stunned, as though royalty had just invited him.

'Yes, why not,' said John. 'Bring along your family.'

The taxi driver looked as pleased as punch.

Sylvie got out of the taxi first. She made her way through the front gate and up the garden path to the house, leaving John to pay the taxi fare and give their friend the date of the party.

'Are you sure you don't want me to wait?' he asked once John had paid the fare.

'You don't want to get stuck out,' he chortled, resuming their little in-joke.

'I'm quite sure,' said John. 'I have a feeling that tonight's going to be my lucky night.'

'You mean you're moving back in together?'

John slowly nodded his head; there was no use denying it.

The taxi driver looked at John for a long moment, making him feel uncomfortable under his gaze. It made John wonder if perhaps he was disappointed that Dear John had given it away – how their story ends.

'I hope you don't mind if I make an observation…'

John looked at him curiously. 'What is it?'

'You don't seem that happy about moving back in together.'

John smiled nervously. The taxi driver had made an astute observation; something was on his mind all right, and it had cropped up as a result of spending the last week together in Cornwall. John paid the taxi fare and walked through the front gate, casting his mind back to the week they had just spent in Sylvie's cottage. It had been a nice, pleasant break away, but it came with some unexpected and altogether unforeseen consequences which John hadn't anticipated.

Their holiday in Cornwall was the first time they had lived together for some time. Increasingly, as the week went on, John found himself getting irritable and short-tempered with Sylvie. He couldn't imagine that it went unnoticed, even though she didn't once bring it up. Now they were home, he found himself in a quandary; that week together in the cottage made him realise that although he still loved his wife and didn't want to lose her, he didn't want to give up his apartment, either. He just didn't know how to tell her that.

Sylvie rolled over in bed to find John wide awake. She switched her bedside table lamp on and noted John's furrowed brow, his serious expression. 'What's wrong?' They were in her bed, in her apartment downstairs, and it was four o'clock in the morning.

'I don't much care for your décor.'

'I know,' said Sylvie.

Alfie wormed his way around the bedroom door that was slightly ajar and jumped on to Sylvie's bed.

John attempted to push him off. 'And I don't much care for pets in the bedroom.' He raised an eyebrow in disdain. 'Or on the bed – for that matter.'

'I know,' said Sylvie.

'But I do care for you, Sylvie.' He turned to face her. 'I care for you very, very much.'

'I know.'

'It's just…' John realised, 'I can't live with you anymore.'

'I know.' A smile crept to Sylvie's lips. She'd been wondering when he was going to figure it out.

'Would you mind awfully if I...?' John gestured toward the door.

'Not at all,' replied Sylvie. 'You go right ahead.'

She watched him gather up his clothes strewn over the floor, getting in a muddle with Alfie around his ankles, who thought it was all a game and tremendous fun. The cocker spaniel scampered off with one of John's shoes.

'Come back here right now and give me that shoe!' John exclaimed, chasing Alfie out of the bedroom.

Sylvie closed her eyes, spread herself out in the middle of

her bed, and gathered the entire duvet around her. Bliss. Then she thought she heard something. When she opened an eye, she saw a cup of tea had been deposited on the bedside table before he left.

John neatly folded his clothes away in the wardrobe and lay down in his own bed, after he had put the cat out of his bedroom three times. Somehow, she kept getting around his ankles and appearing on his bed. Eventually, John found himself on all fours inching the door closed so she couldn't sneak in unnoticed. John rolled his eyes. He could hear Mouse scratching at his door.

'It won't work,' he called out. 'I am still not letting you in. If you want to sleep on a bed, you'll have to move downstairs.'

John smoothed his covers down, picked up a book, and decided to read a few pages before turning his light out. After all, this was his usual bedtime routine, even if it was four o'clock in the morning.

John opened the book and paused for a moment. He thought about his neighbour in the garden apartment downstairs. Although they had enjoyed their time together in Cornwall and were both looking forward to returning to the cottage soon, they were equally relieved to return home and get back to normal.

Both Sylvie and John finally understood that for them, living apart together was their new normal.

46

The timer on the oven pinged. John was already standing beside the stove wearing an oven glove in readiness. He carefully removed the pie from the oven and placed it on the hot plate beside the cooker. It smelt delicious. Nothing could beat home cooking, thought John, looking pleased with himself. Although this was his umpteenth homemade chicken pie, he always got the same sense of satisfaction when he lifted it out of the oven, and the smell of home baking wafted around the room.

The table was already set for dinner. John got out a bottle of bubbly from the fridge. She would be arriving home any minute. John waited. He'd left the apartment door wide open so he would hear her come in. He soon caught the sound of heels clicking on the wooden floor. She was home. At last.

Alfie yapped and scampered off to greet her.

John heard Sylvie's voice. Was she talking to Alfie in that baby voice again? How many times had he told her not to treat Alfie like a little person?

John stopped to listen. He heard another voice, deeper this time, distinctly male. John nearly dropped his serving spoon. Last time he checked, dogs didn't answer back, which meant only one

461

thing – Sylvie had company. Male company. John breathed a sigh of relief when Declan poked his head around the kitchen door. 'Hi John, do you need a hand?'

He waved his gloved hand at Declan. 'No, I think I've got it covered.' John glanced at the huge chicken pie cooling off on the wire rack. 'Has everyone arrived?'

'I think so.'

John removed his oven glove and checked the table setting one more time, making sure he hadn't forgotten anybody. He pulled Gertie's high chair closer to the table near the french doors and then looked at Declan standing in the kitchen doorway at the foot of the stairs. John walked over and patted him on the back. 'Take a seat, Declan. I'll be back in a sec.'

Declan ambled over to the table and pulled out a chair.

John was about to go upstairs when he glanced over his shoulder at Declan seated at the table all on his own. 'Is Chloe with you?' John ventured.

'Yeah. She drove in case I wanted a drink.' Declan held up the bottle of wine he'd brought over.

'Ah, that's excellent.' John wasn't talking about the wine. He breathed a sigh of relief as he walked up the stairs. When he phoned Chloe from New York, he got the impression things were not hunky dory between her and Declan. However, it sounded as though they'd patched things up.

John darted up the stairs and into Sylvie's lounge just as she walked into her apartment holding Gertie's hand. She was followed by Jess, Harriet, and Chloe. Dominic was last in the door. Sylvie had driven to the train station to pick up Jess, who had been to visit friends across London. She'd then stopped by Harriet's place to collect Harriet, Dominic and Gertie.

John gave Sylvie a welcome home kiss as soon as she walked in the door and then turned to Gertie. He knelt down intending to scoop her up in his arms, but she came over all shy and hid behind Grandma.

Sylvie turned around and picked her up. 'You remember Grandpa, don't you?' Sylvie smoothed a lock of wavy blonde hair out of her eyes and studied her face. She was eyeing Grandpa warily. Suddenly, her face lit up with a huge smile. She held out her arms and wriggled out of Grandma's grasp.

John smiled at his granddaughter as she came trotting over, arms open wide. But to John's surprise, she ran straight past Grandpa. He turned around. There, sitting on the floor getting a big hug from a little girl was Alfie, revelling in the attention. He licked her face.

Everyone oohed and aahed except John, who was standing there, arms folded, tapping his foot impatiently and frowning at Sylvie's cocker spaniel, getting all the attention. Next up was Jess, rushing over to give the little black mutt a fuss. Then everyone was crowding around the little dog, telling him how much they'd missed him. Even Dominic, who was not overly fond of pets, gave him a pat on the head.

John rolled his eyes and threw his arms up in a *what about me* gesture until he felt something pulling on his trouser leg. John looked down to find Gertie standing beside him, staring up at him with her large blue eyes. Gertie held her arms up.

John smiled as he bent down. 'I've missed you.' He was about to pick her up when he caught Dominic looking his way. John paused. 'May I?'

'Of course, John.'

John picked her up and caught Harriet giving Dominic a

look as if to say, *go on, tell him*. Dominic walked over and stood beside his father-in-law. 'Look, about what happened over Gertie.'

'All my fault,' said John, without hesitation. 'I shouldn't have left her with someone else without asking your permission. I know I was in the wrong and I'm so sorry. It won't happen again. I swear.'

Dominic shook his head. 'It's me who should be apologising.'

John looked at him in surprise.

Dominic stared sheepishly at John. 'The fact is, I flew off the handle, and things got a bit out of hand. I shouldn't have taken her away from you. That was very wrong of me. I see that now. You wouldn't have left her with someone you didn't trust. It's just things have been going on at work. You know the normal stress of a demanding job, that sort of thing.'

John didn't know because his work was not stressful at all. But then he didn't have a hefty mortgage and a family to support. However, he nodded his head sympathetically. John had been down that road many years ago when they had stretched themselves to buy this house, so he could quite understand.

'I know it's no excuse for flying off the handle like that...'

John rested a hand on Dominic's shoulder. 'Is that a bottle of wine for dinner?'

Dominic looked at the bottle of wine in his hand.

'Why don't you take it downstairs? You'll find a bottle opener in the kitchen drawer.'

'Yes. That's a great idea,' said Dominic, relieved that after what he'd done, there were no hard feelings between them.

John hugged Gertie close and asked her, 'Would you like some of Grandpa's scrummy chicken pie?'

Gertie gave a big nod of the head.

John looked over at Sylvie and the three girls. 'Come on everybody, dinner is ready.' He watched in bemusement as Alfie raced past him and down the stairs.

John led the way down to Sylvie's basement kitchen and spotted Alfie standing over his empty dinner bowl, whining. John ignored him and walked straight over to the high chair with Gertie.

'Nooooo!' Gertie shouted. 'Big chair.' She pointed at one of the wooden chairs.

John looked at her in surprise.

Harriet walked into the kitchen and said off hand, 'Gertie doesn't use a high chair anymore.'

'Oh.' John put her down on a big chair. Gertie rested her chin on the tabletop. 'Oh,' repeated John. 'I think you need a cushion – or two.' He scooted back upstairs once everyone had made it down to the kitchen and reappeared with two plump cushions from Sylvie's lounge.

John halted at the bottom of the stairs. He took a moment to savour the scene as he watched everybody take a seat at the table. John caught Sylvie's eye and guessed what she was thinking. Over the years they had sat around this same oak table, in the basement kitchen of their London home, and seen their family grow and change, their children leave home and return.

When they first moved into this house, there were just the three of them – John, Sylvie, and Harriet – sitting around that table. Sylvie had been pregnant with their second child, Jess. Now, many years later, three had morphed into an extended family of nine, including John's soon-to-be new son-in-law, Declan, and Jess' absent partner in Australia. It had been a long time since they were all together, sitting around the kitchen table. John and

Sylvie could almost be forgiven for thinking nothing had changed. But everything had changed.

John and Sylvie exchanged a knowing smile as he walked over to the table with the cushions for Gertie. They had never been happier or more together than they were at this moment. They had gathered their family together, for the first time since the conversion, to tell them the news: Mum and Dad were no longer living together. They were living *apart* together. They wouldn't feel obliged to say any more than that. For them, living apart together had saved their relationship, although they didn't know it at the time. It had enabled them to grow and find themselves beyond the boundaries of their marriage; living apart had ultimately led them back to each other. If it wasn't for that, Sylvie and John had no doubt they would have split up for good.

John took a seat at the table, wondering what they would all make of the announcement about their permanent living arrangements. He glanced at Jess, Harriet, and Chloe, and caught Sylvie doing the same. The girls already knew Mum and Dad were back together after they saw them on the rooftop garden that night. That's why there were no awkward silences up the dinner table as they all took their seats, but animated conversation and wine corks popping. As far as everyone was aware, they were here to share a celebratory family meal. It was just left to John and Sylvie to tell them that although they were indeed back together, they weren't moving out of their respective apartments.

Sylvie and John weren't anxious about telling them they were living apart together. It wasn't any of their children's concern how they chose to live their lives. However, John was anxious about the other thing he intended to tell them all. Something even Sylvie didn't know about.

His eyes drifted to Gertie tucking into her chicken pie, and then Sylvie, who was under the misapprehension that there were no more secrets between them. His eyes settled on Harriet and Dominic. It wasn't that long ago John recalled he couldn't wait to tell them what he'd been up to during Grandpa duty; taking Gertie along to photo shoots to model children's clothes and star in television commercials. And making quite a bit of money to boot. He had Gertie's first savings book tucked in his pocket. There was quite a princely sum now deposited in her bank account; far more than John hoped to have when he finally spilled the beans and surprised them with it.

It's just that he never seemed to find the right moment to tell them what he'd been up to with Gertie. Since that episode when Dominic had discovered John's friend, Barbara, looking after Gertie, and then banned John and Sylvie from seeing her, branding them bad grandparents, John had been reluctant to tell them at all.

Before losing access to Gertie, it never once crossed his mind that they wouldn't be thrilled about their daughter earning all that money. Now, looking at them both across the table, John wondered what their reaction would be. In fact, he wished he'd never got himself in this predicament in the first place. If it hadn't been raining that day, he would have just taken her to the park and not bothered with the photo shoot.

But such is life. John heaved a sigh. It only started out as a bit of fun. Now his grandchild was verging on becoming a minor celebrity in her own right. Unbeknown to Sylvie, John had taken his laptop with him to Cornwall and gone online after she went to bed, catching up on his emails. That's when he discovered an email from the modelling agency. They'd been approached from a casting agency who had spotted Gertie in a commercial. They wanted her to audition for a part in a children's television programme. It was quite a commitment. It was also worth a lot of money. And it could even be the start of something Gertie might enjoy doing with her life in the future – acting.

John had got himself up a gumtree. Did he have the right to turn it down before giving Harriet and Dominic, even Gertie, a choice? John believed not. He sat there thinking about how a simple thing like a rainy afternoon had led him here, squirming in his seat, wondering if he was about to lose Gertie all over again because he simply hadn't bothered to ask them if they were happy to sign her up with a modelling agency. In hindsight, he realised not asking them first had been a bad idea. Now he was staring at Harriet and Dominic, wondering what the fallout would be.

Even if he took her off their books now, and cancelled all her up-and-coming auditions and shoots, he couldn't pretend it never happened or hide all her work that was already out there. In fact, what had surprised him was that her parents had not found out yet. But they would – of that, John had no doubt. He'd seen her on the television in a commercial just the other day and her face plastered on a gigantic poster on the side of a London bus. John had even spotted her in a national newspaper in an advertisement for a major high street chain.

They were bound to find out, and John would rather they heard it from him. He looked around the table. This should be a celebratory meal. He really didn't want to throw a spanner in the works, but he knew it was time to come clean. He took a deep breath and tried to get a word in over the din up at the dinner table, but everyone was deep in conversation.

John put his knife and fork down and stood up.

'A toast,' said Sylvie, raising her glass, mistaking John's intention.

He glanced at Sylvie. 'Oh, I wasn't—' he began and then caught everybody else raising their glass.

'Speech. Speech. Speech,' shouted Chloe and everybody joined in.

John's shoulders sagged. 'All right.' Standing at the head of the table, he picked up his glass. 'So, I guess you already know why we've gathered you here this evening, apart from sampling my delicious chicken pie.'

Everyone nodded their heads as they looked from John to Sylvie and back again.

John glanced at Sylvie before proceeding to tell them the details. 'As you've already gathered, Sylvie and I have patched up our differences and—'

'What are you going to do about the house?' interrupted Chloe. 'Are you going to rent out the garden apartment? Can't you rent out yours upstairs, Daddy, because I'll miss sitting around this table in Mummy's kitchen.'

'Can't you put it back to the way it was?' suggested Harriet. 'You don't need the rental income – or two apartments now you're back together.'

John opened his mouth and looked at Jess, waiting for her to give her pennies worth.

Jess eyed her dad for a moment, and then turned to Chloe. 'I don't think you need to worry about us not getting together in Mum's kitchen.'

'So, you're moving downstairs,' concluded Harriet, looking across the table at John.

'They're not going anywhere,' said Jess, turning to Harriet. 'Don't you see?'

Harriet folded her arms. 'No, I don't see.'

John smiled at Jess. 'Jess is quite correct. We're living apart together.'

'Living. Apart. Together?' Harriet shook her head in confusion. 'But what does that actually mean?'

'Just what it says on the tin,' snapped John, giving Sylvie a sideways glance.

Sylvie shrugged. She didn't expect them to understand.

'You're keeping your own apartments?' Chloe looked at her parents and clapped her hands. 'Just like Julia!'

'Well, not exactly,' Sylvie chipped in. 'Julia and Tom don't live in a house. They live on houseboats.'

'Yes – I know that,' Chloe shot back. 'But you know what I mean, Mum.'

'Of course I do.'

Jess raised her glass. 'To Mum and Dad, we wish you every happiness – living apart together.'

Chloe quickly raised her glass.

Harriet reluctantly so.

Declan and Dominic raised a glass, both thinking there was never a dull moment in the Baxter household.

47

'Harriet. Dominic. I've got something to tell you.'

Still standing after making that impromptu speech, John reached into his pocket and produced Gertie's saver book.

Sylvie looked at him curiously.

'What's that, Daddy?' asked Chloe.

John passed it to Harriet.

Harriet glanced at Dominic and reached across the table to take the book. She opened it. John watched her eyes go wide.

'It's a savings book in Gertie's name.' Harriet showed Dominic. 'Oh Daddy, you shouldn't have.'

'Shouldn't have what?' asked Chloe, eyeing the savings book.

'Daddy deposited all this money for Gertie.'

John realised Harriet and Dominic had jumped to the wrong conclusion.

'No, I'm afraid that's not my money, that's Gertie's.'

'I know, Daddy. That's so kind of you. I hope this isn't about trying to make up for things after... well after that episode with Barbara because that's not necc—'

John banged his fist on the table. 'STOP!'

The room went so quiet all they could hear was Alfie's

frightened doggy whimper coming from his hiding place under the kitchen table.

'John, what on earth...?' began Sylvie.

'Look, before you thank me, Harriet, I need to tell you something. The fact is Grandpa has screwed up. Just please don't take her away from us again.'

Sylvie stood up. 'Oh, John. What on earth have you done?'

John pointed at the saver's book. 'That is Gertie's money. She earned it – every penny.'

Sylvie stared at him. 'What are you talking about, John? She's two? What on earth can a two-year-old do?'

'Child modelling,' answered Harriet.

John turned to Harriet and stared at her. 'You knew?'

Harriet nodded her head.

John sat down and poured a large glass of wine.

'Modelling?'

Dominic turned to Harriet. 'What do you mean – *modelling?*'

'It's not like catwalk modelling, if that's what you're thinking,' said Harriet. 'She does photo shoots for the big high street stores wearing their latest clothing ranges. She does commercials too. It's a wonder you haven't spotted her yet. That's how I found out – from a television commercial.'

John nodded his head, not in the least bit surprised.

'You knew about this, and you didn't tell me!' said Dominic.

'I didn't tell you, Dominic, because I knew what your reaction would be.'

'I'm bloody livid, Harriet. That's my reaction.'

Harriet rolled her eyes at her husband.

John stared forlornly into his empty wine glass and considered pouring another. This was just the reaction he had been expecting. Dominic rounded on John. 'I can't believe you used our daughter to make money.'

John pointed at the passbook. 'I didn't touch a penny. It's all there, I swear.'

Dominic wasn't listening. He turned on Harriet. 'I knew it! We still can't trust them.'

'What do you mean *we still can't trust them*?' Sylvie cut in. 'I didn't know a thing about all this. Don't lump me in with him!'

'I've got the receipts,' continued John, impervious to the fact that no one was listening to him.

Dominic glared at Sylvie. 'He's *your* husband. You should have known what was going on. Oh, hold on a minute, you didn't have the first clue what he was up to because you weren't around looking after Gertie like you said—'

Harriet slammed a fist down on the table. 'Dominic, shut-up!'

Dominic shut up in an instant.

'I've got an announcement to make.' Harriet stood up.

'Daddy, with your kind permission I'd like to take over.'

John was just reaching for the bottle of wine. He looked across the table at Harriet. 'Take over?'

'I'd like to take Gertie along to her auditions and photo shoots.'

John stared at her, dumbfounded. 'You don't mind that I took her along?'

'Of course not. I just wish you'd told me sooner. But after what happened with Barbara…' Harriet glared at Dominic. 'I can understand why you were reticent to tell us about it.'

John smiled at Harriet and then caught Dominic scowling at him.

Harriet continued, 'I saw the breakfast cereal commercial

when I flicked on the television one morning before work. At first, I thought the little girl was Gertie's doppelgänger because no child of mine would behave themselves in front of the camera. That was, until she smacked her lips and said *yum, yum.* Then I knew it was my Gertie. Although I still couldn't quite believe it.'

John smiled to himself. He remembered sitting in the studio when she was filming that television commercial and how stunned he was when she did exactly as she was asked by the director. There was no grumpy face or whiny niggles the like of which Grandpa used to get whenever he asked her to do something.

'I went to see the agency.'

John had no idea Harriet had visited the modelling agency.

'Don't worry, Dad. I didn't tell them that I wasn't aware what you and Gertie had been up to. I understand you told the agency to hold fire on any further assignments while you sorted out some family issues.'

John glanced furtively at Dominic and nodded his head. He couldn't very well tell the modelling agency he'd lost access to his grandchild; on top of the fact that he didn't have the parents' permission to sign her up with the agency in the first place.

'I took Gertie along with me to the agency,' continued Harriet. 'When they gave me a breakdown of what she'd been earning, I was shocked. But that wasn't what I was there to find out.'

Dominic turned to his wife. 'So, what *did* you want to find out?'

'I took Gertie along to see if it was something she wanted to continue doing. She's almost three. She's got a mind of her own.

I guess perhaps it might have been a novelty for her to begin with, but now she's had a break from it. Was this something she still wanted to do or had the novelty worn off?'

John sat there, nodding his head. Harriet had a point. He looked at Gertie finishing her chicken pie and dolloping generous titbits on the floor for Alfie.

'I took her along to a screen test for a new children's television series.'

'A television series?' said Dominic in surprise.

'Oh, you should have seen her, Dominic. She isn't fazed by all the people on the set. It's like she understands everybody has a job to do, including her. She is so attentive. Gertie listens to the director and then gets to work. It's amazing to see how well she copes with it all at such a young age.'

John said, 'That's why she's one of their most successful child models, Harriet. I wish you'd been there on her first photo shoot.' John smiled ruefully as he told them all about the day he walked into the job centre looking for work and walked out with a job interview for Gertie.

They all laughed at that. Even Dominic managed a smile.

Harriet turned to Dominic. 'She's a natural in front of the cameras.'

John glanced at Gertie. 'Did she get the part?' He knew it was a silly question. More to the point was whether Harriet and Dominic wanted their daughter to go down this road. Although she was almost three, it didn't mean her future was all mapped out – child actors didn't necessarily grow up to be actors. But then some did. This was potentially a different future to the one they thought they had planned for Gertie. But what did it matter in the long run if she was doing what she loved?

'I've been thinking it over, and I'm going to let Gertie continue, as long as she's enjoying herself.'

'You are?' John and Dominic said in unison.

John frowned at his daughter. 'I don't want to be the one to put a dampener on things, but it is quite a commitment.'

John knew this from experience, ferrying Gertie around London to her assignments. You weren't paid a chaperone's fee for nothing. He imagined with Gertie acting in a television show that would be even more of a commitment. There would be long hours hanging around the studio while Gertie was filming.

John had to be honest. He didn't think Harriet really understood what she was getting herself into. He said bluntly, 'Harriet. I don't know how you'll do it working full time.'

'I won't be working full time.'

'What?' Dominic's head swivelled in her direction. 'When were you going to tell me this?'

'When you couldn't talk me out of it.'

'But what are we going to do for money?'

'I've got a new position – part time.'

The only one at the dinner table who wasn't surprised by this news was Sylvie. She knew how unhappy her daughter had been since she returned to work full time, even though Harriet hadn't come right out and said it. The fact was, she missed Gertie terribly, but they needed the money. Sylvie had offered them some financial help, but Harriet wouldn't hear of it. What Sylvie did was mention to her friend and boss, Marcia, that if an opening did arise…

'I've got a new job working as an assistant editor for Marcia Hunt – Mum's boss.'

Dominic looked at her in surprise. 'When did this happen?'

'Just last week, actually. Since Mum started at the magazine their workload has increased so they headhunted me and I got offered a job.'

'But surely that's a demotion,' said Dominic.

Harriet didn't care one jot about that.

Dominic frowned. 'You still haven't answered my question, Harriet. What are we going to do about money?'

Harriet ignored Dominic and turned to John. 'My priority is Gertie. I've decided I'd like to take her to the studio and any other auditions and photo shoots that come up. I worked out that the chaperone fee will make up for what I would have been earning full time. Is that okay with you?'

John beamed at Harriet. His new writing career was taking up a considerable amount of time, and John wanted to spend more time with Sylvie. He wasn't sorry that Harriet was returning to part-time work. As much as he loved looking after Gertie, doing that every day was exhausting at their age. Besides, John didn't think he should be expected to be around 24/7 – a parent, a grandparent at his children's beck and call. He glanced at Sylvie. They had a life to lead of their own, beyond the confines of their immediate family. John was getting the impression that Harriet now understood that.

John frowned. 'Can I still have a regular day or two?' He couldn't imagine going all week without spending time with his grandchild.

'Of course you can, Daddy. If you wouldn't mind looking after her on the days I'm at work?'

'Absolutely.' John glanced at Sylvie.

'Count me in,' said Sylvie. 'We can look after her together.'

That was music to John's ears.

'What about me?' Dominic whined. 'Don't I have a say in all this?'

Harriet shrugged. 'You can say what you like, Dominic, but my mind is made up. Oh, and by the way I've decided to get a pet.'

'A pet?' Dominic threw his arms in the air.

Chloe turned to her fiancé and said, 'Declan, can we get a pet, too?'

Declan glanced helplessly at Dominic and said, 'I suppose we could.'

Chloe squealed in delight and turned to Harriet. 'What are you getting? I rather fancied a kitten myself. Are you going to get a dog like Alfie? He is so cute.'

As if on cue, Alfie scooted over to Chloe and jumped up with his two front paws on her lap.

John caught Alfie misbehaving. 'Down!'

Alfie sat by Chloe's chair and gave her the sad puppy-dog eyes routine. That elicited plenty of attention from Chloe.

John rolled his eyes at Alfie. He was all too familiar with the cocker spaniel's *modus operandi*. It worked every time.

After Alfie had walked those sad puppy-dog eyes around the table and got a fuss from everybody apart from John, the three girls got into a discussion on the merits of pet dogs versus cats. Dominic and Declan talked about footie. And Gertie threw more chicken pie on the floor for Alfie when no one was looking.

John leaned towards Sylvie and whispered, 'Are we still okay?'

Sylvie frowned at John and cast her hand around at her family seated at the kitchen table.

John followed her gaze around the table and understood he didn't have to ask that question.

Sylvie smiled and whispered back, 'I think we're more than okay – don't you?'

John couldn't agree more.

48

A box arrived for Sylvie by FedEx from America containing the last item that had been bequeathed to Sylvie in her father's will. They had all debated what it could be. Perhaps it was something meant for the cottage? Or an item he'd kept that belonged to Sylvie's mother? But what it turned out to be was intended for his daughter.

There was a letter addressed to Sylvie, from her father, telling her that inside that box were his most prized possessions: the journals that he wrote when he was a prisoner of war in Cornwall, up until the summer of 1952, the summer he spent with her mother before he immigrated to America. How strange that it turned out she had also inherited her father's penchant for writing.

Sylvie had organised another girls' night in. They were fast becoming a bit of a family tradition in her apartment. Harriet, Chloe, and Jess all arrived at the same time. Jess had decided to stay on for a fortnight before she returned to Australia, much to Sylvie's delight. Julia had joined them, bringing her cocker spaniel, Holly, along too.

They were going to spend a quiet evening in reading her

father's journals and finding out all about the POW from camp 115 in Cornwall, who turned out to be Sylvie's father, and the girls' grandfather.

In the apartment upstairs, John was not alone. Not to be outdone, he'd organised his first ever lad's night in. His son-in-law, Dominic, was there. He had also invited Sayid, the stay-at-home dad who he met in the park, and had become good friends. He'd also asked the taxi driver. John didn't know his home number, so he had called for a taxi, knowing who would turn up.

John insisted on paying for the taxi for the entire evening, even though he knew he wouldn't be stepping foot in his car. Instead, he invited him in. Then there was Alfie, sitting on his sofa. John walked past him, carrying a plate of nibbles, and came to an abrupt halt. He backtracked and stood there staring at Alfie.

Alfie was chewing the corner of John's throw. The spaniel looked up at John with a guilty expression.

John shrugged, picked up a bite size sausage roll and gave it to Alfie.

Alfie wolfed down the sausage roll and yapped exuberantly at John.

The last guest to arrive was John's future son-in-law, Chloe's fiancé, Declan. John rushed to the door. 'Did you bring it?'

'You bet.' Declan had brought the all-important Wii.

Sylvie was reading her father's journal when she was interrupted by the sound of people jumping up and down on the ceiling above her head, voices shouting victoriously. John's voice was the loudest. Declan had already introduced him to the joys of the Wii. John had even suggested bringing a Wii on their next holiday together in Cornwall, to which she had said no – in no uncertain terms. Chloe had warned her not to give in, even if it was just for a holiday; she had lived with that damn thing until she had moved out, and she was glad to be rid of it.

Chloe stopped reading, too. She cast her eyes heavenward, shaking her head; would they ever grow up?

Sylvie glanced across the room at Chloe and caught her staring at the ceiling and frowning. She knew what Chloe was thinking: *will they ever grow up?* By the look on her face, Sylvie guessed she was glad to be rid of the Wii. Sylvie smiled at her youngest daughter, feeling a mixture of excitement at the forthcoming wedding and relief that Chloe had finally sorted out her problem.

Chloe and Declan had got engaged on the day Chloe moved out of the house they had bought together. They'd had a heart-to-heart about how they could make this relationship work in the long-term and came to a joint decision. They both did a lot of research on the internet before they took the plunge and discovered they were not alone. Living apart together, or LAT living, as it was affectionately called, wasn't for everyone, but Chloe and Declan knew it was for them. If it weren't for her parents, her mother in particular, Chloe would never have thought of it. If it weren't for John vacating his apartment and giving Chloe his keys before he left for New York, Chloe would never have experienced it. And neither would Declan.

One week later, after deciding to live apart, the terraced house next door came on the market; it was as though it was a sign. Chloe walked into the estate agent and made an offer the very next day. Excited at the prospect of buying her very own place and living apart together in the house next door to Declan, she then set about planning their wedding. Harriet thought they were bonkers. However, there were times she caught herself wistfully looking around her mum's apartment, wondering what it would feel like to be somewhere on her own. To close the door and just please herself for a change. She certainly felt like that when the in-laws turned up on her doorstep to look after Gertie and she thought she'd never see the back of them.

Even though things were back to normal at home with the in-laws gone, Harriet still thought there was a lot to be said for LAT living. Perhaps they weren't bonkers after all. Harriet would never admit that to Chloe, though.

Chloe caught her sister looking around Sylvie's apartment. The look on her face suggested there was something on her mind; maybe she was thinking there was something to this LAT living? Perhaps deep down she felt they weren't bonkers after all.

Chloe didn't bother asking her sister what she was thinking. It didn't worry Chloe what other people thought of her living arrangements, as long as it worked for her. Chloe smiled. For the first time since she got engaged, she was looking forward to the wedding. And she couldn't wait for the honeymoon; Chloe had already asked her mum if they could spend two weeks in the cottage in Cornwall after the wedding.

Sylvie had resorted to buying a calendar to make a note of the dates family and friends would be down in the cottage, so there weren't any double bookings. Harriet wanted to take Gertie down there in the summer holidays with Dominic. Chloe was already pencilled in for her honeymoon. Sylvie had promised Julia and Tom a holiday down there, too. And Jess was hoping to bring her boyfriend over from Australia to meet her parents for the first time and then travel down to Cornwall with him to have a break away, just the two of them, in Sylvie's cottage by the sea. Sylvie had looked at her calendar and realised that at this rate her long summer break in Cornwall with John would probably be pushed back to September. That didn't bother Sylvie because she knew the cottage would always be waiting for her.

But for now, Sylvie wasn't thinking of the summer several months away. What was at the forefront of her mind was tomorrow. She could already feel herself getting emotional over the forthcoming nuptials.

49

'Stop fiddling with your tie, John. You're making me nervous.'

'*You're* nervous!' exclaimed John, turning to Sylvie and fiddling with his tie. 'You haven't got the responsibility of giving away the bride!'

That was true. Thinking of John giving her away, Sylvie got out a tissue. She thought she might burst into tears at any moment.

'Please don't cry, Sylvie.'

'Oh John, I thought I'd never see the day…

'Neither did I,' remarked John.

They were standing together at the back of the church, waiting for the bride-to-be to make an appearance.

Sylvie looked around the hexagonal interior of St. Saviour's Church. When they first arrived, she wasn't sure what she thought of the plain 1970s brick church next to Warwick Avenue tube station. But as soon as she walked inside, she was struck by the bright and welcoming interior of St. Saviour's, the parish church in Little Venice.

John leaned in close to Sylvie and whispered, 'I know this is probably not the appropriate thing to say at this point, but let's hope the relationship lasts this time, especially as she's getting married!'

'John, I have every confidence that this time she's found the one.'

'The one?'

'Just a figure of speech, John.'

'But—'

'Shush Daddy!'

John glanced at Chloe, the chief bridesmaid. She was standing beside him with a finger to her lips in a shushing motion.

Gertie, the flower girl, was standing in front of Auntie Chloe in a pretty floral dress, holding a basket of petals. She looked up at Grandpa and put her finger to her lips, copying Auntie Chloe. 'Shush Grandpa!'

'Sorry.'

They all turned at the sound of the church door opening behind them. 'Here we go,' said John, glancing nervously at Sylvie.

A moment later the bride-to-be walked into the church looking radiant in a simple but elegant ivory wedding gown and a matching bolero.

John smiled as he stepped forward and held out the crook of his arm.

Sylvie dissolved into tears at the sight of her best friend walking down the aisle with John. The processional music Julia and Tom had chosen for their wedding only made Sylvie even more emotional as she listened to the song, 'We've Only Just Begun,' by The Carpenters. Sylvie dabbed her eyes.

John smiled at Gertie walking down the aisle a few paces in front of them. She was throwing petals from her basket. Ahead of them, John saw Dominic seated in the pew next to Harriet. He was holding a hand-held video camera filming his daughter. Harriet, sitting next to him, was wiping her eyes with a tissue as her daughter approached.

Gertie stopped at their pew, just as they'd practised a week ago before the ceremony, and waited for the bride to pass her by before taking a seat with her parents.

John winked at Gertie as he made his way up the aisle and got a stern look from his three-year-old grandchild that said, *behave yourself, Grandpa, and don't be silly.*

John stopped at the altar and took his place to one side, handing Julia over to her husband-to-be. He glanced over his shoulder and threw Sylvie a smile; he'd made it. The last time he gave a bride away was at Harriet's wedding almost fourteen years ago. They exchanged a knowing smile. This was good practice for Chloe's wedding in the summer.

The best man turned and gave Sylvie a smile.

John caught that smile and frowned at Bertram.

Bertram gave John an apologetic shrug.

John offered him a smile in return. He knew all about how Julia had sent Tom's good friend, Bertram, on a blind with Sylvie at The Rooftop Café. Lucky for John, it turned out Bertram wasn't the one.

Friends and houseboat neighbours lined the canal path. Some tourists who were taking an evening stroll along Regent's Canal in Little Venice stopped along the towpath, wondering why a large group of people had gathered. There was a hushed silence when Pete, one of Julia's good friends and houseboat neighbours, announced he'd received a text from Chloe to say they were on their way.

Although it was December, and it was already dark when they left the church at four o'clock after the ceremony, Julia wanted to walk along Warwick Avenue back to her houseboat. Fortunately, it wasn't raining, and there was hardly a nip in the air as it was so mild. Those who attended the ceremony at the church jumped in their cars and drove the short distance to the end of the Avenue above the canal, leaving Julia and Tom to take a romantic stroll hand-in-hand from the parish church, under the misapprehension that everyone had gone home.

Julia had not organised a wedding reception. Not that she didn't want one; Julia loved a party. It's just that over the years she'd never had to book a venue because she always hosted her parties at her flat. Julia wasn't the most organised person, and rarely planned things, so she didn't realise she had to book well in advance to secure a venue in London for her wedding reception. Now Julia was living on a small houseboat, she couldn't invite all her friends over for a good knees-up; there just wasn't the room.

Unbeknown to Julia, Sylvie and Bertram had got around that problem and organised a reception for them. It might be a little unorthodox. Sylvie knew it was a lot different to most wedding receptions – but then, wasn't that Julia all over? A little different. A little unorthodox. Sylvie knew, if nothing else, it would be a wedding reception to remember.

Sylvie smiled as she and John clambered out of the back of Chloe's car. Up ahead, other cars were pulling up and parking near the steps leading down to the canal. There was the clunk of car doors and hushed voices as friends and relatives who were at the church left their cars and joined John and Sylvie. They all quickly made their way down the stone flight of steps to the canal below.

'I thought you left a light on in your houseboat?' Julia was saying as she made her way down the stone flight of steps.

'Didn't you leave your lights on either?' Tom was saying.

'I thought I did.'

'How strange that there isn't a single light on in any of the houseboats,' Tom pointed out.

'Yes, isn't it dark.'

The word *dark* had barely passed Julia's lips as they both stepped on to the towpath, when someone shouted, 'It's them! Now, Pete!'

Pete, on one bended knee in the dark, connected the power to the generator on his houseboat.

There were gasps, and oohs and aahs from Julia and Tom as the towpath was lit up by thousands of twinkling fairy lights running like streamers up and down the dozens of houseboats that lined the quay. But it wasn't the twinkling fairy lights that captured their attention but two houseboats, their houseboats, moored next to each other. While they were getting married, their friends from neighbouring houseboats had got together and festooned Julia and Tom's houseboats with streamers, paper lanterns, and more fairy lights to mark the occasion.

To say Julia and Tom looked stunned was an understatement. Sylvie and John were spying on them from a porthole window on a neighbour's boat, along with everyone else who was in on the surprise, hiding in the darkened houseboats lining the canal.

'Do you hear that?' said Sylvie, turning to John.

He nodded. That was their cue. Chloe and Declan had set up a sound system on one of the houseboats. It was playing the married couple's song, 'We've Only Just Begun,' by The Carpenters.

'Come on,' said Sylvie excitedly. 'Let's welcome the happy couple to their wedding reception. Let the party begin!'

Everyone was waiting for the signal. Lights blinked on in the houseboats and doors opened, people spilling out with bottles of wine, food and festive cheer to congratulate Julia and Tom, and welcome them to their wedding reception being held at a very special venue indeed: in dozens of houseboats on the canal in Little Venice.

John caught Sylvie staring at him as he walked up to the deck. 'What?'

'I never thought I'd see the day that John Baxter was enthusiastic about attending a party.'

John looked at Sylvie thoughtfully. 'I think what you're trying to say is that it wasn't that long ago you'd have to drag me to hell and back before I agreed to go to a party with Julia.'

Sylvie smiled. 'You took the words right out of my mouth.'

He breathed a sigh. 'If I hadn't been so obstinate and pig-headed over the years, and just once given in and come along with you to one of Julia's infamous house parties back in the day, maybe…'

'You might have enjoyed yourself?'

John raised an eyebrow. 'Yes. I think you're right. If I hadn't been so inflexible maybe it wouldn't have taken all these years for Julia and me to patch up our differences.'

That was another first, thought Sylvie, John admitting that Julia wasn't the problem.

Sylvie followed John up the wooden steps and out on to the deck. She smiled to herself. Thanks to Bertram's discovery that her phobia of boats originated from her fear of motion sickness, Sylvie had no problem standing with John on the deck, watching Julia and Tom's stunned faces as their friends and neighbours greeted them. Sylvie had popped a motion sickness pill before the wedding.

They moved forward as one, stepping off the houseboat to join the wedding reception. The party lasted well into the evening. Sylvie and John joined the crowd lining the towpath and waved as Julia and Tom set off on their honeymoon together. Sylvie smiled and wiped a tear from her eye as the houseboats manoeuvred away from the towpath, tin cans tied to the back bobbing on the water.

John put an arm around Sylvie's shoulders as they watched the two houseboats, one following the other, the gentle phut, phut, phut of their engines growing more distant as they moved slowly down Regent's canal.

'Look!' Sylvie pointed. There were two enormous banners, one attached to the back of each houseboat. The word 'JUST' written on hers and 'MARRIED,' on his.

'It makes me think about renewing our wedding vows,' said John, surprising himself and Sylvie with an idea that had just popped into his head.

Sylvie looked up at him. 'I think that's a wonderful idea.'

'You do?'

'Absolutely.' Sylvie stared at Julia's houseboat in the distance, following Tom's down the canal. 'Do you think we could do it anywhere we like?' Sylvie wanted to renew their vows somewhere meaningful, magical, and very special.

'I don't see why not,' answered John. He looked at his wife. 'I think you already have somewhere in mind.'

Sylvie said, 'I'd have to check the calendar first. It's pretty booked up, you know.'

'I know,' said John, thinking of her Cornish cottage and the garden overlooking the sea, where he imagined they would renew their vows.

They stood together for a moment before joining the crowd on the towpath to make a toast to the happy couple. Sylvie smiled affectionately at her husband. For the first time in years, Sylvie knew what the future held – and it was good.

A round of applause went up from the crowded towpath as a neighbour on one of the houseboats let off some fireworks. People started dancing. The party had resumed.

Sylvie walked with John along the towpath, slipping her hand in his as they mingled with the party revellers.

'What a day, eh?'

'Yes, it's been quite a day,' agreed Sylvie.

Listening to the music, he turned to Sylvie and asked if she would care for a dance. Her answer surprised him. 'Not right now, John.'

'Oh, I thought you enjoyed dancing.'

'I do, it's just—'

'Ah. I think I've been rumbled.' He had an idea what was wrong. 'Okay, I'll admit I'm a one-trick pony when it comes to dancing. I'm afraid I've yet to master anything other than the waltz.'

Sylvie wasn't surprised; he hadn't been dancing for long. But that wasn't the reason she didn't want to dance. Sylvie was wearing a new pair of designer shoes with ridiculously high heels, and she was wary of taking a tumble so near the canal. She smiled at John. She still couldn't believe he had learned to dance – just for her. Sylvie had an idea. 'Would you like to take dancing lessons with me?'

'Sylvie, I'm game to do anything with you.'

'Anything?' Sylvie recalled a list she had once started writing months ago, soon after John was forced into early retirement. It was all the things she wanted to do with her husband, just the two of them. That list had been binned ages ago when Sylvie discovered he wasn't very keen on any of her ideas, meaning he wasn't very receptive to the thought of spending time with her. Now all that had changed. He had changed. They both had.

She smiled up at John. Sylvie decided it was time for a new list; all the things Love on the Rooftop and Dear John could do living apart together.

50

Sylvie rolled her eyes. 'It looks fine, John.'

He took a step back. 'Are you sure? I could just put another one up over there…' He caught Sylvie folding her arms and throwing him a disapproving look.

She glanced at her watch and tapped her foot impatiently. 'They are going to be arriving any minute.' Sylvie looked at the floor by her feet and sighed. 'You need to clear this lot away before someone trips over it.' She cast her eyes around the rooftop garden. John had done a splendid job hanging up all the fairy lights. He got the idea for decorating their rooftop garden from Julia's wedding reception the other week when her neighbours had hung fairy lights and colourful paper lanterns that glowed in the dark.

John had got carried away and bought too many lights. Now he was on his hands and knees packing away a set of fairy lights that Sylvie had told him not to get out of the box and unravel. He had already hung more than enough twinkly lights.

Sylvie had just finished bringing up the plates of party food from John's kitchen and arranging them on the wooden table under the gazebo. She thought they might have a glass of wine together before everyone arrived. Instead, Sylvie sat down on the swing seat for two on her own, with a glass of wine, and watched John getting irritated as he tried to pack away the lights that refused to fit back the box from whence they'd come.

Watching him, Sylvie put a hand to her mouth and stifled a laugh.

John heard Sylvie snort and looked up sharply. 'It's not funny.'

'Oh, but it is.'

John smiled ruefully. 'I should have listened to you when you said I bought too many lights.'

Sylvie patted the seat next to her. 'Come, sit with me for a moment.'

'Okay.' John got up from his knees. 'You know, I think it would take less time to put these up somewhere than try to pack them away.' He stared at Sylvie sitting on the swing seat for two. A smile crept to his lips.

Sylvie narrowed her eyes. John had an idea – she could tell. She cast her eyes heavenward.

Five minutes later, Sylvie was just finishing her glass of wine while she stood under the gazebo staring out over the London rooftops, when John called out, 'I've finished. You can look now.'

Sylvie turned around.

John was sitting on the swing seat for two, beaming at Sylvie. 'Well, what do you think?'

What Sylvie thought was that he should have packed them away like she asked him to. On the other hand, it did bring a smile to her lips when she saw the swing seat decorated in fairy lights.

'There, you see. I knew that extra set would come in handy.'

He motioned to the seat next to him. 'Come here. I want to give you something.'

Sylvie put her wine glass down and walked over to join him, wondering if he was going to give her an early Christmas present. She hoped not. She hadn't thought to give John a present on Christmas Eve.

John turned to face her. He stared into her eyes for a moment.

Sylvie was just about to ask if something was wrong when he got out of his seat and knelt in front of her. 'John – what on earth...?' began Sylvie. From behind his back, he brought out a little black box and held it up.

Sylvie stared at the box.

Arm still outstretched, he slowly opened the velvet lid to reveal what was inside.

Sylvie looked at him in surprise. 'Are you proposing?'

John coughed, 'Ahem.' He glanced at the ring, looked at Sylvie and then said, 'You think I'm a silly old fool – don't you.'

Sylvie shook her head. That was the furthest thought from her mind at this moment.

'We're already married, I know. But in the spirit of renewing our wedding vows, I wanted to do something special. And so...' John took a deep breath. 'Sylvie, you're the love of my life. And, to borrow a phrase, you're the one.'

That made Sylvie smile.

'Will you re-marry me?'

Sylvie stared at her husband and turned her head for a moment to gaze around the rooftop garden. The guests would arrive at any minute. It wasn't just a Christmas Eve party. John wanted to host another housewarming party for friends and family; a small gathering to celebrate new beginnings – living apart together.

This time they weren't going to hold the party in one of their apartments as before. Instead, John wanted the party in their communal living space, on the rooftop terrace garden. Sylvie knew why. It gave him a chance to show off an area of the house nobody else had seen, and the part of the house conversion that John was the proudest of.

Sylvie turned her attention to her husband. He'd spent hours decorating the rooftop garden. She stared at the ring and realised he hadn't done all this for the party guests. He'd done it for her. That's why he'd been on at her to pop out on Christmas Eve and do some last-minute shopping, or visit friends, or anything but follow him up to the rooftop while he was preparing for the party. What he was really doing was preparing their rooftop garden for something else.

He must still love me very much, thought Sylvie as she leaned forward to take the ring.

'Is that a yes?' asked John as he handed over the ring.

Sylvie nodded her head vigorously and managed a hushed 'Oh, yes.' It wasn't often she was lost for words, but Sylvie had not, in her wildest dreams, expected John to do all this for her.

She removed the plain wedding band she had worn since they first married because at the time that was all they could afford.

'Read the inscription on the inside of the ring, Sylvie.'

'There's an inscription?' said Sylvie in surprise. She held up the ring. 'Oh, darn, I can't read it. I need my glasses.'

'Here, borrow mine.' John slipped them off the bridge of his nose and handed them to Sylvie.

Sylvie popped them on.

'Before you read it, do you mind giving me a hand?'

Sylvie helped him up. He sat down next to her on the swing seat, rubbing his knee. 'I don't remember feeling this stiff the first time around.'

'Well, the first time around you weren't sixty years young, John.'

'That's true,' he replied with a smile. 'Now, where were we?'

'I was about to read the inscription.' Sylvie held up the ring. She slowly turned the ring as she read the inscription. When she finished, Sylvie looked at John, looked at the ring, looked around her rooftop garden, and burst into tears.

'Oh no,' exclaimed John in surprise. 'What have I done?'

'What you've done is made me incredibly happy.' Sylvie slipped on the ring with the inscription, *Love on the Rooftop*. 'One of these days, I'll tell you all about a recurring dream I once had about finding love on a rooftop.'

John raised an eyebrow. 'I'm guessing your dream came true.'

'Yes, all thanks to you.'

Sylvie was sitting on the swing seat for two, admiring her new ring and wiping the tears from her cheeks, when she thought she heard voices in the garden.

Jess appeared in front of them with a concerned look on her face. 'Is everything all right, Mum?'

'Perhaps we should go,' said Chloe.

'I told you to press the doorbell again instead of just barging in, Chloe,' scolded Harriet.

Chloe frowned at her sister. 'But they weren't answering the door,' she protested, throwing a glance behind her.

All the guests had arrived and followed them upstairs. They

were admiring the rooftop garden. John left Sylvie to show off her new ring to the girls while he saw to the guests.

It was only a fortnight since they had returned from Cornwall, and barely a week since their respective girls' and lads' nights in, but John wanted the party to go ahead as soon as possible to make sure everybody could be there, including Jess before she returned to Australia, and John's brother, Dave, before he went on holiday. Dave and his wife were going on another make-or-break holiday together, taking advantage of Sylvie's cottage in Cornwall. John wanted all the family here to celebrate this special occasion – Sylvie and John were back together.

The party wasn't just for the family; there were also friends, old and new. Julia and her husband were among the first to arrive. Sylvie was over the moon when she found out that Julia and Tom had moored up their boats a little way down Regent's Canal, postponing their honeymoon so they could come to the party. Sylvie imagined that once they set off on their honeymoon, who knew how long they would be away.

Bertram and his family had come at Sylvie's invitation. John was pleased to discover that Bertram and Amy had reconciled after their falling out in New York. Amy was still having her engagement party and wedding in England. However, there were two additional guests on the guest list now: her mother and father. An awkward moment followed when John was introduced to the woman on Bertram's arm – his wife. 'Oh John, how lovely to see you again,' she said.

'You two know each other?' said Bertram in surprise.

They furtively glanced at each other, deciding now was not the time to get into the why's and wherefores of how they'd first met, or that she'd stayed the night in John's hotel room in New York. Some things, John decided, were much better left unsaid. 'You must be Amy,' he said, greeting Bertram's daughter and attempting to evade answering Bertram's question. 'I'm John – Sylvie's husband.'

'You're the writer, Dear John,' said Amy.

'That's me.'

'Have we met before?'

John stood there looking innocently at Amy, hoping to goodness she didn't recognise him from her engagement party in The Hamptons. 'No, no. I don't believe we have.'

'Strange. I'm sure I've seen you somewhere before…'

Gertie chose that moment to spot Grandpa in the garden. She came charging up to him.

'Hello, my sweet,' said John, scooping her up in his arms.

'Boy!' shouted Gertie at Rory, who was standing beside Amy, holding her hand.

Amy's eyebrows shot up. 'I know where I've seen you before!' She stared at the little girl in John's arms. 'You were at Daddy's hotel in London. You walked past me in the lobby.'

'Well, Gertie needed to use the facilities,' John replied, avoiding Bertram's gaze. That was another thing he didn't want to get into: the whys and wherefores of spying on a man he thought was dating his wife. Once again, John decided some things were better left unsaid.

'Amelia told me you had a hand in getting her and I back together,' Bertram said off-hand.

John shot Amelia a look, wondering how much she'd told him about what went on in New York. He could feel himself growing hot under the collar.

Bertram held out his hand. 'I want to thank you. I get the impression that if it weren't for you, I wouldn't be standing here today with my wife.'

John took his hand.

Bertram said, 'I'm glad things worked out.' He glanced at Sylvie mingling with the other guests. 'No hard feelings – eh?'

John raised an eyebrow. He realised what Bertram was referring to; no hard feelings for chasing after another man's wife. A loaded handshake followed, which they both knew was all about putting the past to rights and moving on.

Sylvie turned around and saw them shaking hands. She smiled. This was what she had hoped for. Despite her assurances that there was nothing between them, John hadn't been that enthusiastic when she told him she was inviting Bertram to the party. She was delighted they had settled their differences and John was putting that episode behind them, especially as it wouldn't be long and they would see Bertram again at Amy's wedding. Bertram was a good friend. Sylvie wanted to keep in touch with him and his family.

Sylvie left the rooftop garden and headed downstairs through John's apartment and out on to the landing. She gazed over the banisters to the communal entrance hall below to see if anybody else had arrived. Sylvie walked down the stairs to check the front door she had left propped open hadn't blown shut. She paused at the sign she'd attached to the banisters with sticky tape.

Sylvie had come across the *party this way* sign Chloe had made for her months ago when she had her own housewarming celebrations soon after she moved into the flat downstairs. Sylvie hadn't invited John, so she had Chloe make the sign which pointed to her apartment door to avoid any guests wandering upstairs by mistake. She stared at the colourful sign now pointing up to John's apartment. Sylvie smiled as she gazed at the new ring on her finger. Who would have guessed, thought Sylvie, that all these months later they would throw a party on a communal rooftop garden to celebrate living apart together?

'Hey, Sylvie!'

Sylvie turned around to find Marcia marching towards her. She flung her arms around her star writer. 'I've missed you.' She let go of Sylvie. 'We all have.' She stepped aside to reveal the rest of the editorial team who worked at the magazine, whom Sylvie counted as friends.

Marcia said, 'We're all dying to meet your partner in crime.'

Sylvie laughed. 'You'll find John upstairs on the rooftop garden where we're throwing the party.'

'Come on everyone.' Marcia started up the stairs. 'Let's go and meet Dear John.'

Sylvie watched them head up the stairs before turning around to see some more familiar faces arriving. Sylvie hadn't forgotten her old social circle she used to meet up with for coffee mornings in the days before she was too busy with her new career.

A few of Sylvie's old friends had taken her up on the invitation to her party. They had also brought their husbands along, with an ulterior motive; they were keen to show them around Sylvie and John's apartments, eager to show their husbands what LAT living might potentially do for their relationships.

Sylvie welcomed them in and closed the front door. Everybody had arrived. She led them up the stairs, pointing out her apartment on the ground floor with the door wide open. They were welcome to have a nose around if they wished.

Up on the roof, Sylvie ushered her old friends into the garden and offered them a glass of wine and some nibbles. She saw John surrounded by her work colleagues, all taking their turn to shake his hand, chatting amiably to Dear John.

Sylvie cast her eyes around the rooftop garden, taking in some friends John had invited. Before he retired, he didn't really have any friends apart from work colleagues. Sylvie recalled that he had hardly anybody to invite to their original housewarming party, soon after he'd completed the conversion on the house. Now John seemed to have no shortage of friends.

Sylvie had already been introduced to Sayid, the stay-at-home dad, who had arrived along with his wife and three children. He was now working from home thanks to Chloe, who had passed I.T. contracts his way. According to Chloe, he was now building up quite a reputation for himself as an I.T. consultant. Sayid had found that work-life balance he so desperately wanted.

John's new friends from the grandparent-toddler group at the local library had arrived soon after, followed by John's favourite taxi driver and his family, his wife appearing star-struck when she was introduced to the two famous writers.

John and Sylvie tried to convince her they weren't celebrities. They were just an ordinary couple from West London who had converted their house into two apartments, and along the way made a journey of discovery about themselves and each other.

It wasn't long before the party was in full swing; everyone was enjoying themselves. Nobody noticed the two hosts were absent from the rooftop garden. Sylvie and John had drifted downstairs. They sat outside on the front steps of their house, wine glass in hand. They had sat together like this once before, right here on these steps many years ago, and toasted the beginning of their new life together in this house. Today they toasted once more to new beginnings, to a new life – living apart together.

Epilogue

The next morning Sylvie and John met up on the rooftop terrace garden. Sylvie appeared first, with Mouse following her into the garden. She'd woken up to find John's cat fast asleep, nestled on her duvet in the centre of the bed. This wasn't unusual. Like her owner, Mouse was a creature of habit. And she was one bright button. Sylvie always went to sleep with Alfie at the end of her bed and woke up with Mouse in his place. That's because Mouse knew Alfie's morning routine. Like the cat, Sylvie wasn't the only one who liked a lie in. John and Alfie, on the other hand…

They hadn't been home long, and John had slipped back into familiar routines – walking Alfie first thing in the morning before breakfast, even on the days Sylvie wasn't working.

John walked into the garden with Alfie hot on his heels, both looking wide awake and raring to go.

Sylvie rolled her eyes at them and looked at Mouse curled up on her lap purring softly; she was already settling down for another catnap. She wasn't asleep though, Sylvie could tell. Her tail bristled at the sound of Alfie scampering across the wooden decking towards them. Alfie wagged his tail and yapped at Sylvie.

Alfie got a *good morning* and a pat on the head from Sylvie. He got an angry flick of the tail from Mouse for daring to come too close. Alfie backed away from the cat and scampered back over to John's side of the table.

John was setting two mugs down on the garden table. Sylvie knew which one was hers because it had her name on the handle. It was one of a pair of souvenir mugs he had thoughtfully bought in the gift shop on Ellis Island. He passed Sylvie her first morning cuppa of the day.

'Thank you, John.' She smiled. Gone were the days when she was up with the lark, making John his morning cuppa, fetching his daily newspaper from the doorstep, and taking them up to her husband in bed. Now he collected his own paper from the local newsagents every morning on his way home from the park with Alfie.

'Are you sure you don't want to come inside? It's a bit chilly out here.'

Sylvie wrapped her coat more tightly around her. 'No. I'm fine.' They were seated opposite each other at the garden table under the gazebo. The rooftop garden was still festooned with the decorations and twinkly lights from the party last night. John had turned on the twinkly lights for some atmosphere and lit the garden stove for some warmth on a cold crisp Christmas Day morning.

Despite the warmth from the stove, John was right: it was much warmer inside the house. When Sylvie eventually got out of bed, the first thing she did was put the turkey in the oven. Now her kitchen was warm and toasty. As she passed John's kitchen on the way to the rooftop garden, she noticed the homemade Christmas pudding he had prepared last night was simmering on the hob.

Preparations were already underway for the Christmas dinner they were cooking together for their family. Indoors, their homes – the two apartments they lived in – were cosy and warm and full of the paraphernalia of the Christmas season; they each had a tree, decorations, and there were presents yet to wrap and things still to do before the family descended on them later that day. However, they'd both left any last-minute preparations for now. There was something important they wanted to do together on Christmas morning.

Sylvie looked over at the swing seat for two that John had decorated with the last set of twinkly lights. She glanced at her ring and said, 'I wanted to do this here, on the rooftop garden.'

John nodded. 'I understand perfectly.' They placed their empty mugs on the garden table. Sylvie had finished her tea. John had drunk the last of his coffee. They'd both brought their laptops with them. They set their laptops down on the table in front of them. Sylvie and John logged on to their blogs.

They had yet to update *Dear John* and *Love on the Rooftop* since their appearance on *The Who's Who Show* in New York. Their fans were still clamouring to hear how their story ends.

They paused to look at each other across the table, a knowing smile passed between them.

John flexed his fingers above the keyboard. 'Shall we?'

Sylvie nodded. 'Let's do it.'

It was time to tell the rest of the world how their story ends.

If you enjoyed *Love on the Rooftop* I would be grateful if you'd leave a review on Amazon.

For further details about the author and her novels visit
www.elisedarcy.com

Also by Elise Darcy

The Sunrise Coast Series
New Beginnings at the Harbour Inn
The Secret of the Summerhouse
The Cottage by the Sea

The Living Apart Together Series
Living Apart Together
It Takes 2 to Tango
Dear John
Love on the Rooftop

Standalone Novels
Lola & The Man
A Mallorcan Affair
We'll Meet Again
The Villa in Sicily

Printed in Great Britain
by Amazon

41642493R00293